Three Letters to Pine River

Canada

Borealis Press gratefully acknowledges the support of the Government of Canada through the Canada Book Fund (CBF).

Library and Archives Canada Cataloguing in Publication

Griffin, Harold, 1936-
Three letters to Pine River / Harold Griffin.

ISBN 978-0-88887-429-0

I. Title.

PS8613.R537T57 2011 C813'.6 C2011-905211-3

Excerpts from the House of Commons Debates (Hansard) of February 22, 1966 on pages 286 to 294 reprinted with permission.

Cover design: David Tierney

Printed and bound in Canada on acid free paper.

Three Letters to Pine River

Harold Griffin

BOREALIS
BOOK PUBLISHERS

Borealis Press
Ottawa, Canada
2011

For “Vesty”

I would like to thank Martin Griffin for his invaluable advice in my preparation of this project. Also to June Wilkins, my cousin and "techie". To my brother Dan Griffin, I am grateful for his input and counsel in my development of the characters in this venture. My gratitude to my "readers" and critics: Dylan Griffin, Amy Fecteau, Paul Shallhorn, Aidan Griffin, Joseph Griffin, Claire Duchesneau, Anne Henderson, Maudie Swinden, Richard Griffin, Carmelle Bordeleau, Kathleen Boyer, and Dr. Anne Fitzpatrick. Thank you to Erin Singer for the roadwork and research. I am grateful to my editor Janet Shorten for her shrewd and sound guidance. And lastly, thank you to Frank and David, the irrepressible Tierneys, for their kindness and support.

Harold

Prologue

September, 1966. My name is Francis Carroll and I am the eldest son of my schoolteacher father, Thomas Carroll. My mother, Teresa Lawson Carroll, is an artist of some renown in the Quebec City area. I have been blessed with many of the aptitudes of my mother and I work as a commercial artist.

My father has a very strong connection to his family's Irish history, an attribute that I have chosen to emulate. As a young teenager, I spent a lot of time at my Uncle Mike Carroll's farm in Pine River, an Irish community north of Quebec City. I have learned to love the people there very dearly and still visit the area when I have the opportunity.

Some of the Irish immigrants who arrived in Canada did so before the Great Potato Famine of the 1840s. Waves of early Irish settlers, disenchanted and disenfranchised by their treatment at the hands of their English landlords in Ireland, sought a new way of life in North America. Upon arriving at dockside in Quebec City in the early 1820s, would-be tenant farmers were met by agents employed by the French Seigneur, a landowner who sought settlers to open up virgin territories. I cannot imagine that these immigrants had been able to save large amounts of money or property to bring with them. From very humble backgrounds, they would have struggled heroically just to save the money for the fare across the ocean to their new, chosen country. But they felt that they were indeed fortunate to escape a land where over eight million Irish peasants were forced to subsist on farms of very small acreage tending small potato patches, their main food source. Yet, once landed in Canada, they pined for their beloved Ireland, a land of a reverie, and spoke and sang of its beauty.

The promise to the newcomers in Lower Canada was that they could eventually take ownership of plots of land of considerable area, perhaps 200 acres or more. The aim of the Seigneur was to get the territory developed so that the natural resources, especially the forest, could be tapped and the resulting products supplied to the growing urban populations.

In many cases, the Seigneur would provide a cow and seed, and some farm implements, to get the Irish families started. A modest cabin would be available for the newcomers in some instances. Otherwise, improvised wooden huts would be hurriedly built for the families, many of whom had very young children. This housing, although meagre, at least furnished some protection against the bitterly cold winters—something that the Irish arrivals had not experienced with any regularity.

Once the land had been cleared and the acreage was eventually billowing with the planted grains, potatoes, and other basics, more elaborate housing would be erected by the settlers. The supply of wood to afford warmth and allow construction was abundant, thanks to the extensive stands of balsam and pine and spruce, as well as an array of deciduous trees.

One of the first projects embarked upon by the Seigneur was the building of roads to allow the settlers to reach their suppliers, churches, and markets, and to have contact with the neighbouring villages and the big city.

No rent was assessed to the settlers until after three or four years and no capital was required to pay for the land. Over the ensuing decades, the Irish farmers, after much toil and sacrifice, did acquire ownership of their properties.

From the anecdotal accounts that have been passed down to my father, it was a dream realized to inhabit a new country with its seemingly endless space. There were no more barriers to their method of worship, their Catholic faith being shared by their benefactors, the Seigneurs. Many could not believe their good luck and thought that there might be a catch somewhere in this deal. After all, this land was governed from England, whose laws had subjugated the Irish people for centuries. But the French seigneurial system had been able to maintain itself and even flourish, with certain vestiges of power and ownership, in compliance with English law.

So there was no deception lying in wait for the settlers, just hard work and creative self-deprivation in a colder configuration of seasons.

Living in their new Canadian expanses, away from the rule of the laws that kept them humiliated and illiterate, there was little to hold them back. There was no risk of discrimination if they chose to practise their religion. Education and professions were open to them once they could build their own schools and begin educating their offspring. They would eventually organize their community and establish municipal councils. They had the right to own their land and to buy and sell any product that was produced.

The Irish of Pine River, north of Quebec City, originally referred to their new home as the St. Patrick Mission. They were soon supporting their own parish church and establishing an Irish enclave surrounded by the French-speaking population.

Although electricity was not installed until 1947 for most of the residents of Pine River, the community blossomed into a close and productive entity. Farms had their own supply of water from wells close to their houses. They also had access to the Jacques Cartier River and the Rivière aux Pins. Vegetable gardens and potatoes were planted together with the fields of timothy and oats for their animals.

As the years and decades went by, the Irish farmers of Pine River adapted to the economy of the country. Farm properties were bought and sold. Subsequently, some descendants of the early settlers accumulated larger acreage.

The inheritance of a farm often went to the eldest son of a family. Siblings, searching for their own niche in life, moved to the city close by or to other areas of Canada and the United States.

But for the inhabitants of Pine River, all was not nirvana. At the outset of the First World War, the Canadian federal government decided to expropriate some of the properties to add to the

Valcartier Military Camp just adjacent to Pine River. This move by the government dislocated some farming families, who were compensated but were unhappy to have to seek other employment or move to alternative locations in the community. Houses and barns and stables they had erected were taken away in one swoop, the structures not easily movable.

Again in 1965, the federal government decided to expropriate yet another huge section of Pine River property. Once more, the compensation did not measure up to the intrinsic value of this heritage, even if some of the acreage had not been very productive. In the minds of many of the Irish residents, it was a terrible blow. Ramifications from this take-over were felt in the House of Commons in Ottawa, with heated debate raging for many hours. Initially, the federal government expropriated over 38,000 acres. After a tumultuous reaction, the government did return some territory, but the deed was done. As predicted years before by many of the older farmers, the Irish heritage of Pine River was decimated, many third and fourth generation residents dispossessed. Land expropriated by governmental institutions such as the military establishment strips the descendants of the cumulative worth of a family heritage. Had they been allowed to keep what they rightfully possessed, the residents would have been in possession of land of enhanced value. But since they were just farmers, people without real wealth, they were easy victims of the power and wishes of the federal government.

Consistent with my intense interest in the past events of Pine River, I have tried to reveal some of the recorded and oral history of the people in this farming community. This is the background against which my story recounts certain occurrences not devoid of misfortune and tragedy.

Chapter 1

I took the bus out to my uncle's farm, north of Quebec City, in late June of 1952, after school had recessed for the summer. I was fourteen at the time. It was a one-hour bus ride, and I enjoyed sitting in the seat next to the window and looking at the houses going by. There was nothing quite as comfortable as that seat. I was enveloped in my own world, at peace, away from my brothers and sister, in solitude. I wondered about the people who lived in those houses. I considered the buildings to be very solid and colourful, sitting on sizeable plots of land, and I tried to imagine what it would be like living in one of them. I could appreciate the beauty of the properties from my lofty position in the bus, seated high above ground level with almost a bird's eye view.

The bus driver dropped me off at the end of the line for that particular route. I was the last person to get off, at a quiet fork of sandy roads, Scott's Corner in Pine River. As the bus turned around and went back toward the city, I was left alone in a primal calm with the soft wind purring through the trees. A solitary abandoned house stood nearby, some loose material flapping and interrupting the eerie stillness. Then I immediately began the considerable walk to my uncle's homestead with my travelling bag strapped to my shoulders, soon passing several farms with cows and horses grazing, walking by the tall growths of balsams and spruces with their dark green hues.

The farmhouses were few and far between, but I loved the wide-open terrain that represented a sort of liberation for me. This was something that wasn't available in the city, living with my family in a second-storey flat amid an endless series of rented digs inhabited by working people who did not have the means to buy their own homes.

Since I made these trips mostly in the summertime, the countryside would normally be bathing in a swelter of sunshine, hot but not unusually so for our temperate climate. I loved to watch, as I walked along, the puffy white clouds skimming across the sky and going beyond the mountains that surrounded the area. The mountains were high and impressive-looking, dark green against a deep blue sky. But these hills were inaccessible to everyday folk, for the most part still thickly wooded and uninhabited.

The road was solid, yet a dirt, sandy stretch, and the passing of a car would cover me with a thin layer of dust. But when the dust settled and the air cleared again, that welcome peace and tranquillity of the countryside would surround me like a welcome and soothing blanket.

There was fencing on both sides of the road to mark the boundaries of the properties as well as to prevent any pasturing cattle from wandering into the path of a car.

Sometimes I would get a lift from someone in an automobile, maybe a cousin of my own family. But it did not happen this time, so after a one-hour walk I reached my uncle's acreage, sitting between rows of tall trees.

When I went into the farmhouse by the screen door off the kitchen, there was no one present in the house. There was no thought of locking doors in this community. That would have suggested that visitors were unwelcome. It would have been unthinkable that someone would invade the unlocked houses in this community and steal something.

It was as if time were standing still as I paused in that country house, a contented feeling running through me, the hush pressing against my skull. My Uncle Mike would likely be out in the fields somewhere, maybe repairing fences to keep the cattle contained, or perhaps working in the barn or stable.

The house was simply built and unassuming. The main room upon entry into these country houses was the kitchen, usually the largest room. All of the action took place in the kitchen. My uncle's house was no exception, a large wooden table and wood stove dominating the space and many chairs scattered about.

Most homes had A-frame roofs, many with sheet metal covering. When it began to rain, one was immediately aware of the steady patter, hard against the tin.

My uncle was a widower since his wife had died shortly after giving birth to their third child. She began to haemorrhage badly after getting home from the hospital. She weakened, then tragically succumbed while they were trying to arrange to take her back to the hospital. In those days, the mid-1930s, medical help wasn't organized like it is today. It was a terribly traumatic few hours for my uncle and his young sons, he trying to reach a doctor with the help of neighbours and the boys watching their mother fade away. There was no car available to him at this time and telephones had not been installed as yet. He later suffered much guilt and second thoughts at how he had handled the situation, he told my father more than once.

I went back outside and looked across the early summer fields of hay and oats and pasture to see if I could catch sight of my uncle, then went back inside and waited, eventually seeing him through the window, sauntering back across the yard.

"Francis!" he said as he came into the house to see me sitting there.

"Hello, Uncle Mike."

"So you're off for the summer. And how was your school year?" he inquired.

He shook my hand then, with that grip of steel. I knew from past encounters with his handshake that it was going to be a bone-cracking experience. I supposed that it was his way of showing enthusiasm for my arrival. That was the one thing I dreaded about greeting him. Otherwise, I was always happy to see him because he usually treated me, with that big smile of his, like I was a soldier returning from war.

"School's fine," I assured him.

"And what grade are you in now?"

"I'll be going into grade nine in September."

"My God, Francis. You're growing like a bad weed!" he marvelled.

He must have said that to make me feel good, because I didn't think that I had grown sufficiently.

"I played lots of hockey during the winter," I said. "We made the play-offs in the city league, but we got beat in the semi-finals."

"You know, Francis, I've got to get down to see you play. Your father tells me that you're quite the athlete."

"Oh, I guess I'm not bad. I'm a pretty good skater."

He sat down at the big wooden kitchen table across from me. His skin was already tanned even though it was still June and the grain was just beginning to reach some height in the fields. My Uncle Mike was a wiry man of medium stature with a set of piercing blue eyes. I always found his eyes to be remarkable. He wore grey overalls, a red shirt tucked underneath with the sleeves rolled up to the elbow, exposing a thick pair of muscular forearms.

My Uncle Mike had three children, the two older sons all grown up, into their twenties, and working in Montreal. His third child was Janice, who went to school in Quebec City every day travelling by train, and who was on holiday for the summer just as I was. She was sixteen years old and very attractive.

My uncle and I talked about my family situation for a while. I gave him the latest news about the goings-on in Quebec City. He always had lots of questions

I had been told by my parents to thank him for inviting me to spend time at the farm, so I did that.

"Where's Janice?" I asked, subsequently.

"Oh, she went off with her friends Sheila and Teresa. I think one of them is fishing. I told Jan I'd fix her up a rod, but she said she wasn't interested in fishing."

"Most girls are not too crazy about fishing, I guess."

"Well, are you hungry, Francis? Can I fix you a cup of tea and a sandwich or something?"

"No, Uncle Mike. I'll wait for supper. I'm just fine."

"Janice will be home soon. She's the chief cook and bottle washer and I'm sure she'll make something good for supper. Well, Francis, I've got to go back out and finish the job I was doing. I just came to pick up some tools. So I'll see you in a little while."

He went to the kitchen sink and poured himself a large glass of water, taking deep gulps, then exhaling heartily.

"Can I help you with anything?" I asked.

"Well, I'm just repairing some of the fencing over by the army property. A few of the cows got out and were feeding themselves over by the pine trees there. So you can come along and keep me company if you want. Or you can just stay here and wait for Janice. She should be back soon."

My Uncle Mike's spread bordered on the Valcartier Military Camp property. The Canadian federal government had started building the camp during the First World War. Some of the Irish farmers lost their land in the expropriations that the government felt were required. The military needed additional territory because they had plans to begin firing rounds of artillery shells into Pinkney's Mountain, one of the prominent hills that looked down on the Irish community of farms that dated back to the early 1800s. The mountain had a huge scar of barren rocky disfigurement as a result of this onslaught.

The farmers could do little to prevent the expropriations and some considered it just another example of the English taking away the rights of the Irish at will. The Irish had come to Canada to escape the institutionalized prejudice of the British and here they were, again serving as victims.

Although this "land grab" had occurred some forty years before, it was as if it had just happened. The Irish are like that; they have good memories. The farmers worried that the Military Camp would want to further expand and take more land. There were choice pieces of property that the army could use to simulate battle conditions. One group of farmers tended to be pessimistic about the future and felt that the Canadian government would eventually succeed in destroying their heritage.

I went with my Uncle Mike to where he was repairing the fencing. We walked toward the border of the Military Camp property, across the edges of the fields of grain, some of it timothy, much of which already had budding little flowers on the stems.

Uncle Mike and I chatted as we crunched across the field on the hard crispy shoots. My uncle had coaxed and nudged the cows back earlier, and I could see five or six of them; their heads bent down to the sod, chewing away at the young grass of a pasturing section across the field. Anyone who has seen the paintings of the pastures of England, with the cows and calves feeding and the large trees in the background, could appreciate the verdant beauty of this land amid these hills. I loved to look at landscape paintings of the countryside and I would soon begin to appreciate the profound beauty of the colour of the outdoors and attempt to re-create this panorama on canvas.

I left my uncle and wandered around the meadow and trees in the warmth of late June, enjoying the immense blue sky. At my uncle's farm I always had that great fondness inside me, where I could breathe easily and had an appreciation for every living creature and blade of grass. Some of the trees just outside of my uncle's farm border were soft-needled pines, pleasant to the touch. Many needles had fallen to the ground below the trees over the years and had created a spread of reddish soft smoothness in the cool shaded umber underneath. I stretched out on my back, full length, feeling that I could easily fall asleep in this setting. I did not want my uncle, who was working close by, to see me doing this. It was as if I was safeguarding a secret. Had he seen me make love to the land as I did, he might have considered me some sort of a fool, I thought.

But I eventually came to realize that I had underestimated my Uncle Mike. I'm sure that my love for this countryside would never measure up to his. I would see him from the kitchen window leaning up against a fence picket and staring out across the fields. He would stand there for quite a long time, hardly moving. He loved his horses, especially Dolly the old mare, and would stand in the pasture head to head with her as if spending time with an old friend—which she certainly was.

It was also said that my Uncle Mike had a terrible longing for his deceased wife, Annie. This was a yearning that did not seem to want to leave him.

When we got back to the house, Janice was in the kitchen setting the table, a rich aroma of cooking filling the room. Janice gave me a sort of hesitant hug and I could detect a mild fragrant scent from her. She was the same height as I was and beginning to fill out nicely. Her hair was tied up in the back and she had a slim athletic look with surprisingly broad shoulders. I thought her to be more beautiful than ever in her blue denim pedal pushers and white blouse. I'd met her more than a few times in town that year, and since she went to the girls' school down the street, our paths didn't cross very often. But when we did meet perchance around either her school or mine, she always made a big fuss over me, telling her girlfriends that I was her first cousin and that I visited her family's farm during the summer.

Of course, I was hopelessly in love with her. I wanted to kiss her full lips and allow her to hug me forever. But unfortunately, she was my cousin, as well as being two years older. I dreamed about her some nights. These dreams allowed me some intimacy with her, the details of which I certainly would not discuss with anyone. I suppose that if you think about someone often enough, you'll begin to have dreams about that person.

In the evenings after supper, Janice and I would sit outside on the old creaky swing's blue wood benches, facing each other, our knees touching sometimes, and talk about school and other things. I enjoyed hanging around with her and I wondered if she noticed how I fawned over her, something that I hoped to control. She was into basketball a little bit, playing during school gym periods, and I loved hockey, so the competitive aspect of sport was fun to talk about. Her dark eyes glistened in the ebbing light of evening. As the sky darkened and the stars revealed their brightness, Janice would suddenly get up and leave me sitting alone. I usually felt slighted as she left. I could have sat there all night with her. So I'd stay there for a while by myself listening to the steady cacophony of the bullfrogs coming from the nearby swamp and the lonely bark of a dog in the distance, perhaps.

My Uncle Mike was "between dogs," his old and lovable collie having passed away in the spring. He wanted one just the same and was on the lookout for one.

It was 1952, and the United Nations, led by the United States, was fighting in Korea. Canada was contributing to this war effort, so the Valcartier Military Camp was very busy. During daytime the constant rumbling of artillery cannons, mostly 25-pounders, could be heard above all other sounds, the echoes reverberating across the countryside. Puffs of white smoke would appear at regular intervals on the scar of Pinkney's Mountain, with the sound of impact following seconds later—something that fascinated me at the time. The milder staccato of machine gun fire would also resonate from beyond the pines.

The trajectory of the shells was not always arced properly, and some of them would impact the fields of some of the farms close to the border of the Military Camp. This raised concern in the minds of the local farmers, and complaints were issued, but most of these incidents caused little harm, injuring no one and causing minimal damage. Whenever this happened, a military team would be sent from the camp to "clean up the mess."

It was said that the constant rumbling of the cannons became a source of annoyance for certain residents. During damp weather the boom would sometimes shake some of the houses close to the border of the camp. The training of artillery regiments was an intrinsic part of camp activities and had gone on for many years.

It was said that certain residents grew tired of listening to the roar and reverberation and talked about moving away. But few ever took their dissatisfaction to that extreme.

I was never short of companionship on my stays at my Uncle Mike's farm. Several of the farm families had boys of about my age, so if my uncle had no chores for me to do, which was fairly often, I would use the telephone to make contact with them and arrange to meet. Some of these boys attended the same school as I did. They would take the train to town daily. There were at least a dozen boys and girls who made this daily commute to the English-language schools in Quebec City.

I was on good terms with the Kelly brothers, Patrick and Tommy, who lived on one of the farms bordering my Uncle Mike's place. You could not see the Kelly spread from my uncle's farm because of the arboreal growth in between. There was a feeling of isolation in this general area, the farms tucked away in their own corners, the wide fields emitting an aura of autonomous spaciousness. When I visited the Kelly boys, whose house was about a half-mile walk away, I wanted to come back to my Uncle Mike's before dark. If I stayed out too long, as young guys will do sometimes, I found myself walking down a silent, dark, and murky country road with the obelisks of towering trees on either side. On some starless nights it would be so pitch black that I feared the unknown, and imagined wild beasts bounding from the undergrowth to attack me. Of course this never happened, although I had heard stories about some residents having close encounters with black bears. These tales may have heightened my apprehension.

The telephone in my uncle's kitchen was an ever-present marvel to me. It was a "party line." The telephone was constantly ringing during the day and evening, but with different ring signals for each house. My uncle's ring was "three long ones." Many of the people had memorized the "rings" of their neighbours, and news and gossip travelled fast and easily with this manner of communication, since neighbours could tune in to a conversation taking place between two other parties. Some people were said to have spent half their day listening to the dialogue on the phone, surreptitiously taking in the information as a means of entertainment. Of course, the people conversing on the phone knew that they probably were being listened to, so they likely spoke in a sort of code, nuanced and subtle perhaps, to camouflage certain facts. All the residents had to accept this system, the only one available to them at that time. On occasion it would take a long time before the line was available for use, with two parties talking about insignificant matters. One would think that this would have caused some bitterness between telephone subscribers, but it didn't seem to make much difference. The eavesdropping factor may have been more important than anything else, in that it was an unintentionally "indispensable" part of the system, supplying a diversion for all. Since I didn't use the telephone all that often, the party line system didn't affect me too greatly.

In the evening I had to go into the pastures and urge the cows back to the stable area where my uncle would milk them, his hands skilfully working the udders that jettisoned spurts of milk into a clean pail. He had me try it out a few times, but since he usually had five or six cows to milk he didn't waste too much time teaching me a technique that I didn't have that much enthusiasm for, being the perpetual neophyte town boy.

While the milking was taking place, the cow would likely be lashing out at the flies with her tail, my uncle always concerned about being hit in the eye. He told me that he had once tied the tail of one of his cows to her leg, but then the cow had attempted to kick at the insects pestering her, and had upset the milk pail, with the milk wasted on the floor and the cow's foot narrowly missing my uncle's nose. After that close call, he decided to endure the risk of the flicking tail.

The milk we drank at the farm was not pasteurized, a fact that my mother worried about. And since my uncle did not have a refrigerator, the milk was usually lukewarm. But this resource was magically renewable and freshly available twice a day. So I grew to love the fresh milk from the cows.

Cream and butter were often kept in the frigid water at the bottom of the well, to preserve their freshness, and were lowered in a bucket on a regular basis, using a thin rope. Some of the farmers had built a "dairy," which was a small building erected in a cool area where the butter and cream and other perishables were kept.

Most of the jobs that my uncle gave me involved the vegetable garden at one side of the farmhouse. Occasionally, Janice would work in the garden with me, mostly telling me what to do, but since she did the housekeeping she would be busy in the kitchen much of the time. Mainly, I was to make sure that the weeds did not overrun the garden, and that the potato bugs were kept at a minimum on the leaves of the plants. I filled many large glass jars with the little red and black devils. Old Willie Connors down the road identified them as the "Baltimore Beetle," but I never really checked to see if this was correct.

The potato, of course, has always been a life-preserving resource for the Irish farmer. In the early days, potatoes were planted as soon as the land was cleared. They were a very important part of the diet of the first settlers. Eventually, the farmers were able to grow large quantities of this starchy tuber, a product that they sold at markets. Some of the potatoes were kept for seed and usually stored in pits for the next crop.

My uncle's garden was a large plot and produced a considerable amount of vegetables, which were consumed well into the fall and early winter. Most of this produce was kept below the kitchen in a cool cellar, which was accessed by a trapdoor in the floor. When this heavy trapdoor was opened, usually with the supervision of my uncle, a waft of cold air would rise. A precipitous stairway led down and a small light could be switched on to reveal the shelving on which the vegetables and preserves were stored.

One of the problems in the cellar was the presence of the occasional rat. It was an ongoing battle for my uncle to keep this curse under control. At least once, I had seen him emerge from below holding a trap with a large rodent dangling. At such a time, my uncle would have a triumphant look on his face.

"They're pretty smart," he would say. "They knock over and smash the glass bottles. Then they have a feast."

There were many containers of jams and jellies and jars of preserved pork and beef in the cellar. Janice had learned how to prepare preserves under the tutelage of my Aunt Mona who lived about five miles from my uncle.

Janice was a treasure to her father in many ways. Not only had she developed into an excellent cook at the tender age of sixteen, but she had acquired many other skills that she seemed to practise with an obvious joy. My uncle did not treat her as a slave. Rather, he seemed to have a grateful look on his face whenever he spoke about her. And when he talked to her it was as if he were addressing an older person who might give him advice. I found this aspect of their relationship to be extraordinary.

She also operated the cream separator where the freshly drawn milk was poured into the top receptacle. Janice would turn the handle and the milk would "divide," separating into either cream or skim milk. The cream was stored down the well to cool and the skim milk, more often than not, was fed to the pigs. The separator had to be kept very clean: it was washed twice daily, because the cows were milked twice a day.

As a child, Janice had been partly raised by my Aunt Mona, my uncle's younger sister, who had cared for her with great love even though she had five children of her own. Janice had been coddled and fussed over by my Aunt Mona's family, who came to accept her as a "sister."

My father and Uncle Mike had two older sisters, but they had moved to the United States as young women and had married and were raising their own families in New Hampshire. Both had volunteered to take Janice in and nurture her but my Uncle Mike naturally preferred to keep Janice close to him. My Uncle Mike's deceased wife, Annie, had been the only daughter in a family of four children, so after she died it was considered more practical because of circumstances that Janice should be raised by my Aunt Mona.

My Uncle Mike's two boys, Charlie and Lawrence, were a great comfort to him as they grew into manhood. They emerged as strapping young men who were "joined at the hip," very close in their relationship. They had suffered terribly with the loss of their mother, but the support of their relatives and friends had buoyed them up sufficiently that they finally accepted the death. When they graduated from high school, however, both boys began making plans to move away from the farm, get work in Montreal, and take night courses. My uncle always felt that both boys associated the farm with the most distressing time of their lives and that they wanted to get away. He had hoped to leave the farm to one of them when he passed on, but he wondered how he was going to do it since neither of them wanted to manage a farm operation. He secretly hoped that one of them would grow tired of urban life and return to Pine River, but the prospect did not seem likely.

At the farm, Janice wore blue denim most of the time, with the leg bottoms turned up—fitting them snugly, I felt. At times I would sit around the kitchen talking to her while she baked or made butter with the churn or prepared preserves of strawberry jam. She would seldom look at me during these conversations, always totally absorbed in what she was doing.

I played a lot of scrub softball at the ball field with the guys. Our primitive diamond was located near the dance hall and church. We usually were five or six kids and would play the whole afternoon long if the weather co-operated. Then we'd sit around and talk, often about girls and about school.

Some of the guys liked to fish and I would tag along; we would fight our way through the brambles and swat at the mosquitoes that left bite marks on your skin. I used to joke with my buddies about how the flies and mosquitoes liked the taste of a city dweller since it provided them with a different variety, after having to put up with the blood of country hicks, a boring and tasteless diet. I remember, while spending a weekend at the farm, I had gone fishing with some of the kids. I was then about ten years old. I had been bitten so often that my arms and face were simply covered with red marks, to the extent that everyone at school thought I had measles or chicken pox or some other vile communicable disease.

I was pretty close with Tommy Kelly, a tall kid with a kind of scrawny look. But he was as strong as an ox. He was one of the boys who travelled by train to school in Quebec City every day. We both went to the same high school but he was one year behind me, so I didn't get to see him very often at school, except during recess time. He always had to leave right away after dismissal to take his train back home. But when summertime came and I could come out to my Uncle Mike's, I would meet Tommy and spend a lot of time with him. His younger brother Patrick was only eleven years old and I didn't hang around with him too much, although he was a hell of a good ball player for a young kid. Patrick, at the time, was going into grade six and went to the Pine River village school.

My friend Tommy was pretty intellectual in his approach to life even if he had just started high school. He was very interested in current events, keeping scrapbooks of the activities of world leaders such as Russian dictator Joseph Stalin and American president Harry Truman, and following the progress of the Korean War closely. He liked to talk about these things and I was a good listener, partly because of my admiration for him. When we would go fishing or be walking down to the ball field, Tommy would always be rattling on about some world event that most of the boys knew little about, and didn't care to comment on. Not that Tommy wasn't interested in other things. He was a good softball player too, and probably the best hitter in the group.

I usually stayed at my Uncle Mike's for a few two-week periods during the summer. My two brothers also liked to visit him, but since space in his house was limited, he only took us one at a time. My brothers were also younger than I was, so they needed to be watched a little more closely. At least, that's what I heard my Uncle Mike say to my dad one day while Mom and Dad were visiting. So during much of the summertime one of the boys from my family would be out at the farm until school started again in September.

My uncle considered me to be more independent, and also capable of doing more of the chores around the fields and stable, like feeding the calves with pails of milk or fetching the cows or helping him with the hay and oats.

The haying season was the busiest time for my brothers and myself, although that summer I wasn't at the farm while most of the hay was cut and gathered. My uncle used a horse-drawn mowing machine to cut the hay and it was our job to rake it up into piles so that it could be easily forked into the hay wagon for delivery to the barn.

When I took the bus back home after two weeks at my uncle's, I always felt somewhat disheartened. Not only did I have to deal with life in a noisy city once again, but I wasn't sure when I would be permitted to head back to my uncle's place for another stay.

Chapter 2

Quebec City is a beautiful place to be in the summertime. The temperature is usually quite agreeable, and we get a pretty fair supply of sunshine. My family—Mom and Dad, my two brothers and one sister and myself—lived in a six-room flat facing the Provincial Parliament Buildings near the Plains of Abraham, a large park of historical significance.

Going to my Uncle Mike's farm was like visiting another country, in a sense. I wouldn't hear a word of French during the whole time I was there. My uncle's neighbours were of Irish descent for the most part and spoke English in their own way, some with Irish brogues they'd inherited from their ancestors, many of whom came to Canada over 140 years ago. So getting back to Quebec City was always a reawakening to the reality of life for me. All of our neighbours in Quebec City, with few exceptions, were French-speaking. Naturally, I had learned to communicate in French from the time I was very young, roaming around our neighbourhood. Some of the French-speaking kids who lived on my street were always ready for a game of street hockey, or for all the shenanigans that growing boys engage in.

The old city is also a tourist Mecca of sorts, with thousands of visitors, mostly Americans, coming every year. The peak season is from June to September, and droves of walkers can be seen during the day, traipsing along the high walls or through the narrow streets of the old fortified section, part of the renowned Citadel, often with guides recounting the historical data to them. Much of the history of the old city is related to the Battle of the Plains of Abraham in 1759 when the British army of General Wolfe defeated the French defenders under General Montcalm. It is more than likely that there were Irish soldiers in both armies at this famous battle. Even before this historic fray, some Irish had been present in Upper and Lower Canada under the French regime. The British army and navy did a lot of recruiting in Ireland. It was one way that young Irishmen could escape the institutionalized poverty imposed upon them by their masters. Some would have been attracted to the long scarlet coat and the three-cocked hat—uniforms worn by the thousands of men who made up the phalanxes of the English army. The French army also hired Irish mercenaries, both nationalities being strongly attached to the Catholic Church.

Thus began the influx of the Irish in the Quebec City area.

During the Great Irish Potato Famine of the 1840s, the exodus led to Canada for many of the Irish. Some of them ended up in Quebec City, others in Montreal, but many died en route as a result of disease contracted on the ships, not to mention the horrific suffering and death in Montreal and Quebec City as typhus ravaged these two communities. Thousands of Irish immigrants are buried on Grosse Isle, an island close to Quebec City, a quarantine station set up by authorities at the time. Those who made it through safely settled in very well with the French-speaking population and found employment in Quebec City. But more of these newcomers moved on to alternative areas in North America.

Many Irish children who lost their parents to typhus and related diseases during these calamitous times were adopted by francophones. These orphans were legally allowed to keep their names, though later being assimilated into the French culture. There are many French-speaking citizens in Quebec with Irish surnames.

By the late 1800s, a large proportion of the Quebec City police force was of Irish extraction. This was an indication of how well the Irish were accepted as part of the social life of the city. The English-speaking proportion of the city's population was quite sizeable during that era, but had reached its apex. Since then, numbers of English speakers have declined steadily.

The building of a reinforced Citadel, the walled-off fortification, was undertaken in the 1820s by the English Regime and held a position above the St. Lawrence River atop the promontory. In the old days heavy cannons were perched on this advantageous point, capable of firing at ships that might be ill-intentioned. However, since the construction of the elaborate new Citadel, completed in 1831, there has never been a need to defend the city from attack.

Horse-drawn two-wheeled calèches and four-wheeled victorias, often preferred by visitors as a way of observing the points of interest, are frequently seen on the ancient streets of the old city as well as on the Plains of Abraham. In the city itself, these carriages interfere with the regular flow of traffic, but everyone accepts it as being a necessary evil to accommodate the benefits of the burgeoning tourist industry, an indispensable component in the economic life of the city.

Since a horse spends many hours pulling its load through the streets, it does what horses always do under natural circumstances and leaves a trail of defecation in the middle of many of the thoroughfares. This always produces a unique odorous essence that some people say contributes to the atmosphere and ambience of the old city. Of course, the oldest people are accustomed to this odour, having been raised at a time when the horse was the main mode of business transportation and amusement.

When I got back home from this trip to my uncle's after a two-week stay, it was well into July. My mom and dad were naturally curious as to how my visit went. My father, Thomas Carroll, was a teacher at the elementary school level at that time, although he was enjoying a two-month summer rest. His class was in the same building as my high school, but in a different section of the complex. I was still simmering with the moroseness of being back home, after having spent two weeks in heaven, so I wasn't too talkative.

My mom, who was Teresa Lawson before she married my dad, was born in Verdun, near Montreal. She met my dad at a bowling alley in Montreal where Dad's parish bowling team had gone to play Mom's parish team. This rivalry took place every year, part of a socialization program organized by the churches.

I'd arrived back from my uncle's just as my family was about to sit down for supper. I'd walked home from the bus station.

"So how's your Uncle Mike?" my mom asked.

"Oh, pretty good, I guess,"

"Did you go fishing?" my kid brother Eamon asked. He spent a lot of time fishing when he visited my uncle

"Just once," I said. "Mostly we played softball, and I helped Uncle Mike with a few things."

I really didn't want to talk much about it. It was bad enough that I was caged in at our flat again after leaving the wide-open spaces of the countryside.

My younger brother Eamon was twelve at the time and just going into high school. My other brother, Stephen, had just turned ten and was going into grade five, where my dad would teach him. I also had a kid sister, Eileen, who was then just starting school.

Eamon and "Stevie" had a love-hate relationship dating from as far back as I could remember. They did a lot of things together, spending time on the street, playing hockey with the neighbourhood kids, travelling to and from school, and having to share the same bedroom. At times they would actually physically attack each other over some trivial matter. My parents were quite concerned about them and would frequently give one of them "penalty time," as my dad called it. Surprisingly, they were both about the same size as they approached their teens, Stevie seeming to grow at an accelerated rate. He would eventually grow to be well over six feet tall. But their problem disappeared as they advanced through high school. Stevie had enduring admiration for his older brother, who would make the school football team, and he cheered himself hoarse at all of Eamon's games.

My dad would not speak to me right away about my trip to the farm, but would leave his young family the time to get certain questions out of the way. Later in the evening, he would sit down with me on the living room couch and ask about my trip. He was always concerned about his older brother, and felt that Uncle Mike should not be living "alone," unattached. But my Uncle Mike had been a widower for over sixteen years and there seemed to be little chance that he would ever hook up with another woman.

My dad also said that he envied his older brother who was living on his own piece of land in the country. But my dad could never have been a farmer. How would he have been able to spend his time reading if he were obliged to look after a 300-acre farm with cattle and horses and hens and pigs and the general upkeep of an enterprise that kept my Uncle Mike busy from dawn to dusk?

My dad held deep respect for the family farms of the nation. These were the people who supplied us with the sustenance of life, he would remind us. The farmer was under appreciated, underpaid, and disrespected, my dad always said.

Now that I was back in town and since I had a lot of free time on my hands during the summer break, I decided to look for a way to make a few dollars. Following the example of some of my schoolmates, I went down to the old city section where there are at least three large hotels and a plethora of small rooming houses for tourists. Many of these houses are architecturally similar, with stone front facades and slanting roofs built in a traditional European style. The streets in this area are very narrow and were configured many years ago for horse and cart rather than for cars and trucks. So during summertime this section of the city is in a constant snarl with tour buses, taxis, horse-drawn rigs, and the regular traffic. But despite these drawbacks, there is a great atmosphere, with the dominating Chateau Frontenac Hotel and the boardwalk and the open squares and the elegant old churches all perched on the relic of a city above the St. Lawrence River.

The electric streetcars are gone from the city now, but back then, for some people, the trolleys contributed to the spirit of the old capital. In my mind's eye I can still see them grinding up the main streets. During hot summer nights, with the windows of our flat wide open, the sound of the trolleys seemed comforting. When the foul-smelling buses replaced the trolleys, people who lived in main street dwellings yearned for the odourless, if noisy, streetcar whine that had been a constant presence in their lives. Miles of wire grids were removed from above the streets with this change in city transportation. This gave the streets a less cluttered look, according to the city fathers.

Many tourist rooming houses on the narrow streets do business at economical rates. They are close to the big hotels and the boardwalk. Several of my school friends had secured work in this type of establishment helping visitors with their luggage and doing ancillary work for the owners. Certainly, in most cases, the proprietors of these houses weren't going to carry the suitcases of their patrons up the narrow staircases of these older buildings.

Earned income for this sort of work depended upon the generosity of the tourists, who usually tipped you for toting their luggage. There might also be a small salary given to you by the owner for running errands, or helping out in any way with the business of handling American visitors. Being able to speak English was an asset in securing such employment.

One of my school buddies, Jackie Farrell, a guy I played hockey with, told me that he was leaving town with his parents for a three-week period and he asked me if I was interested in replacing him at the tourist home where he worked. Naturally, I agreed, and he brought me down to the Manoir de la Porte to introduce me to the owner, a Madame Gingras. She seemed to be a very nice lady at first, although I discovered later that she could get quite cranky. For ten dollars a week, I was to perform the regular work of a "bellhop" as well as making sure that her clients had places to park their vehicles in the back lot of the rooming house. Because of the cramped streets, very few parking spots were available. However, there was room for about ten cars in her parking lot. Visitors were constantly checking in and out of Madame Gingras's "maison touristique," a three-storied structure with about a dozen rooms to rent.

I usually got to the rooming house at eight o'clock in the morning so that I could help people as they were checking out. My mom would make me a lunch for noontime. I went back home at four in the afternoon. Madame Gingras would berate me for not being present when clients registered in the evenings. Then the visitors had to carry their own suitcases up the stairs.

"I'm sorry, Madame Gingras, but my mom and dad want me to be home before five," I would explain to her.

I did not want to spend more time waiting around for people to decide to rent accommodations at Manoir de la Porte. There were many hours of boredom when I would sit on the cement outer stairway hoping for some action. Madame Gingras did not want me hanging around inside her house. She had many precious artefacts sitting on antique pieces of furniture. I felt that she never trusted me and thought that I would perhaps steal the original Québécois oil paintings from her walls and sell them. I fell in love with some of these works of art and when I passed one while doing a job, I would sometimes linger before it, gazing at the elegance of the colours. Madame Gingras would look at me suspiciously as if to say: "Get outside, and don't loiter inside my house."

She also demanded that I come to work looking presentable, with a clean white shirt and long trousers. This rule was a nuisance on hot summer days. And she expected me to be there six days a week.

So I was relieved when, after a three-week period, Jackie Farrell arrived home from his trip and naturally wanted his job back. It just so happened that I was able in August to return to my uncle's and spend the rest of the summer break there.

Chapter 3

One of the amazing things about being in this Irish country community for a lengthy period was being exposed to the hospitality and generosity of the farm folk. Everyone knew that I was the eldest son of Tom Carroll. My father was held in high regard and was considered a success story. As a young man he had left his father's farm, an inheritance later passed down to my Uncle Mike, who was the elder male of the family. My dad worked in Montreal and eventually enrolled in college to qualify for the teaching profession.

Both my Uncle Mike and my father were absolved from serving in the Second World War. In my uncle's case, it was because he was a widower with three young children to raise and because he was a farmer and a producer of food products. My father was also married before 1940 and was the father of two children. Even so, he wanted to be involved, but failed the eye test after volunteering to join the Royal Canadian Air Force.

Many of the people in my uncle's neighbourhood were cousins of mine and whenever I met them there would be invitations to supper. The welcome was unsparing and lavish. I can remember that, from the time I was very young, I was always made to feel very special when I visited, usually accompanied by my Uncle Mike and Janice. It was during this time that I began to play euchre at these homes. This card game could include six players and usually was pursued with much enthusiasm, including loud exclamations and table thumping by some of the men, a few of whom had huge callused and sunburned hands—capable of splitting a kitchen table in two, I worried. After the card game, everyone would sit around the kitchen, the men drinking beer or whisky. Some of my father's cousins were very good singers and knew the old Irish folk songs. It was quite comical to hear them coax each other into a song.

"Jim, sing 'The Wild Colonial Boy.'"

"But I'm not sure of all the words," my dad's cousin Jim Foy would say.

"Go ahead, Jim. You start and I'll help you."

And Jimmy Foy would start the song, run into trouble with the words, and others would prompt him with the next verse to help him keep singing. More often than not, everything was sung without accompaniment. Not that there weren't accomplished musicians in the community. More than a few of the locals played fiddle or accordion.

Those who sang would chant these old Irish songs that I had never heard before, many of which told tragic tales about the struggles against the British usurpers. Songs like "Mrs. McGrath," a tale about a young man who comes home to his mother after serving with the British navy. Both of his legs are missing after a battle at sea. It may have been these songs that spurred my interest in Irish history and awakened something deep inside me. I began to realize that there were other things in life besides hockey.

There was little wealth among these people, the farm operations providing comfort and security, but not much more. The land itself tended to be sandy at its base and rocky on its surface and therefore not suitable for growing certain produce. Much of the income of these farmers was acquired by selling butter and cream in the nearby towns or by the raising and sale of cattle or pigs or turkeys. A certain amount of wood-cutting for fuel and logging for sawmills also could provide earnings, since many of the farm properties had acres of land populated by stands of strong, sturdy evergreens as well as birch, maple, and an assortment of others. Some residents had acquired employment at the Military Camp, doing maintenance work or on construction projects.

The United States of America had always been a source of attraction to the Irish immigrants who had initially come to Canada. Some would use Quebec as a stopping-off point with the intention of finally moving south. This attitude was quite prevalent in the minds of the newcomers, the growing economy of the U.S. being a great source of wonderment. With the limited prospects that the toil of farming presented, there was much dislocation toward the American land of unlimited opportunity. It was not extraordinary for all the children of certain families to leave for the south, so that some of the original Irish names in the early influx of immigrants would simply disappear from the social fabric of Pine River. But for many, life in Pine River was more than satisfactory. The day-to-day work of running a farming operation held its attractions.

The slaughter of some of the livestock furnished the farm families with meat for the long winter months. All farms had their dairy cows that supplied milk for cream and butter, and most farms raised hens to provide eggs for themselves and to sell or barter in neighbouring towns.

Hog-raising provided the farmers with a guaranteed income at very little expense. The Irish had always had great respect for these creatures and referred to the pig as "the gentleman who paid the rent." The oats grown in the fields, the skim milk, and the discarded potatoes were all mixed together to nourish the hogs. These ingredients were often brought to a miller who ground this compost into "meal." This ingredient was also fed to the chickens and turkeys.

The farmers were very close to their animals, in a sense. All of the horses had names, of course, and even some of the cows were nicknamed, often by the children. I noticed that when I went with my Uncle Mike to the stable to give him a hand with something, he would be forever talking to the horses as if they were people.

"How are ya today, Jess?" my uncle would say. "You got enough to eat there? We're gonna let you go out in a minute, it's such a lovely day today."

And the horses would be happy to see us, their heads moving up and down and back and forth, their feet shuffling.

In some cases it was very difficult for a farmer to "put down" a cow. There were those in the neighbourhood who specialized in doing this work. My Aunt Mona's husband, Matt Hayes, was one of these men. Everyone knew that he was very good at dispatching an animal very quickly. I had seen on one occasion a carcass hanging by its hind legs from the large doorway of my uncle's barn with the stomach split open to be disembowelled and the other entrails removed before the butchering. It was not a pleasant sight, yet we all knew of the necessity of this work.

But even if there was little chance for the accumulation of wealth, little poverty occurred among these people. They were resilient and proud and willing to help one another when difficulty arose.

Devotion to their church had become a solid and enduring force in these agrarian people. My Uncle Mike drove me and Janice to Sunday Mass whenever I was at the farm. The parishioners showed great respect for the priest who said the weekly Mass—Father Emmett Lynch. Father Lynch was actually a chaplain at the Military Camp. The relationship between the pastor and the people could be very strong. Back in the 1890s, a curate at Pine River had been transferred by the bishop of the diocese to a distant parish. Several of the farming families sold their holdings and followed their pastor to his new parish many miles away. The attachment could be very deep.

The get-together after Mass was an opportune time for the Irish Catholic community. For most, it was the only period during the week when they could interact as neighbours. Some would chat for over an hour, telling of the latest events in their lives. After all, farming was a solitary occupation, each farmer, day after day, grinding out the routine of caring for his land and animals. A farmer could not afford to be sick. The cows could not wait to be milked, the grain and produce had to be reaped upon ripening, the farmer had to be a jack-of-all-trades, forever subservient to the operation and maintenance of his enterprise. He had to deal with unexpected eventualities, unavoidable in a farm operation. The farmer was his own boss, answering to no one but his family.

Thus, the gathering on Sunday outside the doors of the church was a period of renewal and rediscovery for them.

Another important social event took place at the community centre on many Saturday nights. This was a square dance with hired musicians, usually accordion and fiddle players. The building literally rocked with the sound of bouncing feet, with couples swinging, twirling around at a furious pace—a highly appreciated skill. The man and woman had to have perfect balance in order to spin on the spot. I wondered how they were able to accomplish this feat without falling. This technique seemed to be designed to hold the partner up using a kind of centrifugal force. The other couples would stop dancing and gather around the expert "swingers," clapping in rhythm, with many howls thrown in.

Whatever drinking took place was done outside the hall. Many of the young men would stand around, swigging beer and talking about cars. On the balmy summer nights, there was something magical about standing outdoors in the moonlight, listening to the music from inside the dance hall and hanging around with your friends.

While I was in Pine River that summer, my Uncle Mike drove Janice and me down to two of these affairs. I usually hung around the outside of the hall with Tommy and the other guys, but occasionally we would go inside, sit on the benches along the wall, and watch the show. More than a few times Janice would coax me to be her partner, but I was quite shy about trying this kind of dance, especially one of them called the "Lanciers." I finally relented and went through the motions, struggling to keep up with the rest, Janice pushing me forward, mostly amid adults who had been doing it for decades. The "swinging" part of it was the most challenging. I was relieved when the set was finished, even if I sort of enjoyed it and wished I knew the moves a little better.

I heard talk of an almost mythical figure from decades before, a man by the name of Willie Carson, who was said to have frequented these barn dances. He was an incredibly imaginative practical joker who drove the people crazy with his antics. In the old days, all the farm families arrived at the dance hall with their horses and rigs and tied the horses to a rail not far removed from the building. At the height of one evening's festive dancing, Willie managed to sneak out of the dance hall unnoticed. He released nearly all of the horses that were tied to the rail, slapped them on the rump, and sent them off. Just about all of the horses, familiar with the territory, headed home. When the dancers inside got wind of what had happened, they were not sure who was responsible for this exasperating deed. Many had to walk or hitch rides home, several miles, in most cases to find their horse and empty rig waiting for them at the stable door of their homesteads. It gradually became known that Willie Carson had been at work again. They would have killed him had they caught him on the night of his caper, but time soon dulled their anger. From that point on, he was watched with great care wherever he turned up.

I got back to my Uncle Mike's on August 10th. The understanding was that I could stay until the end of the month. The haying season was over. My younger brothers both had helped my uncle with the gathering of this crop. But there was still work to do in the fields. After the oats had been cut and bundled by the machines, I had to gather these together into shocks so that they could be easily loaded on the wagon for the trip back to the barn. I found that working with the stalks of oats was a little unpleasant because of the bristly nature of these strands of grain. I remember the hay being easier to handle, and when it was piled in the barn you could jump from a high perch and land with little chance of injury. We used to spend time in Tommy Kelly's barn doing somersaults from one of the high beams into a soft bed of hay.

It was on this visit to my uncle's that Tommy Kelly and I were to witness an event that would haunt us for many months.

On Sunday morning, August 17, after Uncle Mike had driven Janice and me home from Mass in his old Ford, Tommy telephoned wondering if I was interested in going fishing in one of the brooks that ran through the farms on what is known as the 7th range. This land area has a long, winding sandy road that stretches through a mixture of forest and open fields of planted grain. Tommy told me that his father had suggested there might be rainbow trout in some of the rills that flowed into the Rivière aux Pins, the principal waterway in the area.

Because my Uncle Mike was not likely to need my help on this particular Sunday, and since I wouldn't turn down a chance to spend the day with Tommy, I agreed to meet him close by and we would go up the 7th range road.

It was a gorgeous day with a cool breeze blowing as Tommy and I set out to find our way to the spot suggested by his father.

As usual, Tommy was talking about the Korean War and how the United Nations forces, led by the Americans, had twice repelled the Communist armies, first the North Koreans, then later the Chinese army which had entered the war and had initially thrown the American army back. He said that the big hero at this stage of the conflict was General Matthew Ridgeway, who had succeeded General Douglas MacArthur, a stubborn man who fell out of favour with the Truman administration. Now, Tommy said, the war was at a stalemate and negotiations had been started with the Communist powers to bring an end to the fighting. The partition line between the two opposing armies was just about at the same spot as it had been when the war started. As a member of the United Nations, Canada was committed to aid in this conflict and would eventually send more than twenty thousand troops to Korea. Tommy was going on about the utter stupidity of war and told me that he could not understand how a Chinese soldier would seem to have so much hate instilled into him that he was willing to die in order to kill the Americans. He told me that great masses of Chinese soldiers would storm American positions, sometimes at night, and hundreds of men would be lost out in the open—much as in the First World War.

The Cold War was well under way at this time and, with both the United States and the Soviet Union stocked with nuclear weapons, there was a climate of expectancy and fear throughout the civilized world. The Russians did not trust the United States, partly because the Americans had used the atomic bomb against the civilian population of Japan in the Second World War. Tommy was worried that the Korean conflict would spiral into a Third World War. He said that humanity seemed to learn nothing from history. Here we were, Tommy said, just seven years after a war in which untold millions were killed, and yet the politicians of both sides were once again testing the frontiers of insanity.

Tommy's expression of these military and philosophical points was very enlightening to me, and I wondered how such a young person could have such a grasp of world events as well as a jaundiced view of human behaviour.

We trudged up the sandy road for a mile or so and went across a field into a partly wooded section. I had never been in that area before, a mixture of pasture and forest that buzzed with the sounds of summer. In most cases there was an unwritten agreement that young people could wander around these tracts of land, where they usually fished in the brooks that lazily made their way to the larger stream—the Rivière aux Pins. I noticed that, in this particular sector, there was some fencing, no doubt erected to prevent cattle from getting lost or disoriented or roving into neighbouring growths of grain.

Although I felt somewhat adrift in our search for this "famous" brook, Tommy seemed to know where he was going and, sure enough, as we tramped around a copse of young trees, we began to hear the sound of running flow, fleeting at first, then louder as we approached it. What we came upon was a stream of blue and brown easy-flowing water, almost creek-sized, lustrous in the intermittent rays of the sun. We followed it until it had smoothed out into a calmer drift on flatter land, half forested and half meadow. We decided to set up under the shade of a tall pine, and sat on the moss-covered banks, thankful that there seemed to be fewer mosquitoes in this more open area. Our fishing rods were quite primitive—long pieces of branch that had been chosen and trimmed, not too heavy but sturdy. Tommy had accumulated quite a few of these branches which he kept handy in the shed near his house, and he had chosen one for me. Tommy always seemed to be on the lookout for suitable limbs of trees. If we were walking down a road or in a field he would suddenly stop and work his way into a growth of shrubs or trees to snap off a desired offshoot.

For fishing line we used a tan-coloured hemp string rolled off a spool and attached a fishing hook.

We sat down and began furling some fat red worms around our hooks. Tommy had gathered them earlier from the manure pile behind the Kelly barn and had put them in a tin can.

Then the wait began. I was told by Tommy to talk in hushed tones so as not to disturb the tranquillity so vital in the brook-fishing process. He said that if we spoke softly our voices would blend into the natural sounds of the wind and the trickle of water and the various calls of creatures. Although Tommy was younger than I was, I was quite willing to listen to his counsel.

As we sat in this tranquil location, after having dipped our fishing hooks into the languid flowing water, we began to hear the sound of raised voices in the distance, voices with a tinge of anger. Then there would be a few seconds of silence, but the voices would rise in resonance again. It was obviously an argument between two men.

Tommy and I looked at each other wondering what the fuss was all about. We laid down our fishing rods, rose, and began to walk, somewhat stealthily, to where the voices seemed to be coming from. We looked down upon a large field of oats to where a sort of path was elevated upon the remains of what Tommy told me was an old railway that had been in operation many years before.

From a cluster of trees we could see two men standing and talking to each other across a fence. They both looked to be middle-aged. Tommy recognized both men almost immediately.

"I'm sure that's Paddy Connors with the blue shirt," Tommy said. "He has a farm farther down. The guy on the other side of the fence is Mike Ferrigan, and his property starts right there at the fence."

We noticed that two children were walking away from them, about twenty yards down the railroad bed from the two men.

"So you know both of these guys?" I said.

"Yeah, sure. Paddy is my mom's cousin. You know, I think these two guys are related to each other, too."

As we stood there talking just above a whisper, behind a tree, at a safe distance, the argument of the two men took on new energy, and one of them half-leaned across the fence, waving a finger, and seemed to be threatening the other man. We could understand them quite clearly as they raised their voices once again.

"I don't want to see you on this path any more!" Michael Ferrigan was saying loudly.

"But we all use this path. What's the harm in that?" Paddy said, just below a yell.

"The fence is across the railway bed to keep the cattle out," stormed Mike Ferrigan. "People are passing by, opening the fence, and won't put it back, and the cows come in through the gap. Everybody is doing it on purpose and I'm getting damn tired of it. Dunigan's cows are feeding on my oats and I have to send one of the kids out to chase the cows back."

"Mike, I don't want to fight about this. We have a legal right to pass here."

"I'm not putting up with this any more!" Ferrigan said emphatically.

"This is a public roadway. We have to come this way, otherwise we'd have to take the other road which is twice as far."

Ferrigan seemed to grow more agitated during the discussion, more threatening.

"I don't want you coming back this way, or it'll be bad for you to do it. Go around by the other road. This is my property and you're trespassing on my property. Don't come back this way or you won't go back to the same tune as you came!" he said, waving his finger once again at Paddy Connors.

"You can't stop me from walking on a public road," answered Paddy. "I always put your fence back up after I pass."

"No, you don't! I'm warning you, don't come back this way!" said Mike Ferrigan, and he walked away up the track toward his house which I could not see from behind the trees but which Tommy said was about half a mile away.

Paddy Connors also turned, and started walking down the railroad bed the opposite way. He cupped his hands over his mouth and called out the names of the two children who had gone ahead.

"Marianne! Hughie! Wait for me!" he shouted.

But Mike Ferrigan wasn't finished talking. He turned back toward Paddy Connors and began yelling something that I couldn't understand perfectly, but it think it was, "You get yourself a good man and I'll get one too and we'll see if you're able to smash my mouth."

Paddy half turned, stopped, and yelled back, "Get one yourself!" and then kept walking down the old track toward the children.

I could see that both of these farmers were pretty big men, and I wouldn't have liked to intervene if they got into a scrap.

"Those two guys can't stand each other," said Tommy. "They've had a few arguments before. My dad said that he had to help keep them apart at a council meeting a few months ago. Paddy Connors wanted to take Ferrigan outside and fight him. Paddy said that Ferrigan was not paying enough school tax or something and Mike Ferrigan called him a goddamn liar. That wasn't the first time they had a run-in. They haven't been civil with each other for years."

We started back to our fishing spot after both men had disappeared from view.

"And you say that they're related to each other?" I asked.

"Yeah, distant cousins, I think. Mike Ferrigan has about ten kids and he owns another property farther down. But nobody likes the idea of him putting a fence across that old railroad track. Everybody uses that track to pass through because Mike Ferrigan doesn't really own the land where the railroad track is. It belongs to the railroad that used to pass here years ago. The railroad never really gave up that land. People have used it as a walking path for years. I guess that when people pass with their horses they don't put the fence back up after they take it down. Everybody tells Ferrigan to rearrange his fencing, but I guess he doesn't want to be bothered. My dad thinks Mike Ferrigan is a little wacky. It seems to run in his family."

I found it somewhat surprising that two neighbours in these peaceful surroundings would be on such bad terms. It was unexpected to hear of such a confrontation in a community where the farmers were from families who had lived together in harmony for generations. The threat by Michael Ferrigan was ominous in its tone and we both sensed at the time that what we had witnessed was not the end of it; that, as Tommy said to me, "there were going to be very bad feelings and perhaps some violence" as a result.

"Mike Ferrigan's got an awful temper," said Tommy. "He actually killed a man about fifteen years ago with an axe, but they decided that he had done that in self-defence, so they let him go free. And my dad says that Paddy Connors was a little wild when he was younger and got into some scraps in Quebec where he worked for a while. Anyhow, he's not afraid of Mike Ferrigan and would stand up to him anytime."

That additional information made me feel uncomfortable, now that we had witnessed the threats from Ferrigan.

As we got close to where we had been fishing, we were a little careless and were walking in the open between some tall trees. We heard the steps of someone running and looked down to the railroad bed again to see a young lad jogging toward Mike Ferrigan's fence. The boy noticed us and slowed down to a walk and then stopped, looking up to where we were. He may have been about a hundred yards away from us. It was a peculiar little scene with the boy staring at us while we stood still and stared back down at him. He was a big kid wearing shorts and a sweater.

"That's one of Mike Ferrigan's boys. There's five or six of them," Tommy said softly. "That's Joey; I remember him from the village school. But I never hung around with him."

"How old is he?"

"He's about our age. I'm not sure."

We were both stopped and continued to look down at him, but not a word was exchanged. Then he ran to the fence, scaled over it, and kept running along the railroad bed toward his house.

Tommy and I sat there by the side of the brook for a few hours in the afternoon of a grand sunlit day, but we weren't successful in landing any trout. We did catch a few catfish, those ugly-looking hairs sticking out of their mouths. Tommy said he could spot a few rainbow trout far down in the depth of water, but my untrained eye didn't see anything.

As we ambled back down the 7th range road, we had half-forgotten about the verbal altercation between the two farmers. We talked about other things. Tommy was never at a loss for words about the world situation and he seemed to have advice for all the politicians and leaders on earth concerning their irrational political stances. He talked about General Douglas MacArthur who wanted to bomb Chinese cities, possibly with atomic weapons, in retaliation for their entry into the war, and he commented on the eccentricities of Kim Il Sung, the leader of North Korea.

Chapter 4

By the time I got back to my Uncle Mike's, Janice had already put the Sunday tablecloth down and was waiting for my uncle to come back from visiting his sister, my Aunt Mona.

"So, did you catch anything?" Janice asked me.

"No. Just a few catfish," I told her.

"Did you bring them home?"

"We just threw them back in."

"I don't know how you guys can sit there for hours, just waiting for some dumb fish to bite your hook," she said.

"Tommy's dad told him that we could catch some rainbow trout in one of the brooks up there on the seventh range."

"You mean up near the old railroad track?"

"Yeah. How did you know?"

"Oh, I went up there with Teresa Dunigan a few weeks ago. She likes fishing, would you believe it?"

"It's a lot of fun when you get a bite," I said.

"You guys are pathetic!" she laughed.

Janice was wearing a dark green tartan skirt and a blouse because she'd been to Mass earlier with us. I loved the way she laughed. It was a sort of a little girl's laugh. She bounced back and forth in the kitchen while talking to me and had the wood stove going with a large pot simmering. I loved to watch her moving around with her perfect young lady's body and a frequent smile showing her perfect teeth. I tried to imagine myself as her boyfriend, putting my arms around her and holding her close. I kept thinking these things while I was talking to her and I wondered if I was normal or some twisted love-starved moron who was mentally deranged. I found myself repeatedly having thoughts of intimacy with her, and then asking God's forgiveness. It was a vicious circle.

"We saw two guys having a big argument up on that railroad path," I told Janice.

"Oh, yes? Who were they?"

"Tommy told me one of them is Mike Ferrigan and the other guy's name is Connors, I think."

"Paddy Connors?"

"Yeah, I think so."

"That Mike Ferrigan is a real trouble-maker. I'd stay away from him. He's got a bad temper. I heard that he murdered some guy years ago and the police let him get away with it; something about it being in self-defence. Of course, Dad said that the police didn't know him so he went free. But everybody around here knows him, believe me! A lot of people think he's pretty unbalanced."

"He was warning Paddy Connors not to pass that way again or he was gonna do something to him," I said.

"Yeah? Well, everybody uses that path, even if it passes through Ferrigan's property. If they didn't they'd have to all go around by the main road. For Paddy that's at least two miles longer. I'm sure he will go back home by the same way, so there might be trouble."

"Paddy had two kids with him."

"He's got five kids in all. I guess he was going down to his dad's place. He usually visits his mom and dad on Sunday with some of his kids. His parents live just over here near the sixth range road."

"They're both huge guys. I'd hate to have to step in between them."

"It's too bad, 'cause Dad says that Mike Ferrigan seems to be a good father to his kids, but he's got this bad temper and not many people are fond of him because of that."

Janice began setting the table and she reached over close to me several times, placing the plates and utensils. She had beautifully shaped arms, lightly tanned, and I always got that whiff of her, a very slightly perfumed scent that gave me a singular desire to be closer to her.

It was while I was sitting at the kitchen table that I could hear two men talking outside. We both went to the screen door and looked out to see my Uncle Mike conversing with a man in a blue shirt.

"There!" exclaimed Janice. "That's Paddy Connors! He's the guy you said was in the argument with Mike Ferrigan."

We both went outside.

We tentatively approached my uncle and Paddy Connors, who turned their attention toward us.

"Hello, Janice," said Paddy.

"Hi!" said Janice, and she advanced and shook his hand.

"Boy, you sure are growing up!"

Janice laughed.

"And this must be one of Tom's boys," said Paddy, looking at me.

"Yes," my Uncle Mike said, "this is the oldest boy, Francis."

Paddy Connors reached out and shook my hand.

"You know, Francis," he said, "I used to chum around with your father a lot in the old days. We spent plenty of time together. We did some fishing up by the River O Pah. When you get back home tell your dad you were talking to Pat Connors."

"You know, Paddy," my Uncle Mike said, rekindling the previous conversation, "I wouldn't worry about Ferrigan. He's just a blowhard. He's always threatening someone."

"Yes, well, he told me on the way in this morning that if I came back by the track he'd be ready for me, whatever that means."

"Well, Paddy, he's a big guy and he likes to intimidate people."

"It's just that I'm with the kids and I don't like them to have to listen to him trying to bully people."

"Look, Paddy, he's got no right to prevent people from using that track. We all know it passes through his land but we all know he doesn't own the part that the track was on. And, by rights, he shouldn't be putting a fence across that path."

I wanted to tell Paddy Connors that Tommy and I had heard some of the argument, but somehow the cat bit my tongue. I felt at the time that we had overheard something that we should not have been privy to.

"Still, I'm gonna ask Earl to come with me as a witness, 'cause you never know what he's up to," said Paddy.

"Will you have a cup of tea with us, Paddy?"

"No thanks, Mike. I'll be off now. I've gotta pick up the kids at Dad's and head home. I've got a big day tomorrow."

So Paddy Connors said goodbye to us and walked back down the road toward his parents' home. He was a tall man with husky shoulders and a youthful-looking face. We stood there a minute and watched him trudge along. My father may have mentioned Paddy Connors at home when he reminisced about life as a farm boy, something that he did pretty often. But I couldn't remember having heard the name Paddy Connors. My father talked about lots of people from his country birthplace, but I had lost track of most of their names.

I learned later that Paddy had an old '38 Ford, but it was in disrepair so he often harnessed up one of his horses if he had things to pick up. With the rig he would usually use the main road, which was a bumpy ride on its sandy surface, full of rocks and potholes. But on a sunny Sunday afternoon, there was no need to go to the bother of pulling a big rig. Paddy Connors had walked down to see his parents many times on a Sunday, using the old track, with a few of his children. Sometimes he would hitch up one of the horses to a cart for the railroad path, stopping along the way, probably telling his little ones what he knew about certain wildflowers and trees and the odd critter they would see bounding across the open spaces between the trees. Or exploring some of the swampy bogs along the way, the children looking for a bullfrog to catch. From what I understand, he was a self-educated man, an avid reader, and everyone in the neighbourhood spoke glowingly about him.

As my Uncle Mike, Janice, and I went back into the house, we didn't realize that it would turn out to be the last time that we would see Paddy Connors alive.

From the information we gathered later, Paddy Connors collected his two children at his father's house and began heading back home to his own property. Paddy had likely thought of what my Uncle Mike said about Michael Ferrigan and started back home without his brother Earl. He would be using the railroad path, the same way he had come. He must have kept his young daughter and son close to him as they went along when, less than a mile out from his father's house, cautiously aware, he caught a glimpse of a person in the distance, he said. That person he took to be Mike Ferrigan, who had emerged from a clump of bushes holding what Paddy thought to be a rifle in one hand.

Paddy immediately stopped, turned around, and headed back to his father's house.

It must have been after four o'clock on that bright Sunday afternoon and, from what we heard, Willie Connors, Paddy's father, was sitting with his wife Ellie on the porch of their house. They soon spotted Paddy and the two children coming down the road toward their house again, and got up from their chairs to go down and inquire as to why Paddy had returned.

As they approached him, Paddy was saying, "I just saw Ferrigan! I think he's got a gun in his hand!"

"Are you sure it's him?" asked Willie.

"Who else could it be? He told me this morning that he'd be waiting for me," said Paddy.

As it was told to us, Earl Connors, Paddy's younger brother, came out from the house at that moment. He lived with his parents, was still single, and did most of the chores at Willie's farm as well as holding down a job at the Military Camp.

"Ferrigan's carrying a gun," Paddy said to Earl. "I just saw him up the track a piece. You'd better come up with me until we get past his property. If anything happens, you'll be a witness and we'll get the law after him."

"All right," said Earl.

Ellie pleaded with Paddy to take the long road. "Don't go that way, Paddy. He's a crazy man. He'll just frighten the children."

Hughie, Paddy's eight-year-old son, already had tears in his eyes because of what was happening, even though he didn't understand it. Marianne was apparently more stoical about the situation.

"Maybe you should take the road, at least until things calm down a bit," suggested Willie.

"I think I have to have it out with him once and for all. He can't stop me from using the path. I'm gonna stop in at Coughlins' on the way up and ask Terry to come with me," went on Paddy. "Then there'll be three of us, so he won't be so courageous. Anyway, I have no fear, so don't worry about it."

And Paddy and Earl and the two children set off again, dropping in at the Coughlin homestead on the way up through the 7th range and enlisting Terry Coughlin, Elmer's son, to accompany them along the old track path through Mike Ferrigan's property. They soon met 16-year-old Dennis Cleary who, after having been informed about the prospect of trouble, agreed to go along with them as an additional witness.

So there they were: three adults, a boy in his teens, and the two children moving up the track.

Earlier in the afternoon, as Mike Ferrigan sat with his wife Maggie in the kitchen of their home, they had no doubt discussed the problem he had with the people using the path and taking down his fence. He had frequently sent one of his sons out to check and see if the fence was still up and, if not, to chase any cattle that might have wandered into his oat field back out and off his property. The idea that he could not rest guaranteed that his fence would be secure infuriated him. His wife tended to back him up, although she must have worried about his quick temper. She knew of his past, but took a certain pride in his mostly successful effort to curb his old habit of violence—outbursts that could erupt at the drop of a hat.

We do not know how much Ferrigan had spoken to his wife about meeting Paddy Connors earlier in the day. But she was loyal to him, staunchly supporting him in his efforts to maintain the integrity of his property and his fields of grain. She felt that the neighbours had discriminated against him and their children in the past.

Sometime after three-thirty, they received a visitor. Raymond Coughlin, a cousin of Terry Coughlin, drove up by the main road in his new Chevrolet and stopped in to see the Ferrigans. He knocked and came in through the front screen door and, after salutations, inquired as to whether some of the Ferrigan youngsters would be interested in going to a dance the next weekend at the town hall. If so, Raymond could provide them with the tickets. The Ferrigans had several teenagers, some of whom had permission to attend social events. As the conversation went on, Raymond was asked to stay for tea. They sat down at the kitchen table while Maggie rustled up an early supper, with a group of the younger children present.

From the kitchen windows of the Ferrigan household, there was a distant view of the railroad path that ran up to the back of their house and continued on. As the Ferrigans and Raymond Coughlin sat eating and drinking their tea, Maggie looked out the window and spotted someone in the distance. It appeared to be an adult with two children, although she said she could not be certain.

"Look, Mike, that could be Paddy Connors! Don't let him get away this time without warning him about the fence," said Maggie.

Michael Ferrigan went to the window and stood there for a few seconds staring out into the vague distance. He then left the kitchen hurriedly and went back toward the inside of the house, closing the door. He did not leave the house by the front door, yet he did not return to the supper table.

Raymond Coughlin remained at the house for a good half-hour after Michael Ferrigan had left the kitchen. When he took leave in his car again, Michael Ferrigan had still not reappeared.

According to his brother Earl, Paddy Connors did not seem to be worried as he walked up the railroad path. There were four of them, along with the two children. The children ran ahead as they often did, and the men talked about unrelated things as they went along.

Dennis Cleary, with his sharp sixteen-year-old eyes, was the first to spot Mike Ferrigan, who was running along the upper side of the track, coming in their direction. He was carrying a rifle and seemed to be making a feeble attempt to conceal himself among the trees. But the group soon caught a glimpse of him hovering above them. Then he would run ahead toward another spot closer to them. If he thought that they had not seen him, he was badly mistaken.

The group continued to walk along the track. Paddy Connors called ahead to the children to wait for him, which they did almost immediately. They came to Ferrigan's fence stretched across the track, the adults climbing over it, the children crawling under.

As they approached a small bridge on the path over a running brook, Ferrigan, having come down to the track, was walking toward them. The group was close together, but moving forward.

"Go back! Go back!" Ferrigan bellowed, even though he was only about ten yards from them.

Paddy Connors and his group stopped, rather stunned by the urgent and almost hysterical roar of Ferrigan's voice. The angry man was standing but five yards from them, both hands on his rifle held against his chest.

"Go back!" Ferrigan cried again.

"I will go back, but first I'd like to have a word with you," said Paddy.

But there was no more time for words. Ferrigan simply raised the rifle to his shoulder, pointed it at Paddy Connors, and pulled the trigger.

No one could have described the scene that followed, with the children bent over crying for their father to speak to them, pulling at his chest and holding his face in their hands, imploring him to respond. Paddy Connors lay, a white handkerchief in his hand, his body contorted, a scarlet gaping hole in his skull already oozing blood onto the grass.

Unwilling to believe what they had just witnessed, Earl Connors, Terry Coughlin, and the young Cleary boy stood just feet away from the motionless victim.

Earl Connors, in a foolish act of instinctive anger and desperation, rushed at Ferrigan and grabbed his gun, attempting to wrench it away from the shooter. But Ferrigan, a larger and hulking man, was able to swing the butt end of the rifle, striking Earl on the arm and forcing him to let go.

"God-damn you, you'll never hang me!" he cried as he backed up and seemed to be preparing to reload the rifle.

The inherent need for self-preservation then seized the group and all fled the scene and ran back down the railroad track, the children whimpering, being prodded by the adults. It was a scene of commotion and utter panic.

A macabre dance of evasive and frantic movement followed, according to the witnesses to the crime, with Ferrigan running after them and aiming the rifle, cocking it back and forth and shouting threats and obscenities. All had heard rumours of the bouts of insanity that Ferrigan had demonstrated, that he was capable of brutal violence, having axed a neighbour to death in a previous act of frenzy. They had all been made aware that insanity seemed to run in the family. Ferrigan's brother James had had to be physically prevented from committing acts of assault upon his own family. On one occasion, neighbours had been sent to find him, quite naked, chasing his own mother inside the house, intent upon beating her, she fending him off with a length of heavy rope.

There was an indescribable fear of Michael Ferrigan and of what he was capable of doing. The body of Paddy Connors, lying on the railroad path, was proof of this ghastly possibility.

The only one to offer token resistance to Ferrigan was Earl Connors who, at the height of the chase, hurled several fist-sized rocks in the killer's direction.

Ferrigan then gave up his pursuit and went back toward his own home.

The emotionally anguished men and still wailing children made their way down the track to the nearest house, which was the home of Joe Dunigan, who had also experienced run-ins with

Mike Ferrigan. All were emotionally drained and breathing heavily from their great distress.

What the men had to do quickly was to get a wagon and go back to retrieve the body of Paddy, the possibility being that there might be some small chance that he could be saved. But since Joe Dunigan had no horse at that time, it was decided that Earl would run down to his parents' house to fetch a wagon. A call was made to Willie Connors telling him that his son Paddy had been shot by Mike Ferrigan and that his body was lying on the railroad path still and that he must be very badly hurt.

The provincial police were also called and they said that officers would be sent immediately.

The news of the alarming event began to spread quickly through the community, and the telephone rang constantly as I sat in my Uncle Mike's kitchen with Janice. A tragedy such as this in an agrarian Irish farm setting was rare indeed, and few could comprehend how such a calamity could be visited upon them. While it was true that Mike Ferrigan had committed a killing more than fifteen years previous to this, that event had been considered completely anomalous behaviour, the first act of extreme violence in that community since its origin. But now that it had been allowed to happen again, the people began to ask themselves how they could have permitted this violent man to live amongst their families.

A resentful anger began to escalate among these people within a matter of minutes, as the news quickly spread by telephone.

When Willie Connors and his wife Ellie discovered their son, still lying as he had fallen on the track, the dire feeling of dispossession was expressed in tears of devastation by both of these elderly parents.

How could this have happened? Why had they allowed it to happen? Why had God permitted such a terrible cross to be cast upon them?

The dead body of Paddy Connors was placed in the wagon and the horse slowly made its way back to Willie's house where the corpse was placed on a bed.

Within the hour, two squad cars from the provincial police came rushing down the sandy road in a huge cloud of dust, sirens at full blast, headed toward the location of the killing. They managed to drive their automobiles close to the crime scene. The area was soon cordoned off, after which, at the prodding of the people who had gathered, one car was dispatched to the house of Mike Ferrigan. Several other local cars followed, and had it not been for the quick action of the authorities, the life of Ferrigan would have been in danger. The seething anger of the relatives of Paddy Connors, of which there were many, was such that a lynching was narrowly avoided as the police took Ferrigan into custody. A few of Mike Ferrigan's siblings had already gathered at the house and had encouraged the police to take their brother.

The wife of Paddy Connors, Eleanor, had still to be notified of the tragedy. She had not gone down with Paddy to visit her in-laws that Sunday afternoon. One of the children was not well and Eleanor had decided, while her sister Mamie was visiting, that they would bring the children out across the fields and have a picnic amid the trees beside the lake bordering the farm.

As the two women returned from their outing, walking across the field with the three youngest children of Paddy Connors, a car drove up and parked in front of their house. She recognized the car from a distance as belonging to Terry Coughlin and she wondered why he would be there.

"Paddy has been badly hurt!" Terry told her.

He could not bring himself to tell her the truth.

"Oh my God! Where is he? Where are the children?" she cried.

"They're all down at Willie's now."

"What on earth happened?"

"He had a run-in with Mike Ferrigan."

"Take me down there, Terry. I must go. Mamie will stay with the children."

When Eleanor entered her father-in-law's house, where many of her relatives were standing on and around the porch, she immediately sensed the gravity of it all. As she then saw the body of her husband lying on the cot, she threw herself upon him and sobbed uncontrollably. In doing so she called out his name several times, and all outside the house could hear. Many were weeping. Paddy Connors had been indeed loved in his community as a decent family man, brother, and friend. It was a terrible loss.

Janice and I were among the mourners at the home of Willie Connors that evening. His home was but a half-mile walk away. I had never been as physically close to someone who had been murdered soon after, of course, and my memory of that day is etched in detail. Janice was bereaved beyond consolation, and she wept also, her head bent down, her hands covering her face. I had never seen Janice cry, a sight that flooded my heart with an undying empathy and aroused in me a palpable anger. How could anyone inflict so much hurt and sorrow on his neighbours? I couldn't remember having ever met Paddy Connors before that day, yet I felt that I had known him. I knew also that, upon hearing of this tragedy, my father would be terribly distraught.

During early evening, the police sent for Quebec City officials to examine the body, including a doctor and some plainclothes detectives. The remains of Paddy Connors were then transported in a dark van to Quebec City, where an autopsy was later performed . Afterwards, an inquest would be held.

Tommy Kelly and his family had also come down to the house of Willie Connors to lend the family support. Paddy Connors had been a relative and close family friend to the Kellys. Tommy and I greeted each other, but this wasn't the time for chatting. The silence of most of the people spoke volumes. The wake and the ceremony of loss had begun. The realization of such a dastardly deed had to sink into the souls of the friends and relatives of Paddy Connors. An aura of incomprehension reigned, the most evident reaction of these people being to try to understand how such an unspeakable crime could erupt in the midst of their community.

When we came back to my Uncle Mike's later that night, the telephone was still ringing at a furious pace, but my mother managed to get through to us. Evidently, news of the shooting had spread to Quebec City. She expressed utter dismay about the tragic event to my Uncle Mike and said that my dad was too upset to talk to his older brother and would call him later. I spoke to my mom then and she asked me if I wanted to come home. I told her that if it was all right with my Uncle Mike, I would prefer to stay.

The following morning many newspaper and radio reporters descended upon the community, along with a television crew, seeking out the witnesses to the killing and attempting to interview nearly anyone who knew Michael Ferrigan or the victim, Paddy Connors. Pictures were taken of the spot where the shooting had taken place, as well as photos of an Irish neighbourhood in mourning.

In the early afternoon Janice and I walked up to the scene on the railroad path where Paddy Connors had been shot. On the way I helped Janice pick wildflowers of different colours, wild thyme and mountain laurel mostly. She made a kind of bouquet. When we got to the spot, the area was still cordoned off, and a few police officers were inspecting the ground closely, bent over. I supposed that they had not been able to complete this the previous day since darkness had set in too quickly.

As we stood there we noticed a cross had been put up, made of wood and tied together with ribbons, so Janice laid the bouquet beside it. Then we bowed our heads and said a few prayers. As we stood there, side by side, Janice suddenly took my hand in hers. I didn't look at her and pretended that this was not extraordinary. I felt that it could be a symbol of family solidarity in the face of a very difficult time for her. But it was also a truly tender moment for me. Her hand felt warm and full, and since I had never held it before, there was a beautifully foreign feel to it, yet something intensely personal. She then threw her arms around my neck and held me, pressing her cheek to mine, and instinctively, I responded and held her around the waist. We maintained the position for at least a minute. With the exception of my mother, I had never held another person in this way. It was an unfamiliar yet ethereal feeling, something I will always remember.

On the way back to my Uncle Mike's, Janice said, "Didn't you tell me yesterday that you and Tommy heard them argue?"

"Yes, why?"

"Well, you know, Francis, that could be very important information to the police when they start this investigation."

"Yes, but I'd sooner stay out of it."

"But Mike Ferrigan will have to pay for this crime. I'm sure that they'll probably charge him with murder."

"Did you tell anybody what I told you?"

"No, I haven't said a word. I thought of mentioning it to Dad but I'd prefer it if you told him."

"It makes me nervous just thinking about this," I said.

"You should think about saying something just for the memory of Paddy Connors. The whole story has to come out, and you and Tommy can be very important in getting to the truth."

Janice had told me that she wanted to be a lawyer, but I didn't expect her to be already practising law.

That evening after supper I walked up to the Kelly farm to speak to Tommy. The Kelly family had a large rambling house with brightly painted walls, as well as recently whitewashed structures—a barn and stable, hen house, and garages for a tractor and other farm vehicles. Tommy's father, Allan, was a skilled mechanic as well as a farmer. Other farmers frequently hired him to repair broken machinery. The north side of the Kelly spread led up to a tree-covered hill from which a swift brook tumbled. Tommy's dad had erected a waterwheel, one part of which was submerged in the flowing water, which filled the buckets in the wheel causing it to turn. This age-old contraption enabled him to install indoor plumbing in his house, turn the butter churn, and do other tasks. They were among the few families in the area to have these "modern" conveniences. Allan Kelly also had a sawmill operation going, the mechanics driven by a gas-fuelled engine.

The Kelly family was badly shaken by the events of the previous day. Allan Kelly and Paddy Connors had been close friends for many years, since their school days. Tommy's mother, Katherine, was a second cousin of the murdered man. The atmosphere in the Kelly household was very quiet and subdued.

I didn't know what to say to these people. I wanted to offer them sympathy but I was worried that I would say the wrong thing. So I sat in the kitchen for a while with Tommy and his parents and Patrick, his younger brother, hoping that my silence would convey my condolences.

Tommy and I soon went outside and sat on the steps of the veranda.

"I told Janice yesterday that we heard the argument. I suppose that I shouldn't have said anything."

"Was this before the shooting?"

"Yes."

"Well, you didn't know then what was going to happen."

"Did you say anything about it to your family?"

"Naw. Mike Ferrigan is always arguing with somebody. That was nothing new, so I didn't mention anything about it."

"Janice said that I should tell Uncle Mike about what we heard."

"I don't think it makes that much difference what we heard," said Tommy.

"Janice thinks that we might have to go to court and testify."

"There may not be a trial. He has no defence for what he did." Tommy had a trace of anger in his voice. "There was a bunch of witnesses who saw everything. But maybe you're right. If he pleads not guilty, he'll want a trial by jury. I don't see how he could defend what he did. He was paranoiac."

"What does paranoiac mean?"

"You know, he never trusted anyone and thought everybody was out to get him. We'll just have to wait and see. If word gets out that we heard Ferrigan threaten Paddy, then we could be made to testify. I suppose we should tell people what we heard. I guess I'll have to tell my dad and you can tell your uncle if you want."

As the evening sun went down, we walked over to the stable area to look at a new calf just recently born. Patrick, Tommy's brother, had already chosen a name for the little female who looked up at us from the stall. "Molly" stood on still shaky legs, a black-and-white little beauty with soft misty eyes. Patrick had been assigned by his father to care for her.

"Life begins and life ends," said Tommy, a slight tremor in his voice.

He bowed his head in contemplation for a moment.

"I'm gonna tell my dad about what we heard," he said then.

So we both decided that we could not keep quiet about what we had witnessed. Our silence would have been unthinkable and stupid. It was the least we could do for the memory of Paddy Connors. If the need ever arose that we would have to testify, we were ready.

We did not discuss what we would say if called to court, but I resolved to be honest and try my best to relate what we had heard. I think both of us were aware of the gravity of the situation at the time. We wanted to do the right thing, but I was quite nervous about the prospect of appearing at a public trial.

As the sky darkened Tommy and I stood leaning against the barn wall.

"I spoke to him just about an hour before he was shot," I said. "He came over from his dad's to speak to my Uncle Mike and ask his advice about dealing with Ferrigan."

"What did your uncle say to him?" asked Tommy.

"I think he told him not to worry, Ferrigan was just a bully."

I remember feeling very reflective that night. I had seen deep sorrow up close for the first time in my life. There were moments when Tommy and I just gazed up at the immense star-filled sky, always a source of wonderment to me, a lad from the city.

"I wonder if God knew about what would happen here yesterday and, if so, why he allowed it to happen," said Tommy.

It was a statement that only Tommy could make, and it didn't surprise me too much.

I didn't worry about walking back to my Uncle Mike's in the dark that night. I remember that the moon was a lovely white crescent.

Just before I left, I said to Tommy, "You remember that kid we saw on the path yesterday?"

"Yeah, that was Joey. Why?"

"I was wondering. Do you think he told his father that he saw us close to where the big argument was?"

"Yeah. That's a good question. Maybe he didn't know about the argument, I don't know."

"So the family might know that we were around there and Ferrigan and Paddy were yelling at each other pretty loud," I added.

"I'm not gonna worry about that."

By the time I got back to my Uncle Mike's the house was quiet. I thought that Janice and my uncle had turned in, having learned from my visits to the country that farmers are early risers, up shortly after dawn to milk the cows and see to the routine chores caring for the livestock.

I enjoyed listening to the radio in the kitchen before going to bed. I would have the sound down low, with the voices of Bing Crosby and the Andrew Sisters and Frank Sinatra and Vaughn Monroe singing their ballads. I felt a little guilty about doing this the day after Paddy Connors had been killed, but I was trying to deflect the sombre and disturbing thoughts of the killing.

As I turned the dial of the radio, it seemed that there were hundreds of radio stations available in this big sky country. The clearness of the American stations was dazzling to me.

Janice came in then, making sure that the screen door wouldn't slam. She'd been down the road to see one of her girlfriends. She came over and sat on the sofa beside me.

"Hi," she said softly.

I'm sure that the pace of my heart quickened at times such as this, when she looked at me and smiled. She playfully reached over and patted me on the forearm.

"It's incredible how many American stations you can pick up out here," I said. "It's much better than in the city."

"So what do you like to listen to?" she asked.

"I can get the Brooklyn Dodgers baseball games and WWVA in Wheeling, West Virginia."

"That's not a sports station, is it?"

"It's a country and western music station, mainly."

"So who's your favourite singer?"

"Oh, probably Frank Sinatra, but they wouldn't play his stuff on the Wheeling station. Do you like him?"

"Oh, yeah. He's kinda cute."

"Tommy Kelly really likes Sinatra," I said, and immediately regretted mentioning his name.

"Oh! Does he? I like Tommy. I talk to him a lot on the train on the way to school. He's very smart."

"He's only thirteen years old," I reminded her.

"Yeah, but he's very mature for his age. Some of the guys at your school act like real idiots. But Tommy's not like that."

That was the first time that I was convinced of what I had suspected—that Janice had a thing for Tommy Kelly. I had noticed how they seemed to gravitate toward each other when the people gathered outside the church after Mass on Sundays. I would have thought that, due to the difference in their ages, Tommy would consider her to be like an older sister. But it was more than that. He would say, "Let's go over and talk to Janice," and he was off, elbowing his way through the crowd of worshippers with me following like a lapdog.

I was just a little vexed at the idea of Janice and Tommy hitting it off, although I had to admit that they complemented each other—Janice with her bright and witty personality and great looks, and Tommy, the tall gangly kid, wise beyond his years. His easy style of talking and his perceptive intelligence reminded me of a very young James Stewart from *Mr. Smith Goes to Washington*, a movie they had shown us at school.

Yet, I wanted to keep Janice for myself, and not attached to some other guy. True, she was a first cousin of mine, but maybe life would allow us to be an exception and we would eventually marry. Of course, I knew down deep inside that this was another pipe dream of mine and I likely felt that if Janice ended up with anyone, Tommy would be a good choice.

"Would you like to practise?" Janice said, suddenly.

"Practise? What do you mean?" I blurted.

"You know, practise swinging."

She stood up and went into the centre of the spacious kitchen and sort of crooked her finger to me.

"But we have to be quiet. We don't wanna wake up Dad," she said gently.

And so she placed my hands just above her hips and put her hands on my shoulders, and we practised "swinging." We moved around in a clockwise direction, trying to get our feet to move simultaneously. We had no music to accompany us, but we were able to get into a rhythm with her counting. After a little while I started to get it. We moved around a little faster, she nimbly intertwining her fingers behind my neck and I holding her at the small of her back. If my Uncle Mike had been awake in his bedroom upstairs, he would have wondered at the shuffling of feet and the giggles and the panting, not at a very propitious time. But we were younger then and full of life even in difficult times. My uncle never mentioned a word of it. He was a good sleeper, I suppose.

Chapter 5

The autopsy on the body of Paddy Connors was completed on August 18, the day after the killing.

"I discovered," began Coroner Gilles Charest, "a hole just to the right side of the victim's nose, which seemed to correspond to a larger jagged hole at the rear of the skull. Of course, the skull was fractured. There were no other signs of violence on the body. When I opened the skull there seemed to be a sort of passage tunnelling with some grey matter imbedded."

The doctor went on to state that the heart, lungs, and other vital organs of the victim were sound, so that he attributed the death of Paddy Connors to the bullet that entered his head. The coroner said that death had likely occurred instantaneously. He could not state exactly from what distance the victim was fired at, but suggested that it would have been from less than ten feet. He had found traces of blood in the facial creases and fissures and understood that the face of the deceased had been cleansed after the shooting by members of the family.

The coroner's inquest, also held under the direction of Dr. Gilles Charest, took place the following day. The jury for this preliminary inquiry was chosen from the inhabitants of the farming locality and Quebec City. After the coroner had described the wounds of the victim, witnesses of the killing testified, giving details of the violent event.

Earl Connors, the brother of the deceased, was asked to give an account of the events of the fatal Sunday afternoon. He stated that his brother, the victim, had asked him to come by the railway track and through Michael Ferrigan's property. Paddy had seen Ferrigan with a rifle waiting for him to pass. Earl said that on the way up they dropped in at the Coughlin house and enlisted Terry

Coughlin to accompany them, and then later were joined by sixteen-year-old Dennis Cleary. As they all walked up the track with the two children they soon saw Michael Ferrigan with his rifle. Ferrigan ran toward them telling them to go back and then he raised his gun and shot the victim. Earl Connors said that he attempted to take the rifle away from the shooter without success and they soon all ran down the track as they thought that Michael Ferrigan was about to shoot at them.

Terry Coughlin and Dennis Cleary were then called to testify and they corroborated the statements of Earl Connors in similar detail.

Other witnesses were called to tell of the aftermath of the shooting and how the body had been transported to the home of Willie Connors, the victim's father.

Once the testimony and medical evidence had been produced, the jury recommended that Michael Ferrigan be charged with "wilful murder."

The coroner concurred with the arrest of Michael Ferrigan who was already safely lodged in the Quebec City jail. The coroner then impressed upon the witnesses to be available to give evidence at any forthcoming proceeding.

Ferrigan was arraigned before the judge on August 19.

Ferrigan's defence advocate, attorney Gerald Nolan, entered a plea of "not guilty." Lawyer Nolan had already defended Michael Ferrigan in the previous criminal proceeding after Ferrigan had killed another man with an axe.

The judge in charge of the case, the Honourable Justice Roger Sévigny, scheduled the trial for October 15—time enough, he felt, for the prosecuting attorney, Leslie Power, to prepare. Gerald Nolan, Ferrigan's lawyer, unsuccessfully pleaded with the judge for more time.

Judge Sévigny decided that the accused should be held in custody and denied bail. This determination was made because of Michael Ferrigan's previous violent episode of 1934, as well as to still the passions of many of the residents of Pine River.

The body of Paddy Connors was returned from Quebec City on Thursday, August 21. A wake was held at the home of Willie and Ellie Connors. The house had a large front kitchen area that could accommodate many mourners, as well as a spacious veranda where people could gather to quietly comfort each other.

Eleanor, Paddy's widow, did not want the body of her husband exposed at her home, but at the same time she felt that the wake should not be held in a commercial funeral parlour far removed from the area. Initially, Eleanor wanted an open coffin so that the family and friends of Paddy could see the damage that the killer Ferrigan had perpetrated upon the visage of her spouse, but she was counselled that, for the sake of the children, the coffin should be kept closed. Of course, two of the children, Marianne and Hughie, had already seen the results of Ferrigan's work and the outcome of the violence laid bare before them, together with the last gasps of their beloved father.

The heart-breaking gathering was overwhelming for all, yet the communion of solidarity allowed acceptance to rise to the surface. Many families brought food to the home of Willie Connors during the wake, and the teakettle was constantly boiling. Some people stayed for hours, edging out of the house to the veranda and then back in to say another prayer, perhaps, as a sign of utter respect for this highly respected man. Many tears were shed at the small pew that was placed before the coffin. Vases of flowers, as well as a few larger more formal wreaths, surrounded the body, the brown-wooded coffin topped with a black rosary.

The funeral of Paddy Connors, held six days after the killing, was also difficult for the community to accept. Hundreds attended as Father Emmett Lynch extolled Paddy Connors as an exemplary family man and friend who would surely be on our minds for many years to come.

Caught up in the emotion of the burial, I felt deeply moved, especially when I saw the coffin being lowered into the ground before the eyes of the older children, Marianne, Hughie, and Gerald.

I can still remember, quite vividly, the plaintive sounds of Father Lynch's voice near the end of the funeral service as he intoned the "Dies Irae."

My father rented a car and attended the funeral, sitting with me in the pew. He had to drive back to Quebec immediately after the service because my mother was ill and she was looking after the three children at home. My dad was visibly upset during the funeral and he shuddered a few times during the burial, his hand over his eyes.

During the next week at my uncle's before school started we managed to finish with the oats, now stacked in the barn to help supply the needs of the horses and the cows during the lengthy winter season. The family, cousins, and friends of Paddy Connors continued to mourn, their disbelief finally easing into a painful acquiescence. The events had caused an equally emotional burden upon the families of the Ferrigan clan.

But the anger in the community smouldered, the embers of resolve simmering as the wheels of justice took their inevitable course.

I told my Uncle Mike about the argument Tommy Kelly and I had witnessed on the morning before the killing, and the threats that Ferrigan had made toward Paddy Connors. Tommy had also spoken to his father about it.

"Is that so, Francis? My God, that could be very important information when the trial rolls around," my Uncle Mike said.

"Do you think that Tommy and I would be called to court to tell about what we heard?"

"I couldn't say, Francis. But I'm glad you told me about this. We should certainly let the police know that you heard these threats being made. The lawyers would be interested in this too, I'm sure. Anyway, Francis, I'll speak to some of the officers as soon as I can."

If there was anyone who could be designated as a peacemaker during this time, it was my Uncle Mike Carroll. He had never relished the ongoing feud between the Ferrigans and the

Connors family and the Dunigans—something that had gone on for years, mainly for petty reasons. My uncle had been close to the Connors family just as his father had been before him. He had always been on acceptable terms with the Ferrigans even with their disturbing history and questionable sanity. He understood the anguish that the Ferrigan family was suffering, with one of their own accused of murder and the forthcoming trial on the horizon.

It was not out of the ordinary for certain Irish families to show great disdain for each other. Some had brought these feuds with them from the old country, as unbelievable as it might sound. An Irish family could be on very poor terms with another, the underlying reasons for which had long been forgotten. There was also the religious factor that, in some cases, would exacerbate already icy relationships. The Catholics tended to choose to settle in areas where they were predominant and the Protestants did the same, each group being clannish and choosing to associate with others in their own group.

Yet these components were not noticeable to me as a visitor. I tended to look at the people and the countryside with rose-coloured glasses, the beauty of the land and the warmth of my friendships overwhelming any other consideration.

It was not surprising that the Ferrigans would drop in to see my Uncle Mike on occasion. Since my uncle was a former mayor, there were always matters to discuss with regard to municipal and school taxes and property regulations relating to the Military Camp along the border of some of the farms.

My uncle, Janice, and I were seated at the kitchen table having supper one evening during my last week when a car drove up to the house. My Uncle Mike recognized it as Mike Ferrigan's car. He left the supper table and went out to speak to the two people who got out of the car. One turned out to be Patrick Ferrigan, Michael's younger brother, and the other was Maggie Ferrigan, the wife of Michael Ferrigan.

Janice and I could not hear what the conversation was about but we could see from the window that it seemed to be a tranquil exchange. After about five minutes, Uncle Mike came to the screen door and called in to me to come outside.

Maggie Ferrigan was a slender woman in her early forties who spoke quietly, saying that she was pleased to meet me and that she knew my father. Patrick Ferrigan stood next to her, staring at me without let-up, which made me feel just a trifle uncomfortable.

"My son Joey says that he saw you on the Sunday just a few hours before the shooting," Maggie said.

"Well, I was with Tommy Kelly and we saw this boy running up the track and Tommy said it was Joey Ferrigan," I explained.

"We were just wondering if you heard my husband and Mr. Connors talking that day," she went on.

My Uncle Mike interjected, "You know, Maggie, we should not be talking about these things now because of the investigation that's still going on."

Patrick Ferrigan did not speak, but stared at me quite resolutely, as if trying to penetrate my thoughts.

"It's all right, Mike," Maggie said. "We were concerned that he may have seen or heard something."

"Francis is heading back home in a few days and he should be starting school again next week," said my uncle. "Isn't that right, Francis?"

"Yes, Uncle Mike," I said, feeling the tension that was just beneath the surface of this rather strange encounter.

"All right, Francis. You can go back in now," said my uncle.

After I went back into the house, Janice and I noticed that the conversation went on for about five minutes more, then the two got into their car and motored off.

My Uncle Mike had already spoken to one of the detectives assigned to the case concerning what Tommy Kelly and I had overheard on that fateful Sunday. Ferrigan's defence lawyer soon got wind of it and both he and the prosecutor agreed that Tommy Kelly and I were not to communicate with each other in any way until after we had testified in court, if we were to testify. All of this was revealed to me a few days before I went back home at the end of my stay. The prosecuting attorney, Leslie Power, telephoned my uncle and told him that he wanted to see me when I got back to town. My uncle said that any arrangements of this nature would have to be made through my dad.

I had meant to get together with Tommy and some of the other guys to play a last game of softball before I left, but the new court conditions prevented us from doing that. I did not see the logic of this directive at the time, since both Tommy and I planned to tell the truth about what we had heard.

So I stayed around the farm property for the last few days, helping my Uncle Mike with a few chores and harvesting some of the garden vegetables with Janice.

"Are you nervous about testifying in court, Francis?" Janice asked.

"No. It doesn't bother me too much," I said, a little dishonestly.

"You'll be all right. Just tell them the truth."

"What do you think they'll ask me?"

"They'll ask you to recount what you heard, I'm sure. They don't want you to talk with Tommy before the trial about your testimony."

"If that's what they want I wouldn't speak to Tommy about it. But why should we have to stay apart? That's crazy."

"This'll all be over in a few months," she reassured me.

I would often be on the edge of tears during those last few days. I wanted to go for a walk in the fields away from the farmhouse and cry my eyes out. Had Janice not been around I'm sure I would have wanted to go back home to Quebec City, but I wanted to be with her for the remaining few days. She always seemed to be so well grounded and in good humour.

On the morning that I left the farm to go back to town, my Uncle Mike drove me to the bus stop at Scott's Corner. Janice came with us. I always had a melancholy feeling upon leaving, and the tragic occurrence seemed to have lowered my already low morale. We sat in the car talking while we waited for the bus to show up. When it did, my uncle and Janice got out of the car with me and walked me over to the open door of the bus.

I shook hands with my Uncle Mike and then Janice hugged me and kissed me on the cheek. I felt suddenly that I would lose my composure, but somehow I held on and clumsily tried, without success, to return the kiss. It was the first time she had ever kissed me and I went up the steps of the bus in a daze. On the ride back to the city I was less interested in the architecture of the self-contained houses. My mind was more preoccupied with Janice and with what had taken place over the previous two weeks.

As I went up the stairs of our flat in Quebec City, the door opened at the top of the stairwell and my mother waited for me to reach the top, then she threw her arms around me before I had a chance to put my kit bag down. I completely lost it, and the tears came gushing from my eyes. I couldn't remember having ever sobbed like that.

My kid sister, Eileen, was standing beside my mom.

"Mommy, why is Frankie crying?" she said.

Chapter 6

My parents had already been informed that I might be a witness in the forthcoming legal process. I had always been well treated by my mom and dad, who were both disciplinarians but seemed to know when to offer emotional support to all of their children. In the ensuing weeks, before the trial, there seemed to be a strong effort on their part to treat me with kid gloves. They realized that I felt somewhat uneasy during this time, and the emerging prospect of possibly being put through the burden of testifying at a murder trial made me a little over-anxious. The idea that I couldn't speak to one of my best friends seemed rather bizarre. I had looked forward to seeing Tommy Kelly on the first day of school, and to think that I wouldn't be allowed to even look at him bothered me.

On the whimsical side, I asked myself, who was going to keep me informed about what was going on in the world? How would the negotiations between the United Nations and the Communist nations turn out with regard to Korea? Was this the year when the Brooklyn Dodgers would finally beat the New York Yankees in the World Series? Tommy had kept me engaged about these matters during the summer and I prayed that the trial would be over soon and things would get back to normal.

I had trouble getting to sleep at night during this period. My mind was a jumble of emotions, the thoughts sometimes merging into a miasma ranging from sadness to affection to lustful fantasy. My musings and expectations kept me awake and jittery.

Not all of it was godawful. There was the vision and remembrance of a group of boys in the country prancing down the road to the ball field, laughing and commenting at what was said and what we saw. Some of the kids had bikes but we used to like walking down. There was Tommy Kelly trying to turn the conversation his way, but at the same time identifying the birds to us—red-winged blackbirds and grackles and chickadees and barn swallows and nuthatches and cowbirds. He seemed to know all of them. There was Will Poole with his stories about which driver was the biggest drinker in the community and who had totalled their cars.

Then there was Artie King's big dog, Scratch, who always tried to follow us down to the ball field. Artie would spend the whole time trying to shoo him back home. The mutt seemed to love Artie so much that he could not think of leaving him. Artie would finally throw a handful of sand at the dog. That was the final straw. The pooch would hang its head and head back home as if the victim of a great insult.

As we walked, we were spread across the sandy surface of the road carrying our bats and softball gloves and canvas bags, containing our sandwiches and milk bottles, slung over our shoulders. When a car came zooming up the road, causing a small dust storm, we would separate to allow it to pass, trying to identify the driver and the make of car.

"There goes Jimmy Foy in his old Plymouth," Will Poole would say. "He's driving straight, so he must be sober. 'Course it's still early in the day."

Norman Rockwell, the famous American illustrator, would have relished depicting us in our summer duds and ball equipment, heading to the playing field. Or, for that matter, portraying some kids walking through the fields of the farms with the breeze bending the hip-high lengths of grain, the golden colours giving off that lustrous sheen.

At times, on a brisk windy day, the shadows of clouds would race down the sandy road like silhouettes in a pursuit.

It was funny how I had begun to picture everything as an artist would before he began a painting. I loved the colour of the outdoors and the light and dark cast by the sun.

There were my somewhat disturbing mental meanderings concerning Janice and what I would like to do with her lying on the soft red pine-strewn needles at the edge of the evergreen stands. I hoped I could forever feel her arms around me, pressing her lightly tinted pink lips to my cheek. I thought her to be the most beautiful creature on the face of the earth, blossoming into a desirable jewel, full of smiles, laughter, and sexual allure. When would I see her again? When would I be able to walk across the summer fields with her as we had done a few times, both of us looking up at the white and fluffy configurations of clouds? Would I have to wait a whole year before I could sit facing her on the old blue-wood garden swing again? I ached at not being able to hold her and feel the soft roundness of her breasts against me.

But most of all, I thought about the looming possibility that I would be brought to court to testify against a man who could be executed for his crime. There was talk that he would be hanged. The courts hanged people for murder in our country. I had seen pictures of people being hanged as well as the depiction of some men about to be executed in some western movies.

My desire for revenge and for the ultimate measure of justice being carried out was tempered. But Canada was still executing murderers, and I had to accept that.

As I fell into a half-sleep, the boom of cannon fire pervaded the background of my anxieties like a slow-beating and abrasive bass drum.

Thankfully, school had begun and with it the preparations for the upcoming hockey season.

My homeroom teacher for grade nine was Brother Norbert, a stocky, jocular man who loved literature, especially the works of William Shakespeare. On the subject of poetry he would say, "I love to read the odes of Byron, Sheets, and Kelly." His humour was a little beyond a lot of the kids in the class, but I imagined that Tommy Kelly would have enjoyed Brother Norbert greatly, and indeed was taught by him in the ensuing high school years.

Since my father taught at the elementary level in my school building, my parents felt that all of their children should naturally be exemplary students. My younger brothers Eamon and Stephen competed with each other, their test results usually up in the nineties. I seemed a little less gifted.

But I enjoyed the comradeship of school, especially when we would head to the indoor arena on Saturday mornings for hockey practice. My best friend and buddy in town was Jackie Farrell, who played with me on the Bantam school team. As line mates the previous year, we had combined to score quite a few goals.

Quebec City, as the summer warmth begins to ebb and fall rolls around, calms down and the number of tourists in the hotels decreases. The trees slowly turn lighter green, then yellow and orange, against the backdrop of the older sedate grey buildings, many of which mimic Gothic-style architecture, with large windows and ornamental and symmetrical features. This is one of the outstanding aspects of the old historic capital city.

I had been told that Michael Ferrigan's trial was to take place at the Quebec City courthouse, so I walked down with Jackie to the Place d'Armes, the city square where the building is situated. It's a large dignified-looking four-storey structure taking up half a block of city space. Just across the street is the stately Chateau Frontenac Hotel. At the adjacent side of the square sits a large monument of the founder of Quebec City—Samuel de Champlain. Then beyond is the boardwalk, that magnificent walkway more than two hundred feet above the St. Lawrence River.

I had never been inside that courthouse and, looking at the tall dark windows standing like impenetrable facades, I wondered about how my testimony would be accepted.

I tried to tell Jackie what the trial was all about, swearing him to secrecy. He said that he envied me, but I would have given the whole experience to him had I been able.

Religion was an ever-present feature of my youth, both at home and within the Irish-Catholic community in Quebec City. My parents made certain that all of their children attended Mass on Sundays and Holy Days. Since we all went to a Catholic school, there was the religious regimen to contend with—retreats, the

Sacraments, and daily prayer. So I was quite willing to ask for God's help during this trying period of my life.

God was seldom out of our sight, so to speak. I felt Him to be a continuing witness to what I was doing. If I was about to get involved in some mischievous activity, my conscience was there to remind me of my frailties.

Indeed, as a teenager growing up during the early fifties, I made my share of mistakes, experienced some peer pressure in early high school, and caused my parents a certain amount of concern, just as all kids do. But taking an active role in sports helped to feed my fantasies during those years, and I managed to avoid any serious trouble.

I always walked with my younger brothers to school, in part as a safeguard. There were always groups of French-speaking kids who liked to taunt us as we made our way up the streets speaking English. These kids did not seem to realize that a lot of our friends near our flat were French-speaking neighbours with whom we got along very well. My family was very well accepted around our neighbourhood, partly because we could all speak French.

I believe that many young people during the early fifties were much the same as I was. We were more introspective, in the spiritual sense, than present-day young people. We were aware of others, and knew that our behaviour affected others. Extended family ties were very important.

Young people were being made aware daily of the precarious hold that the human race had on survival. There were many more parishioners in churches. We prayed to God to deliver us from a possible nuclear apocalypse. The Cold War between the United States and the Soviet Union could easily burst, we felt, into an unprecedented conflagration. The constant jockeying between the two great powers sent shivers through all civilized people.

As I grew up, I always understood that my life and experiences centred in my home. Conditions there were almost ideal, so I was deeply attached to my family and I felt that I was fortunate in many ways, even if I may have taken my good fortune for granted at times. My parents, who were both well educated, though not well-to-do, expected their children to acquire skills that would serve them well in a professional way, and steer their energies toward improving their social status. What my parents were trying to do was to allow themselves and their children to break out of the cycle of lower-class work, a situation that for centuries prevented many Irish-Catholic families from rising into professional occupations. This was the background from which I was expected to cope in the upcoming test, where an ordinary young person would be pressed into an uncommon experience.

There was also the personal and intimate side of my family life. I tended to be very sensitive witnessing the relationship between my mom and dad. I did not like to see them argue. There were a few schoolmates of mine whose parents were divorced or separated. Although I could not see this happening to my parents, the sense of dread at the possibility was somewhere in the back of my mind. I secretly relished any show of affection by my mom for my dad and vice versa. It was not something that I wanted to watch necessarily, but something I hoped would always be there. It was not the love they showered on me that was important, but the love they showed to each other.

The newspapers reported that, in a separate pre-trial hearing, the defence lawyer for Michael Ferrigan had made a sudden request, to the judge in the case, for a change of venue for the upcoming trial. Defence Lawyer Gerald Nolan was insistent as he made his request.

"Where do you suggest that the proceedings should be held?" Judge Sévigny asked lawyer Nolan.

"I think that Montreal would be a better and fairer situation for my client," lawyer Gerald Nolan argued.

"How do you see Quebec City as being an unfair site for the trial?"

"There is a virulent and instilled prejudice against my client, Michael Ferrigan, in this immediate area. There is much vindictiveness against him among the relatives and friends of Patrick Connors in this city as well as Pine River, which is close by. The media have also played a large role in castigating my client and pronouncing his guilt on an almost daily basis. How can my client get a fair trial under these circumstances?"

"And how do you see a venue such as Montreal being a more suitable place for conducting the trial? Have not the news media right across the country been covering this case?" asked the judge.

"Your Honour, there are many factors in this case that would be better served some distance away from the site of the shooting. In the selection of the jury, for example, there is a lesser chance that jury members chosen from another area of the province would be already prejudiced against Mr. Ferrigan. The measure of hate against my client is so great, the desire for revenge is so high, that a trial here would be a mockery of the judicial system. My client is being pre-judged by the general population before all the facts of the case have come to light."

"Mr. Nolan, we cannot prevent the media from covering this trial in the usual way. This story is already being told across the province and the country. As for the prejudices of the relatives and friends of the victim in this case, we cannot change the thoughts and feelings of people who feel strongly about the killing. The jury selection will be made carefully as per procedure, a jury of the peers of the accused. They will be carefully screened. No one with preconceptions about the case will be permitted. The jury is not likely to be influenced by the spectators who attend the trial, and the jury will be told that they are not to discuss the case outside of the jury room. All witnesses for both the prosecution and the defence cannot be present at the trial before they testify. I cannot see where you will improve the situation for your client simply by changing the geographical location inside this province. Mr. Nolan, I will give your request some thought, but as things stand now, the trial has been set to begin here on the predetermined date."

Judge Roger Sévigny was a rather corpulent man with a great tousle of grey hair. He never raised his voice, but would speak in a monotone—a rather detached manner that sometimes gave people the impression that he was bored with the case. But his alertness betrayed his seemingly nonchalant appearance. He listened to everything said during the pursuit of this case with rapt attention. More than once, later on, during the actual trial, he would ask both defence and prosecution lawyers to repeat questions that he had not fully understood, and frequently complained about the low tones of the voices of some of the witnesses.

The request for a change of venue by Defence Lawyer Nolan was soon refused and everything was scheduled to proceed as planned.

Leslie Power, the prosecuting attorney, called my father in late September and arranged a meeting with us at his office which was situated on the second storey of a building on Grande Allée. We went there at the end of a school day. Leslie Power's office was quite sumptuous, with black leather chairs and brown varnished bookcases, glass fronted, filled with legal tomes. He was a tall man with a thin moustache and was dressed in a full suit with a starched white shirt, vest, and a bright green tie. My dad had never met him before, but had heard of him from reading newspaper reports of previous criminal trials.

"Thank you for coming, Mr. Carroll, and thank you, Francis, for volunteering to help us with this case," he said.

It was the kind of "volunteer" work that I was not too keen about.

After shaking hands all around, we got right down to business.

"Francis, could you give me an idea of where you were on the day of the shooting of Mr. Connors?"

"Well, Tommy Kelly and I were trout fishing in a brook near Mr. Ferrigan's property. I didn't know we were next to Mr. Ferrigan's farm at the time, but Tommy told me."

I was pretty nervous when I started talking to this lawyer. But I think that as the meeting went on I got more relaxed. I was happy that my dad was with me.

"So your friend Tommy Kelly and you have not been talking to each other since you were asked not to?"

"Yes, that's right, sir."

"Because we don't want Mr. Ferrigan's lawyer to think that you two have coordinated your stories. So, go ahead, Francis, tell us what happened after you started fishing."

"Tommy and I heard these two voices talking pretty loud, so we left our fishing rods by the brook and went toward the sound of the voices and saw two men arguing across a fence on the old railroad track they have there."

"And did you know who these men were?"

"No, I couldn't remember seeing them before, but Tommy told me who they were. One was Mr. Ferrigan and the other was Paddy Connors."

"What time of the day do you think it was when you heard these two men arguing?"

"Well, it was just when we started fishing after we got home from Mass, so I guess it was sometime pretty close to twelve o'clock."

"And from what you remember, what was the argument about?"

"Well, I think that Mr. Ferrigan was pretty mad at Paddy Connors and other people because he said that they were trespassing on his land and taking down his fence on purpose and not putting it back. He told Mr. Connors not to come back that way again or he'd do something to him."

"What else did he say?"

"I remember him saying that if Paddy Connors came back the same way, Mr. Connors wouldn't go back to the same tune as he came."

"And what did you think that meant?"

"Well, it sounded like Mr. Ferrigan planned to do something pretty violent if Paddy Connors came back again."

"How many times did Mr. Ferrigan threaten Mr. Connors?"

"Oh, three or four times."

"Did Mr. Connors threaten Mr. Ferrigan?"

"No, I didn't hear that. Mr. Connors was trying to reason with Mr. Ferrigan and saying that the railroad was a public road and he had a right to pass. At least, that's how it seemed to me."

"Is there anything else that you remember from the argument?"

"Well, when Mr. Ferrigan was going back to his house, he yelled back at Mr. Connors to get another man so they could fight."

"And what did Mr. Connors say?"

"He told Mr. Ferrigan to get one himself or something like that."

"Was Mr. Connors alone that day?"

"No. There were two children with him and they were standing and waiting on the track about twenty or thirty yards ahead of Mr. Connors."

Leslie Power told me that at the trial he would ask me the same questions and he wanted me to answer them the same way. It was funny because it was like we were rehearsing for a play. So we went over the questions again and I tried to answer them in a similar way. Then we talked about the upcoming trial, with my dad getting into the conversation. Lawyer Power described the courtroom to me and told me where I would be sitting when I testified. I realized at that moment that it was a sure thing now, that I would certainly be a witness in this murder trial.

Apart from a few questions, my dad said very little during this meeting. He told me afterwards that I had done very well.

We were with Leslie Power for about thirty minutes and I was very relieved when the meeting was over. He said that I would be called to testify a few days after the trial began unless some unexpected matter developed.

Chapter 7

The only time that I felt released from the worry of the approaching trial was when I was playing hockey. This game is so all-encompassing and free-wheeling that while playing you are totally freed of any extraneous thought.

At the time I was rather obsessed with hockey and skating and just about anything wintry.

While I was growing up in Quebec City, there were many outdoor rinks during wintertime. Nearly every school had a rink beside its building with snow piled up to bank the carefully tended sheets of ice surrounded by boards. A house league hockey schedule was a part of after-school activities on a daily basis in most schools. This was true of my school as well as for hundreds of other schools throughout the province. There were also quite a few recreational outdoor rinks not attached to any school, but there purely for the amusement of people. For a small fee you could skate for two hours or so, all skaters going around in an orderly fashion in the same direction. For the first hour we would skate counter-clockwise, and reverse to clockwise for the second hour. Most of the rinks were flooded by the end of November and were in operation until well into February.

I was happy to have hockey playing in my life because at every other moment of the day my thoughts were on the upcoming trial. There was a measure of dread in my thinking. I wanted with all of my being to have this experience over with.

In the fall of 1952 my hockey coach was Brother Martin of the order of teaching brothers of St. John the Baptist de la Salle. He was a stern man, but just while he was coaching. He and my teacher, Brother Norbert, knew some of the players on the Detroit Red Wings of the NHL, whom they had gone to school with. When the Red Wings came to Quebec City to play exhibition games against the Quebec Aces of the Quebec Senior League, the Detroit players would come up to our school and put on a show for us. Those were heady days for hockey fanatics such as myself. We were permitted to skate on the ice with some of the best hockey players in the world.

Jackie Farrell and I loved to skate or play hockey, almost every day during the winter months, and would often go to public outdoor skating rinks during the weekends. There were several in the old Quebec City area, including one at the Chateau Frontenac Hotel and another at the Esplanade Park. It was a beautiful setting in both cases, with the old walls of the city lit up at night-time at the Esplanade and the smaller rink at the hotel beside Dufferin Terrace, the snow-covered boardwalk with the river below. Leaning on rails, hundreds of people would be watching kids using the huge slide that was erected for visitors.

It was at these public rinks that we grew accustomed to asking pretty French-speaking girls to skate with us. You'd just sort of sidle up to her and ask if you could skate with her. At most times girls were more than happy to be asked. Then you would wrap one arm around her waist and she'd wrap her arm around yours and you would skate in tandem around the rink and practise your French. It was a rather intimate way to introduce yourself to a girl, to immediately be holding her close to you. But that was the custom of the time. Once a girl found out that you were English-speaking, a different world seemed to open to her and frequently she'd be trying out her English with you. Of course, some of them were too shy to speak English, so you'd just speak French to them.

On October 15, the trial began with the process of choosing a jury. Many of the candidates for jury service who were called to court stated that they had no prejudice against the accused personally, but considered him guilty of the crime with which he was charged. All those who professed this belief were disallowed. One man was found to be a kin of the deceased and was also disallowed. Another claimed to have done some business transactions with Michael Ferrigan, so he was also excused. Other candidates called to jury duty stated that they were opposed to capital punishment and felt that the country should not be hanging its citizens. Since hanging was included as part of the law of the land, these men were disallowed. After several days, the court, with the assent of the prosecution and the defence, finally decided who would make up the jury. The actual trial then was set to begin.

Another factor in the choosing of the jury was the language issue. Michael Ferrigan knew little French, so a jury member had to be familiar with the English language to be accepted. The rules recognized that half of the jury members should be English-speaking, and the remainder should have a facility with English. The trial, with interpreters available, was conducted in both languages, the defence and prosecution lawyers both being fluently bilingual. But most of the public who attended the trial were English-speaking, many having been raised in an Anglo-Irish culture very close to Quebec City geographically, but isolated within their own English-speaking enclave. Few of these Irish agricultural residents had the chance to communicate in French since their realm of activity was usually restricted to their own community.

There was much interest in the trial among the population of the old city as well as the inhabitants of Pine River. Citizens of Quebec City, many unknown to the accused and strangers to the Irish of Pine River, wished to attend the trial but many were turned away for lack of room. The relatives of Michael Ferrigan and the late Paddy Connors were generally given precedence.

Eleanor Connors, the widow of Paddy, attended regularly with other members of the extended family of the victim. My mother was present for some of the sessions, as well as my Uncle Mike and other relatives. The wife and siblings of the accused were in attendance constantly, once the trial got under way. With the daily presence of the newspapers and the briefings that we got, we were kept up to date regarding the events. The dialogue between lawyers and witnesses was covered in much detail.

The courtroom was packed at all times, with people lined up in the morning to get into the building. Bailiffs constantly warned the spectators to be perfectly quiet and not to show any expression of emotion while testimony was being given. These officers of the court stood with their eyes trained on the observers and would not hesitate to expel anyone who disrupted business in any way. This was the protocol in the court that Judge Sévigny ran.

The day after the composition of the jury had been agreed upon, the prosecution of the case began, with the room filled with spectators, totally absorbed and expectant.

The accused, Michael Ferrigan, was led into the courtroom and seated at the front, flanked by two officers. He was wearing a dark-coloured suit with a white shirt and tie. To someone unfamiliar with the proceedings, he could have seemed like an unassuming gentleman who held a clerical job with some firm. But to all in the court who knew him, he was what he was, a large man of considerable strength who had worked hard all of his life. Beneath the dark suit was the muscular body of a farmer, a man who had been through the courts before, a man again charged with the most serious of all crimes—wilful murder. There was little pride in his bearing as he sat in the box of the accused, his head frequently bent forward as if to examine his shoes. He had a full head of hair, cropped short. At first he did not make eye contact with anyone in the court, but then his eyes momentarily searched the section where his wife Maggie sat with some of her kin.

Judge Sévigny came into the chamber immediately after, and proceedings were set to begin.

Lawyer Leslie Power, for the prosecution, gave the opening statement to the jury. Speaking in both languages, he called upon the jury to perform their duty and listen to the evidence against the accused with utmost care. They were asked to deal dispassionately with the charges against the prisoner and to set aside all prejudice.

Leslie Power then immediately got into the details of the happenings of Sunday, August 17. He said that the victim had met with the accused in the morning on that date and the latter had made threatening remarks to the victim. These threats would be corroborated by witnesses whom he would produce for the court. He said that the threats were serious and could very well be characterized as death threats.

Defence Lawyer Gerald Nolan objected to this part of the opening remarks, stating that the prosecuting attorney was already using prejudice against his client. Nolan said that on the occasion of the morning meeting between the two farmers, there had been threats on both sides. The defence attorney edged in these objections at the outset, as if to suggest to the jury that there were extenuating elements to that first meeting between the accused and the victim on that Sunday.

The judge seemed vexed at the interruption, but told Mr. Power to be careful with his opening remarks.

Prosecuting Attorney Power then got around to describing the second encounter, later in the afternoon of the same day. There were two adult witnesses and three minors who had seen with their own eyes the cold-blooded killing of the victim after absolutely no provocation had been made toward the accused. He told the jury that Michael Ferrigan approached the victim and the group of witnesses on a public road that ran through his own property and fired the deadly shot, fulfilling the threats he had made earlier in the day. This public road, the prosecutor said, does pass through the property of Michael Ferrigan but everyone has used it for decades and continues to use it to the present day for multifarious purposes. Lawyer Power went on to say that the accused had constructed a fence, illegally, across the railway road, a throughway open to the public and still owned by the railway. This cumbersome fence had to be removed and then replaced when anyone passed with a horse and rig. The underlying reason for the anger of Michael Ferrigan was that part of this fence had been taken down. He had murdered his neighbour because of a gap in a fence.

The prosecuting attorney drew distinctions between manslaughter, killing in self-defence, and the killing that the law defines as "wilful murder." He could see no rational reason why the charge of murder would not be appropriate. He described the killing as a pre-meditated act precipitated by a person who had no respect for another human's life.

Leslie Power stated that if nothing would occur, before the end of the trial, to lift the dark cloud that rested upon the prisoner, he should be held fully responsible. And if nothing was produced to destroy the evidence and the weight of the testimony of the witnesses, he could not see how any verdict could be returned other than "wilful pre-meditated murder."

To conclude his remarks, the prosecuting attorney appealed to the jury to do their solemn duty in accordance with the terms of the oath that had been administered to them.

The early witnesses for the prosecution were the police officers who had arrested Michael Ferrigan at his house. Some of the police officials had questioned and taken statements from the accused at the city jail. It was firmly established by the police that Michael Ferrigan had admitted to the killing after being taken into custody, but the accused had claimed that there were extenuating circumstances involved. It was only after these statements made to the police that Michael Ferrigan sought out the counsel of Gerald Nolan.

The rifle used by Michael Ferrigan to kill Paddy Connors was exhibited. It proved to be a .303 calibre model once commonly used by soldiers at the army camp.

There were some objections by Defence Lawyer Gerald Nolan about the fact that the police had taken statements from the accused before he could call his lawyer. Upon questioning, the police said that when Michael Ferrigan came into the police station on that Sunday evening, no one could shut him up. He talked continuously and freely, repeating that he had not meant to kill Paddy Connors. There was much haggling on this issue, with the judge twice calling the two lawyers into his chambers and asking the jury to retire to their room.

Dr. Gilles Charest, the coroner, then took the stand and recounted the chronicle of clinical details of the autopsy that he had summed up at the inquest. The technical description of the mortal wound of the victim did not fail to have an impact on the spectators in the court. The short summation that the doctor used to delineate the massive head trauma to Paddy Connors, not embellished nor dramatically stated, had the desirable effect, at least for the prosecution.

Both lawyers had perfunctory questions for the doctor after he had completed his testimony, the questions of the defence lawyer being very brief. Attorney Nolan did not want endless attention paid to the brutal and deadly aspects of a coroner's report. That would have severely damaged his case, he must have felt.

The court recessed after that first day of testimony. The following morning the first witness sworn in by the prosecution was Earl Connors, the brother of the victim.

"What is your occupation, Mr. Connors?" asked attorney Power.

"I am a farmer and construction worker, and I reside at my father's house in Pine River. I am a brother of the victim, Patrick Connors."

At this point the judge told the witness to speak louder and more slowly, that his testimony should be clear to all in the courtroom.

"And who is your father?" went on lawyer Power.

"My father is William Connors."

"Could you give the court some idea of the area where the events associated with this trial took place?"

"My father's house is about one mile from the prisoner's house which is along the seventh range road. The victim's farm is on the other side of the prisoner's farm about four miles from my father's house. When my brother visited my father he used the old railroad track road to come. Part of this old railway road goes through the prisoner's property, for about ten acres."

The prosecution brought out a large sketch showing the relative position of the properties concerned. The chart was placed on an easel at the front of the courtroom. The defence objected to the use of this sketch because of its "unreliability," but the judge said that the drawing was suitable for the time being so that everyone could get a general idea of the distances between the properties. There was some verbal jousting about this issue, with the lawyers talking quietly to the judge in front of his large raised desk.

The questioning of Earl Connors continued.

"Would you describe in your own words, Mr. Connors, the events that led to the death of your brother?" asked Power.

"My brother, while visiting our father's house, told us about the warning that the prisoner had issued to him earlier in the day. He asked me at about four o'clock in the afternoon to accompany him and his children back to his home up through Ferrigan's property. My brother, the deceased, told me that he had just seen Michael Ferrigan waiting for him to pass and that Ferrigan was holding a gun in his hands. He said that if Ferrigan tried to do anything to him, we would get the law after him. We used the railway path. On the way up we called in at the Coughlin house and asked Terry Coughlin if he would also come with us. He agreed and we then met the Cleary boy, who also came. There were six of us in all as we walked up the old railroad track."

"Now, were you worried that something was going to happen as you all walked up the track?"

"Well, we knew that Michael Ferrigan had a bad temper and my brother told us that Ferrigan was pretty mad when they had met earlier in the day, so yes, we were a little concerned. But we felt that because we were three men he wouldn't do anything foolish."

"So you continued to walk up the track. What did you see next?"

"We spied someone up in the bushes and he was holding a rifle in his hands, but we kept walking up the track. He then came down to the track to confront us and advanced toward us. We were all walking close together. The prisoner, Michael Ferrigan, came along the track half running and yelled, 'Go back! Go back!' and he was only about ten yards from my brother and he yelled 'Go back!' for the third time. My brother said, 'I will go back, but I'd like a word with you.' Michael Ferrigan then raised the gun and shot my brother dead. My brother, as soon as he was shot, immediately fell down. He had a handkerchief in his hand. He never stirred nor spoke after."

There was a moment of silence in the courtroom as Earl Connors lowered his head and ran his hand through his hair.

"And what did you do then, Mr. Connors?" lawyer Power continued his questioning.

"I ran at the prisoner and tried to take the gun away from him, but he swung it around and hit me on the arm. Then he said, 'God-damn it, you'll never hang me!' And then he backed up and tried to reload his rifle, so I ran back down the track with the children and the others."

"What did the prisoner do then?"

"He followed us. He ran after us for several acres, then he went back the other way."

"What happened next?"

"Well, we went to Joe Dunigan's to get a wagon to go back and pick up my brother. But Joe's horse had died the week before, so I went back to my father's house and got a wagon there and took my father and mother up to where my brother was lying. Joe Dunigan was there already with the others and we took the body back to my father's house in the wagon."

Leslie Power then told the judge that he had no more questions for Earl Connors for the time being.

The judge cautioned both lawyers again to speak louder, that he did not wish to be constantly straining to hear the testimony.

The defence lawyer, Gerald Nolan, then cross-examined Earl Connors. He had no preliminary questions but got right to the issues.

"Mr. Connors, are there not fields of grain on Mr. Ferrigan's property which are fenced off to prevent neighbouring cattle from straying into his fields?"

"Yes, but these fields . . ."

"Just answer yes or no, Mr. Connors!" said Gerald Nolan.

"Yes, sir."

"Is it not true, Mr. Connors, that people passing on this railway track undo the fence to pass and then do not replace it?"

"No horse or rig can pass without taking it down, and I suppose some people do not replace it."

"Do you pass by this road yourself, Mr. Connors?"

"Yes. When I visited my brother or someone else behind Mike Ferrigan's farm, I have taken a horse and wagon up by the track."

"Have you seen any motor vehicles on this track?"

"I did see a few motorcycles on the track a few times, but the track is kind of elevated and narrow in spots, so it's not suitable for cars."

"And have you ever forgotten to replace the fence after you took it down?"

"Yes, I may have forgotten on a few occasions."

"And did you do this intentionally?"

"I forgot to replace it, sir."

"Mr. Connors, do you know of any other people using the track who took the fence down and intentionally did not put it back? Wasn't it a running joke in the community that people would take the fence down and not put it back up?"

"I am not aware of that, sir."

"Mr. Connors, was there not bad blood between my client, Mr. Ferrigan, and your late brother?"

"Yes, I would say so."

"When did this discord begin, to your knowledge?"

"It may have begun several years ago at the community dance hall on a Saturday night."

"And could you give us some idea of what went on that evening?"

"Well, I think it began over something that happened at the village school. It was claimed that one of Michael Ferrigan's boys was bullying my brother's little girl, so my brother Paddy asked

Michael Ferrigan if he'd talk to his son. Well, it started as a discussion, but then it got out of hand. Both of them were having a drink and a few of us had to step in between them to stop them from going at each other."

"And since that day they were not on very friendly terms."

"Yes, sir."

"And there was another run-in at a school board meeting not too many months ago, was there not?"

"I was not present at that meeting, but I remember hearing something about it."

"Well, let me refresh your memory, Mr. Connors. Your brother, Patrick, accused Mr. Ferrigan of short-changing the school board on his taxes. Is that not what your brother said?"

"Yes, I believe that is so."

"And there were angry words from both sides and your brother said he was going to smash the mouth of Michael Ferrigan if they would only go outside the meeting room?"

"I was not present at that meeting, sir, so I cannot say."

"But you were told about this argument, were you not?"

"Yes, several people told me about it."

"You were told about what Patrick Connors said to my client at the meeting, were you not?"

"Yes, I heard something of that nature."

"It was common knowledge in the community, was it not?"

"Yes, I suppose you could say that, sir."

"But despite all this rancour, Mr. Connors, did your brother and Mr. Ferrigan ever come to blows?"

"Not that I know of, sir."

"Did Mr. Ferrigan ever attempt to do any harm, physically, to your brother during all the years since their falling-out?"

"Not that I know of."

Earl Connors, a tall lean man, was not comfortable in the witness stand, according to my mother who was present in court. He seemed very reluctant to answer the questions of Ferrigan's defence lawyer and nervously fingered his tie as he answered. But he spoke in a clear voice, though at times too softly for the judge, and had a sympathetic air about him, his voice trembling slightly, and a twinge of sadness in the timbre of his words. He seemed to find it difficult to adhere to the judge's wish that he speak louder.

"Mr. Connors," continued Gerald Nolan in his questioning, "did you not have stones in your pocket when you and your brother and the others met Mr. Ferrigan on the railway track before your brother was shot?"

"I had one stone, sir."

"How big was this stone?"

"It was about the size of a baseball, sir."

"And lastly, Mr. Connors, did your brother Patrick Connors own a pistol?"

"I believe he did own a pistol."

"Did you ever see this pistol?"

"Yes. He showed it to me on one occasion."

"Do you know if he had it with him on the day he was shot?"

"After he was shot we found no pistol on him."

"Mr. Connors, while my client was approaching you on that Sunday afternoon, was his rifle pointing in your direction?"

"Not at first, sir. When he ran toward us, he was carrying the rifle against his chest."

"During this time, did you notice when your brother, the deceased, reached into his pocket?"

"I did not notice. We were looking at Mr. Ferrigan."

"Thank you, Mr. Connors. That's all for now."

Gerald Nolan was trying to sow the seeds of doubt in the minds of the jury. Did Paddy Connors threaten Michael Ferrigan in any way on that Sunday in their initial encounter? Did Michael Ferrigan feel that he was going to be shot at and that he was just acting in self-defence?

Before Earl Connors could leave the witness stand, prosecutor Leslie Power had a few more brief questions for him.

"Mr. Connors, did your brother have any weapon visible as he faced Mr. Ferrigan's rifle?"

"No, sir. He had nothing in his hand except a handkerchief."

"Again, did you find any weapon on your brother's person that day?"

"No, sir."

"Thank you," said Leslie Power, and he looked at the jurymen for a few seconds and went back to his table.

Leslie Power's next witness was Terry Coughlin, one of the men who had accompanied Paddy Connors up the track on the Sunday that Paddy was shot.

"Mr. Coughlin, at what time did you first see the victim, Patrick Connors, on the afternoon of Sunday, August 17th?"

"I first saw him sometime after four o'clock when he came by and asked me to go with him past Mike Ferrigan's property."

"What did he ask you to do?"

"He said that because he had seen Ferrigan with a gun earlier waiting for him, he wanted me to go and be a witness in case Ferrigan tried to do something. He said that he was in a hurry at that time because his two children had already gone up the railroad track."

"So you agreed to go?"

"Yes, I did."

"Mr. Coughlin, could you give us an idea of what happened as you accompanied Mr. Patrick Connors up the track?"

"Yes, sir. We started to walk up the track and soon met young Dennis Cleary, who wanted to come with us. So Earl and Dennis and I went up the track with Paddy and the children and we walked about half a mile and Dennis said that he saw someone carrying a rifle up in the woods above us. So we all soon saw him and Paddy Connors said it was Michael Ferrigan for sure. Paddy said to me, 'Oh, there he is along the bush with his gun.' But Ferrigan soon came out from the bushes and came down to the track ahead of us and started running toward us. When he got close to us, about ten yards away, he yelled, 'Go back!' three times. Paddy Connors said, 'I will go back, but first I'd like to have a word with you,' but Ferrigan didn't give him time to say a word. He aimed his gun at Paddy and pulled the trigger. I heard the report and saw the kickback of the gun. Earl then ran at Ferrigan and tried to take the gun away from him, but couldn't do so and we thought that Ferrigan was getting ready to shoot at us again so we all ran down the track to get away from him. We all ran to Joe Dunigan's house. Everyone was frightened and in shock. We wanted to get Joe's wagon to go up and get Paddy, but Joe had no horse at that moment, so Earl ran down to his place and got a horse and wagon. When Earl came with the wagon accompanied by Willie and Ellie, his parents, we picked up the body and brought it down to Willie's house."

"How long did you know Paddy Connors?"

"Oh, about a dozen years, sir."

"Did you notice if he was carrying a weapon that day?"

"I did not see anything in his hand at the time he was shot except a white handkerchief."

On cross-examination, Gerald Nolan asked Terry Coughlin some questions about what happened after the shooting.

"Mr. Coughlin, did you notice while running away down the track whether Earl Connors threw any stones at Michael Ferrigan?"

"No, I did not notice."

"Did Michael Ferrigan fire any more shots toward anyone else after he shot at Patrick Connors?"

"No, sir. He did not."

"Were you aware, Mr. Coughlin, that Patrick Connors owned a pistol?"

"Yes, sir, I was aware."

"Do you know where Mr. Connors acquired this pistol?"

"I believe he got it from his cousin Dominic Farley who served in the war."

"Have any idea why Patrick Connors would want to keep a pistol in his possession?"

"No, I have no idea."

Young Dennis Cleary then took the witness stand for the prosecution and he reiterated similar details to the court regarding the events of the shooting. The defence attorney did not cross-examine him.

Raymond Coughlin was the next prosecution witness called. He had visited the Ferrigans in mid-afternoon on the day of the killing.

"What was your purpose, Mr. Coughlin, in calling in at the house of Michael Ferrigan on that Sunday afternoon?" asked Prosecutor Power.

"The parish committee wanted to organize a dance for the young people to close out the summer, so I dropped in at Michael Ferrigan's just to see if some of his teenagers might be interested."

"And how were you received at the Ferrigan household?"

"Maggie invited me for tea and before I knew it she had all kinds of food on the table and I sat down with Michael and some of the kids to have a bite."

"What did you notice about the behaviour of Michael Ferrigan as you sat down to eat? Did he seem tense or anxious, in your estimation?"

Defence Lawyer Nolan immediately objected to this question.

"Yes, Mr. Power," agreed the judge, "please refrain from soliciting the opinions of the witnesses."

"When Margaret Ferrigan looked out the window," continued Prosecutor Power, "and said that she thought she could see someone coming up the railway track, how did Michael react?"

"He put down his cup of tea and went over to the window."

"What else did Margaret Ferrigan say at that time?"

"She said that she thought it might be Paddy Connors coming up the track and that Michael should speak to him again about the fence."

"What did Michael Ferrigan do after that?"

"He looked out the window for a few seconds, then he went into a room at the back of the kitchen."

"Did you see him again that afternoon, Mr. Coughlin?"

"No, sir. He didn't come back. I left the house about a half-hour after that, but he still had not come back."

Chapter 8

After the court had recessed that day, many of the extended family members of both the accused and the victim took the train back to Pine River in late afternoon. There seemed to be little rancour between the two groups. In a sense, both families were up against the system of justice, both families seeking what they considered to be a just resolution to the trial. They tended to sit in separate cars in the train. Yet some of the Connors clan were still on speaking terms with the Ferrigan family.

The next day, the first witness for the prosecution was Marianne Connors, the twelve-year-old daughter of Paddy Connors. My mother described her as an alert-looking and strikingly dignified girl, with long hair and blue eyes, who seemed to be the most expressive of the witnesses thus far. She spoke in an audible voice that resonated in the silence of the crowded courtroom. The judge had no reason to bend forward to hear her testimony as he had had to do with some of the preceding witnesses.

"Would you state your name and where you live?" began Prosecutor Power.

"I am Marianne Connors, daughter of the deceased. I live with my mother, now that my father is no longer alive. I have two brothers and two sisters, all younger than I am. I remember the day that my father was killed. It was a Sunday afternoon."

"And how old are you, Marianne?" asked Lawyer Power.

"I will be thirteen years old in December."

"Marianne, do you know Michael Ferrigan?"

"Yes, I know Michael Ferrigan. I know his children who went to school with me at the village school."

Prosecutor Power spoke to her delicately, unable to mask the reality that he had a very special witness before him.

"Marianne, so you were with your father on the Sunday morning of the day that he was killed?"

"Yes, I was walking with my father that morning going to Grandmamma's. My little brother, Hughie, was with me at the time of our visit. A good piece from our own house we met Michael Ferrigan. He asked my Da, 'Why do you come on an idiot's land?' My father said he had a right to be there, which Mr. Ferrigan denied. I think Michael Ferrigan told my Da to get a man and he'd get a man and in a fair fight he would beat him. He called my father a name and wanted to know when he could fight. My father then sent us ahead down the track while he was talking to Mr. Ferrigan, and they were arguing pretty loud. Michael Ferrigan was saying that my Da and others were not closing the fence after they passed. Me and my little brother kept walking down the track and then we stopped but they were still talking pretty loud to each other. Mr. Ferrigan was telling my Da not to come home by the track again or he'd be sorry. He said that my Da would go home to a different tune if he tried to pass by again. Then my father joined us and we went to Grandma's and were there three or four hours. We ate lunch at about one o'clock but we didn't stay for supper. We started to walk home, but my Da said we had to go back to Grandmamma's, so we went back and got Uncle Earl and started back home again. Then I guess my father went to get Mr. Coughlin and another boy and when we got close to Mr. Ferrigan's house we saw him running with a gun. We all saw him coming with his gun and he said, 'Go back! Go back!' and then he shot my father dead, and then he said, 'He will never speak again.'

"My little brother and I tried to speak to my Da but he wouldn't answer and his face was covered with blood. Mr. Coughlin soon took me by the arm and we all ran away down the track and went to Mr. Dunigan's."

There was a sigh from the people in the courtroom. One of the bailiffs put his finger to his lips to signal silence.

"Did you ever hear your father making comments in your home about Michael Ferrigan?" went on Lawyer Power.

"No, my father didn't talk about him."

"Did your father make any threats or warnings to Mr. Ferrigan on the morning that all of you first met on the railroad track?"

"No, I don't remember anything like that."

The people in the courtroom were very moved by the testimony of Marianne, in the opinion of my mother, and despite the severe looks from the bailiffs, some people wiped their eyes with their handkerchiefs.

I was not in court that day, but I had seen Marianne on a few occasions. I had seen her at church on a few Sunday mornings but at the time I wasn't sure who she was. I did know that she was a rather beautiful young girl and I had caught her looking at me while the crowd gathered outside the church after Mass. I suppose I would have considered her to be quite young then, but when I saw her again at her dad's funeral and my father had bent down and kissed her cheek, something clicked and I remembered having seen her before. She had those beautiful blue Irish eyes and even at the funeral our gazes met a couple of times.

As with Dennis Cleary, the defence attorney did not cross-examine Marianne Connors. No doubt he did not want to be seen brow-beating a young girl who had the sympathy of all.

The prosecuting attorney called several more witnesses that day, men from the farming community who had met Paddy Connors on his way up the track. He questioned others who had helped to bring the body of Paddy Connors to his father's house. More details of the aftermath of the killing came out. News of the shocking event had travelled fast in the minutes and hours following the shooting, and an incensed crowd had gathered at the scene of Paddy Connors' death. Many had headed to the house of Michael Ferrigan. Fortunately, the police had also arrived and prevented the onset of vigilante justice by immediately taking Ferrigan into custody.

It was shortly after the court was adjourned for the day that my father received a call notifying us that I was to testify the next morning. I could only suspect that Tommy Kelly would be the witness to follow me. If there ever was a time when I wanted to be with Tommy it was that evening. I could have used his support. He probably could have given me some advice on how to handle the whole thing.

I slept little that night. I woke up in a cold sweat a few times and kicked the blankets off and lay there staring at the ceiling. I wanted to go to my parents' room and crawl in with them and have them hold me. Perhaps had I been younger I would have done that.

The following morning my brothers and sister went off to school with their lunches, and my father, who took the day off from work, and mother walked me down to the courthouse. It was a fifteen-minute walk. I felt that I was going to my own execution.

When we got to the courthouse we were ushered in and seated on benches close to the front of the large ornate room. The spectators were then allowed in. They took their seats very quietly and before I knew it the room was packed. The doors were then closed. No more of the public would be permitted entry.

Michael Ferrigan was then brought in with an officer on either side. They installed him at the front of the room in the box seat near the judge's desk. He was a tall man, husky, and even larger than I had imagined. He did not look at anybody but lowered his head. When he did look up, he seemed to be staring off into space, his eyes on no one in particular.

The jury then came in from a side door and seated themselves on the twelve chairs to the right of where we were sitting. One of the bailiffs then announced that the judge was to enter. The magistrate soon walked in quickly and took his seat and gavelled the proceedings to begin. That was the way Judge Sévigny ran things. Everything was soon under way.

Prosecutor Leslie Power immediately called me to the witness stand and I was sworn in. As I was facing the spectators, I recognized many of the people facing me. There was my Uncle Mike and Janice and many of the people I had met on my stays in Pine River. Tommy Kelly's parents were present, of course, since Tommy was to take the stand right after me.

Needless to say, I was very nervous. I was actually on the edge of tears and wondered how I was going to hold up. Luckily, Janice was looking right at me and she winked and gave me a half-smile. That seemed to buoy me up a little.

Michael Ferrigan hardly looked at me after I started speaking. It was as if he did not want to hear what I had to say. I certainly had no desire to stare at him, but seeing him up close was a little intimidating, though not as much as I had expected. He looked to be a rather pathetic figure sitting in his seat.

Things were held up for a while, everyone waiting while Leslie Power was shuffling through some papers. Both the defence lawyer and the judge were looking at him, waiting for him to begin.

Finally, Judge Sévigny said, "Mr. Power, we have a lot of work to do today. Are you ready to start?"

"Yes, Your Honour."

Then Leslie Power began his questioning.

He looked at me and said, "Would you state your name, please?"

"My name is Francis Carroll, sir."

"And Francis, would you tell the court how you came to be present in Pine River on the Sunday of the killing of Patrick Connors?"

"Yes, sir," I said. "Every summer I go and visit my uncle, Michael Carroll, who has a farm in Pine River. I help my uncle out with some of the chores sometimes."

"And you live in Quebec City?"

"Yes, I live here with my parents. My father is a teacher. My father is my Uncle Mike's brother. Anyway, after Mass that day my friend Tommy Kelly asked me to go fishing with him, so we went up the seventh range road and started fishing in the brook there."

"Now, Francis, would you explain to the court how you overheard a discussion between two men on that Sunday morning?"

I went on to tell pretty much the same story that I had already given Prosecutor Power at his office. His questions were almost exactly the same as the ones he had asked me then.

At one point he asked me, "Francis, of the two men you saw arguing that day, is one of them in this room?"

"Yes, one of them was Mr. Ferrigan."

And I was asked to point to Michael Ferrigan sitting in the defendant's box.

When he finished his questions, the Defence Lawyer Gerald Nolan began to cross-examine me.

"Now, Francis . . ." he started. "You state that you had never seen these two men before, these two men who were arguing. Were you not close to one hundred yards away from these two men?"

"Yes, sir. But Tommy Kelly, who was with me, said he knew them right away, as soon as he saw them."

"And how could you be certain of what they said since you were that far from them?" Gerald Nolan asked, looking back and forth between the jury and myself.

"Well, it's very quiet up there and if someone is talking loud, you can hear them very well."

"How long did you hear these two voices before you actually understood what they were saying?"

"Well, maybe for a minute or two, sir."

"So you didn't understand exactly what they were saying for a few moments before you saw them."

"That's right, sir."

"Would I be right in saying that both men were raising their voices to each other?"

"Yes, sir. I guess that's right."

"But you didn't understand all that was said?"

"That's right, sir. Not at the start when we first heard them."

"Do you remember Mr. Patrick Connors saying to Michael Ferrigan, 'I'll throw your fence into the swamp and you along with it'?"

"No, sir. I don't remember hearing that."

Prosecutor Leslie Power objected to this question immediately and the judge sustained his objection and told the jury to ignore the question as well as my answer.

Defence Lawyer Nolan was again trying to implant in the minds of the jury that threats were made on both sides at that morning encounter.

Thankfully, I was then released from the witness stand. I was permitted to stay in the courtroom.

The bailiff then summoned Tommy Kelly and he came into the court with a calm and confident air that didn't surprise me. I'm sure that he felt not less than equal to the highly regarded officials in the courtroom. He sat in the witness stand exuding something between flair and wonder.

Leslie Power seemed to relish asking Tommy questions. I'm sure that he considered the two of them to be a team in the case against the perpetrator of this crime. He would soak up every last drop of worth from this thirteen-year-old witness, a lad who was rather extraordinary in his ability to respond.

"And would you state your name, please?" began Power.

"My name is Thomas Brendan Kelly, sir."

It was the first time that I had heard of Tommy's middle name being Brendan.

"And where do you reside, Thomas?"

"I live with my father and mother and brother on acreage in Pine River on the sixth range road adjacent to Michael Carroll's farm on the east side and Elmer Coughlin's property on the north side. Willie Connors is just down the road from us on the south side. The Valcartier Military Camp border is not far removed and just on the other side of Mr. Carroll's farm."

I am sure that Tommy would have given the court a geography lesson had he been able to continue, but Mr. Power soon cut him off.

"Now, Thomas, what led you to overhear this conversation between two men on the Sunday morning of the death of Patrick Connors?"

"Well, my friend Francis Carroll and I decided to do some fishing in an area that was above the railway track close to the fence erected by Michael Ferrigan. There are lots of tall trees in that area. We set up at the side of a brook that flows down under the railway track path and almost at once we began to hear the sound of raised voices below us. So we got up and went to see who was doing the arguing."

"And who *was* doing the arguing?"

"I recognized them right away as Paddy Connors and Mike Ferrigan."

"Did you know both of these men very well?"

"Yes, I was very well acquainted with Paddy Connors because he was my mother's cousin and he had visited our house on several occasions. As for Mr. Ferrigan, everybody knows him. He owns a lot of the property in that seventh range road and I've seen him around many times."

"Now, Thomas, when you began hearing the voices, could you understand what the argument was about?"

"At first we had no idea what the argument was about. We could just hear two men sort of yelling at each other."

"But once you got within earshot, what did you hear?"

"It was the old story of Michael Ferrigan complaining about people who took down his fence and did not put it back up when they passed by the railway road. Mr. Ferrigan was warning Paddy Connors not to pass that way again or he wouldn't, meaning Paddy Connors wouldn't, go back to the same tune as he came."

"And how did Mr. Connors react to this warning?"

"He said that he had a right to pass there, and that it was a public road."

"Who, in your opinion, seemed to be the more argumentative of the two men?"

Defence Lawyer Nolan sprang up and vehemently objected to the question.

"Your Honour," he protested, "the prosecutor is putting thoughts into the head of this young witness and leading him on."

The judge sustained the objection, and told Leslie Power again to avoid asking for the opinions of the witness.

But Prosecutor Power would not be swayed.

"Of the two men, Thomas, who was shouting louder?"

"Oh, no doubt—Michael Ferrigan. He was furious, while Paddy Connors was more reasonable, I thought. I know that Mr. Connors showed no fear of Mr. Ferrigan and stood up to him."

"And what did you hear about Mr. Ferrigan asking Patrick Connors to get a man to fight him? Did you hear that?"

"Yes, I heard that. He seemed to want them both to get a man and they'd have a fight and they'd see if Paddy Connors was able to smash his mouth, or something like that."

"And what was that all about?"

"My dad told me that Mr. Connors had said that to Michael Ferrigan at a school meeting several months ago. My dad was there at the meeting when he heard that. My dad said that Mr. Connors invited Michael Ferrigan to step outside, but Mr. Ferrigan said that he had a sore arm and did not want to fight."

Defence Lawyer Gerald Nolan rose and asked the judge for a time-out so they could discuss something confidentially. The two lawyers approached the judge's desk and whispered to each other for several minutes and then the lawyers went back to their tables.

Leslie Power chose not to pursue the previous line of questioning with Tommy.

"Getting back to the Sunday in question, Thomas," Leslie Power continued, "how many times did Michael Ferrigan issue this warning to Patrick Connors, that is, not to use the railway road any more?"

"Oh, at least three times, sir."

"Did Mr. Connors make any threats to Mr. Ferrigan?"

"Not that I heard, sir. He was talking loud but he was calmer, in my opinion. He said at one point that he didn't want to fight about the matter."

"Now, Thomas, was Patrick Connors alone in this walk down the railway track?"

"No, he was with two of his children. I think they were Marianne and little Hughie. They were about twenty-five yards or so down the track when we first saw the two men arguing."

"Do you think they would have heard what the argument was about?"

"Oh, yes. They were much closer to the men than we were."

"Now, Thomas, after hearing these threats from Michael Ferrigan, how did you feel?"

Gerald Nolan, this time, casually interjected and asked the judge not to allow that question, to which the judge agreed.

The prosecutor told the judge that he had no more questions for Tommy. There was no doubt that the court was in awe of such a young man responding as he did. All eyes watched Tommy as he sat in the witness stand waiting for the defence lawyer to begin his cross-examination.

"Thomas Kelly," began lawyer Nolan, "how old are you?"

"I will be fourteen years old in January, sir."

"And are you aware of the feelings of the people of your community toward Michael Ferrigan?"

"Yes, I have a pretty good idea of how most of the people feel."

Prosecutor Power chose not to object to this line of questioning.

"And is it your feeling that there is a lot of love and respect for Michael Ferrigan in Pine River?"

"Not exactly, sir."

"Is it not true that most of his neighbours tend to regard him as a hard-working man who owns a lot of property and tends to take good care of his interests?"

It was a question that seemed out of place for such a young witness, but lawyer Nolan knew whom he was dealing with and Tommy was more than up to the test. Prosecutor Power did not object to this question.

"Yes, sir. He owns quite a large acreage in different places and he puts up a lot of fencing to remind everybody."

"Now, Thomas, how do people regard the fact that Michael Ferrigan has placed a fence across the railway track which is used by a lot of people on a daily basis?"

"Well, some people do not put the fence back up after they take it down when they pass. I believe that a few have done this to spite him. People feel that Michael Ferrigan has that fence up illegally and it riles them when they have to replace it constantly when they pass. It's a rather clumsy set of logs and not easy to manage. Of course, it's easy for us kids. We just climb over it, but if you're using a rig of some sort you've got to remove the logs."

"Have you ever heard people scoff at Michael Ferrigan?"

"Yes, I've heard people talk about him in unfriendly ways."

Prosecutor Power objected to this question, and the judge sustained this challenge and asked the jury to disregard it.

Leslie Power then asked permission to approach the judge. The two opposing attorneys were soon whispering back and forth to the judge, who then called for a brief recess and the three of them retired from the court to discuss some matter. The defendant and the jury also withdrew from the court.

When proceedings reconvened, Defence Lawyer Nolan said he had no more questions for the witness. Some felt that the defence lawyer did not want to allow Tommy Kelly much time in the witness box because the lad was unpredictable. His style of speaking had an articulation that startled everyone. He had done admirably well, had spoken in a self-assured style, and his whole appearance had exuded a certain dash. I was indeed proud of him that day and realized that our involvement in the trial would soon be over and we'd be able to speak to each other again. As it turned out we were not recalled to testify, so I was soon back talking to Tommy at recess time in the schoolyard and he was soon putting me back "in touch with things." Other students at the school soon found out that we had testified at the murder trial so we both had to field a lot of questions and to satisfy a certain curiosity. I guess at the time I was impressed with my own importance, but I hope I didn't carry it too far.

I was also made aware that Marianne Connors was attending the girls' high school. Tommy informed me that Janice and he were sort of shepherding her on the train and in town to make sure that she oriented herself properly to her new surroundings. The girls' school was close by and every day after dismissal Marianne took the streetcar down to the railway station with Janice. I had walked Tommy over to where he took the trolley and we met Janice and Marianne while they were standing there waiting.

It was the first time that Marianne and I had spoken to each other.

"Were you nervous when you were on the witness stand?" was the first thing that she ever said to me.

"Oh, yes. I was ready to throw up," I answered.

Everyone laughed at that statement. I had an addiction for getting laughs. My mind was always working so that I could put in a comical retort of some kind.

"Tommy was really great, my mom said," Marianne added.

She smiled up at him admiringly.

After some more small talk with Janice and Tommy, the streetcar soon came and I watched them all get on and stood there as it pulled away with its squeals and grinds.

Marianne was just going on thirteen years of age, but she was very attractive up close. There was also an awareness in her eyes that radiated intelligence. On the emotional level, she had amazed everyone by the way she had dealt with the death of her father. I shuddered to think about how I would feel if I had lost my dad, a sinister and unthinkable vision.

The defence strategy in the trial of Michael Ferrigan began with the summoning of Joseph Dunigan to the stand the following Monday.

Attorney Gerald Nolan began his questioning.

"And what is your occupation, Mr. Dunigan?"

"I am a farmer in Pine River, sir."

"Where is your property located, Mr. Dunigan, in relation to the property of Michael Ferrigan?"

"My property borders on Mr. Ferrigan's for about sixteen acres. I guess you could say it's on the south side of his property."

"Is your property next to Mr. Ferrigan's at the railway road where the shooting took place?"

"Yes, it is."

"Is it not true, Mr. Dunigan, that your cattle, on more than one occasion, have gone into Mr. Ferrigan's property to feed on his grain?"

"Yes, that has happened, but only when the logs were taken down, so the cows went in through the gap in the fence."

"Did you ever take Mr. Ferrigan's fence down and not replace it, Mr. Dunigan?"

"No, sir. I have never done that, nor would I have reason to do that. I don't get back into that area very often. When I do I use the main road."

"Do you know of people who do take the fence down and do not replace it?"

"Yes, I am aware of that."

"Do you think that these people do this purposely? "

"I cannot say, sir."

"Mr. Dunigan, how would you describe your relations with my client?"

"I'd say that they are rather strained, sir."

Joseph Dunigan was an older man who lived with his wife Helen and two daughters, Teresa and Esther. Everyone in the community knew that the bond between him and Michael Ferrigan had been broken years before and that they could not bear to look at each other.

"Mr. Dunigan, can you tell the court how you came to be on bad terms with Mr. Ferrigan?"

Prosecutor Power asked the judge about this question and what it had to do with the case.

"I'm trying to establish, Your Honour, that my client is an honourable man and a good neighbour," explained Gerald Nolan.

The judge disallowed the objection and told Joe Dunigan to answer the question.

"Yes, well, it may have had something to do with Cromwell, a bull that I owned and that I allowed Michael Ferrigan to use on my property."

"How did this arrangement work, Mr. Dunigan?"

"Well, he'd bring his cows over to my field if he wanted them fertilized."

"How long ago was this, Mr. Dunigan?"

"It must be up to five years ago and before that."

"So what went wrong?"

"Well, one of his cows broke a leg somehow, so he had to put it down."

"And how did he react to this?"

"Well, he was quite upset, and he wanted me to compensate him for the loss of his cow. He said that it was the bull that caused the cow to break its leg."

"Do you think that Mr. Ferrigan was justified?"

"Well, no one was around to really see what happened, so I have no idea how the cow broke its leg. Anyhow, he's never forgotten that and he keeps reminding me."

"Mr. Dunigan, how do you feel about the position of that fence which is across the railway track?"

"I have never been in agreement with where that fence is located and I have told Mike Ferrigan as much on more than one occasion. I tried to tell him one day how we could arrange the fencing so that it would not interfere with people passing on the track, but he wouldn't allow me to tell him. I had a proposition to make to him where we could work together and keep the cattle contained on my property and not block the railway track, but he would not even listen to my ideas on the matter. He seems to be a very stubborn man. He said he had no intention to add any additional fencing."

"Did Michael Ferrigan ever threaten you in any way since you had a falling-out with him?"

"Threaten? No, he never really threatened me."

"So how would you describe your relationship with Mr. Ferrigan despite these differences? Was it normal?"

"If you mean by normal, did we ever commit violence against one another, no, we did not, sir, and I suppose you could say that our relations are normal but not very friendly."

With that, Gerald Nolan terminated his questions.

Leslie Power was soon up on his feet.

"Now, Mr. Dunigan, could you tell us of the events that occurred in your presence on the afternoon of the shooting of Patrick Connors?"

"Yes, sir. At about five o'clock on that Sunday afternoon, my wife Helen and I were just about to sit down to supper with my two daughters when we heard a great commotion in front of the house. We all went out and we saw Earl Connors and the boy Dennis Cleary. They both seemed to be very distressed and they told us that Paddy Connors had been shot. Two of the children of Paddy then came running into the yard, along with Terry Coughlin. The children were both crying, especially the boy, Hughie. Earl wanted me to hitch up a horse and wagon to go up and get Paddy. They said he was lying on the railway road. But my horse had died just a few days before, so Earl decided to run down to his house and get his own horse. We telephoned Earl's father to get him to hitch up a wagon. We made a few more phone calls to tell some people what had happened and we called the police. My wife and the girls took care of the children while Terry and I ran back up the railway road to see what we could do for Paddy. When we got to the spot where he was lying, we could see that Paddy had expired. His body was sort of twisted around, so we straightened him out as best we could and waited for Earl to come up with the wagon about ten minutes later."

"Did you see Michael Ferrigan at this time?"

"No, there was no sign of him."

"Were there any other people with you there?"

"Yes. Dennis Cleary soon came back and Paddy's older brother Eddie arrived too. There were a few others there. When Earl came with the horse and wagon, Willie and Ellie were with him. It was very sad. Other people began to arrive soon after and there was lots of talk about Michael Ferrigan and what should be done about him."

As it turned out, my mother said that Lawyer Gerald Nolan erred in putting Joe Dunigan on the stand. Joe spoke in a simple, straightforward way that everyone easily related to. Although he was not dramatic in his tone of voice, his quiet manner of speaking could not hide a slight quaver. The jury fixed their eyes on him at all times during his testimony, no doubt won over by his thoughtful reserve. If lawyer Nolan had been trying to show that Michael Ferrigan had normal relations with his neighbours, the testimony of Joe Dunigan contradicted that notion. Instead, the jury got caught up in the revelation of the events of that deadly afternoon.

Chapter 9

Winter, with its extremely cold snaps and storms that slow down the frenetic pace of a city, is not that bothersome to a young lad. The people who complained more about the winter were the older generation, it seemed to me as I was growing up. Young school kids tend to accept the weather as it comes and make use of the existing conditions to pursue their pastimes.

During the winter months my brothers and I would walk to school every day, a distance of about one mile. Even my little sister, Eileen, was able to do this as soon as she began grade one, when it was always the job of one of us boys to drop her off. Mom always made sure that we were dressed warmly with our scarves wrapped around our necks. My dad, being a teacher, had by this time already gone to school to prepare for class. On some mornings, after an overnight snowstorm, it was rather difficult to walk through the unploughed streets. And then we would walk home for noon lunch which my mom would prepare for us. Then back to school for afternoon classes, and so on.

It was all a hale and hearty regimen, before school buses came into wide use, and with the traffic on the city streets rather minimal.

Our flat was heated with a coal-burning stove that always died out during the night and had to be restarted for the next day. My mom and dad alternately cleaned the inside of the stove early every morning, taking out the old pieces of coal and then rekindling the fire. It was always quite cold on winter mornings in our flat. But soon the new flames would burst into life and the warmth would fill the kitchen and we'd be up and ready for another day. Eventually the landlord had an oil-burning furnace put in at the basement level of the house our flat was in, and we were on easy street.

But for the working person, a winter season in the old city would present certain problems. Calcium or salt was not used to any great extent on the city streets; therefore, a thick layer of hard snow and ice imbedded itself on most roads. There was much skidding and sliding after a snowfall, the plight made more ticklish because the core of Quebec City is built upon the slope of a rocky hill. Movement was slowed down considerably as people tried to get to their jobs. However, citizens had learned to dress warmly when venturing out, and the public transportation system continued to function, and the city ploughs, many of them still horse-drawn, took to the streets. Cities that are exposed to large yearly amounts of snowfall learn to cope with it, and either remove it or deal with it. Quebec City was no different.

Except for the fact that the snow had to be removed from the surface of the ice rink at school, winter after a storm presented few difficulties for us young people. We simply went about our regular routines as if nothing was amiss.

For the Irish immigrants coming to a new country set in a colder climate, winter posed some serious challenges. Ireland is essentially an island whose temperature seldom dips lower than the freezing point during most years. Not that the people of Ireland have not experienced difficult winters. There have been treacherous years of snow and sleet and tumultuous winds. But even if the plots of land in Canada were huge compared to what the immigrants had farmed in Ireland, and the long-term future held great promise, the early years of settlement for the Irish tenant farmers were beset with dire obstacles, especially in terms of the extreme weather conditions.

Amongst the early Irish settlers the bitter winter took its toll. Some were unprepared. In many cases they were poorly clothed to deal with the harsh reality of incessant cold. The records of the parish at St. Augustin, close to Pine River, reveal that "on the eighth of February, 1824, Patrick Fitzpatrick, farmer, husband of Sarah McEvoy," was buried in the cemetery of that parish. He was thirty-three years of age and "was found frozen to death on the morning of February fifth, without any sign of violence," by a group of residents.

And then again, in December of that same year, the parish records the burial of one "Patrick Coyle, seventeen years of age. This boy was subject to epileptic seizures and he was found, quite frozen, on a road not far from his home, with no sign of violence."

In 1826, a 32-year-old woman was found frozen to death, according to the records of a Loretteville church nearby.

To these victims we can add the name of John Landrigan, found dead on the 6th range road in Pine River "by the visitation of God, yet unknown," as the coroner's certificate states. It does not say that he froze to death, but "early March can be pretty cold in this country, so it is very likely that he froze." He was but twenty years old.

Even in the late 1800s, a man named Redmond was found in another man's barn, frozen to death. Though long after the early pioneer time, this case demonstrates the severe circumstances facing these settlers.

It is easy to understand how activities on these farms can change as the winter sets in, usually in mid-November. The snows begin and continue until the following April. It is really a winter of six months. It is a far cry from their homeland. The winters of Ireland can have much rain and wind and unpleasant weather, but it is nothing compared to the winters of the land the Irish farmers chose to emigrate to–in this case, Quebec.

During these wintry months, horses and cattle were kept in the stable, the cold conditions lessened by the natural insulation of the animals' warmth as well as by the buffer generated in the stores of hay and oats in the barn area, usually connected to the stable.

In most cases farmers had horse-drawn vehicles, cutters, and sleighs that were used to transport whatever was required.

A post office was established in the early 1880s in Pine River, the mail being a most precious means of communication, especially through the long months of captivity caused by the mountains of snow. One of the farmers was hired to do the mail run, first on a weekly basis, and later from Monday to Friday, his rig laden with letters and packages. Mail delivery, in most cases a joyous occasion, was a time the people greatly anticipated.

It is said that one of the men who delivered the mail in the early days was a farmer named Ernie Higgins. It was a 25-mile circuit every day for Ernie to distribute the mail, as well as to pick up letters to be sent out. He was an affable man who never turned down the offer of a drink, and sought out the possibilities on a regular basis. He had a penchant, when making deliveries, to "stop in" at the farms, have some refreshments with his "lovely neighbours," then continue on his way. Ernie was known to be a distributor of other products along with the mail. His daily route, to some neighbours, was known as the "liquor run." Most men who were hired to do this mail circuit could do so in less than five hours. Ernie would take as long as eight hours on occasion. And by the time he got back to the post office with the outgoing mail, he would have some difficulty counting out the money he had collected for the cost of the outgoing postage. It was discovered one winter day that the mare Ernie used to draw along his sleigh showed every indication of blindness. This was an animal that knew where all the outside mailboxes were and would stop precisely at each one. Everyone considered it a miracle of sorts that both Ernie and the horse could have performed so well despite their incapacities.

Roads were kept open where possible during the winter—roads to adjacent towns and villages, roads to Quebec City. But for the farmers in some isolated areas it was a time devoid of much social activity; the families hunkered down near the warmth of the hearth, still performing necessary duties around the stable.

On a crisp early March day in 1934, a Friday, Matthew O'Meara left St. Michel, a town south of Pine River, to travel to Quebec City with a load of timber, using horse and sleigh. O'Meara, a lumberman, had a brother who kept a boarding house in Quebec.

Matthew stayed there overnight after concluding his delivery of the wood to a Quebec City furniture craftsman. To travel the road to Quebec City by horse and sleigh at that time was a common undertaking, although the twenty-mile trip took several hours. It was considered wise to stay one night to allow the horse to rest before returning.

The generations of Irish settlers had produced people who were now accustomed to the cold of winter. Much work was now being done during wintertime, including wood-cutting, trading of goods, and travelling along the icy roads between country and city. These were hardy men who did not shirk opportunity because of chilly weather conditions. The road to Quebec City did allow for motor traffic, but many still used the horse-drawn conveyance.

The following day Matthew O'Meara met his younger brother, David, who had also been in the city delivering pieces of birch, and together they decided to travel back home together, each with his own horse and sleigh. Before doing this, the O'Mearas went to a tavern on St. Vallier Street and consumed several glasses of porter.

The O'Meara "boys" were raw personalities, known for their hard drinking and rough and ready ways. They would rarely retreat from volatile situations and therefore indulged in occasional bouts of fisticuffs, whether it was in the taverns of Quebec City or in their own neighbourhood. They were also gregarious men, products of a large extended family. Their circle of friends, many connected with their business, met frequently at social settings where drink and good times percolated.

They also had enemies. One of these was a large, gruff man named Michael Ferrigan, who had inherited acreage from his father in Pine River. Ferrigan was a married man in his thirties who had four children. He was known for his quick temper and his willingness to back it up with the use of force.

The difficulties between the O'Mearas and Michael Ferrigan had begun a few years before over a business deal, a sale of lumber by Michael Ferrigan to the sawmill of Matthew O'Meara. This was one of many deliveries made by Ferrigan, the last few for which he claimed he was not paid. Matthew O'Meara vigorously denied this. A few nasty verbal exchanges occurred as a result of this mishandling of business and, while Ferrigan threatened to take the matter to court, he never quite got around to it and the feud between the two parties festered into a hateful scenario. There were threats and counter-threats and the situation further deteriorated into a fear-filled predicament, where the O'Meara family had great uneasiness about their safety. This was not an issue that could have been settled by an exchange of punches in a bar. It was as if war had been declared between two rivals. The O'Mearas went about their activities in the Irish community with a common watchfulness just below the surface of their daily movement.

During the O'Mearas' return trip to Pine River, on a day that had turned bitterly cold, there would be at least one more stop. Within five miles of home, they met up with Dominic McDonough, a close acquaintance who suggested that they drop in to Mrs. Wild's tavern for a drink. The day was ending, with the sky darkening, and the horses needed rest. There was fear, however, that Michael Ferrigan would be present at Mrs. Wild's tavern, as he was known to be on occasion. As they approached the tavern, Dominic went ahead and entered to see if Ferrigan was there. He was not, so the two O'Mearas and McDonough stopped in for a rest and refreshments.

With regard to the O'Mearas, Michael Ferrigan had his own fears and trepidation. He had heard it said that the O'Meara family had it in for him and that one of them had said at a gathering that some family member should "shoot that son-of-a-bitch Ferrigan." A heavy-set man who weighed well over two hundred pounds, Michael Ferrigan presented a commanding figure as he travelled about the community. Although he was a man of few words, many of these words seemed to be ill-humoured and unsociable in tenor. In short, he did not make friends easily and seemed to have wanted to use his imposing physique as a factor in his previous dealings with the O'Mearas.

From the outset of business relations with him, Matthew O'Meara had considered Ferrigan to be a bully of sorts and a person who should certainly be brought down to size.

Yet, with all these negative attributes, Michael Ferrigan showed himself to be a hard worker and had earned the respect of at least some of his neighbours.

It was ironic that these two adversaries actually lived close to one another. The possibility was very real that they could meet, haphazardly, since both of them used the same road and did business with the same suppliers. To get to their property, the O'Meara family had to pass by the Ferrigan homestead, and did so daily.

When the three patrons, Dominic McDonough and the O'Meara brothers, emerged from Mrs. Wild's tavern after consuming a few glasses of ale, the journey homeward continued. The three horses trotted along, with the attached sleigh bells ringing rhythmically. The night was frigid and the exhaled breaths of all horses likely released a luminous spray of whiteness at short intervals. There is something primitively beautiful in this image, the stars casting the only light upon the unending snow and the clanging sound of the three sleighs moving along unfalteringly through the night.

The three vehicles soon reached a fork in the road, one leading toward McDonough's farm and the other being the main road to Pine River where the O'Mearas lived. After parting with McDonough and before heading to the 7th range toward home, the O'Mearas decided to call at the home of James Kerwin, a man whom both brothers admired greatly. The welcome light of the coal oil lamps had beckoned to them and, leaving their horses by the side of the road, they were soon sitting at the table in James Kerwin's kitchen enjoying one last drink before finally travelling the last lap toward home.

They had been sitting in the front kitchen for a good half-hour, chatting and joking, when one of James Kerwin's boys appeared at the door. He informed the O'Mearas that the horses they had left at the front of the house had decided to head home, the sleighs empty of any driver. All went outdoors without their overcoats to listen to the fading sound of bells ringing in the distance. There was no attempt to run after the horses and the brothers simply decided that they would have to walk the rest of the way home, a distance of a few miles. There was no fear for the horses. These animals knew the roads of that area and would surely find their way back home safely. James Kerwin expressed his fear that the family of Matthew O'Meara would fret when they saw the horses come back alone. He offered to hitch up a horse to his sleigh and take the brothers home. The O'Mearas would not think of putting James Kerwin to all that bother. The walking distance to their home was relatively short.

Before setting off, Matthew O'Meara decided to borrow an axe from James Kerwin. Why he opted to do this he did not know, although in the back of his head was the thought that they would have to pass by the property of Michael Ferrigan. Better to be safe than sorry, he must have figured. So Matthew trudged along toward home, the axe angled down from his shoulder, always at his younger brother's side.

After walking more than a mile from Kerwins' toward home, according to Matthew, the sky seemed to darken as clouds passed under the stars. The brothers heard what they thought was a sleigh coming toward them, its bells tingling faintly.

"Oh, that must be Tom," said David O'Meara, referring to a younger brother who had likely seen the empty sleighs come back with no one in them and had decided to come down the road to find his older brothers.

The O'Meara brothers soon could recognize the outline of a sleigh and horse in the darkness ahead. They could also make out the figure of someone beyond the sleigh. The sleigh itself was stopped and was stationary beside the road. As they approached David saw that the horse and sleigh were his own. Matthew paused briefly to examine the vehicle while David walked on ahead toward the person now in the middle of the road.

"Who is that?" Matthew heard David ask.

David was no more than twenty yards ahead of Matthew.

The dark figure of a person was moving toward David.

"Come on, you bastard. I have you now!" were the next words that pierced the air. Matthew clearly recognized the voice as belonging to Michael Ferrigan.

Matthew O'Meara walked toward his brother. As he approached the two figures, he saw Michael Ferrigan aim a blow at his brother with an axe. Ferrigan held the axe with both hands and struck again, this time to the shoulder area, and then again to the body of David O'Meara. The blows were powerfully and rapidly struck and soon brought the victim to the ground. Matthew then saw Michael Ferrigan strike David once again while he was prostrate. In doing so, Ferrigan sounded a perceivable grunt. With the last blow struck by Ferrigan, Matthew was just a few feet away and he raised his own axe toward Ferrigan.

But then Ferrigan backed off, and Matthew turned his attention to his brother who was struggling to rise. Ferrigan ran to another sleigh that was parked farther down the road. Matthew saw him jump into the sleigh where he shouted "Go on, go on!" and drove off.

As Matthew stated at the coroner's inquest later, his brother lay limp and he lifted his younger brother's head and tried to get him to speak. His brother responded with some sounds and gurgling. His brother did not speak after that. He heard him drawing his breath, and something seemed to be boiling inside of him. After a moment he decided to lift his brother up, noticing the blood on the road beneath him.

"When I lifted him up off the ground into my arms, I perceived he was breathing no more; I thought he was dead. I carried him back down the road toward his sleigh, but he was heavy and slipped from my arms. I picked him up again and carried him another ten yards."

After Matthew had carried his brother's body back to the sleigh, he realized that his brother's vehicle had been linked with thick wire to a picket in deep snow by the side of the road. The horse was still trying to break away from the entanglements. Ferrigan had apparently intercepted one of the O'Meara horses as it had pulled its empty sleigh through the darkness. No doubt he had suspected that the O'Mearas were up to some black-hearted scheme to trick him and to fulfil their plans to waylay him. He had heard some talk, just days before at Mrs. Wild's tavern, that the O'Meara brothers would likely attack him on the road near his home. It was his right to strike them before they had a chance to carry out their evil designs.

With the numbness in his hands, Matthew O'Meara could not loosen the wire that secured the sleigh to the fence picket in the deepness of the snow. In a panic, he decided to leave the body of his brother by the wayside and run home to get help. David O'Meara was soon picked up from the road by the O'Meara family and other neighbours who lived in the area.

It seems that Michael Ferrigan had told his family that he had had a confrontation with the O'Mearas, and that he had left the body of one of them lying by the roadside.

Early the following morning, Michael Ferrigan hitched up his sleigh again and immediately headed for Quebec City. In the aftermath of the previous night's killing, he had decided to seek legal help. Meanwhile, the police had been informed of the death of David O'Meara at the hands of Ferrigan, and they were on the lookout for the perpetrator of this crime. He was soon arrested on St. Louis Street in Quebec City near the office of Gerald Nolan, a lawyer whom Ferrigan had just met with. Ferrigan had told the lawyer that he had been out making purchases the previous day and that on his way back home, he found two men named O'Meara waiting for him in the darkness on a country road near his home. He said that they both ran forward and struck him several times, after which he had taken an axe from his sleigh to defend himself and that after the incident he had informed people about what had occurred. He repeated this story to the police, who now kept him in custody. Ferrigan said that he had come to town to talk about his involvement after he'd heard that David O'Meara had died.

The police had been given two versions of the killing and the circumstances around which it had occurred. The question of who was the aggressor in this event had to be answered. The body of the victim, David O'Meara, had been horribly mutilated, the right arm "almost severed from his body, and his stomach area being opened to such an extent that the entrails protruded." He had died almost immediately, and the police had later taken the body to Quebec City.

A few mornings later, the police left town with the coroner to go to Pine River. Michael Ferrigan was made to accompany them. The inquest into the affray took place at the home of James Kerwin, whom the O'Mearas had been with just before the killing.

The results of the autopsy were aired, the details of which were very difficult to bear for the O'Meara family.

"I examined the body of the deceased and noticed five incised wounds," Coroner Charles Fortier began, as it was published in the newspaper. "The first was at the root of the neck on the left side and extended from the edge of the sternum and penetrated through the clavicle and through the first rib at its curvature toward the spine. The second incision penetrated the left side of the chest, about three inches in length, and separated part of the cartilage of the sixth and seventh ribs and part of the sternum diagonally. The third was situated on the right side, penetrating the abdomen through the cartilage of the false rib. The fourth was situated on the left side of the spine and separated the long muscles on the side of the spine, and penetrated the body at the last dorsal vertebra, which is deeply indented by the instrument. The fifth wound was situated on the upper third of the length of the arm, and penetrated into the bone.

"On opening the thorax, the left cavity was found to contain about three pints of blood, the lung was collapsed, the heart empty of blood. Both lungs were free of any trace of disease. The stomach contained a moderate quantity of food, appeared quite healthy, as did the other organs contained in the abdomen, with the exception of the liver which exhibited a long deep incision that corresponded to what I noticed on the right side. A small quantity of blood was found in the cavity of the abdomen. I opened the skull, and examined the brain and its membranes, which were found to be in perfectly normal condition. I am of the opinion that the first wound I have described was, inevitably, the mortal wound, and that in combination with the other wounds described, was the cause of death."

It was a report that clearly illustrated the extent of the massive wounds, as well as the brutal intentions of the assailant. One of the witnesses at the inquest, Edward Cleary, stated that the accused had visited his house on the night of the killing. Michael Ferrigan had told him about the confrontation; he quoted Ferrigan's claim that the two O'Mearas had attacked him on the road near his home and one of them had called out for the other to shoot him.

The jury at the inquest recommended that Michael Ferrigan be held for trial, and he was brought back to Quebec City and incarcerated.

The trial in the case of the killing of David O'Meara began three months later. It was of a surprisingly short duration. The witnesses for the prosecution were virtually the same people who had testified at the inquest. There had been only one witness who had actually seen the crime—Matthew O'Meara. But his testimony was marred by the probing questions of Ferrigan's defence lawyer, Gerald Nolan. In his answers, Matthew O'Meara admitted to the court that members of his family had discussed the matter of Michael Ferrigan on several occasions, and some of them had felt that the latter was a person who should be dealt with severely. At least one other witness had already confirmed that these discussions had gone on.

Matthew O'Meara also admitted that, on the night of the killing, he had been carrying an axe as he walked down the road with his brother. Why had be bothered to borrow such a destructive weapon from James Kerwin?

Much scepticism arose as testimony was given at the trial. There was conjecture as to who had initiated the violence on the occasion of the death of David O'Meara. There had been menacing words coming from both sides prior to the killing. The court was in a quandary as to which party should be held responsible.

The jury deliberated several hours and came back with a verdict of "not guilty." Michael Ferrigan was set free. The general consensus was that since the prosecution could not prove that Ferrigan had intended to kill anyone, he had acted in self-defence.

Michael Ferrigan was released back into his community of Irish families, who could not understand how such a level of violent savagery could surface within their peaceful environment. How were they to regard a neighbour who was capable of hacking a fellow human being to death?

More than seventeen years would pass before the violent and extreme traits in Michael Ferrigan's personality would emerge once again.

Chapter 10

I first took a hockey stick in my hands when I was five years of age. My dad had given me one for Christmas, along with a standard-sized hockey puck, and I would go out on the icy street and shoot the puck against a fence near my home. It did not take long for one of the French-speaking neighbourhood kids to join me. My French skills were not very good at that time, but we had one thing in common—a great love and admiration for Maurice "the Rocket" Richard. His name was likely the first one in hockey that I was familiar with. Other names soon became part of our hockey lexicon, names that were pronounced similarly in both languages—Butch Bouchard, Kenny Reardon, and Bill Durnan.

Playing street hockey was indeed a uniting factor, and most of the neighbourhood boys took part. The French-speaking kids had adapted certain English hockey expressions that they had heard on radio broadcasts, yet since there were more French kids playing, the language of the majority prevailed. That was how I first began to speak French.

I cannot properly express the joy that I felt as I began to play Pee Wee hockey in the house league at school. If I had a game scheduled after class, the thoughts in my head were totally preoccupied with the coming event. I had considerable difficulty applying myself to my schoolwork during such a day. The teacher would frequently awaken me from a deep dream where I was skating full belt down the ice and shooting the puck into the net of the opposing team.

We warmed up to the hockey season in much the same way as a young person to the south would look forward to the baseball season. We saw no obstacles in living with the snow and ice and cold temperatures.

By the time I got to high school, I was on the school's Bantam team which played inter-school hockey throughout the city. In these city-wide leagues, we were the only English-speaking team, so the French schools tended to consider a game against us as a truly special contest. The French-speaking kids were great hockey players at all levels. They were marvellous skaters and puck handlers. It is no surprise to me that many of them rose to great heights in professional hockey. The game came to symbolize Quebec itself, where thousands of kids skated daily on thousands of outdoor rinks scattered throughout the province.

During the fall of 1952, at the height of the trial and after I had testified, my father rented a car for the day on a Sunday and drove our whole family out to Pine River to see my Uncle Mike. I enjoyed this trip even if I didn't get to hang around with Janice, by ourselves, or see Tommy Kelly. My brother Eamon and I did visit the site of the shooting that afternoon. The area had an unnatural feel to it, with the oat field cut low and some of the other fields nearby lying fallow. My Uncle Mike said that the people who passed by the railway road were now always replacing the logs of the fence. After what had happened, no one would appreciate the humour of not doing so.

A sombre mood still permeated the homesteads of Pine River. The interest in the trial was still at fever pitch, with the defence lawyer of Michael Ferrigan trying to regain a foothold. The prosecution had mounted a seemingly insurmountable case against the defendant, with witness after witness having pointed to the unprovoked killing by Ferrigan. The threats made by the defendant early on that sad Sunday had been overheard. It certainly seemed at the time that Michael Ferrigan would be found guilty of "wilful murder" and that he would be forced to pay for his crime.

From the early days that Michael Ferrigan had been held by the police for the murder of Paddy Connors, there had been a spate of newspaper articles exciting prejudice against his client, Defence Lawyer Gerald Nolan wrote to the court. That had been one of the reasons that Nolan had sought a new venue for the trial. While the accused had admitted being responsible for the shooting, this was no reason for the press to be writing articles referring to Michael Ferrigan as a cold-blooded perpetrator, according to Nolan.

Lawyer Nolan wrote that there was also evidence that the deceased Patrick Connors was a powerful and quarrelsome man, not as innocent as he was portrayed, and known as "Big Connors."

In this written submission to the court, Gerald Nolan also issued a complaint that strongly suggested that brothers of the deceased Paddy Connors and relatives of the earlier victim David O'Meara may have been seen with certain members of the jury that was trying Michael Ferrigan. Although he had no knowledge of jury tampering, he implored the judge to take the steps necessary to remedy this "interference."

Gerald Nolan's plan for the defence was to show that Paddy Connors was a man with an explosive temper. He wanted to get the jury to believe that the deceased had demonstrated on more than one occasion that he was ready to use violence and had shown this trait toward Michael Ferrigan as well as others.

The next defence witness that Gerald Nolan offered was a maintenance worker at the Valcartier Military Camp whose name was Dominic Farley.

"I understand, Mr. Farley, that you were involved in the fighting during the war," began Nolan.

"Yes, we went in with the Allies at Normandy on June 6th, 1944. That was my first experience in actual combat after spending many months training in England."

Leslie Power, the prosecutor, chose not to object to this line of questioning, something that was obviously aimed at developing sympathy for the coming testimony of the witness. He would be the last to earn the wrath of the court and jury by downplaying the words and honourable service of a returning Second World War veteran.

"And how long did you serve with the Canadian Army during the war?" continued Nolan.

"I joined in 1941 and received my honourable discharge in 1947, two years after the war ended."

"Could you explain to us how you came into possession of a German pistol?"

"During the campaign in France, I confiscated it from one of the men in my platoon who had taken it from a captured German officer. As the sergeant of the platoon, I was to be in control of all captured weapons."

"So you kept it as a souvenir, so to speak."

"That's correct, sir. That's the only weapon I kept."

"And for curiosity's sake, Mr. Farley, what sort of pistol are we talking about here?"

"It's commonly known as a Luger, sir."

"Now, Mr. Farley, how did Patrick Connors come into possession of this weapon?"

"Well, I showed it to him once and he always expressed a lot of interest in it, so one night while we were playing euchre we made a bet as to which team would win the game. I told him if his side won the game he could have anything he wanted, within reason, of course. I suspected he would ask for the pistol even before we lost the game. Anyhow, I intended to give it to him from the time that he first saw it."

"So this happened how many years ago?"

"Oh, three or four years ago. I'm not sure of the date."

"Did you have any regrets having given away this souvenir?"

"No, absolutely not. It was just sitting there in my drawer. I never used it for any purpose. Besides, Paddy Connors was a very close friend of mine and I felt that if he wanted the pistol, then he could have it."

"So, Mr. Farley, did Patrick Connors still have this pistol in his possession at the time of his death?"

"Well, he still owned the Luger. Whether he had it on him on the day in question, I have no idea."

With this witness, Gerald Nolan had established to the jury that Paddy Connors did certainly own a pistol.

Leslie Power had a few questions in cross-examination.

"Mr. Farley, do you know if Patrick Connors ever practised firing this pistol?"

"Well, he could not have practised with it because there were no rounds in its chamber nor anywhere else. The Parabellum 9mm rounds are not readily available here. I never bothered to buy any and I never heard that Paddy did either."

"So for all practical purposes, this weapon could not have been used at all."

"That's correct. Unless Paddy ordered some bullets on his own. I'm not aware that he did. I never heard that he actually got around to firing the pistol."

"So even if Patrick Connors did have the pistol in his possession on the Sunday of his death, he could not have used it since there were no rounds in the weapon?"

"I suppose you could say that, but I cannot be absolutely certain. He may have planned to use it to warn or intimidate Ferrigan. There was not much love between those two."

Gerald Nolan had a slight grin on his face, no doubt feeling that lawyer Power had dug a slight hole for himself, according to my mom, who was in the courtroom. How was Michael Ferrigan to know whether Paddy Connors had bullets for his pistol or not?

Nolan next called a man named Hubert Cowley to the stand.

"Mr. Cowley, have you ever made the acquaintance of deceased Patrick Connors?

"Yes, sir, I did in a way."

Hubert Cowley was a stocky young bartender and part owner of a hotel in Cartier Village, a town close to Pine River.

"Could you give us some idea of what happened when you first met him close to one year ago?"

Leslie Power asked that the judge not allow these questions as they had no relation to the events of August 17, the day of the death of Paddy Connors. He said that the witness was referring to something that had occurred more than a year before the killing.

"But, your honour," responded Gerald Nolan, "I'm just trying to show that the late Patrick Connors was involved in a few altercations in the past and that he was not as peaceful as the prosecution would have us believe."

The judge overruled the objection and told the witness to answer the question.

"Well, Mr. Connors came into the bar," related Hubert Cowley, "with two of his brothers to have a drink, and they soon got into a heated discussion with a group of young men from the village. These fellows were asking the Connors boys what they were doing there. They suggested that the bar was not on Catholic territory or something to that effect. There is no love lost between certain groups up there, you know. Anyway, Paddy Connors invited them to come outside and the issue would be settled. So they all went out to the front of the hotel near the entrance and the battle began, with punches exchanged, and it went on for about ten minutes before some of us managed to put a stop to it. A few of the participants were cut and everyone was breathing pretty hard and I guess they were all exhausted from all the wrestling."

"And what was the role of Patrick Connors in all of this?"

"Oh, he was in the thick of it."

After Nolan had finished with this witness, he looked at the jury for a second and sat down, with a look of confidence on his face.

Prosecutor Power said that he just had a few questions for the witness.

"Mr. Cowley, is religion a big divider in the general area of this Scottish/Irish farming community?"

"Well, it may be, but on that particular night there seemed to be a sort of peace agreement started."

"How do you mean?"

"Well, after the fight they all sat down and started drinking together and praising each other for what good boxers they were. I found it to be pretty remarkable at the time."

Defence Advocate Nolan's attempt to paint Paddy Connors as a man with a violent temper ended rather amusingly, at least in this particular instance.

The next witness for the defence was one Malachy Lonergan, a farmer who lived to the north of Michael Ferrigan's property.

He was one of the few of Ferrigan's neighbours who seemed to be on friendly terms with the accused.

"Mr. Lonergan, did you and Michael Ferrigan ever discuss the situation regarding his fence?" asked Defence Lawyer Nolan.

"Oh yes, on several occasions, sir."

"Could you give the court a general idea of how Michael Ferrigan felt about the situation?"

"Well, he would get quite infuriated about the whole thing. He said that people were taking down the logs on his fence and not replacing them. He thought that they were doing this to laugh at him. He told me that he had to send one of his sons down the track to check on the fence very often. I remember that in the months before the shooting he told me that he and his boys had to chase cows out of his field on several occasions."

"Could you tell us, Mr. Lonergan, whether Michael Ferrigan was aware that Paddy Connors owned a German pistol—a Luger?"

"Oh, yes, sir. Most people around knew that Connors had this pistol and that he got it from Dominic Farley."

"Do you think that Michael Ferrigan ever felt threatened or endangered about confronting Patrick Connors?"

"All I can say is that both of the Connors, Paddy and Earl, had left a gap in his fence several times after passing down the track. There was some animosity between the Ferrigans and the Connors family, and I believe everyone was aware that Paddy and Michael had a few arguments where insults were exchanged. There was some talk about the two of them having it out once and for all, but Michael told me that there would have to be people present to make sure that everything was fair. They were like two schoolboys, being spiteful to each other. I chastised Michael about this but he didn't pay much attention."

"Did Michael Ferrigan know that Patrick Connors had no bullets for this pistol?"

Leslie Power objected to this question and the judge agreed.

"Did you see Michael Ferrigan on the day of the killing of Patrick Connors?"

"No, I did not, sir."

Prosecutor Leslie Power did not cross-examine Malachy Lonergan.

While there had been no proof shown that Paddy Connors had had a pistol on his person on that lethal Sunday, the Connors family were the ones who had picked up the body of Paddy and had transported it back to the house of his father. It would have been a positive factor for the defence lawyer had he been able to create suspicion that the pistol had been removed from the clothes of Paddy Connors. If the court was convinced of Michael Ferrigan's fear for his life on that day, there would be a legitimate argument for a plea of self-defence or, possibly, a reduced charge of manslaughter.

Michael Ferrigan's past history did not help his cause. After all, he was the man who had hacked his neighbour to death on a frigid night eighteen years before. Even if Ferrigan's previous bout with explosive passion was not summoned up during this trial, everyone knew about it. Buried deep in the minds of all—the judge, both prosecution and defence lawyers, and most of the jury—was the image of someone who had managed to evade punishment for a previous act of extreme violence. Admonitions by the judge against the mention of the first killing did not lessen the bald suspicion of this man—again accused of an unprovoked act of mortal and unrestrained wilfulness. Reminders of Ferrigan's past transgressions appeared regularly in the press.

My mother was almost consumed by the events of this trial. After sending her children off to school in the morning, she would head down to the courthouse and attempt to get a seat. She did not always succeed, but more often than not she did gain entrance. My mom always gave my dad an up-to-date report in the evenings, usually during suppertime. The newspapers covered the events of the trial regularly and my mom would read observers' analyses faithfully, and she would then expound her own opinion to my father.

Chapter 11

In the meantime, I was immersed in the routine of school activities. I was deeply impressed with my teacher, Brother Norbert. He was "a man for all seasons," in a way. There was an intellectual bent to his personality, he had an unending appreciation for the prose and poetry of the English language, but he was also a great hockey fan with a deep understanding of the tactics of the game. Once in a while, usually on a Monday morning, he would talk about a match held the previous Saturday night between the Montreal Canadiens and some other NHL team, and explain to us why one of the teams had been victorious, even though many of the kids weren't in the least interested in the game. He'd fill the front blackboard with diagrams of the winning plays, pointing out the strengths and weaknesses of each team and explaining why, ultimately, the victorious team had prevailed. How he could acquire this information from a simple radio broadcast was always a mystery to me. The Brothers did not own a television set as yet.

I noticed Brother Norbert talking with some of the hockey coaches at the school rink, advising them on how they should conduct practices. Having attended the same school with two members of the Detroit Red Wings, he saw to it that several of the team's players came to give hockey clinics at our school. It was quite amazing to see members of an NHL team skating on our outdoor rink and giving us tips on how to move the puck quickly up the ice as a team. Speed and finesse were the two keys to success in hockey and that was how victory was achieved, they said. So hard work was required to attain both of these skills, and although I never made it as a big-time player, I'll never forget the unselfish behaviour of these professionals and how they helped to instil a life-long love for the game of hockey into our very souls.

One of the key witnesses for the defence of Michael Ferrigan, someone whom Lawyer Gerald Nolan decided to call to the stand, was a man named Sars Fogarty, a sawmill operator who also farmed on a 10th range property close to the acreage of the victim, Paddy Connors. Fogarty had always been on acceptable terms with Michael Ferrigan.

"Mr. Fogarty, would you say that you are a friendly neighbour of Michael Ferrigan?"

"Yes, I suppose you could say that, sir."

"And are you the brother of Seamus Fogarty who is a magistrate in Cartier Village close to Pine River?"

"That is correct, sir."

"Could you tell the court about a meeting between your brother Seamus Fogarty and Michael Ferrigan, a meeting that was held several months ago?"

Prosecutor Power rose and asked the judge why the court should accept such a leading question and why Magistrate Seamus Fogarty was not available to give testimony.

"Your Honour," explained lawyer Nolan, "Magistrate Fogarty has been hospitalized for some time now and is not able to be here, but he has vouched for the sworn testimony of his brother and will give the court, on this day, a copy of the sworn statement by Michael Ferrigan."

Judge Sévigny allowed Nolan's questions to continue.

"Yes, my brother told me," continued Sars Fogarty, "that Michael Ferrigan had gone to his office, my brother's office, and had sworn a complaint against Patrick Connors. In the complaint he stated that Patrick Connors had physically threatened him at a school meeting. He also claimed that certain members of the Connors family were interfering with the security of his property by taking down a fence and leaving a gap so that the cows of his neighbour were invading his grain fields. He told my brother that he was sure that Patrick Connors carried a weapon on his person much of the time. He said that he feared for his safety and the safety of his family."

"Was anything done as a result of this complaint?" asked Gerald Nolan.

"Nothing that I know of, sir."

"Thank you, Mr. Fogarty."

Leslie Power did not choose to cross-examine this witness.

Gerald Nolan had long considered putting Michael Ferrigan on the stand in his own defence. He must have thought that there was little to lose. Up to this point in the trial it seemed almost certain, because of the graphic details of the shooting supplied by several witnesses, that the defendant would be found guilty. The reasoning behind allowing Michael Ferrigan to testify on his own behalf was to show that he had feared for his own life on the day of the shooting. He had been threatened and challenged and harassed and victimized. In his own mind there seemed little doubt that his adversaries were prepared to use violence against him, even lethal violence. They could easily have been armed with a pistol, and rocks big enough to bludgeon him. He had a family of ten children to care for and a property to protect.

Defence Attorney Nolan must have wondered how the jury would perceive Michael Ferrigan. There was a deep and singular hope that the defence would have the verdict reduced to manslaughter.

Ferrigan was a large man, but he had begun to lose weight since his arrest. He had always been a healthy, robust specimen, but the odious ordeal had mutated him. Ferrigan was not the same man now that he was lodged in prison. He was no longer in control of his life. He yearned for the company of his wife and children.

But would he be able to arouse any sympathy in the minds of the jury? Would they be able to empathize with him and understand the pressure that he felt with his back to the wall in the face of his adversaries? Would he be able to reproduce himself as a normal human being who had simply collapsed psychologically when faced with the prospect of another confrontation?

During the trial Michael Ferrigan had sat in the prisoner's box, with his lawyer close by, his seat perpendicular to the spectators. He clearly wanted to show that he had great respect for the judge and the court. Most of the spectators could see his reaction to the statements of those who testified against him. For the most part, he tended to sit with a slight slump, moving very little. His family usually took the seats at one side of the chamber, but he would seldom turn to acknowledge that they were there. His wife, Maggie, attended court every day, sitting several rows from the front of the chamber, almost hidden amid her relatives. She frequently had her head down as if she did not wish to be recognized.

Lawyer Gerald Nolan reluctantly decided that he would allow his client, Michael Ferrigan, to speak to the court as a witness on his own behalf. There was considerable risk in pleading his case in this way. Ferrigan did not have any of the charm that would endear him to a jury. In his many conversations with him, Nolan had noticed the surliness of the man. Ferrigan's responses tended to be terse and without humour. Nolan conferred with Michael Ferrigan on the night before his testimony, the lawyer telling him about the nature of the questions he would be posing.

Michael Ferrigan was not beyond sympathy. He was first and foremost a family man with a large brood, who visited him frequently at the city jail. His wife, Maggie, was steadfast in her support for him and his fight for vindication. When visiting him she would always bring at least one of the children.

As things shaped up during this climactic stage of the trial, it would be the last forceful effort to get the court to relate to the predicament of his client, Nolan felt. He had to put the jury in the shoes of Michael Ferrigan. He must tread carefully, trying to camouflage his client's rough-hewn characteristics. There were going to be no second chances.

Allowing Ferrigan to testify also meant that his client, with certainty, would be cross-examined by the prosecutor. This was one of the strongest arguments against putting Ferrigan on the stand, but Nolan was prepared to take a chance.

After Michael Ferrigan was sworn in, he sat down in the witness box, facing everyone seated in the court. This was the first time some had seen him head on. A few in the court were surprised by the gauntness of his look. He seemed to be a subdued man, done in by his own rash behaviour. But he was not yet defeated. He looked steadily at his defender, Gerald Nolan, and seemed energized and anxious to get on with the task of giving his side of the story.

"Would you state your name and occupation, sir?" began lawyer Gerald Nolan.

"I am Michael Ferrigan, and I am a farmer living in Pine River," he answered. His voice was audible, but tinged with a rasp, a trait that continued as he spoke, nearing the end of this trial.

"And do you have a wife and children, Mr. Ferrigan?"

"Yes, I am married to Margaret and I have ten children, five boys and five girls."

"Where, Mr. Ferrigan, is your property situated in Pine River?"

"I own two properties, one to the north of Joseph Dunigan on the seventh range, and another two hundred acres north on the eighth range, which I acquired some time ago."

"And how did you acquire these properties?"

"My father left me the farm, and I bought the other property."

"So you pay taxes on both of these properties?"

"Yes, sir. I am now paying my taxes on both."

Gerald Nolan had been able, to start with, to establish Michael Ferrigan as a tax-paying, family man in the Irish community. This was the correct way of proceeding, surely, thought Nolan. Keep it simple.

"Now, Mr. Ferrigan, can you tell me if your property is fenced off from other farms? I'm referring to your property on the seventh range."

"Yes, my property on the seventh range is fenced off from Joseph Dunigan's property on the south side and there is also some fencing on the north side where Malachy Lonergan's property begins."

"You did put some fencing across the railway track path."

"Yes, well, I felt that I had to put the fence across the railroad track because my land is on both sides of the track and if I didn't put the fence across the track, Mr. Dunigan's cattle would come in through the gap."

"How did you think that your neighbours would react to this?"

"Well, I didn't mind people passing on my property as long as they put the fence back up after they passed."

"And how difficult is it to put this fence back up, Mr. Ferrigan?"

"It's very simple. Just take the two logs down, pass the horse and cart through, then put the logs back into place."

"Are these logs very heavy?"

"No, they are not. My young son Joseph who is fourteen years old can lift them up very easily. They're light and would be too small to use at the sawmill."

"Now, Mr. Ferrigan, if I can change the topic a little, would you tell the court about your relationship with Patrick Connors? First of all, were you not related to him?"

"Yes, I was. We were second or third cousins."

"I am told that your relationship with Patrick Connors was quite good up until a few years ago. What happened?"

"It goes back to a few years ago when he complained about my son Joey pestering his daughter at school."

"So how could that have caused such a break in your relations?"

"He wanted me to chastise my son over this, but I told him to let the kids work out their own problems."

"And where did this discussion take place?"

"It was on a Saturday night at the dance hall."

"And from what I understand, this discussion led to a pretty serious situation and it took several people to prevent you from going at each other."

"Yes, I suppose that's correct."

"And then, not too many months ago, you and Patrick Connors had a confrontation at a school meeting."

"Yes, that's right. He claimed that I was not paying my fair share because of my two properties. I told him that he was lying and then he said that if I went outside with him, he would smash my mouth. I told him that I could not fight him at that time because I had a very sore arm."

"Now, Mr. Ferrigan, getting back to the fence across the railroad track, didn't Patrick Connors pass through your property on a pretty regular basis?"

"Yes, that's right. His farm is a few miles to the north up on the eighth range and instead of taking the main road he would take the shortcut through my property:"

"Did you have any objections to his doing this?"

"No, I did not, as long as he replaced the fence after passing through with the horse and cart."

"And did he always replace the fence after he passed through?"

"No, he did not. And the same for his brother. Whenever we saw them pass up the railway track, I would send one of the boys down to check on the fence."

"And the fence was never replaced?"

"Many times it was not."

"Did other people use this track road?"

"Oh, yes."

"And did they replace the logs in the fence?"

"Well, some did and some didn't."

"And for what reason would anyone be using this track road to begin with?"

"Well, in the summertime the track is very handy to haul wood or hay or anything else. Not everyone has a truck to go by the main road. If you had a truck you couldn't drive it on the track. The track is too narrow and bumpy in places, I think. So I allowed people to pass on my property, but I wanted them to realize that if they left the gap open, then the neighbour's cows would come into my fields and trample and eat the grain."

"Do you think, Mr. Ferrigan, that some people left the fence down after they passed just to goad and harass you?"

"Yes, I believe so. Some people seem to have a great hatred for me."

"Now, Mr. Ferrigan, let's go back to the morning of Sunday, August 17th. Could you tell the court what happened?"

"I thought I saw some cattle in the oat field down where the fence is across the railroad track, so I went down to see if it had been left open. When I got there I saw the logs were down and they were thrown to the side and some of Dunigan's cattle were in my field. About ten minutes later Paddy Connors came walking down past my house with two of his kids. It was Sunday so I knew he was headed down to see his father Willie."

"So what did you say to him?"

"I asked him what he was doing on my property. He said he had a right to pass there. I agreed with him but I showed him that the fence had been taken down and not replaced. He denied ever having left any gap open and told me he'd throw me and my fence into the swamp and if his kids were not there he would beat the hell out of me. I told him to get two men who could referee and we'd see who would beat the hell out of who."

"And did you warn Patrick Connors not to come back by the railway track?"

"I told him that if he wasn't willing to put the logs back into place, not to come back through my property."

"Mr. Ferrigan, were you aware that Patrick Connors owned a pistol and sometimes carried it with him?"

Prosecutor Power was on his feet immediately after this question and asked the judge to disallow it, stating that Nolan was injecting speculation into the trial.

Judge Sévigny decided to allow the question.

"Yes, I had heard that," answered Michael Ferrigan.

"And did you ever suspect that he was capable of using it on you?" asked Nolan.

"Of course, I worried about that."

"Why did you feel that way?"

"Because he seemed to have a lot of spite against me and

had threatened me. So I was worried that if I tried to defend my rights that he or someone in his family would do me some harm."

"Now, let's move forward to the afternoon of that day. Could you give us an idea of how the final confrontation took place?"

"Yes, well, my wife Margaret and I were sitting at the kitchen table with Raymond Coughlin who was visiting us. Margaret looked out the window and said she had spotted a man with two children coming up the track. I went back to my room and picked up my rifle and ran down toward the track to meet whoever was coming. When I got close to them I thought they might have noticed me, so they turned around and went back down the track the other way."

"Why did you take your rifle with you?"

"Because I was worried about my safety,"

"What happened next, Mr. Ferrigan?"

"Well, I hung around the trees above the track, waiting to see what would happen, and about twenty minutes later a bunch of them came up the track. There were four men and the two children. I ran down to the track to meet them and told them to go back. Paddy Connors reached into his pocket, so I fired a shot at him."

"Did you have the intention of killing Patrick Connors at that moment, Mr. Ferrigan?"

"No, I did not. I meant it to be a warning shot, but sadly it hit him. I had no intention of killing him."

"Did Earl Connors come after you then?"

"Yes, he had a large stone in his hand and I thought he would try to hit me with it. He tried to take the gun away from me, so I pointed the rifle at him and chased him down the track for a few acres. Then I turned and went back toward home."

"And did you fire any shots at these people?"

"No, of course not."

"And did you then look at the victim, Patrick Connors, after everyone had left the scene?"

"Yes, I did. I tried to revive him. I realized what I had done even though I had no intention of doing such a thing. Then I went back home."

"And did you regret what had happened, Mr. Ferrigan?"

"Yes, I had very strong regrets."

And with this last exchange, Gerald Nolan completed his questioning of Michael Ferrigan. Had he been successful in painting his client as a threatened man who justifiably had been concerned about his safety? Did the jury believe that Ferrigan had not meant to kill Paddy Connors, but had fired a careless shot that had inadvertently struck the victim? Was there a possibility that self-defence could be successfully pleaded for Ferrigan? If not, surely manslaughter would be the worst scenario.

Michael Ferrigan had been surprisingly lucid in his answers. His responses had sounded rational and logical. He had not sounded like the man who had axed someone to death in a previous demented act.

Nolan's questioning of Ferrigan had been fairly short. The lawyer did not want to get into much detail about the tragedy.

But had Ferrigan spoken the truth (Nolan must have thought)? Had he subtly coloured his testimony so that he would appear to be an average human beset by the prejudice of his neighbours, bullied and menaced because he had tried to protect his interests? The young people who had testified against him had given a different story about that Sunday morning encounter. The court had been especially impressed by the testimony of Marianne Connors since she was present during the exchange of angry words and had heard them all. Her description of the conversation between Michael Ferrigan and her father had been articulated differently. Added to that was the testimony of the two of us, Tommy Kelly and myself.

Nolan did not really know if Ferrigan's testimony would be believed. According to the statements of the three of us, Michael Ferrigan had been much more aggressive in his warning to Patrick Connors on that Sunday morning. The words we used to describe what we heard would be very difficult to disavow. Michael Ferrigan had made threats and had carried them out later in the day. How could he claim he felt in danger simply because the victim Patrick Connors had reached into his pocket to retrieve a handkerchief? In all likelihood, Ferrigan was the only person who was truly armed in that final encounter.

The court recessed and lawyer Leslie Power would have overnight to think about his cross-examination.

Chapter 12

My mother is a very talented woman. As we grew up, she knitted beautiful sweaters for my brothers and myself. She worked at tatting, did crochet, needlework, and embroidery. At our parish church she was considered the "crafts lady" and had organized quilting parties and planned craft goods bazaars to raise money. She also had a great love for oil painting. Many of her canvases hung on the walls of our flat and she gave many paintings away to friends and relatives. My mother usually painted using photos that she took around the city and on my uncle's farm in Pine River. Whenever she visited the farm with my father, she would disappear with my little sister, Eileen, and roam the fields and woods taking pictures with her little camera, using black-and-white film. She would eventually turn these photos into gorgeously coloured works of art.

I was deeply influenced by my mother's talent. She had bought me a "starter" kit for oil painting—a few brushes, some tubes of paints in an array of colours, solvent, and linseed oil—for my fourteenth birthday. At first I did not touch the kit, being a little intimidated by my mother's natural abilities. But, slowly, I began to dabble with the colours, and then tried painting a few small canvases, mostly still life set-ups I had organized on the kitchen table. My mom would frequently stand behind me offering suggestions. Gradually, I began enjoying it. My mom coaxed me and my brothers up to the art museum and we all stood before some of the Impressionist landscapes of the French masters and marvelled at the richness of the colour and the contrasts of light and dark. In many ways it was a revelation to me. I began to realize that I had a strong feeling for the visual arts. This was not within the normal interests of a high school kid who loved hockey and other sports, but I attributed this realization to my deep respect for my mom.

We also had an art teacher at school. While she couldn't afford to supply oil paints to the students on her limited budget, she did give us sketching paper and told us to buy charcoal sticks. Mrs. Edna O'Hara taught us about perspective. She would place a large picture of a series of buildings on an easel at the front of the class and ask us to sketch it, then go around offering pointers on how we could improve. We soon began to appreciate the sense of visual depth that our drawings could bring out. Very often I would take my finished sketch home and use thinned-out oil paint to put colour to the street and buildings. After the painting had dried, I was able to use a rag to rub out any trace of charcoal. My mom was pretty impressed with this technique and began to hang some of my "oeuvres" on the kitchen walls.

But my love of painting was not something that I talked much about at school. I did speak about it to Tommy Kelly when we got a chance to get together at recess time. Some of my classmates would refer to me as a "lacquer-loving linseed nut" because I made the mistake of bringing a few canvases to school one day to show to the art teacher, Mrs. O'Hara.

The seasons of the year are well expressed by nature in the old city. In autumn, millions of dead leaves lie on the streets and sidewalks, the colours fading, the residue crisp. But somehow we all loved autumn because it was the season for football. Our school fielded a team in a city league. There were both English and French high school teams in this league. Most games were held on Saturday afternoons on the sprawling Plains of Abraham, so after hockey practice on Saturday mornings I was off to the football game. Hundreds would gather at the field. I never made the high school team, mostly because I never seriously tried out for it, yet I loved to watch the games. During the fall of 1952, Tommy Kelly began staying at my house on Friday nights so that he could attend the football game the following day. He wanted to be playing when he got to the senior grades. I figured, looking at him, that he would probably be too skinny to play tackle football, yet I never under-estimated Tommy, and maybe as he grew older he would fill out and gain some serious weight. He eventually did play for the team as quarterback and set all kinds of records in passes completed and touchdown passes thrown. He was a very brainy tactician, as I remember, with a great sense of when to make certain calls, and he drove the opposition crazy with his draw plays and screen passes.

But in October of 1952 we were just spectators, in awe of the high school guys in grade eleven and twelve who had made the varsity team. We would yell ourselves hoarse, encouraging the team to make a first down, or score a touchdown, or call to the defence to hold at the goal line. It was all great fun for Tommy and me.

Unfortunately, I remember the football field as the place where my heart was first broken.

Tommy came down to the hockey arena to watch my hockey practice one Saturday morning. We arrived at the football field in the afternoon, the game got under way, and I noticed that my cousin Janice Carroll was standing at the sidelines with a group of her friends. Tommy had told me that she planned to travel in to attend one of the games, so I wasn't exactly surprised to see her. During half-time Tommy and I sort of sidled over to talk to Janice, who introduced us to some of her pals and we exchanged banter for a while before the second half began. Then I sort of got lost in a football match that went down to the final wire and the visiting team came out victorious.

As the crowd began to disperse at the end of the game, I noticed that Janice was standing at midfield talking to one of the players from our school team. He was a tall, gangly guy named Jim Larkin. He was one of the leaders of the team, with a reputation as a rough-and-tough competitor who played as an end and caught lots of passes and would run down the field using straight arms to attempt to ward off would-be tacklers. Tommy and I noticed that he was smoking a cigarette and standing very close to Janice. She seemed to be enjoying the attention greatly as she looked up at him. He then put his arm over her shoulder and she put her arm around his waist and they walked toward the edge of the playing field, Janice again looking up at him admiringly.

I was devastated, and felt that something precious had been taken away from me. Although I saw Janice infrequently, I felt very close to her and had fantasized about her quite regularly.

"Now I know why Janice wanted to come in to see the football game," said Tommy.

It didn't seem to bother Tommy that Janice had found the love of her life. Neither of us had known that she had someone special.

It seems that Janice had met Jim Larkin at a lunch counter that some of the high school students frequented at noon hour. I thought about the prospect of not having Janice in my future. All the plans I had made in my mind had to be cast aside. They were replaced with a vapid emptiness. It took me several months to come to the realization that I would not be able to love her completely.

The trial resumed on Wednesday, October 22, with the cross-examination of Michael Ferrigan. Every available seat was taken in the courtroom, as usual. There was a great sense of expectancy on the faces of the assembled spectators, expressed in the energetic intensity of the family supporters on both sides of the case.

As soon as everyone was seated, Michael Ferrigan was marched into the courtroom by the two officers. He sat at his customary position and was immediately approached by his lawyer, who whispered something to him.

Minutes later, all stood as Judge Sévigny entered, setting up at his bench and gavelling in the proceedings.

Prosecutor Leslie Power immediately called Michael Ferrigan to the witness stand, where he was sworn in once again.

"Mr. Ferrigan," began Prosecutor Power, "you have stated that you put this fence up across the railway track to prevent cattle from coming onto your property. Is that correct, sir?"

"Yes, that is correct."

"Did you not know, Mr. Ferrigan, that doing this was an illegal act?"

Defence Attorney Gerald Nolan objected to this question, telling the judge that Michael Ferrigan was not being charged with illegally putting up a fence.

The objection was disallowed and the judge told Michael Ferrigan to answer.

"Yes, well, I wasn't sure about that, but it would have been very costly for me to do it any other way."

"Mr. Ferrigan, did the railway not compensate your father many years ago for the lease of the strip of land that the railroad was built on?"

"I was not aware of very much compensation."

"Do you know, Mr. Ferrigan, that the railway has never given up this ownership, and that theoretically, they still have title to this strip of land?"

"Yes, I have been reminded of that on a few occasions."

"Didn't your neighbour Joseph Dunigan propose a way to fix up the fences so that his cattle would not stray onto your property?"

"I don't recall Dunigan saying anything worthwhile about that."

"His solution would have solved this problem, would it not have?"

"I am not in the habit of doing business with him. I have not had good luck in my dealings with him in the past."

"Your neighbour, Mr. Dunigan, has testified that he tried to get you to agree to work with him to solve this problem. Is this not true, Mr. Ferrigan?"

"I don't recall anything worthwhile coming from Joe Dunigan. He is not an honest man, in my estimation."

"Did he not suggest to you that a fence could be put up on his property to keep the cattle in and that he just wanted your help in doing this, to share the work and expenses?"

"I have good reason to be suspicious of anything that Joseph Dunigan proposes."

With these responses, Michael Ferrigan began to show the vindictiveness in his character, that he was a venomous man with a serious chip on his shoulder.

"So it was easier for you to illegally put a fence up across the railway track, wasn't it?"

Lawyer Power was persistent.

"I had no intention of committing an illegal act," answered Michael Ferrigan.

"Now, Mr. Ferrigan, when you first met Patrick Connors on the Sunday morning in question, you stated that your fence had been taken down and not replaced; is this correct?"

"Yes, that is right."

"Your statements seem to indicate that you were blaming Patrick Connors for this."

"I was not blaming him for doing it that morning, but for all the other times that he and his brother did not replace the fence."

"So you were infuriated that the fence had not been replaced and you were treating Patrick Connors as a scapegoat."

"I don't understand."

"I mean that you were blaming Patrick Connors for something that someone else had done."

"Paddy Connors was not innocent in this matter. I know that him and his brother have both left a gap in my fence on more than one occasion. I have proof of that."

"So you made some very serious threats to Patrick Connors at that time. You told him not to pass that way when he came back home after visiting his parents. You said that if he did come back the same way, he would not go back home to the same tune as he came. We have the sworn testimony of three young witnesses who heard you make these threats. Your words were not the idle words of someone in a heated discussion, but ominous warnings, Mr. Ferrigan. And you repeated these threats several times, according to the witnesses. What exactly did you have planned for Patrick Connors if he did return home by the same route?"

"I had no plans. I was just angry at him and all the others who did not replace the logs."

"And what did you mean when you said that he would not 'go home to the same tune as he came'?"

"There is no meaning. They are just angry words."

"And, Mr. Ferrigan, you have sworn in your testimony that Patrick Connors told you on that morning that he would, and I quote your exact words, 'throw me and my fence into the swamp and if his kids were not there he would beat the hell out of me.' Do you stand by these statements, Mr. Ferrigan?"

"Yes, I do."

"Well, how is it that not one of the three young witnesses heard such a remark coming from Mr. Connors? On the contrary, their testimony states that Mr. Connors was conciliatory and did not want to fight with you about this matter."

"They did not hear everything that was said."

"And, Mr. Ferrigan, why did you yell out, according to the witnesses, to Mr. Connors to get a man as a witness and you'd get one too and you would see who would smash someone's mouth?"

"That was because Paddy Connors told me a while ago that he would take me outside and smash my mouth. So I meant that if there would be witnesses we could have a fair fight."

"You have stated, Mr. Ferrigan, that you were seated at the kitchen table on that Sunday afternoon with Raymond Coughlin, and that your wife Margaret spotted someone coming up the railway track. Is that correct, sir?"

"Yes, we were having an early supper."

"So what did you do immediately after?"

"I went to my bedroom and got my rifle and went down to see who was coming up the track."

"How did you leave the house? You did not leave by the front door, nor by the side door, according to Mr. Coughlin. How did you leave the house?"

"I left by the gallery at the back of the house."

"But, Mr. Ferrigan, there is a six-foot drop from the balcony at the rear of your house and there is no stairway. Am I to believe that you jumped down from the rear balcony?"

"Yes, that's what I did."

"Why, Mr. Ferrigan, did you not leave the house by the front or side door? Could it have been that you did not want anyone to see you with the rifle?"

"I did not want the children or my wife to see me with the rifle, so I left the house by the gallery."

"So when you went down to see who was coming up the track, did you recognize who it was?"

"Yes, I was sure it was Paddy Connors and his two kids, but I thought that they saw me so they turned around and went back."

"And did you see a father and his two children as a threat to your well-being?"

"I was always suspicious that there might be other people with him."

"And you say that you hung around the trees and waited to see if they would come back again?"

"Yes, that's right."

"And then after a while what did you see?"

"Well, I saw Paddy Connors come with three other men and the two children."

"So you ran down to the track to meet them."

"Yes."

"And did you know who these people were?"

"I saw that Paddy's brother, Earl, was with him and there was one of the Coughlins, and the young Cleary lad with the two kids."

Michael Ferrigan seemed to be somewhat agitated as Prosecutor Leslie Power fired these questions at him in rapid fashion. He shifted positions in the stand and looked away from Power and off to the side as he answered.

"What, Mr. Ferrigan, did you say when you got close to them?"

"I told them to go back."

"Did you hear Patrick Connors say to you, 'I will go back, but first I'd like a few words with you'?"

"I only saw him reach into his pocket so I fired a shot in his direction."

"I repeat, Mr. Ferrigan, did you hear Patrick Connors say, 'I will go back, but first I'd like a few words with you'?"

"He might have said that but I do not remember it."

"Now, Mr. Ferrigan, you have stated that you did not mean to hit Patrick Connors with that rifle shot, but that you only wanted to warn him."

"Yes, sir. That's right."

"And how far away from him were you when you fired the shot?"

"I was perhaps ten feet away from him."

"How did you think you would miss hitting him when you were that close?"

"I fired the rifle very quickly in his general direction. I did not mean to hit him."

"Now, Mr. Ferrigan, one of the witnesses who was present at the scene of the shooting has testified that, immediately after you fired the fatal shot at Patrick Connors, you said, 'He will never speak again!'"

"No! No! That is not so!" Michael Ferrigan bolted up straight in his chair and glared at lawyer Power.

The prosecutor continued. "And another witness who was present at the scene of this shooting has said that he went and tried unsuccessfully to take the gun away from you and you said, 'You'll never hang me for this!' Mr. Ferrigan, how could you have said this if you only intended to fire a warning shot at Patrick Connors?"

Michael Ferrigan looked downward and answered, "I did not mean to kill him."

"How could you have shot Patrick Connors, without any provocation whatsoever, in front of his two young children?"

"I did not mean to hit him. I was very upset, and I regretted shooting him."

There was a moment's pause in the courtroom while Leslie

Power went back to his table and looked briefly at his notes. Dead silence filled the chamber.

The prosecutor had a few last questions.

"Mr. Ferrigan, did any of the witnesses throw any rocks at you before the shooting?"

"No, sir." Michael Ferrigan answered, his head still bent forward, his eyes looking downward.

"And did you see any of the men you confronted carrying weapons?"

"No, sir."

"I have no more questions, Your Honour," said Prosecutor Power.

Defence Lawyer Gerald Nolan immediately rose and received permission from the judge to ask a few additional questions of Michael Ferrigan.

"Mr. Ferrigan," asked lawyer Nolan, "when you met Patrick Connors for the first time that Sunday morning, did you ask him to get a man and you'd get a man and you'd have it out once and for all?"

"Yes, I did."

"Did you want to have a fair fight with Patrick Connors at some time in the future?"

"I did not want this, but I was willing to do it to defend myself. But I wanted it to be a fair fight."

"So you planned to have this encounter some time in the future, is that right?"

"Yes, sir. If I had to fight him, I would have."

"Did you ever, Mr. Ferrigan, have any plans to shoot Patrick Connors?"

"No, I did not, sir."

"Did you plan to kill Patrick Connors when he came back up the track on the afternoon of that Sunday?"

"No, I did not."

"Thank you, Your Honour," Nolan said, looking at Judge Sévigny.

Michael Ferrigan was told to step down from the witness stand and he returned to the prisoner's box, not looking at the spectators even for a second.

Chapter 13

There was much concern among the people of Pine River about the welfare of the wife and ten children of Michael Ferrigan. The accused man had been incarcerated for over two months and his prospects for release did not seem good. Everyone took the children of Michael Ferrigan to be blameless in this tragedy. Several of them were attending the village school. Two of the older children, daughters, were being taught at the girls' school in Quebec City, one of them in her senior year. Life had to go on for this family. The siblings of Michael Ferrigan managed to organize and complete most of the reaping of the grain. His older boys were very capable of seeing to the needs of the cattle, doing the milking, and preparing the wood for the upcoming winter season.

Michael Ferrigan's wife, Margaret, travelled daily to Quebec City to attend the trial. She also chose to visit with her husband at the jail during the pre-trial period and on weekends. No doubt she found the whole ordeal to be almost unbearable. Her husband tended to be quite depressed as he sat in his cell while the trial was not in session. How had this calamity occurred? How could her husband of twenty years have proceeded so rashly? Why had she allowed him to embark on this path of self-destruction? Of course, she had had no way of knowing that he would still be capable of such an impulsive and deadly act. She thought he had learned his lesson eighteen years before when he had been involved in a terrible conflict ending in the death of a supposed enemy.

But she had to stand by him, to use all her energies to see that he was fairly treated. This for the sake of the children, the youngest ones still mystified about the disappearance of their father, a stern but powerful force in their lives.

The farmers of Pine River, almost to a man, had little compassion for the likes of Michael Ferrigan. He had brought ignominy upon the name of their community, not once but twice. They felt that he had escaped a prison term for his part in the hateful enmity that he had been partly responsible for in the death of David O'Meara eighteen years before.

Where did this man come from? How could such a violent creature emerge from a peaceful agrarian climate where neighbour valued neighbour and children were raised in peace and serenity?

Now that the witnesses had testified and the setting was in place for the final statements of the lawyers, would Michael Ferrigan once again escape justice? Could his lawyer, Gerald Nolan, manage to convince the jury that Ferrigan was only acting in the defence of his interests and his person when he shot Paddy Connors? Many suggested that he would be convicted of a lesser charge, and not "wilful murder." There was a strong suspicion that the law did not always act in the interests of the victim.

I was not at the courtroom at this stage of the trial. But the details of the proceedings were cited daily in the newspaper. My mother was also still focused on the events at the courthouse and was up to date in her knowledge of even the most insignificant details. When she could gain admittance to the chamber, she always had a recap of the testimony for my father, and was surprisingly detailed in her account. She also remembered what everyone was wearing for court appearances. My father would stare at her in wonder that she could recall these details. She also had great admiration for the judge and both lawyers in the case.

Tommy Kelly also followed the trial closely, from reading the news accounts and getting information from his parents who came into town to attend the trial on most days. Tommy worried about the possibility of Michael Ferrigan being hanged for this killing. He considered capital punishment to be an outdated form of retribution by the state. How could a court find a person guilty of killing someone, and then turn around and execute him in a barbaric fashion? Tommy had already studied the history of hanging in the Americas. He would tell me about it. He would read me articles he had discovered in reference books.

There were a number of ways that prisoners were hanged. Before 1850, the method used was called "short drop" hanging. A condemned man would be placed on a horse or a vehicle that was then moved away and that left the prisoner dangling until strangulation took place. Ladders and stools were also used to achieve the same effect.

Later, more modern methods took hold, such as the "standard drop," a product of the English judicial system. This was better than the "short drop" because it was claimed that it immediately broke the person's neck, causing paralysis and unconsciousness. The standard drop was used to execute some German Nazis after the Nuremberg trials.

Another practice was called the "long drop," in which the condemned person was allowed to drop from four to ten feet, depending on the weight of the prisoner. This was designed to deliver the force of over a thousand pounds, which fractured the neck at the cervical vertebrae. The result was decapitation, in some cases, so the length of the drop was shortened. This unspeakable and gory result prompted some American states to switch to the gas chamber as a means of execution.

After the hanging itself, and following the prisoner's lapse into unconsciousness, movements of the body and limbs could occur for a while due to muscular reflexes. Death was usually pronounced once the prisoner went into cardiac arrest. This may have taken from four to fifteen minutes. The sphincter would relax and urine and feces would be evacuated.

I found Tommy's descriptions and readings to be rather disgusting, yet we did not laugh about it because of our personal involvement in a trial where the accused was likely to be executed by hanging if found guilty.

There was also a measure of regret at the fact that I had testified against Michael Ferrigan. I did not know the man. Apart from seeing him in the courthouse, I had only seen him once before that, at the railway track where Tommy Kelly and I had overheard the argument between him and Paddy Connors. I had seen the burden of sorrow that he had inflicted upon the people of Pine River, yet I did not hate the man. I felt pity for him and his family. Like Tommy Kelly, I did not want to see the authorities execute him for his crime. Better that he should be able to live out his days in prison where, at least, his family could visit him. Even if his children would have to live with an absentee father, they could still write to him or telephone him. Putting a father to death leaves a residue of abhorrent memories for his children, to say the least.

Yet, time seemed to dull any feelings of guilt I may have had about my testimony at the trial. As its progress moved into its final phase, I became more of a spectator than a player. Young people can feel detachment pretty quickly about certain people who are not closely related to them. If Michael Ferrigan had been my father, I would have had to live with the horror of seeing a loved one facing a barbarous ending. I could not contemplate such a spectre occurring in my household.

Thankfully, there were many distractions for me during this period. For the first time in my life, I had a real appreciation for sport and art and the good humour of my teachers, whom I actually looked forward to seeing every day. Not that I was a great student, setting all sorts of academic records, but I was an easy-going kid, as I remember, and I think my teachers had a liking for me.

Of course, I wasn't a saint. I had a reputation for being a "dirty" player on the hockey rink. I had been and still was the most penalized player on the school team and even if I had great adulation for the scoring wizardry of Maurice "the Rocket" Richard of the Montreal Canadiens, I secretly wanted to play like Ted Lindsay of the Detroit Red Wings. He was the pest on the rink who got on the nerves of the opposition, along with being a very skilled player. I wasn't the biggest guy on the rink, but I wanted to be the most willing to "mix it up." Hockey seemed to stir something in me. I got a special thrill when I could nail some guy on the other team with what I figured was a good clean check. I didn't care if I got a penalty. This kind of play seemed to bring out a second nature in me, a relatively quiet guy at school who was the brunt of a good bit of teasing from my classmates and team mates.

My father had seen many of the hockey games I'd been in, but he seldom commented on my style of play. He complimented me if I scored a goal or got an assist, but he never criticized me for spending time in the penalty box for repeated infractions. He knew my hockey coach, Brother Martin, and I surmised that they both felt that other teams in the league were wary of me, that I was adding an extra element to our team that distracted the better players of the opposition. Fighting was frowned upon at the level I was playing, and if you were an instigator in a punch-up you were banished from the game and suspended for the next one. So I had no wish to get into any fights or to try punching my opponents.

But I loved the act of skating. There was something valiant in gliding across the ice, with all your equipment on and a hockey stick in your hands. Before a match, I would feel like a warrior about to enter a life-altering contest. I felt strong, invincible, and unstoppable. None of the players wore helmets in those days, yet there seemed to be few head injuries. Sticks were held lower and not used like battering rams as they are now. The most admired players were the best stick-handlers, skaters, and shooters.

During hockey practices we were encouraged to skate on the rink with the same facility as we ran on the playing field, stopping and starting with power and ease, skating backwards with comfort and confidence. These were all skills that our hockey coaches helped us to develop by putting us through routines that we repeated for a half-hour before we scrimmaged. We'd be exhausted after a practice, but we loved it. When you're young, there's something unrefined and magnetic about being out of breath. Once you have a drink of water, you're ready to go again.

Tommy Kelly never actually saw me playing in a hockey game, although he'd seen me a couple of times practising at the arena on Saturday before we went to the football games. His regular commuting to school every day did not leave him the time to get involved in hockey. But he followed the NHL teams very closely, knew the names and scoring statistics of most players on the six NHL teams, and was a diehard fan of the Montreal Canadiens.

Football was Tommy's favourite sport and he loved to throw the ball around at recess time in the schoolyard and while we were at the football games, at half-time and after the game was over. From the first time I'd tossed the football back and forth with him, I noticed how well he threw it, a beautiful spiral that soared through the air like a slow-moving rocket. He had long spindly-looking arms, yet he seemed to get great leverage when he threw the ball and was able to arc it across the field a considerable distance. My friend Jackie Farrell would be amazed at Tommy's prowess and told him that he would soon be throwing passes for the high school team.

We became a sort of threesome in the schoolyard, throwing the football back and forth and yakking about things. Jackie Farrell, well aware that we had been involved in a trial, was naturally curious about our experience, but he didn't press us too hard about it. Tommy and I tended to avoid discussing it and its ominous foreboding, but it was always probing my memory and conscience, even if it didn't bother me that much. The novelty of being involved in the trial, if that was what it was, had certainly worn off, and what remained was a strong desire for the whole thing to end.

Chapter 14

In the case of the Crown versus Michael Ferrigan, Prosecuting Attorney Leslie Power began his final summation with the confidence that he had done his best. Knowing of the strong possibility of a conviction, he must have seen himself as a likely winner, but surely hoped that he had dealt fairly with all the issues.

Leslie Power was a tall slender man, immaculately dressed, with an erect bearing. He was more formal in his questioning approach and lacked the dramatic flair of Gerald Nolan. Yet he was very effective and business-like, without bombastic or exaggerated pretence.

A jury, by its nature, tends to be composed of nondescript individuals, at least in appearance. There is no communication between peers in the courtroom during the trial. There is seldom a show of emotion, no sympathetic or angry looks, little expression of humour or disgust. The "mixed" jury in the case of the Crown versus Michael Ferrigan was made up of labourers and skilled workers, but there was no way of telling the difference between them.

Nevertheless, these were all good citizens who wanted to do a creditable job at something that was likely not to be repeated again in their lives. They were family men for the most part, previously unknown to the accused and, as well as could be fathomed, initially devoid of any discriminatory feelings toward the man they were judging. They were also men of their times, and subject to the mores and scruples of their generation.

"Gentlemen of the jury," Leslie Power began, "you are being asked to do a great task during this time, and that is to judge the guilt or innocence of a man who has been accused of killing his neighbour and cousin in an act of 'wilful' murder. How did this whole eventuality come about? What measure of hate and fear and loathing could have led the accused, Michael Ferrigan, to take a rifle and shoot Patrick Connors dead? What manner of vengeance could enable a man to kill another before the eyes of the victim's children, on a beautiful August Sunday afternoon, in a quiet and peaceful agrarian setting? How was this possible? What level of folly was at work here? Could this tragic outcome have been avoided? Was it the natural result of a dispute that had no solution? It seems that it was decided in the mind of Michael Ferrigan that the killing of Patrick Connors was the only way to resolve a certain problem regarding the positioning of a fence."

Leslie Power paced back and forth in front of the jury as he spoke. He tended to look upward contemplatively, now and then casting a quick glance at the twelve men.

"Gentlemen, it is my intention to impress upon you that Michael Ferrigan, with aforethought and resolve, decided to kill Patrick Connors. This dark cloud has not been removed by the defence in this case. Michael Ferrigan warned Patrick Connors, on that Sunday morning, that he would take the necessary measures to prevent him from ever crossing the Ferrigan property again. He may have used shaded language, but the intent was present.

"We have no reason to doubt the testimony of the three young witnesses who heard these threats loudly and clearly. We have no reason to suspect any conspiracy in their words. They are truthful young people and an honest reflection of their Christian upbringing. These threats made by Michael Ferrigan were death threats. There is little doubt about that.

"When Michael Ferrigan told Patrick Connors not to pass through his property again, he was speaking out of fury and purpose. When he said to Patrick Connors, and I quote the words of the young witness Thomas Kelly, 'you won't go back to the same tune as you came,' Michael Ferrigan meant every word of what he was saying. And his fury did not die down. He had more than four hours to think about that threat. He had more than four hours to reconsider. He had more than four hours to allow his anger to simmer down. But he did not weaken in his resolve. He would not allow the black cloud to lift from his spirit. He planned to settle the issue, once and for all, in his own way. And that was to shoot Patrick Connors down, with aforethought and fatal determination.

"And when Michael Ferrigan sat in his kitchen taking a cup of tea with his wife and children and visitor Raymond Coughlin, he was ready to carry out his plan. When his wife saw someone in the distance coming up the track, Michael Ferrigan went into the back rooms of his house to fetch his rifle and surreptitiously escaped from his house, jumping down from the back balcony. His wife had no way of knowing that he had picked up his gun. Raymond Coughlin states that he waited for Michael Ferrigan to return to the supper table to finish his tea, but there was no returning. Michael Ferrigan had begun his mission to intercept the people who were innocently walking up the railway track. True, these men and children would be crossing Michael Ferrigan's property. But this was a public road, and they had every right to be on it.

"It is outrageous to even talk about the issue of the fence in this matter. How can one man carry out the evil intent and execution of murder because of the positioning of a fence? What scurrilous act can be fomented in the mind of a man, to be willing to end the life of a fellow man because a fence was left open?

"Yet, Michael Ferrigan was dedicated enough to carry out this evil intent. He ran down to meet the people coming up the track, his rifle poised at the ready, his pent-up fury coiled to strike. Michael Ferrigan did not even allow Patrick Connors a brief period of time to explain himself. He was bent upon delivering the final lesson to Patrick Connors—a bullet to the head, in full view of two innocent children who had to witness their precious father shot down in cold blood, never to speak to them again.

"And when the brother of Patrick Connors, Earl, with great courage, attempted to take the rifle away from him, Michael Ferrigan cried out, 'You will never hang me for this!' All of the witnesses attest to this. Why would Michael Ferrigan say such a thing? He would say it because his intention to kill Patrick Connors had been gestating in his mind for a considerable period of time. He knew what he was about to do. He knew, in the darkness of his soul, that he was willing to end the life of Patrick Connors. His anger had consumed him, and he had persuaded himself that this terrible act was justified."

There was a pause in the courtroom. Leslie Power stepped back to look at some papers on his table, a habit of his no doubt designed to allow his words to settle in the minds of the jury. The silence in the courtroom was the silence of a graveyard, almost ear-splitting. It was as if everyone had stopped breathing. A sombre climax had been reached.

"Gentlemen of the jury," went on Leslie Power, "Michael Ferrigan has admitted that he warned Patrick Connors not to pass through his property again, and we all have heard witness to that fact. Michael Ferrigan has admitted that he took his gun from one of his rooms and left his home by the back balcony so that he could intercept the people advancing toward his property. He has admitted that he raised his rifle and shot Patrick Connors. He has admitted that he chased the others, men and children, down the track immediately afterwards.

"There was absolutely no indication that Patrick Connors had a weapon on his person that day. It was testified that one of the men had a stone in his hand. Why should he not have held a stone when he knew that a man with a gun awaited them?

"This killing, gentlemen, was committed without any provocation whatsoever. It was a cruel, vicious, and vengeful act of a man who was obsessed with what he saw in his mind as a need for retaliation.

"An innocent victim has been murdered. The perpetrator of this crime is seated with us here in this chamber. It is now your responsibility to find this man guilty, and for the law to execute the ultimate penalty."

And with that final statement by lawyer Leslie Power, the prosecutorial process had been completed.

The judge recessed the court for that afternoon. Since Defence Lawyer Nolan had asked the court for a little time to prepare his final summation, the judge would wind up proceedings the following morning, before sending the jury out to decide on a verdict.

Defence Lawyer Gerald Nolan was not a classy-looking man for a highly educated attorney. He had a sort of frumpy look about him—his hair was too long, he looked as if he needed a shave, his trousers were baggy-looking, and his tie always seemed to be askew. But underneath this unkempt image, here was a man who was articulate and dramatically inclined. He was able to give much essence and spark to his probing questions. He had a clear and lyrical voice that easily held the attention of everyone in the court.

"Gentlemen of the jury," he began in his final statement, "we have reached a climactic stage in this trial. My client, Michael Ferrigan, is the accused in a matter that takes in all the elements of human experience. In the relationship between the accused and victim of this shooting, there have been threats of violence from both sides. There has been a total lack of meaningful contact between neighbours who have known each other for years. There has been fear and trembling because of these threats and lack of contact. The fear on the part of my client was unmistakable. Michael Ferrigan feared for his life, he feared for his family, and he feared for the integrity of his property, a gift and inheritance handed down to him from his father. Survival in an agrarian setting is based upon very basic rules. A man's first responsibility is to secure and protect what he has. There is no substitute for what a farmer and his family owns. His very subsistence depends upon how he copes with the problems that face him.

"And there is no doubt that my client, Michael Ferrigan, had problems. He had problems with certain neighbours who did not respect the practical boundary lines that he had set up to prevent his neighbour's cattle from invading his fields of grain. He had problems with certain people who falsely accused him of not paying his fair share of taxes to the community. He worried about the lack of respect that the inhabitants of Pine River held for his extended family.

"But, most of all," and here lawyer Nolan paused for greater effect, "he feared that, if he insisted upon safeguarding his property rights, he would be physically harmed.

"This is the plight within which Michael Ferrigan found himself on the Sunday of August 17th. There is no doubt that when Michael Ferrigan first met Patrick Connors on Sunday morning, after his fence had been taken down and the logs tossed aside once again, with the cattle of Joseph Dunigan feeding themselves in his oat field, he was infuriated. He had absolute proof that both the victim Patrick Connors and the victim's brother, Earl Connors, had left a gap in his fence in the past. He had fresh memories of the threats that the victim had made to him. Patrick Connors would have liked to, and I quote, 'smash his mouth.' He felt that Patrick Connors and the rest of the extended Connors family had no respect for him and that they would like to do him harm.

"He also knew that Patrick Connors was the owner of a pistol and Michael Ferrigan felt that Patrick Connors would likely use it on him on the pretext of defending himself. He felt that Patrick Connors' reputation preceded him, that Patrick Connors seemed to welcome confrontation, and that Patrick Connors was more than willing to fight him, having invited him to violence on more than one occasion.

"With regard to the statements of the three young witnesses who claimed to have overheard the Sunday morning conversation between my client and Patrick Connors, I have a few questions. Did the two young boys hear enough of the verbal exchange to be able to give a valid rendition of what words were actually exchanged? How far were they from the actual meeting site of the two men in question? In their own words, they claimed they were over one hundred yards from the two men. How could they possibly be able to give a realistic version of the conversation between my client and Patrick Connors? They claim that they heard two men arguing but could not understand what was said at first. Why should they even have been allowed to testify?

"With all due respect to the testimony of Marianne Connors, the young daughter of the victim, there is also a crucial question. Is not her testimony coloured by the traumatic events that occurred later that Sunday afternoon? And the two children of Patrick Connors, in that Sunday morning meeting, may not have been within earshot and may not have heard or understood all that was said as the two men argued with each other.

"These questions are of the utmost importance and could be a deciding factor in this case. There is much cause for doubt in the submissions of the three young witnesses. I am sure that the testimony, in all three cases, is well intentioned, but there is a basis for scepticism there.

"The underlying questions are: Did Patrick Connors threaten Michael Ferrigan at this early Sunday confrontation? Did Patrick Connors laugh at the fact that Michael Ferrigan's fence had been left open once again? In other words, did Patrick Connors show his derision for Michael Ferrigan on that morning and make little of the latter's desire to safeguard the boundaries of his property?

"We have been made aware, from the testimony we have heard, that Patrick Connors was no shrinking violet, that he seemed to welcome the idea of using physical force, that he was willing to incur the anger of my client and goad him into a feeling of apprehension."

Gerald Nolan paused and went over to his table to take a drink of water. It was as if he wanted the men of the jury to think about the hot-tempered stance that Paddy Connors was known to have demonstrated on more than one occasion.

The jury in the case of the Crown versus Michael Ferrigan was a "mixed" jury, but only in the sense that the men were French-speaking and English-speaking. They were made up of the "peers" of the accused, men of different trades and occupations. There were three farmers, two labourers, an electrician, a pipe fitter, a mechanic, a truck driver, a fisherman, and two factory workers.

Most were middle-aged men, but there was one older gentleman, and a few in their early thirties. All of them were bilingual, a requirement for this case. Attentive and unblinking, the eyes of these men seldom strayed from the judge, lawyers, or witnesses, according to my mom. If they were to eventually decide the outcome of this trial, surely they were giving it their best attention.

"Let us now turn our attention," continued Defence Lawyer Nolan, "to the late afternoon of Sunday, August 17th. There is no doubt that Michael Ferrigan told Patrick Connors, at the morning dispute, not to return home by the same route. It is my belief that he said this more in anger than in resolve. When my client, later that afternoon, went down the track from his house to meet Patrick Connors, who was on his way back home, he did so with great fear. Here was Patrick Connors coming up the track with three men, all of whom had what he felt was a great loathing for him. What did they plan to do if he opposed them? Would they once again ignore his demands that his fence be kept closed? Michael Ferrigan felt that he must show his mettle and defend his rights. He had to confront them and insist that they respect his wishes.

"What happened next will forever dwell in the mind of Michael Ferrigan as a terrible blunder. Surely this matter could have been otherwise resolved. But there is no reason to believe that Michael Ferrigan planned the death of Patrick Connors. Admittedly, he did tell the group of men to turn back. He was carrying a rifle. But when he saw Patrick Connors reach into his pocket, he must surely have felt that his own life was in danger. And when he fired that fatal shot, it was done in a quick reaction to what he felt was a sudden threat to his very being. He did not mean for the bullet to erase the life of Patrick Connors. He had no wish to murder his neighbour. He has vehemently denied that he said, and I quote the young daughter of Patrick Connors, that 'He will breathe no more.' There was no desire in my client's heart for the death of Patrick Connors. It may be true that, according to the witnesses present at the shooting, Michael Ferrigan said, 'You will never hang me for this.' But he had absolutely no way of knowing at that moment that he had delivered a mortal wound. These were just words reflecting the terrible tension that Michael Ferrigan felt. And when one of the witnesses tried to take his rifle away from him, he took that as another threat to his well-being. We all know that Michael Ferrigan did not fire his rifle again despite the fact that a large stone was cast in his direction. I repeat. At that moment my client had no idea that the rifle shot at Patrick Connors had been fatal. Indeed, after the witnesses had gone back down the track, Michael Ferrigan tried to revive Patrick Connors. He felt an undying regret for what he had done. There was a profound sorrow in his heart for the demise of Patrick Connors. My client is a family man himself and he felt the anguish of the children at the scene. But Michael Ferrigan had acted to preserve himself. He felt that, under the circumstances, he had no choice but to fire the shot. The underlying fact is that he did not seek nor plan to kill Patrick Connors. We all know, and this is corroborated by the witnesses, that there was a vague plan at some time in the future to have a scrap with Patrick Connors. This does not add up to a plan to kill the victim.

"Gentleman of the jury, I ask you to think upon the words I have spoken about this matter. Michael Ferrigan did not murder Patrick Connors. He found it necessary to defend his person and his rights, and fired a shot in careless fashion at Patrick Connors with absolutely no wish to kill him. He did this in a situation that he felt was self-defence. At worst, he could be charged with manslaughter, for the irresponsible use of a weapon.

"Gentlemen, I thank you for your attention."

Gerald Nolan went back to his table and sat down. He looked at his client, Michael Ferrigan, and they nodded to each other. The defendant put his hand on his forehead, the hand taut and thick-veined, the hand of a working man beset with a terrible anxiety.

I first began to "notice" Marianne Connors during the summer of 1953 while I was out for a two-week stay at my Uncle Mike's. She was going on fourteen years old, yet she had the quiet manner of a girl several years older. She came down one day to the ball field by bicycle with a few other girls and hung around for a while watching us play. Then Will Poole and Pat Kelly came up with some reason to take a break from playing to spend a little time with the girls.

Marianne had noticeably grown taller over the year. I had not run into her more than a couple of times during school days in Quebec City. There was a picnic bench at the ball field in Pine River where we all sort of sat around and joked and teased each other. Quite honestly, Tommy and I would have preferred to continue playing ball on that day because we felt at the time that the girls were a "little young" for us.

I had developed the habit of bringing my sketching pad with me just about everywhere I went, so while we were sitting on the bench I took it out of my bag and started sketching Marianne. Actually, she was the only one of the three girls who was sitting still long enough for me to make a drawing of her. After about ten minutes I tore the page out and gave it to Marianne. She looked at it, gave a little laugh, and then gazed at me with those blue eyes. I told her she could keep it, and the other two girls were "oohing" and "aahing," looking over Marianne's shoulder at the sketch. The guys were sort of nonchalant about my sketching. They'd seen some of my drawings. But Tommy was very encouraging and had already told me that I had real talent.

The amazing thing about Marianne and myself was that we seemed to have very little to say to each other at that time. It was as if everything had been already said and there was little need to say anything else. Of course, this changed over the years and we got to a point where we couldn't shut each other up.

After I got back to Quebec City that summer I received a letter from her thanking me for the "lovely drawing." She said she was going to have it framed and would keep it always. I suppose I was rather touched by this and wrote her back, briefly telling her that I would like to do a painting of her, perhaps the following summer.

My real "courtship" of Marianne Connors began the next

year. But it was done by mail, for the most part, at the beginning. I began thinking about her quite a bit. We would exchange letters.

In June of 1954 I managed to get a job at one of the biggest hotels in Quebec City as a "busboy"—a sort of waiter's helper in the main dining room. So I didn't get out to my uncle's for more than a few weekends. At the hotel, most of the work I had to do involved cleaning up tables after diners had left. I would cart loads of dishes back into the kitchen, and prepare the table for the next diners, as well as doing jobs inside the kitchen itself. I was paid a fair salary for this work and was quite proud of it. The waiters and waitresses would also share their tips with me, which I thought was quite nice. But the job lasted for only two months before I went back to school in September. I was complimented by the head-waiter on my performance and was told that I would be invited back for the following summer season of 1955. As it turned out, I never worked at the hotel again.

During my school year in grade eleven, I did not see Marianne Connors very often. She was still only fifteen years of age and I was seventeen, so at the time I considered her to be still a little young for me. When I did run into her at the bus stop or at the drug store lunch counter, where some of the high school kids gathered, we would greet each other with a sort of cautious enthusiasm. But since the meetings were very brief, I often would run out of words and stand there, a little self-conscious about talking with a "younger" girl, still a grade nine student at the girls' school, in front of my friends. When I spoke to Jackie Farrell about her, he would always remind me that when I was 83 years of age, Marianne would be 81.

But even as a fifteen-year-old, she was tallish and willowy and quite beautiful, I deduced in my great wisdom. Increasingly, I began thinking about her more than ever and wondered if she thought much of me. I realized that I could speak to her much better using the written word than in person.

Everything sort of came to a head during the summer of '55 after I graduated from grade eleven, which they then called Junior

Matriculation. I had lied about my age and had gotten a summer job as a waiter in one of Quebec City's better restaurants—La Maison St. Antoine. They had been impressed by the fact that I had worked at Quebec City's most famous hotel the previous summer, so they hired me. From observing the waiters at the hotel the year before, I had quickly developed a knack for that kind of work and told Jackie Farrell, with a serious look on my facetious mug, that I was considering it as a lifetime career. When I added up the amount of money I was making in gratuities, perhaps it wasn't such a bad idea.

My day off that summer was Monday and I used it for biking out to St. Gabriel on my "three-speed" if the weather was suitable. It was my only chance to get together with Tommy Kelly, who wanted to throw the football around since he was set to be the quarterback of the school team that coming September. Marianne Connors, from what I could see, seemed to be "keeping the company" of Tommy's younger brother Patrick at that time. I can remember being mildly disturbed when I saw them together on the Kelly veranda as I pedalled up to the house. She was chasing him around trying to tear off his baseball cap.

But she was very joyful upon seeing me and even hugged me. Both the Kelly boys had grown to be big, almost burly, specimens so I wasn't about to impose myself too fondly upon this lovely girl. But I was deeply impressed by her natural beauty, and for the first time I felt a somewhat disturbing attraction to her.

But how would I ever be able to cultivate this seed that was growing within me? After all, I lived in Quebec City, I had a job, and likely would not see a lot of her in the future.

However, there was some promise in the way that she looked at me, her full lips parting easily into generous smiles. I wanted to spend some time with her, alone, when we could explore the depth of our magnetism. I cagily asked Tommy if his brother was serious about Marianne and he told me that they were "just friends with a rather platonic relationship." Upon hearing this I was encouraged a little and began to realize the extent to which I was willing to go to spend some time with Marianne.

At the restaurant I started my shift at 2:00 p.m. and worked well into the night, usually getting home after twelve midnight. I'd usually sleep in till ten o'clock the next morning.

"The Connors girl called last night," my mom said to me one morning, without too much expression.

"Marianne Connors?" I blurted out.

"Who else?"

"Did she call from Pine River?"

"No. Apparently she's spending time with her Aunt Mamie down on Artillery Street. She left her number. It's on the table over there."

"I didn't know one of her aunts lived here."

"Well, that's what your father says. I don't know her side of the family that well."

In two minutes, I was on the telephone.

"Hello," Marianne's voice answered.

"It's Francis. You're in town?"

"Yes. I just came down for a few days."

"Can we get together?"

"Yes, I suppose so."

"I have to go to work in a few hours. So maybe tomorrow morning we can go for a walk or something."

Maureen "Mamie" Gill Bryson lived in a third storey flat at the top of two long flights of inside stairs on Artillery Street. She had a hot cup of coffee waiting for me when I entered, so I sat down with Marianne and her and we began talking about Pine River and the people there. She was a loquacious woman and wouldn't stop chattering until I virtually had to grab Marianne's arm and pull her out of the flat and down the stairs.

Once on the sidewalk, holding Marianne's hand, I would not have changed places with anyone in the world. Marianne would soon be sixteen years of age and she had truly blossomed into a gorgeous young woman. I felt very privileged to be with her and sensed at that moment that there was a God on this earth and that this God was out to see that I was unimaginably gratified.

We walked through the streets of the old city, stopping to enjoy those points of interest that attracted her attention. She'd been down to the historic parts of town just a few times and was not that familiar with the city's antiquity. I did my best to enlighten her, exalted in my position as mentor to this beautiful creature.

As I remember it, the day was cloudy but the rain held off so we must have walked for two hours. I tried to explain to her the historical importance of certain sites. We walked past the courthouse where we had testified a few years before.

Marianne was quite sturdy in build, much like the whole Connors brood. She'd learned to do many of the tasks at the family's farm now that her father was no longer with them. She drove the tractor and milked the cows and helped with the reaping of the grain in summer and fall. Two of her uncles were raising turkeys on their farms and they gave Marianne work looking after the gobblers. They had expanded this business to the extent that they had had to employ another full-time worker.

Naturally, I was on top of the world being with Marianne that day. I loved to watch her move around, her strength and flexibility showing in her walk. She was surprisingly strong. We started to wrestle playfully at one point and I was quite amazed at the power in her hands and arms. We walked through the Battlefields Park and I held her around the waist as we were moving along. When I kissed her on the cheek she pressed her head against my lips. I knew then that I was in love with this girl.

I took her into the Provincial Museum to see the city's most impressive art collection. I told her that my mother had brought me to the museum years before. Since I was somewhat obsessed with art myself, I did not hesitate to give Marianne a quick "course" on what I knew about the evolution of art. I used words like gothic and impressionism and rococo and dada.

"You're a bit of a snob when it comes to art, aren't you?" she said later, after we had left the building.

"What do you mean?" I protested. "These are the things my mom taught me."

"How am I supposed to remember all those terms?" she said.

"You'll remember them. I'll teach you."

"Oh! Francis Carroll the art teacher, is it?"

Then she giggled and squeezed me close to her as we walked along. That was the first time that Marianne showed me what a great sense of humour she had. She loved ribbing me.

I knew that I loved her and yearned to possess her completely, yet, fortunately, there were restrictions in the circumstances of how we were able to be together. Not that I was seeking sainthood in celibacy. Had the opportunity arisen where we would have been isolated together for any length of time, I would doubtlessly have succumbed to the invitation of desire and fulfilment.

With her blue eyes and her dark hair and her slim muscular figure, I suppose I considered Marianne to be a classic beauty. But she would have objected to that designation, I'm sure. She thought herself to be quite average in her looks. There was little sexual aggression in the way she carried herself, as she did not need to be forthcoming in that way. Marianne moved easily, exuding a certain quality of physical and social grace. Because of where she lived and because of what was required of her, she had not participated in sports to any degree, as I had. Still, there was a power in her bearing that always surprised me and that was the natural result of her duties and activities at the farm. As a young woman, in my estimation, she was strength and gentleness personified.

Chapter 15

At the courtroom on the last day of the trial of Michael Ferrigan, Judge Sévigny spoke to the jury before they retreated to their deliberating room to decide upon a verdict.

"Gentlemen, you have listened with great patience, over a rather difficult period of time, to the evidence at this trial. The accused in this case has been charged with wilful murder. You must understand that, if you find him guilty of this crime, he must pay the ultimate penalty. That is what the law of the land stipulates.

"You have heard the testimony by both the prosecution and the defence. We are all aware that the accused, Michael Ferrigan, did take the life of Patrick Connors. The accused has admitted that he alone is responsible for this killing. The defence has contended that there were mitigating circumstances surrounding this shooting. You must decide whether Michael Ferrigan had valid reason to use a weapon for what was implied by the attorney for the accused as being self-defence. The defence has also taken the position that Michael Ferrigan did not mean to kill Patrick Connors, that he meant to defend himself and inadvertently caused the victim's death by firing a reckless shot.

"It has been pointed out to us, time and again in this trial, that this whole sanguine event took place because of a gap in a fence, a fence that had been put up by Michael Ferrigan to prevent neighbouring cattle from eating the grain in his fields. This fence was illegally erected across a public path, a roadway that many people used on a regular basis."

My mother, who attended proceedings on this final day, said that the judge summarized the case quite well for the jury. These men were working men, not familiar with legal jargon. This judge seemed able to speak their language.

"The prosecution has alleged," continued the judge, "that Michael Ferrigan murdered Patrick Connors, in an uncontrollable rage, with premeditation, and without provocation. You have heard the young witnesses state that Michael Ferrigan threatened Patrick Connors at that first meeting on that Sunday, and the prosecution maintains that the accused man fulfilled these threats four hours later, with complete awareness of what he was doing.

"All of you, gentlemen, must agree on the verdict. If you feel, beyond a reasonable doubt, that the accused is guilty of wilful murder, then you must find him guilty. You must also realize that, and I state this once again, if you do find the defendant guilty of murder, he must pay the ultimate price.

"You will now retire to your private chamber."

There were no empty seats in the courtroom that day, as there had not been during all of the trial. During the judge's address to the jury, there was little need for the bailiffs to caution the spectators. A full hush permeated the courtroom, a disciplined silence that allowed the words of this judge to resound in their monotone, but electric, essence.

Michael Ferrigan was immediately led from the courtroom, his head down, a tall but thinner man, with an officer of the court on each side of him. The spectators stared at him, some turning around as he passed them to follow his route out of the door of the chamber. He was led back to a holding cell to await the judgement of the jury.

The courtroom then emptied, the press people and the observers and the concerned family members all vacating a venue that many had become familiar with over the previous fortnight. The press had all but suggested the likely outcome of the jury deliberations in their columns and press releases. Few media people saw any chance that Michael Ferrigan would escape the wrath of the law this time. No one expected the jury to dwell on the issues for more than a few hours, yet no one could predict precisely how long it would take. Many of the spectators took the opportunity to walk to the Dufferin Terrace and stroll back and forth on the boards above the river on a misty, cool, late October morning.

As it turned out, the jury deliberated for a little more than two hours. It was announced that the court would reconvene at 2:00 p.m., when the agreed-upon verdict would be revealed.

A heavy pall of late October clouds covered the sky as all assembled once again, entering the old courthouse to hear the jury's decision. In the courtroom, when everyone was seated, the prisoner, Michael Ferrigan, was brought in and seated himself beside his lawyer, Gerald Nolan. Judge Sévigny then came in and the jury filed in immediately afterwards.

Blank and neutral looks infused the faces of the twelve members of the jury. A tense and severe calm settled into the chamber.

Michael Ferrigan stood to hear the final decision.

The first voice to be heard was a clerk of the Crown who rose and looked at the jury.

"Gentlemen of the jury, are you agreed upon a verdict? Is the prisoner guilty or not guilty of the charge of murder?"

One of the jurymen rose from his seat and pronounced the one word: "Guilty!"

All eyes were instantly affixed upon Michael Ferrigan, who stood staring at the jury, betraying a stunned look of dismay.

The clerk then asked each of the members of the jury in turn if they agreed with this judgement. One by one they all tilted their heads downward, then up again, as a signification of agreement.

Michael Ferrigan sat, his hands covering his face, his elbows on the table before him.

A female voice then called out from the back of the courtroom.

"No! No! This cannot be!"

It was a call from Michael Ferrigan's wife Maggie, who had seated herself at the rear of the chamber among her relatives. She began to sob loudly, her overwrought feelings, so well contained during the public trial of her husband, suddenly giving way. She soon had two of the court's bailiffs at her side. They each took her by an arm and led her from the chamber.

Thankfully, she was spared having to witness hearing the death sentence pronounced on her husband.

Michael Ferrigan stood before Judge Sévigny, who sentenced him as follows:

"You have been charged before the court and society with the greatest crime to be found in the annals of crimes committed. You have been charged with the crime of pre-meditated murder. You have had a trial, a fair one, an impartial one, where evidence has been adduced not only against you but in your favour, to a jury of your peers. The case against you, Michael Ferrigan, is sustained by evidence that leaves no alternative for the court but to perform the painful duty that the law requires of it.

"I cannot imagine how a man of your position and intelligence could possibly have conceived and carried out so terrible a crime. I will not overly recall to your recollection the horrible, sanguinary scene that took place when you slew your victim in the presence of his little children and his friends, and killed him as you did without provocation.

"I remind you that this act committed has been one that you have confessed to. The court has no alternative but to concur with the decision of the jury. You precipitated a father, your neighbour, your own cousin, to eternity without a moment's notice.

"It is now the duty of the court to pass sentence upon you. It is right to say that you cannot expect the slightest mercy.

"I must pronounce that you, Michael Ferrigan, be taken to the common jail. There, within its precincts, on Friday the 9th of January next, you will be hanged according to the provisions of the law, by the neck, until you are dead, and may God Almighty have mercy upon your soul."

It must have seemed unlike Judge Sévigny to make such a dire pronouncement. Although his personality had little charisma, he personified fairness and had allowed the trial to proceed without interference or heavy-handedness.

But he was acting as a judge in the system that was the law of the land. He was doing his job.

After the sentencing, Michael Ferrigan's defence lawyer, Gerald Nolan, approached the judge and whispered something that apparently indicated that his client was ready to say a few words to the court. The judge, of course, concurred, nodding his head.

Michael Ferrigan rose from his chair and faced the judge. There was a moment of delay as he seemed to be gathering his thoughts.

"Patrick Connors had liberty," said Michael Ferrigan, "as well as any other to pass by that road, as long as he replaced the logs of the fence after he went through. I met him on that Sunday morning and told him that he and others were not doing that, but he would not listen to me. If he had always put up the fence after he passed, he would still be alive today."

This post-sentencing statement by Michael Ferrigan contradicted, in a way, the defence strategy during the trial. It was as if he was justifying the killing of Paddy Connors.

"He told me that day," continued Michael Ferrigan, "when I spoke to him about it, that he would throw my fence into the ditch and me along with it. He challenged me to fight again and I told him that I was willing to accept this challenge if he got two strange men with us, but he always had a crowd with him to back him. He threatened me at the schoolhouse and swore by Jesus Christ that he'd smash my face.

"I wanted him to keep the peace, and made a complaint before a magistrate. The papers are still there and will prove these facts."

There was another pause, and no one was certain if Michael Ferrigan had more to say. Then he sat down again.

When I got home from school on that day, my mother told me the news. It was soon all over the radio stations and the television broadcasts and then the newspapers.

It began to dawn on me that Tommy Kelly and I had been partly responsible for Michael Ferrigan's conviction. The next day, while Tommy and I were speaking about it at recess time, we both expressed the hope that the hanging could be avoided. Tommy said once again that hanging was a barbaric practice that should be gotten rid of and that a country should not have to resort to murdering its own citizens. Up to that point I had never given the issue of capital punishment much thought. Tommy said that there was a deep feeling by some people in the country that capital punishment should be abolished. Better that one thousand murderers be given life sentences than having one innocent person executed, Tommy said. That was the danger of having a penalty like hanging as a preventive measure. There was too much likelihood that the law would make a mistake and execute an innocent person. Tommy told me that he was doing a little research on the matter and that he had read that quite a few persons had been wrongly executed in the United States. But few people seemed to give the matter too much thought, and when the wrong person is executed, it is too late for second thoughts. He read that, in some cases, accused people had been given the death penalty on the basis of very slim evidence, something that was called circumstantial. Tommy told me that he was trying to get the school debating society to argue this topic. I can't remember if they ever got around to it.

After Michael Ferrigan had been given the death sentence, his wife Maggie wasted no time in bringing the issue before the authorities. Along with lawyer Nolan, she sought to have the conviction overturned before the Court of Appeals. If this failed, her aim was to have the death sentence commuted to life imprisonment. She made many representations, with the aid of lawyer Gerald Nolan, to local and federal officials and politicians, to save the life of her husband, the father of her ten children.

To say that the trial and conviction had disrupted the lives of the families of the accused and the victim would be an understatement. Both of these farmers, Michael Ferrigan and Patrick Connors, had left young children fatherless. That was the most difficult aftermath of the whole ordeal. Thankfully, all of these bereaved children emanated from unions that had the benefits of extended family support. The Connors clan was quite numerous in Pine River. The brothers of Patrick Connors were indispensable in providing help to his widow, especially in caring for the crops and cattle. For the children themselves, life had to go on. Marianne was going to school in Quebec City daily, travelling by train, and two of the other children, Hughie and Gerald, were attending the village school.

In the case of the Ferrigans, the volatile nature of their existence continued. In the month of September of that year, Patrick Ferrigan, a younger brother of Michael, was arrested for the attempted shooting of a fellow worker. This had occurred before the trial of Michael Ferrigan but after the day Patrick had come to see my Uncle Mike, and, although it did not come up during the proceedings, it could not have helped Michael's case. It became common talk to categorize this family as a wayward clan who seemed to operate outside of the rules of society.

Still, the Ferrigan family, led by a stalwart pillar, Michael Ferrigan's wife Maggie, managed to hold things together. With the help of her older sons and daughters, she was able to keep heads above water on their property as well as pursuing all avenues in a persistent and courageous effort to keep her husband alive. She could not have done more and, no doubt, she earned the respect of her neighbours. There was little ill will toward her and her children among the people of Pine River.

Despite all of these tasks and preoccupations, Maggie Ferrigan managed to visit her husband almost daily at the prison. The court allowed him to be kept in Quebec City close to his family. If all efforts to save his life failed, he would be transferred to Montreal for execution. She encouraged him and expressed the feeling that they would be successful in getting the courts to allow an appeal.

Chapter 16

I went into Senior Matriculation in the fall of 1955. This class, grade twelve, was equivalent to the first year of university; this had been put in place partly as an economical way of starting higher education. Students could still live at home and not be subject to expensive tuition fees and paying for room and board at some distant university.

Marianne Connors was on my mind a lot at the time. She was still travelling daily by train between Pine River and school, but occasionally she would stay overnight at her Aunt Mamie's on Artillery Street. This allowed us the time to perhaps go to the movies or share some other activity together.

I loved the movies. I could not think of a more pleasurable time than sitting in the theatre with Marianne, holding her hand and leaning close to her, our fingers intertwined. After the movie was over, we would stroll up La Rue St. Jean, then duck into a soda bar for a soft drink. She had to be back to "Aunt Mamie's" before 10:00 p.m., a curfew that she adhered to religiously. We did not want to jeopardize this great opportunity we'd been given. She was always in my thoughts, causing me to lie awake at night thinking about her, and I eagerly looked forward to the next time we'd be together.

The grade twelve curriculum required a lot of my attention in those days. I studied chemistry, mathematics, and history. There were no more art classes at school for students in Senior "Matric," but I still sketched and painted when I could. I had saved money from my working summer, so I used some of it to buy art supplies—a good easel, a sturdy wooden case for my paints, and good-quality brushes. If I had another obsession, apart from Marianne and hockey, it was for oil painting. My mom would usually give me Christmas and birthday presents related to painting—books about the painters of the Impressionist period and instructional manuals on how I could improve my "oeuvre."

I remember going to the theatre with my mother to see a film called *Moulin Rouge,* which starred actor José Ferrer as the physically stunted Henri Toulouse-Lautrec. It was a brilliantly conceived production depicting life in Paris in the late 1800s. Lautrec, strongly influenced by the artists of the Impressionist movement, was an exceptional lithographer and painter. The haunting music and "period" costuming of the film filled me with a kind of ambitious desire to pursue art as a career. I cannot think of any factor, apart from my mother, that influenced me more than this movie.

Tommy Kelly was considered to be one of the best quarterbacks who ever played football at our school. He threw many touchdown passes and enabled his team to win the city championship two years in a row. Tall and hard and sinewy, Tommy wasn't the fastest runner, but he could throw the ball on the run extremely well. It was quite difficult to defend against him. His play calling was unpredictable for any defence. He always seemed to be on a different page and no one knew (not even his coaches) what play he would call next.

The school football team held about three practices a week, so Tommy would usually bunk down at Jackie Farrell's house after a practice. He was admired and singled out as a desirable example by all of his teachers as well as the student body.

But Tommy still took the train home on his "off" nights and I was soon made aware that he was spending a lot of time with Marianne. He knew that I had a thing for this lovely girl. I had spoken to him often enough about her for him to be mindful.

I could understand that they would be attracted to each other. Both were very intelligent young people and, no doubt, spoke the "same language" and did not suffer fools gladly. They also had a lot in common in that they'd been indelibly marked by the experience of having to testify at the trial a few years before.

During this time I was not spending much time with Tommy. He was preoccupied with football and I was trying my best to cope with the grade twelve course of studies. The winter of 1955 was a worrisome time for me. I was still meeting Marianne at noontime when possible and still writing to her, our letters being a sort of "journal for two." But since I could not spend much time with her there was an incompleteness about our relationship.

I was still playing hockey for the school team even though my level of intensity for this game as a player began to wane somewhat.

I realized that, if I was going to keep Marianne for myself, I would have to fight for her, but I wasn't sure about how to do this. Tommy seemed to be in a much better position than I to spend time with Marianne. They took the train together, coming to school and returning home, and no doubt managed to get together frequently in Pine River if they wished. How would I be able to compete with that?

Summertime came and I worked at the restaurant again. I could not go to Pine River very often. It got to a point where I was a little embarrassed to go. Apart from all of this, I was making plans to attend college in Montreal that fall and perhaps would be completely out of the picture.

In mid-November of 1952, Mrs. Margaret "Maggie" Ferrigan was in the midst of a "heroic" fight to save the life of her husband. Together with her lawyer, Gerald Nolan, discussions were held about whether there was a possible chance that the verdict of the trial could be appealed. If not, they hoped that the death sentence could be commuted. Realistically, there seemed to be little prospect for success in seeking a new trial. The press had been overwhelmingly in agreement with the verdict, if not the death sentence, and the mood of the public seemed to coalesce into a similar bent.

The drive to secure a commutation of the death penalty began to meet with some support, once the details of Michael Ferrigan's case began to be passed along by word of mouth. Many people began to show a deep disdain for the idea of a government executing its citizens. What was to be gained, depriving ten children of a father by wiping him off the face of the earth, using barbaric strangulation as a method? How would the following generations of the Ferrigans be served by stigmatizing the grandchildren with the scar of an executed grandfather?

Seeing this groundswell of sympathy, Michael Ferrigan's lawyer, Gerald Nolan, did not relent in pursuing an appeal in the cause of his client on at least a few important bases.

The first was that the Connors and O'Meara families were a very influential clique in the Pine River farming community and had been able to prejudice the press, police, and even the jury into leveraging the case against Michael Ferrigan. Beyond the walls of the courtroom, this group had alluded to the previous violence and killing that Michael Ferrigan had perpetrated some years before in the death of David O'Meara. Although the O'Meara killing had not been brought up in the recent trial, the relatives of both victims of Michael Ferrigan did not relent in their often voiced desire to see the killer pay the ultimate price for his crimes. They could never find a place for forgiveness for the atrocities against both David O'Meara and Paddy Connors.

Another consideration that lawyer Gerald Nolan had in mind was the matter of the "irritability" of Michael Ferrigan. This farmer had been hounded by his neighbours for years, about the fence he had installed across the railroad track. These neighbours knew of the fragile and unpredictable nature of his temperament. Yet they had badgered, hassled, and exasperated Michael Ferrigan to the point where he had responded, on cue, to their subtle taunts. They had been, Nolan felt, partly responsible for the killing of Patrick Connors. Had the neighbours dealt with this volatile man with a little more tact, the killing would never have occurred.

And finally, there was the business of the pistol that Patrick Connors may have had with him on the day of the killing. Nolan felt that, with more time, he could discover the truth about this possibility. He thought of a witness whom he had called to the stand during the trial, a man named James Landers, who supposedly had been present at the home of Terry Coughlin when Patrick Connors had stopped there on his final walk up the track. This man, a close acquaintance of Paddy Connors, was said to have had a short conversation with the victim at that time, warning him of the explosive disposition of Michael Ferrigan. The victim had apparently told James Landers that he was prepared to meet Michael Ferrigan with force if there was a need to use it. Lawyer Nolan had called Landers to appear as a witness, but the latter expressed an obvious unwillingness to come, showing great agitation. When Landers finally did appear, he called Gerald Nolan aside and asked to be excused from testifying, saying that he knew nothing about the case. Nolan had noticed that the man was trembling. The lawyer felt that this man knew more than he was willing to tell, and that he feared the vengeance of the O'Meara and the Connors families were he to testify truthfully. When Gerald Nolan finally got him to the stand, Landers bent his head down and professed, under oath, to know absolutely nothing about the events. He had simply told Patrick Connors on that day "to be careful"; he had simply gone to the site of the killing afterwards to help. He had little more to say. His brief testimony was all but overlooked.

However, in approaching the court authorities regarding an appeal of Michael Ferrigan's case, Gerald Nolan was given no hope for a reprieve. The Court of Appeals formally turned down his request for a second trial, stating that the prisoner had confessed to the crime, allowing a guilty verdict supported by overwhelming evidence. Michael Ferrigan would have to submit to the law of the land.

Yet there seemed to be a gathering storm of opinion in the populace, as evidenced by letters to editors, that Michael Ferrigan should have been given a life sentence, as opposed to the ultimate degradation of the human body and spirit by paying the ultimate price for this crime. Information began to surface about the man Michael Ferrigan, information that he was not the insensitive being portrayed by the press, but a father who was faithful to the traditions of his Catholic upbringing. He'd been married in a

Catholic Church, and had seen to it that all ten of his children were baptized as Christians. He also was described as a "friend of education who sought to improve the schools in his district." He was described as "an honest man who ran a respectable farming operation" and who dealt fairly with the people with whom he did business.

Maggie Ferrigan sought some measure of mercy for her husband. She wrote letters to the leaders of the country—political and religious—asking that they use their influence to alter the death sentence to life imprisonment.

Some of this correspondence was later published:

November 28th, 1952
To the Governor-General of Canada
Ottawa

Dear Sir,

It has been several weeks now that my husband, Michael Ferrigan, the father of my ten children, is under sentence of death. He now waits in the Quebec City jail before he will be sent to Montreal to face his executioners.

In my anguish, I humbly throw myself at your feet and tearfully implore you to use your considerable influence with the parliament to come to my rescue. I am begging for a commutation of my husband's death sentence to life in prison. With all of his failings, my husband has been a good father to his little ones. I remind you that eight of our children are below sixteen years of age.

My husband's attorney, Gerald Nolan, is now pleading for consideration with the Supreme Court of Canada.

I deeply desire that Your Excellency will heed my urgent supplication and use your compelling voice to help in any way possible in this matter.

Margaret Ferrigan

I graduated from Senior Matriculation, equivalent to freshman year in university, in early summer of 1956. I had spent twelve years in school, being instructed mostly by the teaching Brothers. Their influence on me was remarkable. They were tough and used discipline in a way that was quite innovative, for the most part. I had great admiration for my hockey coach, Brother Martin; my English teacher in grade nine, Brother Norbert; and my science teacher in Senior "matric," Brother Christopher.

But I especially remembered Brother Sebastian, a man who seemed to be perpetually on duty. He taught every subject from 8:30 a.m. to 4:00 p.m., every school day, with a half-hour off for lunch. He was the football coach, the director of discipline, producer of Gilbert and Sullivan's *H.M.S. Pinafore* and other musical productions, and organizer of the chess club and the floor hockey league.

I also remembered Brother Sebastian as a strike breaker. Some of the goons in Fourth Commercial decided one day to stage a wildcat strike because of their dislike for the bookkeeping teacher, a Mr. Jarry.

The time they chose to walk out on the bookkeeping teacher unfortunately coincided with Brother Sebastian's not infrequent trips to the lavatory, where he used to check up on students smoking in the cubicles.

The confrontation was unexpected, dramatic, and short-lived. There was something beneath Brother Sebastian's black robes and Marine brush-cut that spelled Vesuvius.

At least a few students suffered welts and bruises just scrambling back to the desks in their classroom.

And then, apparently, he delivered to them an oration that could surely rank with the best speeches of John A. MacDonald, Clarence Darrow, and John F. Kennedy.

I did not hear the speech, but I heard of it. One thing about it stuck in my mind. He told the students what his salary was after introducing them to the word "pittance." He said that he made seventeen hundred dollars a year, but that he hardly saw any of it.

His salary went straight to the "Motherhouse." Three of the ring-leaders of the walkout were suspended "for an indefinite period," and were allowed back to school only after lengthy discussions between their parents and the administration of the school.

My father was a history buff of sorts who spent a lot of time searching out volumes at the English-language bookstore in Quebec City. He was meticulous in the care of his books, keeping them in glass-fronted wooden bookcases. Very few pages of his books turned yellow over time since he kept them incubated, away from the dust. He had several of these bookcases in the living room and a few more in his bedroom. They stood almost floor-to-ceiling, the rich wood glaze kept shiny by my father's lemon-scented rub-downs. He belonged to the Book of the Month club. He recently received Winston Churchill's volumes on the *History of the English-Speaking Peoples* as well as the ex-English Prime Minister's books on the Second World War. He had the Will Durant *Story of Civilization* series, and *The Outline of History* by H.G. Wells. There have been scores of books written about the history of Ireland. My father acquired them all.

I am sure, had my father not spent money on purchasing new books, he would have been able to own an automobile. As it turned out, he did not buy a car until he was almost fifty years of age, when I was away at university.

The books that my father had on Irish history began to stir my interest while I was in my last year of high school. I was made aware of the terrible price the Irish people had to pay at the hands of the British.

Margaret Ferrigan wrote to her husband when she could not visit him:

Dec. 14, 1952
Dear Michael,

I am sending this note to you with your brother as I am not able to see you till Monday.

It seems that the courts will not hear your case again and give you another trial, so Gerald Nolan and I have been writing letters to get your sentence changed. I am praying to God that we will be successful.

Things are going very well here, although we had a big early snowfall on Wednesday which blocked the roads so the kids missed a few days of school. I want to take Sean down to the doctor in Loretteville. He stayed awake all night and I think he may have the scarlet fever or something else that Ellen had last year, with lots of redness on his face. The house has been warm enough with the wood stove going, so we stay in the kitchen most of the time. Everything is okay in the stable. The boys are doing the milking.

Sars passed by yesterday morning and said he'd try to get down to see you soon. His brother is very sick in the hospital and they don't think he'll last more than a few weeks. I'm sorry to hear that because he's a good man. I'm saying prayers to the Blessed Mother for him.

Michael, I can't tell you how much I miss you. Johanna is asking for you and wondering when you're coming back home. The house seems to be so empty without you. I said the Rosary with Ellen last night for you and I hope the Lord will answer our prayers.

I am looking forward to seeing you Monday. Don't give up hope. Gerald Nolan is a fine lawyer and is working hard to get some good news for you. I spoke to him on the telephone yesterday and he is very sure that they will listen to him.

In the meantime, God be with you.

Your loving wife, Margaret

Using all of her considerable energy, Margaret Ferrigan pursued her goals with a passion. She managed to convince the Municipal Council of Quebec, through the intercession of one of the city councillors, to send another petition to the Prime Minister and the Governor General seeking a commutation of her husband's death sentence. Meetings of citizens were held, with resolutions for clemency carried and then sent to Members of Parliament and the Prime Minister.

Margaret visited her husband at the prison as often as she could. She soon had enlisted Father James McDonald of the English-speaking Catholic parish in Quebec to begin seeing her husband on a regular basis. The Sisters of Charity, who taught Michael Ferrigan's daughters, impressed upon the children in school to pray for the success of the petitions for clemency.

Michael Ferrigan initially felt confident that he would be successful in having his sentence commuted to life imprisonment. He had great faith in his lawyer, Gerald Nolan. But as the precious days went by with no sign of relief from the foreboding future, his morale weakened. Always a robust man, healthy and still muscular, he continued to lose some weight. He was not the surly man who had confronted neighbours in the past. He seemed to have gained a deep respect from his jailers, men who came to sympathize with him and his desire to continue to live for his children.

He walked constantly in his cell. In the exercise yard, his head down, overcoat buttoned to the top, wearing a winter toque securely wrapped around his head, he trudged steadily in a circular path. His appetite was good, yet he began showing some tremor while handling his utensils.

Mid-December arrived and he was visited by his wife and city alderman Michael McFee. This local politician had taken up his cause. Also present were two of his sons: the eldest, Stephen, who was nineteen years of age, and Joey, who was fourteen. Michael Ferrigan said that he felt somewhat pessimistic about his chances for a commutation, although he had not given up hope and seemed to be very appreciative of their visit. He spoke of his difficulties and said that if times had been good he would have sold his holdings in Pine River and moved to the United States or to the west of Canada. At this stage, Maggie broke down and began to weep, holding her younger son Joey close to her.

The extended Ferrigan family still held high hopes that the Supreme Court of Canada would reach a decision in favour of Michael Ferrigan. The lower courts had not been willing to allow an appeal, but surely the highest court in the land would find it in its heart to commute his sentence. Michael Ferrigan had committed horrendous acts of violence, but in his normal behaviour he had taken a deep interest in all affairs in his community. He was a man who had risen early every morning to work his farm and often worked well into the evening. He had laboured all of his adult life to support his large family.

In considering the plea for a commutation of his sentence, could the Supreme Court avoid thinking of the two killings that Michael Ferrigan had perpetrated? Even if he had been acquitted of the charge of murder in the O'Meara case, was there any doubt that this killing played its part in helping the court to arrive at a decision?

And that decision of the Supreme Court of Canada was to turn down the plea for a commutation of Michael Ferrigan's death sentence.

Chapter 17

In 1956, while working at the restaurant La Maison St. Antoine, a restaurant that specialized in French cuisine, I felt quite fortunate. It was a rather pricey eatery with a solid reputation among visitors to the old city. Believe it or not, the manager of the restaurant suggested that I put on a French accent when I spoke English to the clientele, many of whom were American tourists. I found this request to be rather bizarre, but having heard many francophones speak English, I had no trouble speaking English with a simulated Parisian accent.

I had a very good summer, financially speaking. My salary was not great, but many of the American visitors were very generous tippers. I was able to accumulate enough cash to pay for my university tuition and books, and still have money to help support myself in Montreal, at least for the first several months.

Charlie and Lawrence Carroll, my Uncle Mike's two sons, met me at the train station when I arrived in Montreal on September 2nd. They were very gracious from the beginning. It seemed to be a big deal for them to help me out, getting me started in the big city. They shared an apartment at the west end of Sherbrooke Street, a "three-and-a-half." They told me that I could stay with them until I found a place downtown, closer to Sir George Williams College, the school where I had already been accepted. This school offered the courses in art and design that I wanted to take.

Lawrence, the older of my two cousins, worked for a big insurance company and was studying for his C.P.A. at night school. His brother, Charlie, worked for Simpson's Department Store and was also taking courses. Charlie was a real joker and said that he would show me around town as soon as I got settled in.

It was easy to like these two guys. I ended up spending several days with them before I found a place near the college at a private residence owned by an older woman who had a room to rent "for a serious student."

My cousin Charlie was instrumental in introducing me to the benefits of beer at various pubs and taverns in the brief period that I stayed at his apartment. He wasn't a huge guy, but built along the lines of his father, my Uncle Mike. He had a certain swagger and fancied himself to be a sort of *boulevardier* in downtown Montreal. He was very well known to a cluster of drinking buddies who seemed to enjoy seeing him walk into a tavern, the small tables covered with draft glasses of ale, the loud hum of voices bouncing off the walls.

Charlie was a big hockey fan and took me to see a Montreal Canadiens exhibition game at the Forum. It was the first time I had ever seen a National Hockey League game in person. We had standing room tickets that were cheap, and we stood in one of the aisles leaning against an iron rail. This position was actually closer to the ice than many of the more expensive seats at higher levels.

The Montreal Forum is a venerable old arena which has a colourful history. In the fall of 1956, the Canadiens were well on the way to becoming a dynasty, having won the Stanley Cup the previous season and icing a team that seemed sure to repeat. My interest in hockey as a player was lessening. I did not try out for the varsity team at the college. Yet I felt that I would always be an ardent fan of the game.

But the city itself was a different experience for me. People were continually walking in droves up and down St. Catherine Street, a main thoroughfare, speaking to each other in languages I'd never heard before on such a scale—Asian dialects, Italian and Greek and Spanish, and smatterings of other languages as well. Montreal had a truly cosmopolitan aura.

A few days after I got to Montreal, and during one night of introducing me to Guinness beer, Charlie headed me down, east on St. Catherine Street, past the storefront windows dazzling with stylishly clad mannequins. Charlie commented on the visual attractions as we walked toward a seedier part of town, the St. Lawrence Boulevard section. We ambled north and passed several blocks past older buildings, some near dilapidation. This area of the city had a strangely abandoned look to it, with fewer people on the streets. But the tacky outside lighting of bars and restaurants still offered their enticement. Charlie stopped at one tavern and we entered a grungy-looking large room where men sat alone or in groups at regular tavern tables. Except for two waitresses, there were no women in this establishment. The décor was functional: a bar with half a dozen stools, several small neon signs on the wall advertising various brands of beer. There were ceiling fans, and a large cigarette machine. Charlie was an avid smoker and always seemed to be plunking coins into these contrivances.

I noticed immediately that most of the customers were seated at tables facing a large television screen snugly placed in one corner. Charlie and I sat at one of these tables and ordered beer.

It soon became evident to me that what was being screened was a pornographic film. I had heard of these movies, had heard friends talk about them, knew of the ongoing debate in the media about the admissibility of such films in a free society. But I had never seen a pornographic film until that night.

A succession of acts of acrobatic sexuality was unveiled before my eyes. A nude man with two nude women, interacting to the sounds of groans and whimpers, then two naked women entwined, breasts and crotches exposed. It went on and on. There were no limits to what the camera beheld: visions so blatant they defied description.

I wondered why Charlie had brought me to this specific tavern. I supposed that he considered it a part of my education, that I should be exposed to this exhibition of debauchery. This was all about life in the big city of Montreal. He felt that I should be informed, perhaps.

Even if I wasn't headed for sainthood, I did not want my wandering on the seedy side of Montreal to ever get back to my parents, and I also hoped that my cousin Charlie would not become addicted to strip joints and porn, something he tended to joke about—a trait far removed from the innocence of his childhood.

Yet I survived, and was lined up at the college arena the next morning registering for my first term courses with the hundreds of other students, male and female. It was my first experience studying in the same class with undergraduates of the other variety.

I had been accepted into second year of college because of the Senior Matriculation I had completed after high school.

I decided that I wanted to major in Political Science, exposed to the historical and social machinations of Machiavellian figures practising power politics. I credited my interest in this topic directly to Tommy Kelly, who had stirred in me an unending curiosity about politics; and to my father, whose voracious consumption of historical data had fed a similar inclination in me. But I would use my elective courses to study art and design. I hoped to stay as far away as possible from math and chemistry, subjects for which I felt I could not develop a great love. I wanted to improve my drawing ability, a skill that I felt would serve me well for the rest of my life, since I could not imagine living without being able to conceptualize my view of reality on paper or canvas.

I was positively amazed on the morning of my first drawing class when I walked into the studio with a dozen or so other students, male and female, to see a nude girl sitting on a stool at the front of the room. After Professor and artist Jeremy Cohen introduced himself, he went on to say that any venture in sketching or painting a subject sans model was an invitation to failure, and what subject has more allure, variation, and complexity than the human body? This was very typical of Jeremy Cohen. He was always full of surprises and brought us to the strangest places, to visualize life in a big city and sketch in a real environment. I loved the guy.

I did not have a clear view of what I wanted to do with my life as yet. I still had not considered art as a career possibility, although I knew that I was the most at peace while involved in the solitary craft of sketching and painting. My father had encouraged me to follow my academic interests while choosing my courses, reminding me that I should be developing a set of skills that would allow me to be successful in finding employment. I can't really say that I followed his advice, but I was searching.

Mrs. Louise Taschereau, the woman at whose house I had rented a room, was a widow. She had converted the basement of her duplex into an apartment that she rented out to a young bachelor who worked in downtown Montreal. The other section of the duplex was being leased to a professional couple. These people provided her with some income.

My room in Mrs. Taschereau's section was on the main floor close to the kitchen. She proved to be a very generous soul who treated me like a son almost from the day I moved in. The room was sizeable and had a large desk that had been used by her husband. I had kitchen privileges provided that I "cleaned up after using the utilities and utensils," in the words of Mrs. Taschereau. I could not avoid having a great liking for her as the school year advanced. She always had breakfast ready for me on school days. On the weekends I had to help myself. We watched the television news together after suppertime on many evenings. She demanded that I let her know if I did not plan to show up for evening meals. I had a key to the front door and could come and go as I pleased. All in all, we had a near ideal arrangement. I was a sort of amateur cook, specializing in a few dishes. On the odd occasion, I would prepare a meal for us, the result of my days working at the restaurant in Quebec City, where I had made the acquaintance of a few chefs. She was absolutely thrilled when I did this, of course.

But Mrs. Taschereau was a lonely woman. She had had no children. Her sole companionship with other people consisted of her Sunday attendance at Mass and, fortunately, she served on some of the parish committees, going to the odd evening meeting at the church. She longed to speak about her life with her husband. He had been a judge in the Municipal Court, mostly dealing with infractions to the city's ordinances. They had travelled extensively, to Europe, to Asia, to South America. Mrs. Taschereau felt it necessary to tell me about her trips abroad and offered to show me a series of slides on more than one occasion. I found it rather difficult to listen to her for lengthy periods of time and kept looking for original excuses to drag myself away from these one-sided conversations and back to my room to study or perhaps do a little sketching.

Mrs. Taschereau also suffered from arthritis, which did not restrict her movements but which, she claimed, kept her awake at night. She told me once that she feared the night and she feared the pain and the fear of the pain. It did not take long for her to confide in me in this manner. I began to wonder why she did not seem to have relatives to give her support in her pain and loneliness. I supposed that her plight was not altogether unusual for older people in a large city. I once again realized how fortunate I was, emanating from a large extended family and clan.

It is within the purview of a criminal lawyer, whether that lawyer is a prosecutor or a defence attorney, to use all methods available to successfully plead a case. Yet the prosecution in a case is not necessarily seeking a conviction, but laying before the court all the evidence in a fair manner.

The jury members themselves, often described as "the peers of the defendant," are not necessarily the most suitable people to make vital judgements. When the members of a jury are chosen, who is to know which one can be easily swayed or cowed, which one will lead and which one will follow and sheepishly acquiesce?

There is little doubt that we have, in some instances, seen miscarriages of justice in the courts. Defendants have been found guilty and condemned to death on the basis of flimsy and circumstantial evidence. It would be naïve to think that juries in these cases were not manipulated.

There is also the uneven balance that exists in the courts between the weight of the prosecution and the weight of the defence. The auxiliary assets available to the Crown seem to be endless, with the law and the government and the police and the logistics lined up behind their witnesses. On the opposite side, the defence lawyer, in some cases, stands alone. The sheer magnitude of strength he faces in the court can easily discourage the solitary defence advocate. He will often throw up his hands at the overpowering resources of the Crown and submit to the forces opposing him.

Defendants have been the targets of an uneven array of legal power in the Canadian justice system. Accused people have been condemned to death after trials where the insurmountable contrivances of the Crown attorneys have totally overwhelmed the defence. Defence tactics have been incompetent.

In the case of the Crown versus Michael Ferrigan, Defence Lawyer Gerald Nolan's dilemma lay in how he could convince the jury that his client did not desire the death of the victim, Patrick Connors. In this instance, the situation was pretty straightforward. Here was a man accused of a deadly act of violence, a man who had previously been involved in an affray of ghastly proportions, a man who had been seen by witnesses to shoot his neighbour dead in the full glare of daylight. He had admitted, to the police, to having shot the victim. To attack as false the notion that his client had maliciously sought the death of the victim did not resonate with the jury.

Gerald Nolan had considered pleading "temporary insanity" in his client's cause. He decided that this tack would not have worked out. Michael Ferrigan was a prosperous farmer in many ways, running a smooth operation, in relative terms, and doing a seemingly good job in raising his brood. True, there had been incidents of irrational behaviour among members of his family, but these patterns of his siblings' conduct would not likely have held much sway. Michael Ferrigan was an ambitious farmer who was not likely to come across to a jury as an insane man.

Attorney Gerald Nolan was unsuccessful in his bid to convince the Appeal Court to order a new trial for Michael Ferrigan. The court did not see the logic of reopening a case where a man with a violent past had killed for the second time.

The defence lawyer therefore threw all his efforts into having Michael Ferrigan's date with death commuted to a life sentence.

He pursued his case as far as the Supreme Court of Canada. His appeals to powerful political and religious leaders were passionate and heart-rending.

But all of these attempts failed. The government and the law had to be served. The courts of law had to continue to assert themselves as the ultimate authority of the land. If a citizen broke this law, he had to pay the penalty. Michael Ferrigan was an honest farmer and the father of ten children. But there was no room for compromise when it came to the killing of another citizen "without provocation."

For the Ferrigan family, Christmas of 1952 was a bleak and depressing occasion. In his final days in Quebec City before moving to death row in Montreal, Michael Ferrigan received visits from his wife Maggie and several of the children. He spoke of his unfortunate position and again reiterated that if times had been good he would have sold his farm and moved away. He seemed to be greatly affected by the visits of his young ones.

Michael Ferrigan never gave up on his contention that he had been placed in an untenable position with regard to his fence and property. He claimed to most visitors that some of his neighbours had purposely left the gap in his fence, annoying him greatly.

Yet he seemed to be very repentant for causing the death of his cousin, Paddy Connors. He had had no intention whatsoever to end the life of the victim. It had been a grievous mistake on his part to inadvertently kill him, he declared repeatedly.

Now seeing the hopelessness of his cause, he turned to prayer, welcoming the visits of his spiritual advisor and rising during the night to kneel by his cot in supplication. As a member of the community of Pine River, he had not been in attendance at Sunday church services very often, yet he saw to it that his older children were.

As an inmate at the prison, he was on very good terms with the guards. He spoke to them freely about his feelings and about how nervous he felt about his future. The guards tried to make his cell as comfortable as possible and allowed him to walk in the yard frequently. He did not object to the rules of the jail, expressing gratitude to the guards for the treatment he received. Indeed, some of them told him that they were praying for him, invoking a wish that his sentence would be commuted to life imprisonment. They told him not to give up hope and cited examples of other condemned people escaping the gallows even at the last minute.

The officers in contact with Michael Ferrigan during his last days at the Quebec City jail saw him as a quiet man with a co-operative mentality, and nowhere close to the violent brute described in some press copy. His spiritual advisors, especially the youthful Father Quinn of the "Irish" parish, had visited Michael Ferrigan when Father McDonald was not available. They were seen to be in prayer together on these occasions.

Yet, there were periods when he would grow sullen and take on a depressed look. It was as if he were harbouring a deep secret within himself, revealed in a spurt of thought, perhaps, that would suddenly rise to the surface.

It must have been difficult for him to understand how he could have slipped into these wanton acts of violence. He had been given many attributes—strength, good health, and virility. What had gone wrong?

Chapter 18

Michael Ferrigan's great-grandfather on his father's side, a hale broth of a young man named Vincent, came to Canada in 1822. He eventually married Irene Duffy, whose family had also emigrated from County Kilkenny in Ireland. Not surprisingly, these two families, the Duffys and the Ferrigans, had known each other in Ireland, having lived close together near the village of Ballyhale, not far from the River Nore, and now here they were, neighbours on a new continent, thousands of miles from the land of their birth.

There seemed to have been little squabbling between families during their early days in Pine River. Survival was the first item on their agenda. But this new land was a far cry from what they had grown up with in Ireland, where to be Catholic was anathema, where the Irish language had been forbidden, and where the masses of people lived on farms with very small acreage, subsisting on what they could cultivate—the potato being the main means of sustenance. In North America, there seemed to be little reason for agrarian people to be filled with centuries-old hatreds. For hundreds of years the politicians of England had worked their subterfuge on the Irish, depriving them of their heritage in land, culture, and religion. But for the Irish immigrants, at least in Pine River, there was little discrimination in their new terra firma. The early years of settlement were challenging and harsh, but the initial support system of the Seigneury was benevolent and humane.

Yet some of the Irish who emigrated to the New World came with the baggage of a centuries-old bitterness, easily transformed into a willingness to indulge in retribution against enemies, real or supposed. The influx of Irish into the bowels of the larger cities of America, people released from the age-old rebellion and insurrection of the old country, was not necessarily welcomed. The

Irish were looked down upon as uneducated louts. Work was difficult for them to find. There were many signs on the walls of factories that read "Irish Need Not Apply." They had to compete for jobs, menial though these jobs might be. They were not altogether innocent, but capable of brutish and lethal acts. Strangely enough, it was this isolation that enabled them to gain political power within the confines of their residential areas. After decades of struggle, the Irish were able to assert themselves as a strong political force in municipal and state politics, and later on the national scene.

How can the actions of a Michael Ferrigan be explained? Why did he harbour such a deep-rooted affiliation with violence that he was able to hack one fellow resident to death and shoot a second one in cold blood?

At the dockside in Cork in July of 1822, "Big Vince" Ferrigan was seen off by his parents and cousins on the brig *Town of Ross*, a two-mast ship used to transport lumber from Lower Canada to the British Isles. This craft was headed back to America for another load of timber, a commodity in endless supply, it appeared. It was customary for the captain to fill the empty spaces on the ship, including the hold, with passengers who, for a reasonable fee and in unreasonable conditions, could make their way to the New World. Luckily, this voyage across the Atlantic Ocean happened to be free of the vile afflictions that later assaulted the passengers during the Great Potato Famine. Yet the crossing was not altogether smooth. Most of the Irish passengers, inexperienced with sea travel, lived in great fear of shipwreck and some spent much time in prayer during the wild storms that seemed so frequent during the passage. The captain would assure them of the safety of the sails and rigging and was known to have said, "How can you be in fear when you have the *Town of Ross* at your feet?"

The eight-week voyage thankfully completed, the ship docked at Quebec City, one of the chief entry ports in North America. After passing customs and registering with officials of the host country, those Irish newcomers seeking to be tenant farmers would be introduced to agents of the Seigneur, a man seeking to have his land developed.

A strong young man, Vince Ferrigan was known to have walked from the docks of Quebec City to the St. Patrick's Mission, a distance of over twenty miles. He first began working as a woodcutter and logger. After several years he married into the Duffy family and was accepted as a tenant farmer with a generous acquisition of over 200 acres from the office of the Seigneur. Thus began the genealogy of the Ferrigans in the Pine River region. There were soon children in the hearth, Vince and Irene eventually becoming parents of seven, four boys and three girls. One of the older boys, Edmund, managed to acquire his own acreage next to his father's farm when he grew to be a man, after practising the logger's trade as his father had done. Edmund was the grandfather of Michael Ferrigan. Two of the daughters of Vincent married within the Pine River community. The other children grew up and left home to make their way to the New England area of the United States, where they married and raised their families. When Vincent died, Edmund inherited his father's land, now a homestead of over 400 acres, with the adjacent piece of land. After his marriage to Helen Hewitt, Edmund fathered two sons and three daughters. His elder son, Thomas, who had stayed on the farm with his father, came into ownership when Edmund died. Thomas Ferrigan was the father of Michael Ferrigan, who grew to be a man of impressive proportions. Two daughters of Thomas were also married in the church at Pine River, although both of them later left with their husbands to live in Montreal. Three brothers and two sisters of Michael Ferrigan remained in the Pine River area.

From all indications, the father of Michael Ferrigan was a stern but hard-working man who maintained a rigid hold over the activities of his children. All were put to work on the farm, and had duties from the time they were quite young. As a farmer, Thomas Ferrigan ran a successful endeavour, raising cattle and pigs, earning a fair income from these ventures. But it was also said of him that he would not hesitate to "put the leather" to both his sons and daughters at the first hint of misbehaviour. Ironically, one of his daughters was strongly encouraged to marry because of a pregnancy, induced while she was being courted. There were rumours that Thomas Ferrigan had made veiled threats to his daughter's suitor to ensure the young man was willing to fulfil his obligations in the matter. Many said that this daughter and another younger one moved away with their husbands due to the malevolence in his personality.

Had he lived to see it, Thomas Ferrigan would have observed that his sons could not successfully blend into a sociable light-heartedness within their community. A statement had been sworn in the office of a magistrate that his son James had demonstrated streaks of insanity on several occasions, residents having to enter his house more than once to help keep the peace after he had assaulted members of his own family. The youngest son of Thomas Ferrigan, Patrick, was arrested for the attempted murder of a co-worker.

And then, of course, there was Michael Ferrigan, the inheritor of the farm, a man who seemed to have fallen heir to some of the characteristics of his father, but to a more explosive degree.

Still, with all the baggage that Thomas Ferrigan had left to his children, there is little there to allow us to understand the extremes of violence shown by his son Michael.

Mercifully, Thomas Ferrigan passed away before much of this heinous behaviour surfaced.

My own father, a fifth-generation descendant of Pine River, began teaching high school—mainly History and Literature—in the first year that I went to college, 1956. A prodigious reader, his immersion in the study of the past had reached a sort of culmination for him. Now he could expound daily on a subject that was dear to his heart.

Mom had her first "vernissage" that same year, a showing of about 25 oil paintings, almost all for sale. I took the train down to Quebec City and was so proud of her, watching her talk about her work with all the people who came to the studio that she had rented for an afternoon. I believe that she sold most of her paintings. Many of the oils depicted scenes from Pine River, and my father had Irish music playing in the background during the showing. For a price, the studio catered in wine, cheese, and some finger food. It was a great event, although my mom said that she didn't make a lot of profit from the show. Both my dad and I told her that she should mark up the prices of her work, that she was a little too humble and self-deprecating.

My maternal grandparents still lived in Verdun, a satellite city of Montreal. My mother had prodded me to pay them a visit, which I did one Saturday evening. They lived in a second storey walk-up, one of thousands of flats in three-floor, balcony-tiered row houses.

"So why didn't you bring your stuff down here and stay with us, Francis?" George Lawson, my grandfather, said. "You could have taken Gordie's room. It's just sitting there waiting for someone."

He was a diminutive man with a great sense of humour.

"Well, my place is very close to school, so it's pretty handy for me," I said.

My grandmother, Meg Lawson, sat perched on a little padded straight-backed chair as we chatted in their small living room. She nodded when her husband spoke, uttering soft sounds of agreement. She'd suffered a stroke a few years before and had lost her ability to speak clearly. They were both small, wispy people whose three children had grown up in that same Verdun flat, but were now many miles away from their parents, my mother being the closest and at least still living in the province of Quebec. My grandmother Meg seemed to catch all of my grandfather's barbs and snickered right on cue. She was soon on her feet preparing snacks, moving slowly but resolutely, and casting regular glances back at me. She was obviously willing to indulge me, having previously heard that I was attending college in Montreal.

I could not remember having seen them more than a few times, social visits having been postponed by my grandmother's illness. But they always had been very generous to me and my brothers and sister, sending us postal money orders for our birthdays and at Christmas time. And we all did speak to them on the phone occasionally.

"So you don't see very much of your children any more," I said.

"Well, your mother is good to us, thank God. But we know that she has her own family to raise so we appreciate her telephone calls. But Gordie and Brian are both out west, so it's a little hard for them to visit. It's like a funeral parlour around here much of the time."

And my grandfather was off to the kitchen and returned with two pints of beer. This was rather unusual because my own father had never offered me a beer at home.

"Come on, Francis. You're old enough to be havin' a beer," my grandfather said.

My grandfather had lots of good stories and jokes about the provincial government, Premier Duplessis, and the local politics of Verdun. He was quite amused when I told him that I was studying political science. He said that politics could be brought down to a few basic truths, among them "power corrupts, and absolute power corrupts absolutely." I felt that this adage, coming from him, was likely part of his comic repertoire. Yet, I could not help but value his judgement; he was a working man who had spent his married life in a rented flat but was a keen observer of the political scene.

We watched the hockey game on the small black-and-white television set that they had. We talked about hockey during most of the game and I had a few more beers. When I left the flat after the game ended, I was a little woozy but managed to take the correct tram to get back home. I slipped into my room quietly, then realized I had to use the bathroom, literally creeping down the short hallway, hoping that I wouldn't awaken Mrs. Taschereau who, I was sure, could have smelt the beer on me had she come close to me. But I always had the feeling that she knew exactly when I came in, and in what condition I was.

My contacts, mostly by mail, with Marianne Connors were rather unsettled during my first term of college. She was in her last year of high school. She talked about going to Nursing School, perhaps in Montreal, when she graduated. Her letters were informative, but not very confiding or affectionate. I had no idea what she was doing or with whom she was keeping company. My thoughts about her were not as frequent, although I still imagined her with me, walking down some street, hand in hand. I missed her company but somehow refrained from telling her in so many words, perhaps because I was a little vexed about our disparate situations—something I was mainly responsible for.

From my father I kept hearing that Tommy Kelly was rewriting the record book of football stats in his last year of high school. His school team had won its first few games by lopsided scores, Tommy having thrown about ten touchdown passes. I was a little envious of him—one of the big heroes of the school now, an excellent role model for the younger students. I missed him a lot, and looked forward to the following September when he would register at McGill University in pre-Med.

But were Tommy and Marianne seeing a lot of each other? I had no way of knowing.

It would have been nice to have Marianne visit me in Montreal where I could have shown her around, but that was a lot to ask of a girl still in high school and whose presence was required at her home.

My courses at the college took some getting used to, with the professors having a laid-back attitude that said, "It's up to you to do what needs to be done." The teachers I had had in high school had taken a more hands-on approach, always aware of how well you were doing, and what assignment you had missed, and making sure that hockey was not interfering with your academic results. We were spoiled and coddled by the lay teachers and the Brothers. They saw, in the academic success of their students, a vindication of their efforts. But at the college level there was a less personalized association between the students and teachers.

After several weeks, well into the routine of getting into my courses at various buildings in the college complex, I began to hit it off with some of the other students. I had definitely decided that I was not going to play hockey that year. One of the results of this decision was that my friendships would develop from my interest in other activities at the college. Not surprisingly I began to gravitate to the college newspaper, where I got involved in doing some of the graphics, putting the paper together for each bi-monthly issue, working with the editor. The main reason for this particular involvement was my friendship with David McAuslin, a kid from Griffintown in Montreal. I used to sit near him during some of the political science classes and we got to talking one day about hockey. He'd been through what he called "the hockey mill," trying out for various teams in the hierarchical structure throughout the Montreal area and having vague hopes of making it to the NHL. But he had decided to abandon all of that when other interests got in the way, and now he wanted to be a sports writer or broadcaster.

So David and I had a lot to talk about. We also worked on many of the newspaper preparations, he doing the writing and I helping to set all the articles in place as well as doing some cartooning on the editorial page. It was usually a twelve-page production and it took a considerable amount of our time to meet the deadline. We had a small room in one of the annexes where everything was done with a staff of eight students, six guys and two girls. David and I were the junior members of the staff, yet we felt, after a few months of helping with the paper, that we had a lot of independence in how we worked. David was certainly the best writer on the paper and I did things no one else seemed interested in doing, so we were self-governing.

Unfortunately, after we closed the newspaper office, most of the staff headed down to one of the bars and, with all the talking and arguing and haggling, wasted a lot of time that could have been used otherwise. But that was not unusual for a university experience, I suppose, and when I look back on it I now realize how preoccupied and contented and carefree I was.

Sonia Martel was one of the girls on our newspaper staff. She was a native Montrealer, having been raised in the western end of the city where most of the anglophone population lived. Sonia was petite with curly blond hair and blue eyes. She would accompany us down to our favourite watering hole, but tended to stay out of the animated discussions on politics and sports. Yet she laughed a lot at what was said, acting as a sort of audience for the "macho dimwits," as she referred to us on a few occasions. The guys were all crazy about her and her sardonic sense of humour. She was a full-time student and held a part-time job, yet still managed to find the energy to work at the newspaper. During editorial meetings she contributed a lot of good ideas and seemed to have easy access to the academic faculty heads and the administration of the school. So she was indispensable as far as the paper was concerned. Cute as she was, I could not imagine the brass turning her away if she wanted an interview about school policy. She seemed to have a gift for public relations and never got on anyone's nerves, as far as we could tell. So the editor, Jake Zella, was happy to have her around.

On one cool Friday evening, well into October, I was headed back to my room when I met Sonia on the street near the college.

"Francis? Francis?" I heard this voice calling from the opposite sidewalk of Sherbrooke Street.

"Oh, hi Sonia!" I yelled. And I ran across the street in heavy traffic, dodging my way between cars.

"Well, you didn't have to take your life in your hands," she said when I reached her side.

"Oh, God! You're right!" I said.

"So where you heading?" she asked.

"I was going home to study. I'm about a month behind in my reading. And you?"

"I just got off my shift at the coffee shop."

"Oh! I thought we could have a cup of coffee together."

"Sure, why not, Mr. Carroll? I been serving coffee all afternoon! Why shouldn't I want to see another cup of coffee?"

I'd come to discover that when she called me by my second name, she was trying to make a point.

But still, we did head to a small lunch counter close by and sat side by side on the chrome-coloured stools facing the tall mirror where the food was being prepared. We ordered coffee.

I eventually got around to asking her if she would go to a movie with me. I remember distinctly that Elvis Presley's "Love Me Tender" was playing in the background.

"Are you asking me for a date?" she said.

"I suppose so."

"But we work together. Do you think it's a good idea?"

"It's the best idea I've had since I've come to Montreal."

"I can't see how I can fit such an activity into my busy schedule," she said.

Then she started to giggle.

"Of course, Francis. I'd love to go to the movies with you."

She put her hand over mine and squeezed it a little.

"You're a smart ass, aren't you?" I said.

"You're damn right I am."

We went to see *Lust for Life*, a film about the life of artist Vincent Van Gogh, played by Kirk Douglas. I apologized to Sonia, as we went into the theatre, for dragging her to a movie about a painter, but the production was so beautifully done that I need not have worried. Sonia enjoyed it greatly, especially the performance of Anthony Quinn, who played the artist Paul Gauguin, a role for which he was later awarded an Oscar.

Although I had a great love for good films, I did not get to go very often. There was something subliminally inspiring about sitting in a movie house living out the fantasy of the Hollywood dream-makers. Montreal had quite a few movie theatres, but I had neither the time nor the funds to spend going to the movies. So I kept a close watch on the newspaper reviews of films and selected what I considered to be the best choices.

Sonia and I went to the movies a few times that first term, usually on a Saturday night, her only free evening. We would make arrangements to do this at the college newspaper office.

My “relationship” with Sonia was rather laid-back at first. I appreciated having her company and didn’t expect it to develop into a romance. She invited me to her home at the west end of the city and we sat down and had dinner with her mother and younger brother. Her father had long been divorced from her mother, an independent woman who was a real estate agent.

After dinner, her brother went out and her mother went to bed complaining of being tired, and we were left in the living room watching television. It looked a little bit too convenient not to have been planned.

“Francis?”

“Yes,” I said.

“Do you find me attractive?”

We were seated close together on a small divan.

“Yes, Sonia. I find you very attractive.”

“Well, how is it that you seldom show it?”

“I don’t know. How am I supposed to show it?”

“Well, you could at least try to kiss me.”

‘Oh, all right. I’d like to try that.”

And I put my hand around the back of her neck, drew her close to me, and kissed her on the lips.

Well, we did that for quite a while, and when I took the bus back to my room that night my mouth was a little sore, my lips slightly swollen with the taste and scent of her lipstick still on them. But I’d relished the experience and I had trouble getting to sleep that night, just thinking about it.

It did not take the newspaper crew long to get wind of our little dalliance.

Chapter 19

Michael Ferrigan spent his last evening and night in Quebec City on January 4, 1953. He received a visit from three people. His wife Maggie was accompanied by his younger brother Patrick, who was himself being litigated against due to a shooting incident weeks before and who was out on bail, and by Father James McDonald, Michael Ferrigan's spiritual advisor. The atmosphere in one of the outer rooms where they were allowed to meet was solemn and tear-filled, Maggie Ferrigan always on the edge, a handkerchief frequently dabbing at her eyes. For the most part the meeting was quiet, with a minimum of words exchanged. It seemed difficult to find things to say. While Michael Ferrigan's lawyer, Gerald Nolan, was still trying to get the attention of politicians in Ottawa and promised to do so unrelentingly into the future, the chance of a change of heart on the part of the authorities seemed very unlikely. Maggie promised that she would visit her husband in Montreal as soon as she could make the arrangements. After she and Patrick left, Father McDonald remained with Michael Ferrigan for several minutes, both of their heads bent in prayer.

The condemned man slept fitfully that night, kneeling and praying several times, according to the guards. He rose early, telling one of the other inmates that he felt nervous about departing for Montreal's Bordeaux Jail.

After a breakfast of toast and eggs and tea, Michael Ferrigan was put into a tightly secured black van for the trip to the new jail. The distance to Montreal was over 150 miles. The January sky was still dark as the vehicle departed, the prisoners sitting on the benches perpendicular to the driver and his partner, who were caged off from their passengers. There were two other inmates in the van but they were both French-speaking, so little banter was exchanged between Michael Ferrigan and his fellow travellers. He could speak only a few words in the other language.

For Michael Ferrigan, it was the end of his life as he had known it. He would no longer see his young children. Several were considered too young to travel to Montreal, to a jail where they would be subjected to the vision of a huge structure in which their own father was incarcerated, a man whose presence was sadly fading from their lives.

He felt sealed inside the van, whose small square windows showed only the grey sky as the vehicle raced down the highway. He was a million miles away from the broad fields of his farm, where he had walked in freedom and tranquillity. He'd loved his tractor and had always admired his own adeptness when pulling his machinery, cutting a swath through his hay and oats. But most of all, he would miss his wife and children. She had always been loyal to him—a strong and tenacious woman who saw to the needs of her children without complaint, a woman of incredible energy. He'd consciously tried to treat his young ones with a little patience and gentleness, as far back as he could remember. Down deep inside his soul, he did not want his children to emulate him, with his bursts of anger and his unwillingness to forget old resentments. He knew this about himself but had seemed to be able to do little to change.

As the van approached Montreal, the ride had many stops and starts, waiting for lights to turn green as they made their way through the streets of a large city. The upper windows of tall buildings were visible as the van gradually wound its way to Bordeaux Jail. Near the end of the trip there was the sound of a heavy iron gate opening, guards talking, and then the van moving forward at a lessened speed.

Finally, the van stopped and the engine was cut off. The prisoners could hear the guards disembark from the forward section and begin to unlock the rear door. All three were glad to get out of the van and stretch their legs. As none of the prisoners had been to Bordeaux Jail before, they stood momentarily and gazed up at the bare immensity of the structure.

They were soon marched into the building and were registered and searched. The ominous sound of steel doors opening and closing seemed to permeate the inner surroundings. Everyone talked in French, and Michael Ferrigan understood hardly a word that was said.

The prisoners soon separated, Michael Ferrigan being given a set of clothing and led down a long corridor to a locked-off section—death row. His new cell was a rectangular room with a cot, a toilet, and a table.

He was told to change his clothes. He put on the coveralls he'd been given and was allowed to keep his loafers.

It was in this cell that Michael Ferrigan was to spend the last six days of his life.

Jake Zella, David McAuslin, and I became a sort of triumvirate as far as the newspaper was concerned. Jake was in his last year but he sort of grew on us. He had a quick wit, sending us into fits at times. At the newspaper office, he referred to Dave and me as the "young nitwits." But Jake, the editor of the paper, respected us a lot, treating us like partners. When going to the bar after working at the newspaper office, he claimed he felt guilty about encouraging us, two guys in their late teens, to get "into the sauce" as he called the beer. But both Dave and I enjoyed his company and seldom refused his offer to buy us a round, after which he would say, "And I expect you to buy me a draft right aft."

My courses in Political Science dealt mainly with the study of government and the behaviour of governmental officials in domestic and international relations. We got into the history of political organization, studying Plato and Aristotle and their belief that the structured state could bring out the best in man. We were assigned to read Thomas Hobbes, John Locke, and Rousseau. We were introduced to Niccolo Machiavelli, a diplomat who submitted to the "base techniques in acquiring and retaining political power, much of which involved corruption, fraud, and ruthless force."

Professor Dermott McGrath, who taught two of my credit courses, was an Irishman from Dublin. It was a simple task for the students to steer him away from the esoteric dialectical theory of his forte in political study and divert him to a discussion on the current news events of the day. In late October of that year, there were two issues that dominated the news—the Suez crisis and the Hungarian Revolution.

Abdel Gamal Nasser of Egypt had decided to nationalize the Suez Canal in order to finance the building of the Aswan High Dam. This move seemed to have precipitated Israel to invade Egypt. Israel had not been allowed to use the Suez Canal. In the interest of safeguarding peace in the area, France and Britain ordered Israel and Egypt to cease hostilities. Egypt refused. The north end of the Suez Canal was seized by the Allies, a move which led to much scuttling of ships by Egypt in the canal.

On October 23rd of 1956, the Hungarian people, led by students and workers, sought to break off from the Stalinist grip that the Communist government had on Hungarian life. Some soldiers of the Hungarian army deserted and joined the rebels. After many had died in the fighting, the Russians sent in hundreds of tanks to eventually put down the two-week uprising. The indomitable courage of the rebel fighters against the overwhelming odds of Russian might gave testimony to the will of Hungarians to cast off the influence of Russia in their everyday life. But the insurrection was ill-fated, and finally petered out after a fortnight of struggle. Many Hungarians used this chaotic time to escape from the country. Canada was one of the havens for these refugees.

We spent many sessions in class discussing these events; Professor McGrath actually served on some of the civic groups that helped Hungarian refugees establish new lives in Canada.

Well into fall that first year, I was getting low on funds and knew that I had to be cautious about my spending habits. I wanted to avoid going to my parents to tide me over for the remainder of the school year. Spending money on beer had not figured into my financial planning when I had prepared for college. I would have done better to spend more time on my studies and less time socializing. My cousin Charlie Carroll called me quite frequently to inquire if I was available to join him at the Rymark's Tavern after he finished work. I did meet him on one occasion but our evening together consisted of swilling a half-dozen drafts of beer for a period of several hours and then staggering to the tram for the ride home. Charlie had tried to convince me to accompany him down to one of the strip joints toward the east end of St. Catherine Street. But I had promised myself that I would stay away from him for a while, even if both he and Lawrence had been very generous to me.

There was also Sonia. She usually worked three shifts a week at a small restaurant–lunch counter not far from the college, fitting in her courses outside of her work hours. Her mother sold houses for a living and struggled to make ends meet, although the family lived in a neat bungalow on a tree-lined street. Sonia's father was a dedicated alcoholic who had divorced her mother years before and who was not able to help his children in any way.

I can honestly say that my relationship with Sonia was distracting from the start. But I had gotten myself into the entanglement, and I began to plot ways to extricate myself from her growing dependence on my company. She was very pretty and petite, and I began noticing how people gave her second looks wherever we went. She made frequent calls to me while I was trying to get my work done at my room. Mrs. Taschereau would look at me askance after she answered a phone call for me, disfavouring that familiar "sweet" voice asking if I was available. In a way, I suppose I agreed with my landlady. Sonia's incessant calls were overkill.

But on the other hand, I had become somewhat obsessed with Sonia and the intimacy that we had quickly developed with each other. She was in her second year of college, majoring in psychology. Over time I, unfortunately, got to feel that she was always trying to psychoanalyze our relationship, and my feelings, and her feelings, and how we should explore the depths of our "consciousness" with each other. Whenever she invited me to her house it was with the stipulation that I should be ready to "come across." She wanted to be held and kissed and caressed and coddled. Conditions for this always seemed to be ideal, with her mother pulling a disappearing act and her brother seldom at home. Sonia began to tell me that she wanted to "relate to me." At first, I did not know what this meant, and when its meaning did dawn on me, I was floored.

So I would not have described our first full sexual encounter as spontaneous. Rather, it was a planned and awkward manoeuvre on the small divan of her living room. Had I been involved in a test of sexual expertise, I certainly would have been ranked at the bottom of the class. Sonia was not helpful in our endeavour. She talked the whole time, for the ten minutes or so that it went on, fully alert and devoid of any extraordinary expression of feeling, telling me not to worry, making sure that my "protection," which she had somehow provided, was on properly. I felt that I had failed miserably in showing her what a stud I was. I had not performed with any degree of savoir-faire whatsoever. To top it off, I had given my "unsullied" self to her, a girl who had relinquished her virginity years before, I suspected. Not that I was the saint and she was the sinner, or anything like that. But I certainly had been the buffoon.

"Did you find that satisfying, Francis?" she said afterwards.

"Yes, of course. I was just afraid that someone would walk in the door, like your kid brother."

"Oh, he's gone for the weekend, didn't I tell you?"

"No. Perhaps you should have."

"Did I please you?"

"Yes, of course you did."

"Do you still respect me, Francis?"

"Yes. How can you even ask that question?"

In mid-November, I got another call from my cousin Charlie Carroll, who wanted to have a beer with me at a new Irish pub that had opened in one of the hotels in downtown Montreal. At first I declined, telling Charlie that I had a lot of reading to do and assignments to complete.

"I want you to meet somebody," Charlie said..

"Not a girl I hope, Charlie, 'cause I'm seeing somebody right now."

"No, no. This is a guy that you'd love to meet, I'm sure," he said.

"Well, who is it?"

"You'll have to come down and meet him to find out."

"You're not kidding me, I hope,"

"No, Francis. This'll be a real surprise for you."

So I took the trolley down to the centre of Montreal and walked into the York Hotel to a cosy little pub they had fitted into the first floor.

Charlie was sitting with someone else at one of the tables set in the corner of the bar, the sound of an Irish reel giving the atmosphere a little authenticity.

As I approached the table, they both stood up.

"Francis! Great to see you!" Charlie said enthusiastically and shook my hand.

"Good to see you, Charlie," I said.

Then I looked at the young man who stood next to Charlie, a lad of well over six feet with the thick shoulders of an athlete.

"Francis, this is Joey Ferrigan."

"Hi, Joey," I said, shaking hands with him, but not making the connection as yet.

"Pleased to meet you, Francis, but we've seen each other before at a distance," he said.

As we all sat down together, it suddenly hit me.

"My God," I said. "How did you two find each other?"

"Oh, I've known his older brother since we were kids. Right, Joey?"

"Yeah, Charlie had a crush on my oldest sister," said Joey, "so he was hanging around the house a lot."

"C'mon, Joey. Kathy was just an infant!" protested Charlie.

They both laughed.

What could I say to Joey Ferrigan?

"I'm sorry about what you had to go through, Joey," I remarked.

"Well, it's been hard on my mom and the family. But what could we do? We just had to accept it," he said.

"You know, Joey, that day we saw each other will always be on my mind," I said.

"Yeah, well, I had no idea what had gone on before I got to my dad's fence that morning. I met Mr. Connors with his two children on the track, but he just said hello and walked on. I remember that I could see my dad far up the track near the house, but he didn't tell me that there was an argument with Mr. Connors. I told my dad that I had seen you and Tommy Kelly up on that grade but he didn't make much of it at the time."

"It's quite a while ago now, but I can picture you looking up at us just as if it happened yesterday."

"Yeah, I've got a fairly clear memory of it too," Joey said.

"So, are you working in Montreal, Joey?" I asked.

"I'm working down at the railway shop doing maintenance on the cars and engines. I'm learning the ropes. I'm going to school at night to try and qualify myself so that I can go to college, but it's gonna be a long haul for me."

Joey Ferrigan was a clear-eyed young man with a short haircut, dressed casually, with the already thick arms of a blue-collar worker. I was deeply impressed with him and his friendly demeanour. He had obviously come a long way in a very short time. He appeared on the surface to have been little affected by losing his father. He had gone through a horrendous experience along with his siblings, several of whom were still pre-teens. His mother and older brother were running the farm, two of the girls now graduated from high school and working in Quebec City.

Charlie, Joey, and I talked for a good while, drinking dark Guinness and listening to the live music of three musicians who sang many of the popular Irish folk songs, the genre of music that was beginning to pick up momentum. It turned out to be a memorable evening. This was an improvement over the previous evenings I had spent with Charlie Carroll, drinking and laughing like idiots at the most inane commentaries made by Charlie himself and his cohorts, mostly about sports and the fragilities of politicians. It was all great fun but a total waste of time.

But I wanted to get together with Joey Ferrigan, just the two of us, where I could talk to him about the aftermath of his father's departure. So I made sure that I had Joey's telephone number before I went home that night. He seemed to be similarly interested in talking to me. We seemed to have struck a chord, as I came to realize during the evening, as Joey paid close attention to everything that I said.

How the young son of the convicted Michael Ferrigan could have turned out to be so affable and gracious was a mystery to me. After I had heard all the talk about the elder Ferrigan, I had a fixed idea in my mind of a violent and contentious man, a father who would surely pass on similar traits to his children. But this notion could not have been further from the truth.

I met Joey Ferrigan at the same pub about two weeks later, just a few days before the first term of school ended and as I was about to go home for the Christmas break. He loved the Irish folk music as much as I did, and talked about how he was collecting LPs of many of the Irish singers.

We gradually got around to talking about the days of the trial and the execution of his father.

"It was very hard at the beginning," said Joey. "My little brother and sister cried for weeks, if not months, calling out for their father. Little Patrick would stamp his feet on the floor, angrily, demanding that my mom go and get his father. But, of course, we older kids knew that he was not coming back. My dad may have had his faults, but my mom will never forgive the government for putting him to death. After the shooting, I saw him just twice at the Quebec prison."

"You must have a deep dislike for all the people who testified against him," I said.

That included me, but I didn't have the courage to ask for Joey's forgiveness.

"No. What my dad did was wrong, wrong, wrong. I knew Paddy Connors. I went to school with his daughter, Marianne, and little Hughie. My father made a terrible mistake."

"What was that incident that came out in the trial, about you giving Marianne a hard time at the village school?"

"I don't remember any of that. I thought she was pretty cute and I think I pulled her pig-tails a few times."

"What were you thinking when you saw Tommy and me that morning? I know you stopped running and looked up at us for a minute."

"You know, I was wondering who you were. I mean, I knew you were Mike Carroll's nephew from Quebec, but I wasn't sure which of the brothers you were. But I'd heard that you were a pretty good hockey player, so I was curious. Of course, I knew you were with Tommy Kelly but I didn't know him that well, I didn't chum around with him."

"You didn't go to school in Quebec City, did you?"

"No, my mom sort of home-schooled the boys after we completed grade six at the village school. She's been to high school. But my dad needed me on the farm that last year. Anyway, I'm still studying at night to get my high school diploma. I think I'll be a high school graduate next year if everything goes all right."

"So I guess it's a hard thing to live with, I mean, knowing that your own father has been executed."

"Yes, it's very difficult for all of us, especially my mom. When we talk about it now, we feel that many things did not come out during the trial."

"What do you mean?"

"Well, my dad was sort of off kilter, in many ways, especially in the last few years of his life. He thought that the whole world was against him. My dad used to go into his bedroom and talk to himself quite loud. We could all hear him, speaking in a sort of gibberish that we couldn't follow. We were too embarrassed to speak to him about it. My mom would go into the bedroom to be with him and the loud rant would stop. But we didn't speak to anyone about this. Sometimes my dad would have that vacant look in his eyes and a worried look on his face as if he was carrying a tremendous weight on his shoulders. Of course, I didn't know any better about that stuff at the time but it did worry my mother, I remember. Sometimes I'd walk into the stable and hear conversation, but then I'd realize that my dad was talking to himself. So, in a way, I was a little scared and I did my best to please him and do what he said. He was always sending me down to the field to see if the fence was still up. On some days, I must have gone down four or five times. It was crazy.

"My Uncle Jimmy," Joey went on, "was a bad influence on my dad when he came over to the house. He was always telling my dad that the O'Mearas were out to get him, that they probably were responsible for getting people to leave the fence down when they passed. Uncle Jimmy would say nasty things about some of the neighbours and curse them. But my mom said that Uncle Jimmy had his own demons and wasn't always right in the head."

"Did you feel that all this should have come out at the trial?"

"I think it might have allowed the courts to at least commute his sentence. My dad was very unbalanced and probably suffered from some mental disorder. That's what my mom says now."

"So why didn't his lawyer pick up on this?"

"My mom says she spoke to the lawyer about it, but he decided not to go with an insanity plea, or a temporary insanity plea. If Dad had been able to get another trial, then I think it would have come out."

"What sort of memories do you have about your dad?"

"You know, he was tough with us. He treated the boys differently. With the girls, he could kid around a lot, teasing them about things. He loved the farm. He would walk around the fields in the spring as if he was seeing everything for the first time. He just loved to be on his tractor, pulling a load of something across the property. He was a proud farmer. My dad was also a good mechanic and he loved tinkering around with the tractor and the thresher and the combine and all the other equipment. He taught me and my older brother Stephen a lot about machines."

"How did he get on some peoples' bad side, because there seemed to be bad blood between him and some of his neighbours?"

"A lot of people never forgave him for the killing of the O'Meara guy. But he didn't seem to feel guilty about it. But, you know, how can we be sure? He kept all of that inside him. He never talked about the past that I can remember. He did write me a few letters from prison. I still have them. Francis, if you're interested, you could have a look at them."

I felt privileged and intrigued that he would offer to show me some of Michael Ferrigan's last letters. I supposed that Joey and I had grown close to each other even if we'd met only a few times.

We sat and drank more Guinness and talked about the Irish folk music. Joey seemed to be easy-going, with an uncommon humility for such a big, strong-looking kid. It was easy to warm up to him.

Chapter 20

After their father had disappeared from their lives, life and work for the Ferrigan offspring had to continue. On the cold winter mornings the children would go down the road to the village school. The older daughters, who went to school in town, would be driven to the railway station by their older brother. The cows had to be milked and supplied with feed in the stable. After the frigid nights, Maggie Ferrigan would start the wood stove for the day. She was thankful, in a way, for the winter. It gave the family some isolation from the neighbours, some of whom she would meet on her trips to the grocery store. They tended to greet her in a detached manner, avoiding her eyes. The railway path was closed during the winter, the amount of snow too cumbersome to move on a regular basis. As a result, few people passed close to the Ferrigan household, just the odd car travelling up the main roadway. Though they did not feel they were treated like pariahs, the Ferrigan clan did withdraw from certain social activities in the community. Maggie Ferrigan, beaten down by the judicial system, still managed to maintain her spirit and strength for the sake of her children. Rumours circulated that she planned to sell her holdings and move away, but that didn't turn out to be correct.

Joey Ferrigan was a young man who poured out his heart to you once you got to know him. It was his way, I suppose, of exorcising his deep revulsion for a legal system that took his father away from himself and his nine siblings.

Ten days before Christmas of that year I took the bus back to Quebec City for the holiday break. I had never before been away from my family for months, so it really felt strange to be bunking in with my younger brothers again. They both were big guys now, playing hockey and football at the high school. The rented flat was, at that time, too small and cramped for four men. My mom and dad were in the process of buying a house to move into that coming spring. My kid sister Eileen was eleven years old and she wanted a bigger room for herself and not the tiny-windowed "closet" she slept in at the flat.

I wasn't back home more than a few hours when there was a phone call for me from Marianne Connors. I had written to her that I was coming home on that date. She still had a few days of school before the Christmas break. I asked her if she could plan to stay at her aunt's in town for that coming weekend, but she said that she had commitments at the farm even if it was winter, helping her mother with the chores. It was very hard for her to just take a few days off. It didn't seem practical for us to meet until she'd finished school for the term. So I resolved to get out to Pine River to see her when the holidays started.

I did meet up with Jackie Farrell who was attending school at St. Francis Xavier University in Nova Scotia. He was playing for the varsity hockey team. We met at one of the taverns and drank a few drafts of beer, Jackie telling me about life as a college hockey player. He wondered, with all the practices, travelling, and comradeship, how he would be able to keep up with his academic workload.

On Christmas Eve morning I took the bus out to Pine River, walked to my Uncle Mike's place, and spent some time with him and Janice. When I hugged her, Janice seemed smaller than I remembered and I wasn't as titillated putting my arms around her as I had been years before. She was wearing glasses and had a rather academic look about her. But she still exuded that beauty and inner intelligence that I'd always seen in her. Janice was in her fourth year at Laval University and said she would be studying law as of the coming September, probably at McGill University.

"So how are you coping with the French courses?" I asked her.

"It was tough going for the first two years, but now I'm sorta getting the hang of it," she said.

My uncle was concerned that his son Charlie had not planned on making the trip to Pine River for the holidays.

"Lawrence tells me that he's living the life of Riley up there," my Uncle Mike commented. "Have you been spending any time with him, Francis?"

"Yes, he showed me around town when I first went up but I haven't seen a lot of him lately," I said.

"Well, if he's not gonna be serious he should come back here. I can think of a lot of worthwhile things for him to do," my uncle said, with a grimly humorous look on his face.

My Uncle Mike drove me up to Marianne's house. We said hello and talked with Hughie and Gerald who were playing hockey outside in the driveway, then went in to see Eleanor Connors, the widow of Paddy Connors. Since I had last seen her at the funeral four years before, she had gained some weight. After a rather ebullient greeting toward me, she told me that Marianne was out at the stable. Eleanor Connors knew, of course, that I had been seeking the company of her daughter for quite some time. Her two youngest children were in the house: Francis, who was eight years old, and a little girl, six-year-old Rose, who was the spitting image of Marianne when Marianne was younger.

Stables, in the wintertime especially, tend to have a strong and acrid smell. It isn't exactly the proper place to greet someone you are anxious to see. Marianne, who was brushing the floor around the cows in their stalls, saw me come in the door and virtually screamed.

"Francis! You're not supposed to see me out here!"

I laughed and went right up to her and meant to take her in my arms.

"No, Francis! I don't smell very good! I'm all sweaty and dirty! Don't come near me!"

She held me off with the huge brush she was using.

"I don't care. I just want to hug you," I pleaded.

She finally relented and allowed me to hold her. She shuddered and the tears began. I didn't know if she was crying because I had caught her at an embarrassing moment or because she was just so happy to see me.

Marianne was wearing a thick knitted sweater and a matching toque and she felt warm and powerful as she held me close. I got a little emotional myself and realized how much I had missed her. We held each other for quite a long time, just swaying back and forth slowly and easily, not saying a word, the odour of straw and hay and cattle and horse and pig heavy in the surroundings, but suddenly not unpleasant.

On Christmas Eve, we went to midnight Mass at the chapel in Pine River in the crisp, cold, clear night, the cars and several horse-drawn sleighs parked close to the building, the ceremony kept short out of respect for the comfort of the animals waiting outside. Father Emmett Lynch gave a brief Christmas wish to all his parishioners, then continued with the service. Many people I had not seen since the trial were there, wishing each other a "Merry Christmas" after the Mass was over. A bright moon shone over the cluster of fully clad people, white vaporous breaths emanating. It was a truly felt expression of fraternity between members of a community, many of whom would get through the winter without much social contact.

People gathered at my Uncle Mike's house after Mass, Janice having prepared a small feast beforehand. The Dunigans came with their two daughters. Willie Connors, whose wife had passed away two years before, came into my Uncle Mike's kitchen using a cane but otherwise appearing to be healthy. Marianne and her mother were there.

We all sat around the wood-burning stove, talking and laughing. I was happy beyond words to be sitting beside Marianne, the smell of hay and animals in the stable replaced by the hint of a soft perfume.

Marianne had turned seventeen in early December and had grown to be a young woman who radiated strength yet had a certain delicacy in her nature, a soft feminine way of speaking. I wanted to be with her into the foreseeable future. I could not imagine doing anything without having her beside me. Our little party broke up after 3:30 a.m. on Christmas morning. Janice drove

Marianne and Eleanor home. I went with them in the car and sat in the rear seat holding Marianne's hand. There was a cheerless look on her face. She said that she was not looking forward to trying to get to sleep. She had recently had difficulty sleeping and promised to tell me about it the next day.

Bordeaux Jail, its structure completed in 1912, is modelled after a Philadelphia penitentiary erected in 1820. There are few prisons in Canada architecturally similar to Bordeaux Jail. It was designed to promote isolation of inmates, a practice that is perfectly suited to the confinement of death row prisoners.

It is an imposing Montreal structure that rests on the south side of the Rivière des Prairies, a branch of the St. Lawrence River. Surveyed from a distance, it stands like a behemoth amid the array of smaller buildings. A federal Government of Canada institution, Bordeaux Jail has been the site of the hanging of more than eighty death row inmates since its construction.

The history of executions by hanging across Canada includes public hangings in the early days, staged to attract a tourist population. It has been punctuated by a litany of decapitations and botched procedures by hangmen.

As I write this in September of 1966, there have been 697 men and 13 women executed in Canada since Confederation in 1867. This does not mean that hanging was not used before Confederation. Both the French Regime and the English hegemony practised capital punishment. It was indeed used for what we would now consider absurd reasons: disobeying orders while doing military service, as well as simple theft and other crimes not involving any killing.

The criminal courts, including the Supreme Court of Canada, have not always shown a readiness to respond to requests for a second look at certain cases. The law is the most revered entity and its precepts have to be adhered to. A challenge to the law is a contradiction. One cannot challenge the procedures of the law nor the law itself. It is next to impossible for the courts to admit that they have erred, that they have misjudged, or that they have been too rigid.

The process of trial and execution in the Canadian justice system has also been riddled with incompetence, inaccuracies, and blatant stupidity. What else could explain the judgement on a 14-year-old boy found guilty of murder on the basis of shoddy and circumstantial evidence, as in the case of Steven Truscott, who was told by a judge that he would be "hanged by the neck until dead"? Thankfully, the courts will likely have a second look at this case.

Canada's most recent executions, in 1962, of two men hanged at the same time, back to back, could not be done without miscalculation and ineptness. One of the condemned men did not die instantaneously, the "long drop" having been miscalculated, with the hanged victim nearly decapitated.

It is impossible to relate all of the thoughts of Michael Ferrigan, installed in his death row cell at Bordeaux Jail in Montreal. His lawyer, Gerald Nolan, worked feverishly to get a last-minute reprieve for his client. Many supplications were made for the life of a man who was to leave ten children in mourning. With but a few days remaining before the scheduled hanging, people of faith throughout Quebec City prayed that the Supreme Court of Canada would see the folly of not commuting this man's sentence.

Maggie Ferrigan, accompanied by Gerald Nolan and Michael Ferrigan's eldest son Stephen, travelled to Montreal a few days before the execution. The three were admitted to the huge building and led down a series of corridors and finally ushered into a room close to the death row cells. We do not know the details of this meeting, but from all indications, it was a harrowing time for Michael Ferrigan's wife of some twenty years, his son, and the condemned man and his lawyer.

At the sentenced man's request, Father James McDonald also travelled to Montreal a few days before the day of the hanging to give him counsel, as well as to administer Holy Communion.

Michael Ferrigan wrote his last will and testament during this time, consulting with his wife and lawyer as to the most proper manner of writing his wishes.

It is not beyond reason to believe that Michael Ferrigan did not wish to kill Paddy Connors, that he had allowed his anger to overcome him and had fired a careless shot at his victim in a reckless fashion. It is also understandable that he may have considered himself an innocent man, accused and found to be guilty of murder "without provocation." It is therefore not unlikely that Michael Ferrigan saw himself as a victim of an inflexible system of laws where judges and lawyers and juries did not examine all of the variables of an event where someone had been killed.

There was little that he could change in his circumstances, except hope and pray for a last-minute delay or reprieve by someone in a prestigious political position.

Just a few months earlier, Michael Ferrigan had walked the fields of his farm. He had not become a rich man, but had gained a status in a country place that he loved, the owner of a considerable acreage, the patriarchal head of an impressive brood of children. Doubtless he ached for the sight of the trees, brooks, and pastures that he had seen daily. With a certain measure of pride, he had been accustomed to wandering to the margins of his holdings, thinking about how he would cope with the demands of the seasons.

But now he was mired in a deep chasm of despair, death awaiting him. All that he had worked for would be left behind. They had installed him in a cell, alone, and he would die in a few days, alone, a rope strangling the life out of him.

He would sleep intermittently in those last few nights, awaking frequently. During daytime, the harsh clanging of steel doors closing, the latches loudly finding their grooves, disturbed him greatly. He would pray for the strength to endure, to face the black abyss, to accept what fate had dealt him. But his depression was at its deepest; he was already mourning his own death.

Michael Ferrigan had not been a religious man, although he believed in God and in the hereafter. With Father McDonald, he prayed that God would forgive him for his transgressions, for his bouts with anger, and for the final act of wilfulness that would lead to his demise.

He expressed dissatisfaction to Maggie and to Father McDonald about the isolation of the death row sector of the jail. He saw himself as a minuscule being in a huge apparatus, the guards nervously delivering his meals, peering in on him as if he were a dangerous vicious animal. They did allow him one hour of exercise daily, walking in an enclosed area by himself. Dark thoughts and visions of his destiny pervaded his being. He knew that his young children missed him terribly and he wept at not being able to see them and hold them in his arms.

Yet, he would still have a certain pride in his being, a confidence in the occupation he had practised and given his life to. He had made many good choices in his life, his marriage to Maggie standing at the apex of his achievements. He resolved to go to his death with his head held high, assured that God would forgive him for the folly he had succumbed to, for his uncontrollable expression of anger. He prayed that God would see to the welfare of his children, that they would be able to cope with his final and irreversible departure. He would not expose his fear, but did his best to retreat into a stoical resolve. This stance tugged at his emotions, aroused in him an undeniable underlying tension.

It would be impossible for a witness to portray the unimaginable sorrow that infused the scene of the last meeting between Michael Ferrigan and his wife on the eve of his execution. Speaking as an artist, I would have found such a picture presented to me as an emotional landscape too overwhelming to reproduce.

Earlier in the day, his lawyer had brought word to Michael Ferrigan that the law would have to take its course. At that moment, Michael Ferrigan "was greatly moved and showed signs of breaking down." That last evening, the atmosphere of the room was heavy with disquiet and distress. It was a pitiful sight, yet with Michael Ferrigan sipping a cup of tea, there was a depth of courage in all present. Little was said. When the time came to depart,

Maggie put her arms around his neck and clung to him. Michael Ferrigan "bore up with the parting with great courage," but on seeing his wife take leave of him, never again to meet, he broke down and wept bitterly.

There is something insidious in the law of a justice system that seeks to prolong the viciousness of violence. It is not only that the courts extract "an eye for an eye," but that it has been done in a manner that subjects its victim to the most degrading manner of execution. It is as if the justice system is taking out its vengeance in a fashion that more than matches the bloodthirstiness of the defendant's crime, however it was committed.

Just after midnight, on the date of Michael Ferrigan's execution, seven chimes sounded and the death flag was raised at Bordeaux Jail, as was the custom. Hundreds of people lined the banks of the river close to the massive prison, dressed warmly against the cold winter night, some squinting at the glaring outside lights. Opponents of capital punishment were present: placards were hoisted and chants were intoned. Also on the scene, in smaller numbers, were the proponents of hanging. In their dedication, some from both factions stayed until past midnight.

It seems that Michael Ferrigan, resolute and intrinsically resigned to his fate, slept for several hours on the last night prior to his execution. His spiritual advisor, Father James McDonald, was available to him during all of this time. On waking, the condemned man told Father McDonald and his guards that he felt nervous, but that he was ready. He ate breakfast, consuming all of the food that was laid out before him.

Michael Ferrigan's last living space, a cell set apart from all other prisoners, could be accessed by only a few personages: the warden and the guards, a prison doctor and clergyman. Anyone else admitted to his cell would be allowed only with the written permission of the judge who had presided over the case.

The execution, within the walls of the prison, would be witnessed by the warden and the sheriff and by persons who were assistants to the sheriff. The condemned man's spiritual advisor and lawyer would also be allowed to attend, as well as a limited number of press representatives. The use of cameras was absolutely forbidden. Lastly, the prison doctor had to be present to perform certain functions after the hanged man had expired.

The man required to see to the "devil's handiwork," the hangman, could hardly be described as a witness. Prior to the execution, his job is to reassure himself as to the proper operation of the trapdoor of the gallows and its rapid release. The rope used on the condemned prisoner, usually of hemp, about one inch in diameter and exceeding 25 feet in length, must be softened so that it will not coil. The dry rope is then tied with the hangman's knot so that the noose will slide smoothly. Once all of this has been done the rope is tied in place in the gallows.

But the executioner's preparation work is not complete. He must calculate the proper amount of drop that will make certain that the fall breaks the neck of the victim immediately, resulting in instant death. The inmate must be weighed ahead of time. His medical history must be studied. All of this to ascertain that he will not be decapitated or suffer slow strangulation during the hanging, the two extremes of ineptness.

On execution morning, the condemned man is pinioned and manacled and walked to the gallows, up a flight of stairs to a built-up platform, and placed standing over the trapdoor. The prisoner is then permitted a word with his spiritual advisor and is allowed to speak any last words he may have. The hangman then places a black hood over the head of the victim and his legs are tied together. The prepared noose is then placed around the convict's neck. The hangman's knot is placed behind the left ear, supposedly the preferred spot necessary to break the victim's neck.

On the morning of January 9, 1953, at ten minutes before eight a.m., Michael Ferrigan's executioner came into the cell and, without speaking, tied the prisoner's hands. Father McDonald was present and had just finished a session of prayer with the victim, who seemed to be somewhat disturbed during the hangman's procedure. The hangman then left and returned to the gallows for a last-minute inspection of the apparatus. After a few minutes he returned to the cell. Michael Ferrigan, accompanied by Father McDonald, was marched down a lengthy corridor and into the large room where the gallows had been erected, in its long-standing location where it had been many times used.

As expected, the witnesses present consisted of the sheriff with a group of his officers, the warden of the prison, and the prison doctor, as well as a group of men of the press who had been allowed to be witnesses.

On the platform, Michael Ferrigan and Father McDonald exchanged softly intoned prayers, after which the priest pressed the right hand of the victim. Michael Ferrigan then stepped without hesitation onto the trapdoor. When asked if he had any last words to say he did not respond, except to say farewell to Father McDonald.

The newspaper report of the following day stated that "not until this moment when he stood upon the drop with the fatal noose adjusted around his neck did the doomed man betray any signs of grief and emotion. In an instant he appeared overcome by the most intense agony, murmuring loudly, standing between heaven and earth, waiting and heaving just before the drawing of the mortal bolt. With the black hood fastened, the hot blood must have rushed into his face at the dilatory conduct of the hangman. He would have wanted to gaze at Father McDonald though it would have been painful to witness, and that gaze would have spoken of the extreme torment that must have overcome him. At the moment of the opening of the drop, the condemned man, feeling it giving way, managed to clutch at the tightening rope, his hands and elbows insecurely bound. The man found himself dangling between time and eternity, and was heard to be shrieking 'Oh, my God!' The plummet was thus impeded and prevented the usual break of the victim's neck, and when the victim fell the remainder of the drop, it was to die the slow death of suffocation. It was probable that the man asphyxiated immediately after his fall, but violent contortions of the body proved that life was not extinct until fully sixteen minutes after the moment of the start of the execution."

Needless to say, the witnesses were very unhappy with the obvious ineptness of the executioner. Several minutes later, Dr. Jean Royer, the attending physician, pronounced the condemned man dead, the result of strangulation, relaying the information to the sheriff and the others gathered. The body was then released from the rope and placed in the usual simple coffin.

The newspaper announced that "after the body was cut down the face of the deceased appeared as if it had sustained much suffering, the neck where the rope was tied being of a blackish hue."

Near the time of the execution, several Solemn High Masses were being said for Michael Ferrigan in Catholic churches in the Quebec City area, the Archbishop presiding at one of the services. Many worshippers were in attendance.

The body of Michael Ferrigan was soon buried in St. Patrick's cemetery in Quebec City, in a section commonly known as the "cholera burying ground." This phrase refers to the many deaths that occurred among the Irish immigrants who had succumbed due to the rampant illnesses and the after-effects of the fateful trips across the ocean.

I remember getting home from school on the afternoon of Friday, January 9, in a hurry because I had a hockey game scheduled for that night. As I walked in the door meaning to get my hockey equipment organized quickly, my mom told me that Michael Ferrigan had been executed that morning. I stopped what I was doing for a while and sat down at the kitchen table facing my mom.

"Did you hear about it on the radio?" I asked.

"Yes. He was hanged at eight o'clock this morning at the Bordeaux Jail in Montreal."

I did not know what to say. Being involved in school and hockey as I was, I had not even thought about the trial for weeks. All I could remember was what my mother had previously told me, that Michael Ferrigan could not get a stay of execution from the courts and that his execution was to proceed as scheduled.

When my mother read the accounts of the execution in the newspapers the next morning, she wept.

Chapter 21

By the main road, it was a six-mile walk from my Uncle Mike's to Marianne's house, so Janice drove me back on Christmas Day afternoon. I wished a Merry Christmas to Eleanor Connors, and to the younger children. Marianne and I left the house and walked the snow-covered road, the grip of winter in the air. She seemed a trifle melancholy and I made a clumsy effort to discover the reasons.

"Why were you crying when I met you in the stable yesterday?" I asked.

"Oh, I cry very easily these days. Mom tells me that I was a lot calmer when I was younger. I've been having nightmares lately."

"What about?"

"About my dad's killing and the execution mostly. It's like I keep reliving everything. I can't seem to concentrate in school. I feel so anxious all the time."

We were walking close together, in step. She leaned her head against my shoulder.

"I wish he was still alive so I could ask Michael Ferrigan why he did it. I'd like to go right up to him and look into his eyes and ask him why he did it," she continued.

We were very quiet for a while, the sound of our footsteps crunchy on the hard snow of the road.

"Guess who I met up with in Montreal a few weeks ago," I decided to say suddenly.

I released her, got in front, and walked backwards holding her by her shoulders.

"I have no idea, Francis. Who met you in Montreal?"

She finally smiled, her beautifully shaped lips parting.

"Joey Ferrigan!"

"Oh, my God! I heard he moved up there. What is he doing?"

"He's working for the railroad."

"Joey's so nice. You know, it's really weird. His father shot my father and I know he felt terrible and ashamed about it."

"You've known him a long time."

"Yes. He was at the school here. We still have the one-room schoolhouse. Joey was a few years ahead of me. We had Mrs. Walling then. He used to tease me a little, but apart from that he was just a playful rascal. But in the spring after his father was executed, I used to ride my bike down to see Teresa Dunigan and I always passed by his house. We always said hello to each other, and one day he said he wanted to talk to me and he told me he was so sorry about what happened and he had tears in his eyes. I knew it wasn't his fault that his father was a madman. He asked me to forgive him, but I told him that he shouldn't blame himself for what happened."

"He told me that his father was mentally unbalanced for months before he shot your father," I said.

"I don't like to think about what sort of person he was. He was a very angry man. Everyone knew about him and we were all afraid of him."

"It's good to talk about these things, Marianne. Don't keep it all bottled up inside you."

We enfolded each other, hugging on the deserted country road, the wintry stillness emitting its calm, the bright afternoon sun shining on us.

"Why don't you come into town some day this week?" I suggested.

"I don't know, Francis. It's hard for me to leave. Hughie doesn't like to do the milking, and I don't like my mom having to go out to the stable. She has very poor circulation in her legs. But I'd love to go down for one evening. Maybe I can make some arrangement with one of my uncles."

"We could go skating at the Chateau Frontenac."

"You'll have to hold me up."

"I'd love to hold you."

"I'm so clumsy on skates."

"You could stay at our house."

"I'd better stay with my Aunt Mamie if I go. She'd be terribly insulted if I didn't."

I had no desire to wear out my welcome, so I came back home to Quebec City the day after Christmas. I'd promised I'd go out with my dad to see my younger brothers play hockey on two successive nights. These were both outdoor matches. My father and I stood on the high banks of snow surrounding the rinks and yelled encouragement to my brothers. My youngest brother Stephen had real talent, was big and fast, and had a future in hockey if he wanted. The Junior A hockey team in the city had a serious interest in him and had him on their list of good young prospects.

Marianne took the train down to Quebec City the next Friday morning and I met her at the Palace Station. A cold snap had set in, but there was nothing that would hold me back from showing her a busy time. I didn't want her to pine about anything, or to even have a moment for depressing thoughts. We visited a few of the art salons, went to see an ice-sculpture exhibition, and saw *On the Waterfront*, starring Marlon Brando. I had already seen the movie and Marianne kept telling me to shut up as I was revealing to her what would happen next. I took her to my home for supper and she seemed to appreciate all the attention she got from the males in our family. We went skating on the ice rink at the Chateau Frontenac Hotel above the ice-filled St. Lawrence River. Marianne rented a pair of skates that turned out to be too big for her, which made our little skating party that much more comical.

The tourist industry seems to rebound during the Christmas season. There were quite a few visitors on the rink with us, yelling back and forth to each other in English with Boston and New York accents. Others were using the winter slide at one end of the terrace. We walked over to see the action up close after we finished skating. The huge built-up slide had three icy lanes and used specially designed toboggans that fit into the lanes safely. The sliders, four on each toboggan, would sit, linking legs around the person in front, and glide down the steep grade, hitting good speed, squealing as they went, and gradually come to a stop at the front end of the boardwalk.

I had not been with Marianne very often since my college courses began and, despite her obvious warmth toward me, she seemed to carry a trace of despondency. We sat down at a small restaurant and she talked a little bit about how she felt.

"So how is your mom coping with things these days?" I asked her.

"She still finds it pretty hard. It's been over four years now since Dad is gone, but to my mother it's still fresh in her memory. I'm beginning to understand how terrible it must have been for her. There she was, left alone to raise five of us with the farm and animals to be looked after. Thank God for my uncles, especially Uncle Eddy. He came over to the house nearly every day to help us with the chores. He showed me how to do certain things. I guess I grew up pretty fast in those months after Dad was shot."

"You held up very well, I thought, at the time."

"Yes, my mom says that I hadn't seemed to respond to what had happened. I was getting a lot of attention from everyone and, at first, I don't think I realized how much my dad's death would affect me. But over the last few years it has really dawned on me, opened up my eyes. Back then, after they hanged Mr. Ferrigan, I really felt sorry for his family. A small part of me wanted revenge, I suppose, but then I started feeling the opposite, that he should have been allowed to live for his children. That really depressed me. Can you imagine, Francis? There were fifteen children with no father as a result of this!"

I was rather stunned that she would still be carrying these burdens on her shoulders. After all, she was still only a high school girl. It was not as if she bore any responsibility for what had occurred. It all started to come back to me then, I suppose.

Marianne had been so self-possessed during her father's funeral, the trial, and then as she started going to high school in Quebec City. It was as if she was storing up all of her grief inside of her at the time. Now that she had matured into all of the weight of those despicable past events, there were going to be some after-effects. I felt sorry for her, but that didn't help matters very much. I decided then and there that I would write to her more regularly from Montreal and keep close tabs on her. It was all that I could do.

I could not imagine the emotional agony that Marianne's mother, Eleanor, had gone through as a result of her husband's sudden death. Eleanor and Paddy Connors had had an idyllic relationship on the farm that they possessed, blessed with five healthy children, living without debt on land close to his parents. The operation of their farm would never give them riches, but Paddy was a hard worker and a good provider. He'd been a man who loved to read, was curious about many things, and had great expectations for his children.

Paddy Connors had not been a living saint, no doubt. He loved to have a drink with his brothers, no matter where. They had a bit of a reputation in the community as good-humoured scamps, always ready for practical jokes, and willing to show the wild side of their "Irishness" by submitting to the occasional brawl. Paddy was said to have even precipitated a few run-ins with the "Proddies" from a neighbouring Presbyterian farming community. He'd been a tall man, sturdily built, with the start of a smile on his face at most times.

Eleanor was a product of the Gill family, who had originally arrived in Pine River in early August of 1823. Her great-grandfather, Timothy Gill, had landed in Quebec City with a young wife and two daughters. They had been residents in St. Mullin Parish, County Carlow, Ireland. Unlike many of the other early Irish immigrants of that time, Timothy had a valued skill. He was a stonemason as his father had been before him. He'd had a hand in the building of many structures in the towns of Carlow, especially the renovations to the manors of some of the landowners.

He'd built retaining walls, crafted cemetery monuments, and repaired the foundations of ancient churches. Timothy Gill had always been also strongly desirous of owning a good-sized piece of land that he could call his own. As part of a long-known Catholic family, he knew that he was not eligible to be a landowner. When he arrived in Quebec, he did not tell the Seigneur's agent that he had practised the skill of stonemasonry. He simply enlisted as a tenant farmer and luckily was granted a 200-acre spread of tree-filled land, one side of which bordered upon a small lake.

Unlike many of the newly arrived Irish tenant farmers, Timothy Gill was a well-read man who kept journals, having developed the skill of reading with the help of his father and mother. He had recorded his observations throughout his family's ordeals as they had experienced them. This heirloom, kept in a special wooden case, had been harboured within the families of his descendants in Pine River. It stood as a testament to the years of difficulty in the Irish diaspora, the dislocation of leaving a beloved country, the wild and risky voyage across the ocean, and the sacrifices endured in the settling into their newly adopted land.

"We do not wish to announce to the world that we are desirous to go to Canada," the journal states. "It is a well-preserved secret kept within the confines of the family, including my father who has slowed down his workload to a large degree. As they may register some objections to our departure, we do not want the authorities to know of our plans. I do not see how I can raise my family and give my children the greatest opportunity to develop in a political climate where prejudice is the motivation of many in the upper echelons of power. So after seeing the customs people and taking very few belongings with us, we have decided to embark on the ship *Dover* at Cork, bound for North America."

The English authorities and landowners of Ireland were happy to see the emigration of Irish peasants. Taxes were raised to a point where it was impossible for these poor people to pay. They would thus be evicted from their small acreage. The landowners, after the devious manipulations of the Gombeen Man would then use the repossessed land for their cattle, sheep, and other purposes. Of course, the family of Timothy Gill was excluded from this bias, they being among the builders and enablers of much of the infrastructure of Carlow. It was in the best interest of the Gills not to announce the planned departure of Timothy and his family.

Timothy Gill wrote down his observations of his family's voyage across the North Atlantic. Some of the entries follow.

"Tuesday, June 3rd, 1823

"On this clear and sunny day, we waved goodbye to my father and mother, Kitty's parents, and a few close friends and relatives, and sailed away. Our two trunks and sealed wicker baskets have been stored below the steerage. I have many second thoughts about embarking upon this pilgrimage. Life has not been unpleasant for us in County Carlow, and I am troubled to leave a comfortable reality in exchange for the uncertainty of a future in a strange land. We walked on the deck watching the disappearing houses of Cork fade into a flat green line. The large sails of the ship swelled in the sun's brightness and pulled our craft forward at a good speed. The ship Dover, captained by Robert Crowthers, is a three-mast ship used mainly to haul lumber from Lower Canada to England and Ireland. For the return trip to Canada, the ship is modified to accommodate passengers, mostly in the steerage. There are a few cabins for those who can afford the price but I have decided to preserve my savings. Down below, the families of married couples have their own quarters and the single adults are separated to either end of the steerage.

"Though the sun continues to shine on this first day, waves have begun to heave and pitch the ship from side to side. Many instantly became seasick and emptied their stomachs over the sides of the railings. The children seem to hold up the best in the buffeting, still running around the deck. My younger girl, Sarah, seems to enjoy the bobbing of the ship. We have the use of a large grate on deck to boil our water, cook our oatmeal, and prepare soup. We have made the acquaintance of many families and have organized our meals together. My wife Kitty has pickled fowl for us as well as cake

bread. In these first days, we are eating sparingly but heartily. My understanding is that the ship is holding stores of basic victuals for later in the voyage as the need will be great."

"Friday, June 6th, 1823

"For most of the people on this voyage, it is the first time they are faring on the ocean. Kitty complains of a queasiness, yet we have both managed to retain our food thus far. We also both sense that Kitty may be with child. This would be our third child and this does not help her condition."

"Sunday, June 8th, 1823

"This rocking of the ship we have had to endure for the last few days, making sleep difficult. But it is nothing compared to the terrifying adventure that the first massive storm would bring us commencing yesterday evening. Huge waves crashed against the ship up to the gunwales, sending spews of water down through the seeping hatches of the ship, soaking all of us and our sundry belongings. It was impossible not to consider that the ship would topple over, sending all of us to eternity. Many were violently ill, yet unable to go up on deck to retch due to the danger. They could but empty their stomachs where it was convenient until there was nothing left, yet the retching continued. It was truly a scene out of hell, with the ship bouncing from side to side and to and fro, pots, utensils, and other articles falling to the floor. But all must be endured. Many, when not sitting quietly at their cots in terror, were on their knees praying that God would save them in this ominous and death-taunting trial.

"Yet, the captain and crew seem not worried and go about their duties on the deck, hanging onto the rails and the rigging, taking down the sails to reduce the buffeting, reassuring the passengers that it all will pass, and that they have seen much worse.

"I am one of the fortunate ones, although terrified. I do not have the desire to vomit any longer. I seem to have quickly adjusted to sea life."

"Wednesday, June 11th, 1823

"Life on the sea is in constant contradiction. On this lovely day we are instilled with a calm I have seldom seen, the water like a smooth shining mirror, just the wisp of a breeze, and the ship Dover not seeming to move forward. The cloudless sky casts its own shimmering brightness and the sun is a searing force on the deck and the cause of oppressive heat in the hold. My older daughter Minnie complains of a very sore stomach, but my wife compels her to stay on deck out of the airless steerage."

"Monday, June 16th, 1823

"A man by the name of Mike Devilin has lost his wife to a terrible fever that she has been ill with over the last few days. She has left two young boys behind. There was much sorrow on the ship as Captain Crowthers allowed the canvas-wrapped body to slide into the sea after intoning prayers from the Bible. The young boys seemed to understand the situation only too well and cried piteously as their deceased mother went over the side. There is fear that others will be affected with this malaise."

"Friday, June 20th, 1823

"We are more than two weeks out of port today. The sails are full with a brisk wind blowing. My family seems to be in fair health, with my daughter improving all the time. We are on the deck most of the day holding onto our hats in a crisp cool breeze. The ship rocks back and forth, but we are becoming acclimated to it more and more each day. The large grate where we boil our water and vegetables is not in use today. We make do with cold food—potato cakes and eggs in salt pickle. The drinking water has a very poor taste, although we have a few ciders available but in limited supply."

"Wednesday, June 25th, 1823

"Mister Emmett Hogan passed away this morning after being ill for several days. He was an older man, a widower, who was on

his way to Boston with his two daughters, both in their early twenties. They, of course, are in deep distress. He was sent over the side not more than two hours after his departure, as determined by the captain and his first mate. There is no doctor on board who would be accustomed to these events. The daughters expressed to us that their father had much regret that he could not see a priest while he was very ill and seeming to know that he would die."

"Monday, June 30th, 1823

"We were struck again late last evening by another tumultuous storm that tested our wills and our courage. This deluge swept great swaths of water across the deck. It had arisen suddenly so that the crew of the ship was not able to lower all of the sails. Once again, many passengers in steerage suffered the effects, a steady drain of water descending onto them causing many to shiver with the cold dampness. The storm lasted through all of the night and into today's morning, doing some damage to one of the mainsails. The crew is busy today repairing the tears. The rain has ceased and the wind is dying down as the day is progressing. We have been told that the grate will be lit later so that we can boil water for tea. I have come to have great respect for Captain Crowthers and his crew who are always in good humour despite the difficulties. He is unlike some of the ship captains we have heard about."

"Friday, July 4th, 1823

"We are told that we are at the half-way point in our seemingly endless voyage. Kitty is certain now that she is with child and our prayers are that this journey across the ocean will not bring us bad luck. I thank God for my continued good health and the health of my two daughters. I have made a fine friendship with Michael Devilin, now a widower. He is a singer of many songs and has entertained us on more than one evening. His two sons have found companionship in my children and there is much scampering across the deck on calm sunny days."

"Tuesday, July 8th, 1823

"There is much fog today in the calm waters of the sea. But little wind blowing to propel the ship forward. On days such as this I am thankful that Captain Crowthers has the right instruments to keep the ship on the correct path. We are told that we should be approaching Newfoundland within the next week. Many are already on the lookout for a dark line of land in the distance. We have noticed many large fish in the waters and are told by a tar that they are whales and give birth to their young as we do. We marvel as these great creatures leap from the water and descend with great splashes. It is truly marvellous. Some travellers have spoken of massive icebergs floating from the north, but we have not seen any as yet."

"Friday, July 11th, 1823

"Heat has once again become the bane of all of us trying to find comfort in the steerage. Not only that the air is stifling, but there is a continuous stench emanating from most quarters after several weeks of close and damp conditions. The unsanitary behaviour among many of the passengers is a cause for alarm. We cannot blame those who have been ill, but for those who are still healthy and young, a constant effort should be made to keep their surroundings clean and orderly. Yet, I do not like to pass judgement on people who must endure life at its most arduous. We are clustered together as we had been told that we would be in this kind of harried travel. The hatches above the hold are ill-fitting, although this allows for a freer passage of air. But when it rains we can see that they are not designed to foster human well-being."

"Tuesday, July 15th, 1823

"The fog we have had for a few days lifted yesterday and today finds us in full sunshine with a smattering of white clouds. Some watchers on deck have sighted logs and floating debris amid the ocean waters. This certainly signals that we are close to Newfoundland. Captain Crowthers has decided to ration our supply of water, each family restricted to lesser amounts. The captain has

also ordered all passengers to bring clothing and bed apparel up on board to be aired out. People who are sick must also be brought up on deck. There is a fever that has been circulating for several days with dozens affected, mostly adults. Thanks be to God, my family remains in good health."

"Thursday, July 17th, 1823

"We have seen two fishing boats with several men in both who all waved at us from a distance. They are working out of the ports of Newfoundland. Two infants were born in the past few days, one of them passing away. It is sad that parents could come so far and be so close to their goal and then lose their child."

"Friday, July 18th, 1823

"The island of Newfoundland stands off starboard. There are throngs of passengers on deck, the first sight of a new continent before their eyes. Also to our right a huge mountain of ice stands in the distance. My two children stare across the waters, their eyes widened, without words at the sight of the iceberg. The grand and welcoming sight of Newfoundland we will see to our right for a few days, I am told."

"Sunday, July 20th, 1823

"We are about to enter the Gulf of the St. Lawrence River, always with Newfoundland at our right side. We have passed the French islands and have picked up a pilot who will lead us safely up the river toward Quebec. Cape Breton, to our left, is said to stand majestically high above the water but we have not been able to catch sight of it. The thought still brings warm thoughts to us. We are deeply impressed by the expanse of this great waterway. We pass several more fishing boats, again with the men waving to us, with the children on our craft hollering out across the blue waters. Kitty and I are very thankful to God for our good luck in surviving the voyage across the deep ocean. We are seven weeks travelling on this ship and look forward hopefully to our landing in Quebec

within a shorter period. We must all give great homage to the captain of our ship who has shepherded us through seven weeks of a sometimes woeful experience. We could not have asked for a better leader, a man who showed extreme care for all of his passengers, especially the sick whom he visited and always showed concern for in very difficult situations. We all feel that we are prepared to wrap him in our arms, thankful as we are for safe passage through the temperamental seas."

"Friday, July 25th, 1823

"This early morning, a considerable amount of fog had accumulated on the river as we got closer to Quebec. The haze prevented us from seeing either side, but the pilot has guided us without mishap, as the fog lifts, past the mouth of another great river coming from the north. The lush green banks of the St. Lawrence beckon with a host of dark green trees covering the land. This expanse of river is truly remarkable, larger and more powerful that any flow I have ever seen. Houses of many colours sparkle in the sunshine, almost evenly spaced along the river shore in some instances."

"Tuesday, July 29th, 1823

"We are anchored in the river before the Quebec city. Far off to our right the children point to a high waterfall where one of the smaller rivers empties into the St. Lawrence. The city itself sits gloriously on two levels with a row of houses on the lower level close by the water. The upper level has a cluster of larger buildings, including the spires of a few churches. Farther on is a high promontory with another row of houses underneath, snuggled up against the cliff. Except for the cliffs this city is not unlike the town of Cork we viewed from the water as we left Ireland. We are exhilarated, with the ship resting in the calm waters of a busy harbour, the river narrower here, waiting our turn to disembark. As the ship sits waiting, I am impressed with the sturdy look of the buildings of Quebec, some several storeys high, with slanting roofs made of metal."

"Wednesday, July 30th, 1823

"The surgeon has come aboard and has examined those who are sick before anyone was able to leave the ship. We then were permitted to disembark, but had to pass through the custom house and register. There was much confusion and tumult as most of the passengers were transferring their luggage to another steamship that will take them farther up the river to Montreal. Many boxes, trunks, and precious belongings are spread about the dock with people scurrying back and forth. Included in this trip to Montreal is a company of soldiers and their wives and children. I am told that hundreds of people will be crowded onto this steamship, so that many will have to sleep on deck out in the open. I do not envy these people and pray God that inclement weather will not hinder the last leg of their journey. I am very thankful that my family's travel is about to end and that we have but twenty more miles to travel to the St. Patrick Mission north of Quebec."

Chapter 22

Kitty and Timothy Gill were able to move into a vacated woodcutter's cabin on the lot they had been granted in the Pine River area, where there were several small lakes. Timothy spent the first few months working to improve the structure of the cabin to make it more habitable for his young family. He was soon able to acquire a young mare and a cart and set about building a temporary log shelter for his first acquisitions. The high quality of the pine on the acreage made his work more than pleasurable. In the fall of 1823, he began to cut down many of the trees, making sure to preserve an untouched area close to the lakefront. In doing this work he was able to acquire the help of Vince Ferrigan, a strong young man who had recently come to Pine River. The two men spent the autumn pulling up the stumps with the great effort of the young mare and clearing the land of rocks so that crops could later be planted.

Timothy Gill was not a man who lacked resources. While he accepted aid from the Seigneur as other tenant farmers had, he'd been able to bring some money and tools with him from the old country. He was not close to destitute as some of the newcomers were, but had acquired a marketable skill as a stonemason, something that he would use to his advantage. Seeing the potential beauty of his lakefront property, he worked hard in those first several months to satisfy the requirements of the tenant farmer's agreement with the Seigneur. This he also did through the winter on the days when weather conditions were acceptable. But the early spring saw him travelling by horse and cart to Loretteville, employed in the building of a new church. He would rise before dawn for the three-hour trip to the work site, where he would stay for two- or three-day work periods. He struggled to learn the French language that was spoken by most of the workers, many of whom were working voluntarily.

Mullin Gill, the first son of Kitty and Timothy, was born on a cold winter night in early February of 1824 in the log cabin. Assisting Kitty in the delivery were two women from the area, Kathleen Duffy and Mary Jane Lonergan. The sense of a strong community had taken root in the early years of Pine River, where there was already a desire to share in the difficulty of surviving in the wooded wilderness. The newborn child was the "picture of health" and was baptized two weeks later in the Cartier village chapel after a ten-mile sleigh ride over the snow-laden and rudimentary roads.

Timothy Gill developed a solid reputation within Pine River as a good neighbour, a farmer and craftsman, and a jack-of-all-trades. Catherine "Kitty" Gill produced five children in all, three girls and two boys, whom she home-schooled as they grew.

While still in his early forties, Timothy Gill suffered the misfortune of a debilitating work accident. This sad event caused him to be laid up for several months, but more seriously, prevented him from ever again doing many of the required chores of the stonemason's trade. In truth, he never fully recovered and walked with a noticeable limp for the remainder of his days. It saddened him greatly that he could not travel comfortably for any distance in a horse-drawn rig.

In his correspondence to his family in Ireland, he did not inform them of his injuries. They were told only after his demise—gone from the earth after only fifty-two years.

Early death was not an unknown phenomenon among the early settlers of Pine River and even in the ensuing generations. The death of a child was not an uncommon, nor an entirely unexpected occurrence. In some families, church records show that parents would be burying a young child one year and having another baptized the next. Young adults died with worrisome frequency, struck by virulent diseases often undetected until it was too late. But these tragic events did not interfere with the will of the survivors to go forward and prevail.

At the age of twenty-one, Mullin Gill found himself the inheritor of his father's homestead, now a newly built house and a farm property grown bigger with the acquisition of more adjacent acreage, a heritage that he grew to value beyond anything else. He'd been given many of the talents of his parents as a builder and caregiver and loved practising a skill that he excelled at—the raising of barns and stables. He usually oversaw the construction of community projects such as the building of a school and a community hall. During the summertime, he and his younger brother, Allan, both tried to fulfil their obligations on the farm while taking building contracts throughout the area. In the meantime, Mullin's older sisters had moved away together to Toronto to work and continue their education. Both eventually married, rearing their children in Upper Canada. Kitty Gill and her youngest daughter, Irene, lived at the farm in Pine River until Kitty's death, ten years after the passing of her husband Timothy.

Irene Gill was one of the teachers at the one-room schoolhouse in Pine River, having replaced the original schoolmarm who had fallen ill. It was a singular breakthrough for the community of Pine River to establish literacy as a standard amid these agrarian families. Many of the early arrivals to America from Ireland could not read nor write. After all, the British laws in the old country had forbidden the masses of Irish Catholics to educate their young. Under these circumstances there seemed little ambition for the common folk to acquire the ability to communicate with the written word. To do so would be to break the law. The proof of this undesirable legacy lay in the inability of many of the immigrants to sign the baptismal certificates of their own children, or to sign at their own weddings or as witnesses at marriages and funerals. The age-old records in the registries of many Catholic churches attest to this unfortunate plight. Priests officiating at these religious functions refer in their records to the inability of worshippers to sign their names. It was testimony to the utter humiliation that the Irish culture was subjected to at the hands of the English overlords. Such was the calamitous effect of the penal laws, a document of the 18th century, one clause of which read: "Education of the Irish children is forbidden by law." After many years of living with this law, after the passing of generations, the Irish people were but a shadow of their civilized past, where their culture had safeguarded the intellectual life of the European continent.

Mullin Gill married Rose Marie McCartney in the year 1858 in the Roman Catholic chapel in Cartier. Since Rose was a Presbyterian, a dispensation was necessary from the Catholic archbishop before the ceremony could take place. In a sense, this wedding brought a segment of Catholics and Protestants together—an event that captured the attention of all Irish and Scottish descendants in the general area. However, when it was learned that one of the conditions agreed upon was that the children of this union must be raised as Catholics, the appreciation of this ritual among Rose's people was somewhat restrained.

Mullin Gill was the grandfather of Eleanor Connors. His marriage to Rose in its early years was childless. It should be remembered that Irish men did not necessarily "marry young." Mullin did not marry until his mid-thirties. His elder son James was born in the fall of 1868, followed one year after by their second son, Stephen. The third and last child of Mullin and Rose was Annabelle.

Eleanor Connors, the widow of Paddy Connors, never laid eyes on her grandfather, Mullin Gill, who died in 1903, five years before she was born. Her father, James Gill, had married one of Martin Farley's daughters, Emily, and they had raised six children on the same property that great-grandfather Timothy Gill had been granted in 1823. Eleanor Gill, the third-born of James and Emily, married Paddy Connors on a rainy spring morning at the chapel in Cartier in May of 1935.

By any measure, Eleanor Gill was considered to be a great catch for Paddy Connors, a man with a wild streak who had earned his reputation as a big, strong, rambunctious, and strangely likeable individual. One of the unique features of Paddy was that he had a great love for books and had earned much respect among his peers as a self-educated man. His formal education consisted of six years of grade school, yet he spoke in an articulate voice on just about any subject, much like a man with university schooling. Eleanor was a handsome woman with a composed demeanour, having taught several years at the village school in Pine River until the obligations of motherhood required her to stay at home raising her children.

Much like Eleanor Connors, I do not remember my own paternal grandfather and grandmother, who both died in 1940, before I was old enough to get to know them. Grandfather Peter Carroll was a third-generation resident of Pine River, his grandfather having come as a young boy with his family to the Pine River area in much the same manner as the other Irish settlers. It is rather sad to consider that my great-grandfather and his ancestors were illiterate. There is little written record of their having dwelled on this earth even though they were hard-working farming citizens who raised praiseworthy families, ran their farming operations, and did business with neighbouring communities. Only the Catholic churches hold written indication that they walked the earth. The church held records of their baptisms, weddings, and funerals. Apart from that, the oral history passed down by descendants is the sole record of the experiences of my father's early genealogy. The reliability of oral history can always be questioned. Only aged people really know how short life is. The generations have come and gone. There is no written correspondence from these early periods. There are very few pictures, and where we do find pictures, the men, women, and children cannot be identified in many cases. My father has some of these pictures in an old trunk, but he cannot tell us who most of these people are. They are beautiful black-and-white pictures that were taken by professional photographers. In most cases the subjects sit or stand in perfect stillness, dressed in their finest wear. I cannot help but believe, since many of these people could not read or write, that they did not think about having the names of the adults and children written on the photos. Nor did they remember to have the dates recorded as to when the pictures were taken. It was no doubt a memorable event for a farming family to travel to town to have their photos taken. I have sketched a few of the people in these pictures. The level of wonder and expectancy in the eyes of the children speaks volumes.

My father was witness to the long-lasting courtship of Paddy and Eleanor Connors. I have spoken to my dad about this and he informs me that Eleanor and Paddy would meet and talk after Mass on Sundays in the years before my dad left for Montreal to work and study to become a teacher. They were both attractive young people and the adults would notice how they took to each other.

But these were the difficult days of the Depression and there was a lesser demand for the cream and butter produced by the dairy farmers of Pine River. Many farmers eventually gave up on the dairy business and switched to the raising of fowl. Knowing that his older brothers would take over the family farm, Paddy Connors went to Quebec City and worked on the docks as a stevedore. He had grown to be a powerful young man and had little difficulty gaining the respect of his fellow workers, many of whom emanated from Irish backgrounds and lived in the Cape Diamond sector of the old city. There were rumours that he'd had his share of punch-ups in some of the taverns of Quebec City, but somehow always managed to survive, never changing in his good humour, while enhancing his position on the wharves to become one of the supervisors of the stevedores. It was at this time that he was referred to as "big Connors."

But the great love that Paddy Connors had for Eleanor Gill was eventually to win out. He took every opportunity to go home to Pine River on weekends, even in wintertime, on the pretext of seeing his family, but inevitably to spend time with Eleanor. By this time the brothers of Eleanor were totally immersed in running a construction and renovating business, a now flourishing enterprise. The various levels of government organized many make-work projects during these slow economic times and the Gill brothers did benefit from this injection. As a result, they had little time for farming and a certain measure of neglect was noticeable on the property.

In the autumn of 1934 the future of Paddy Connors was sealed when he moved back to Pine River. He would take over the farm of the Gill family and manage it back to some sense of order and profitability. Paddy lived with his parents and brothers and travelled almost daily to the Gill farmstead to see to its operation. Eleanor, who was teaching at the village school, was now the de facto owner of the homestead, her brothers having relinquished the responsibilities to her.

Meanwhile, Paddy and Eleanor made plans to marry the following spring.

Marianne Connors was born on a cold winter night on December 2, 1939. The first-born of Paddy and Eleanor was a rosy-cheeked child who cried a lot, Marianne tells me, referring to herself.

It took four years for Eleanor and Paddy to conceive their second child, a boy, Hughie. But after that there were three more born in fairly rapid succession. After the birth of Hughie, Eleanor did not return to teaching.

At the advent of the Second World War, Paddy had seriously considered joining the Armed Forces. When Canada declared war on Germany in 1939, the two oldest sons of close friend Keith Malloy had joined the Royal Canadian Air Force. Paddy had read prodigiously about the spread of the Nazi menace and thought it his duty to serve. But as a farmer and producer and father, there was no obligation for him to do so. His heroes were the RCAF flyers who had helped to save Britain from a German invasion. He felt that he could easily have been part of this noble and courageous effort, his sense of patriotism gaining strength as the war progressed. Finally, with the pregnancy of Eleanor and the birth of his second child, he eased himself into an acceptance, satisfied that he would have willingly served his country had circumstances been different.

The daily boom of cannon fire was a constant reminder to him and his fellow farmers that there was a war being waged against the vile plague of Nazi expansionism. Bordering on the east side of his property across the lake, the Military Camp emitted its rattle of gunfire and the blast of impact into Pinkney's Mountain. The training of artillery personnel went on through the war years and into the post-war period. It was a nuisance that all the country folk were forced to live with and that dispirited some. Paddy's feelings of contentment, as he walked the fields of the family's acreage, were disturbed by a sense of foreboding when he contemplated the future. There were rumours that the camp would eventually want to expand, that the farms west of the camp offered excellent terrain for the training of infantry soldiers, that the lakes of the district offered a dimension that the army desired.

After he married, it did not take long for Paddy Connors to begin to exult in his good luck and in his love for his wife and growing family. The Gill farm that he worked was a mixture of fields and trees and lakeside beauty. There was a "rolling countryside" feature to the whole property, with the grove of pines reaching down to the side of the lake. The family had long owned a canoe fashioned from cedar and Paddy was in heaven as he paddled the edges of the still waters. His own family's ancestors had long farmed the acres of Pine River, eking out a living from its lean offerings. The land was not a bountiful resource, tending to be sandy and rocky and suitable only for a rather limited yield of grain and vegetables. Yet the forest was filled with coniferous dark green trees, useful for many purposes. If this abundance could be managed frugally, it would remain a lasting and priceless benefit for the Pine River community. Farmers considered the winter to be more profitable for them than the summer, since much of this forest resource was required by the neighbouring towns and the nearby city. Paddy Connors felt strongly that, although this country place was not ideal agriculturally, it was a heritage well worth preserving for the Irish descendants of the early settlers who had wrenched a livelihood from it.

Having worked in Quebec City for a few years, Paddy realized how close it actually was to the Pine River area. The thousands of acres of fields and foliated green shades in their isolated location did not deceive him. He could see that the city was already encroaching upon the outer areas, with farmland being bought and developed to satisfy the needs of the growing population. He sensed that, within another few generations, the landscape of Pine River would be forever altered. He was nobody's fool. He knew of the exponential real estate value of the Irish heritage in Pine River.

Paddy Connors, his wife Eleanor, and the neighbours would often discuss these matters. All knew that the local people had to prepare themselves to confront the future. If they were to preserve their heritage and the prospects of their fellow farmers, they must be ready to confront those who would no doubt be bent upon seizing their lands, whether this came from the army or the pressure of urban sprawl. The political structure of the area had to be solidified. The school system had to be anchored, with improvements to the building and the transportation of the students. The federal and provincial governments must be made to understand that Pine River was an entity that was stable, productive, and immovable.

Chapter 23

In their private domain, Paddy and Eleanor Connors emerged as creative and energetic parents. Their children were reading before they were old enough to attend school. The land that they farmed had returned to its dynamic best, with Paddy and Eleanor co-managing the operation with innovative insight. They had stuck with dairy farming and worked with a herd of more than a dozen cows from which they extracted the milk that made the butter that they sold to neighbouring boroughs, building up a reputation for delivering a good product. They raised pigs and turkeys and gained a measure of profit from this venture.

Paddy Connors, forever interested in the economic outlook of Pine River, served on the town council, whose job it was to collect the taxes that went into the support of the village school. His continuing hope was that a sense of unity would inhabit the spirit of Pine River, providing for a sound future for all of its farmers. The desire was that they would be able to give their children a good educational start and prod these children into furthering their level of learning.

To the great joy of all, at the end of the Second World War in 1945, Pine River settled into the softer existence of post-war peace. The activities of the Army Camp ebbed into a quieter and less frenetic pace, with fewer vehicles entering and leaving the facilities. The constant pounding of artillery shells into the bald scar of Pinkney's Mountain was heard only at irregular intervals. Surely this had been, once again, the "war to end all wars" as the nations of the world settled into a less aggressive cadence.

In truth, the new spectre of confrontation began almost immediately, with the refusal of the Soviet Union to retreat to its own perimeters. The lines of possible engagement in Europe had been drawn even while the Americans were considering how they would try to re-develop the economy of Germany and its neighbours.

As a member of the municipal council of Pine River, Paddy Connors and his colleagues had long been lobbying the provincial government about the promised installation of electric power throughout the area of Pine River. It would have been a boon to the farmers had electricity been put in years before, especially since the Military Camp next door was fully powered. Many letters regarding the matter were written to the provincial Member of Parliament for their electoral district.

Paddy Connors, with another councillor, paid a visit to the office of their representative on a spring afternoon in 1946. Paddy's partner in this undertaking was Michael Ferrigan, a neighbour and cousin. It is not beyond the realm of possibility that these two rather imposing figures had some effect upon Mr. Parent, their elected member of the provincial government.

A further promise was made by the politician to present the propositions to the cabinet of the provincial government. One year later, the Quebec Power Company began installing the electric power wiring for the residents along the sandy roads and into the once-isolated areas.

Michael Ferrigan and Paddy Connors were fellow residents in the back ranges of Pine River. Their families had known each other for ages; Michael Ferrigan had married Paddy's second cousin, Margaret Gaffney. There was a healthy respect between these two men, although Paddy did consider Michael Ferrigan to be a brooding individual who had had trouble with the law before the war. He had killed David O'Meara with an axe on a frigid winter's night in 1934. This incident had occurred many years before and, although everyone in Pine River knew of this history, few held any grudge against Michael Ferrigan. Certainly, the O'Meara clan had not forgotten about the killing, but most other residents preferred to think of it as just a sad event to be kept on the back burner.

Paddy would meet Michael Ferrigan at council meetings or at the occasional dance on a summer Saturday night, a regular event that both sometimes attended. The weekly dance was held in a festive atmosphere with lots of the farmers milling outside the dance hall and discussing politics or the business of getting out the lumber and vegetable produce to buyers in the surrounding towns. The fiddle and accordion music from inside the hall would prompt more than a few to join the ladies, who usually went right into the dance hall upon arrival. Some of the younger men tended to stay outside, sitting around and exploring the possibilities of drink.

It was on one of these Saturday nights that the once-abiding relationship between Paddy Connors and Michael Ferrigan would be forever altered.

From what I have been told by my father and from what was revealed during the trial of Michael Ferrigan, the quarrel between the two men started out rather harmlessly, with both men talking about the needed repairs to the village schoolhouse and how the work should be organized. There were several farmers gathered, some adding their input to the discussion. Most of the men were holding bottles of beer and swigging, some on their second or third bottle. There was an easy-going spirit to the discussion, with much willingness to contribute to the forthcoming school project.

What started out as a friendly discussion soon reverted to a one-on-one verbal exchange between Paddy Connors and Michael Ferrigan, according to the bystanders.

"By the way, Mike," Paddy said, in an off-the-cuff manner, "your boy Joey has been bothering my little girl at school. I wonder if you'd have a talk with him."

"Oh, yes? And just what happened?" queried Michael Ferrigan.

"Oh, it's nothing big. My wife Ellie says he's been pulling her hair—you know, her pig-tails."

"Come on, Paddy. You don't want me to get excited about that, do you? What are we, old women?"

"It's not a question of getting excited. I just want you to have a word with him, that's all."

"Which of your little girls, Paddy?"

"It's Marianne. She's nine years old."

"Holy Christ, Paddy. So my eleven-year-old kid is pulling your nine-years-old's pig-tails. Why should we worry about that?"

Apparently he laughed at his own comments, and looked at the others for affirmation.

Paddy Connors did not appear to be amused. He stared at Michael Ferrigan, a serious look in his eyes.

"Mike, you know how sensitive little girls are. Marianne says that it's gone on for a while now, and it's bothering her."

"Lookit, Paddy," Michael Ferrigan said, "I've got nine kids at home. If you think I'm gonna take this seriously, forget it. Let the kids do what they do. Let them work it out."

"Well, I think a responsible father would take it seriously. I'm just asking you to tell him to stop doing it."

"I'm not even gonna mention it, Paddy. I got better things to do with my time."

Michael Ferrigan then turned to walk away from the conversation and took several steps toward the dance hall.

"I'm gonna have to talk to Maggie about it," Paddy said loudly to Michael Ferrigan.

Michael Ferrigan turned around and came back toward Paddy.

"Don't you mention a word to my wife! She doesn't have to know about everything that takes place in the schoolyard," he said, his voice raised.

He approached Paddy to within inches of his face and glowered at him. Paddy raised his hands and shoved him away, pushing against his chest.

It was then that the others moved between the two burly farmers and strained to separate them from each other. The group of men included Earl Connors, Paddy's younger brother. There were no punches thrown, no grappling attempted. But the glaring looks they gave each other indicated that a physical scuffle had been narrowly avoided.

It did not seem to be a serious conflict at the time. As Michael Ferrigan left to return home with his wife, he was seen to nod at a group of men that included Paddy Connors. Everyone soon put the incident behind them

But a bad seed had been sown between the two men.

In the weeks that followed the work on the school was begun, most of it being done on weekends so as not to interfere with the children's study schedule. The farmers who helped out on this project noticed that Paddy Connors and Michael Ferrigan were not exactly on good terms. They seldom spoke to each other and tended to work separately. Their discontent with each other was further hardened over the next few years by the issue of the old railway path that ran through Michael Ferrigan's property for several acres. It vexed Paddy Connors that a fence had been placed across the path, supposedly to keep cattle out of Michael Ferrigan's field.

This old railway path was recognized as a public road, used by farmers to short-cut the distance between their properties. Paddy could have come up with a number of ways in which the path would not need to be fenced off. His father had given him some of the hay from his own fields to use since his father had only two cows to feed. While Paddy transported the grain to his property, it irked him that he would have to climb down from his high perch on a hay wagon, take down the logs of the fence, lead the horse across, replace the logs on the fence, then have to climb back up onto the wagon to continue his trip. He had been made aware that Joe Dunigan had offered to work with Michael Ferrigan to re-configure the fencing so that the railway path was not blocked. On a few hot summer days, with the sweat pouring from him, Paddy had left the logs on the ground after he passed through.

"Let him put the god-damn thing back up himself!" he likely said.

Michael Ferrigan was usually clued in as to when his logs had not been replaced. He watched the railway path closely, and routinely knew who passed through his property. More often than not, his son Joey was sent down to check on the fence.

The intense rancour between Paddy Connors and Michael Ferrigan reached its peak at a monthly school board meeting in early April of 1952. All of the councillors were present.

The agenda of the meeting dealt in part with a proposal to increase the salary of the schoolteacher. In order to do this, costs would have to be cut, and likely rates would have to be slightly increased. In the interest of keeping Mrs. Sarah Walling on the job as teacher, a woman who was considered a wonderful classroom innovator, the councillors unanimously passed a motion to achieve their purpose.

It is difficult to reconstruct the verbal events that led to the latest confrontation between Michael Ferrigan and Paddy Connors. There were a half-dozen versions from the half-dozen councillors present. It began with a discussion to update the assessment rates to the farmers in Pine River according to property size.

It seemed appropriate that farmers who had acquired new acreage should have their assessment increased. Michael Ferrigan was a case in point. He had purchased a lot of over 200 acres north of his original property the previous year.

"I do believe," said Paddy Connors, without mentioning any names, "that those of us who have acquired more land should pay a bigger share. Our taxation system is based upon the size of one's property, is it not?"

Michael Ferrigan sought a delay in assessment since he had just bought the acreage.

"Most of the acres up there are full of rocks and I had to pay some men to do some of the work clearing the property," said Michael Ferrigan. "I think it is unfair that I should have my taxes increased for the time being. The council could at least wait until I get something going up there. I'll likely use it to put potatoes in, but I'm not certain as yet."

There was that hint of intimidation in the words of Michael Ferrigan, as there had always been. It was easy to be cowed by his commanding voice and size.

Paddy Connors would not drop the issue.

"I'd like to remind you, Michael, that the previous owner of this property, Dermot O'Neill, paid his fair share, and I don't see why things should be different since you purchased the lot. We are all assessed at the same rate, so why should it be different with you?"

Alan Kelly, one of the councillors, could see the volatile nature of the dialogue and he tried to defuse it.

"I think we could allow for a grace period where Michael could be assessed later, at least until he can make use of the lot."

But Michael Ferrigan had built up some steam over the matter and stared at Paddy Connors.

"I have always paid my share. I have supported this school board with hard work and my taxes," he said, his voice louder and somewhat self-righteous in tone.

"We must all pay our fair share," said Paddy Connors.

"I would think that you could god-damn well look after your own business, and let me look after mine."

The promise of invective had crept into this latest exchange, but there was little that the other councillors could do to stop it.

"You cannot short-change this school board," retorted Paddy Connors. "It is well within your means to pay what you are required to pay."

"How in hell do you know what I can pay?"

Obvious anger became the brunt of Michael Ferrigan's stance.

But apparently, Paddy Connors would not be put off either.

"You will pay your dues or else you cannot claim to be a councillor in good standing," he said.

The other men in the room sat as if dumbstruck. They had not seen such intense wrangling in all the years they had served on the board.

"Well, you can't scare me with your stupid words, Connors! I've always paid my dues and been proud to do so! You can go straight to hell!"

Those were fighting words, and Paddy Connors was more than up to the challenge. He'd dealt with similar situations in the past. Michael Ferrigan, with all of his bellicose and aggressive posturing, did not frighten him. If there was anything in the personality of Paddy Connors that invited trouble, it was a risky trait he had invited upon himself in the past but that he seemed to have laid aside as he aged.

"Mr. Ferrigan, if you would just step outside, we'll see who is going to hell. If you just give me the chance, by Christ I'll smash your mouth. Just come outside and we'll settle this!"

Michael Ferrigan was not accustomed to being challenged so brazenly. He usually had his way with people that he dealt with.

At this point, several of the other men rose from their seats and decided to placate the combatants. Michael Ferrigan said something about his having a very sore arm and that he was not able to give Paddy Connors a fair fight. The tumult soon died down.

But immeasurable damage had been done. There would be little hope of repairing such a level of conflict between these two men. That particular school board meeting broke up with the councillors making sure that the two rivals did not come close to each other.

It would be several months before these two would again speak as neighbours. They did so on a Sunday morning in the sunshine of August, their loud argument piercing the quiet of the countryside.

Chapter 24

When I got back to college for my second term in January of 1957, I tried to get into the habit of writing to Marianne at least a couple of times a week. I did not necessarily wait for a reply. I had decided to write to her on a regular sort of schedule. She did respond to my letters about once a week, usually writing on a Saturday.

Jan. 12th, 1957
Dear Marianne,

I'm back to the routine of classes and I got the results of my first term exams. I'm averaging about a B-. My Art teacher, Prof. Cohen, allows us to grade ourselves (partly) and I gave myself an "A," which was overly generous, of course.

I'm back with the newspaper guys again. My buddy here on the paper, Dave McAuslin, got a part-time job at one of Montreal's radio stations, which is a great break for him. I think I'm gonna have to look for work myself because I'm getting kind of low on funds.

I hope you're feeling well and getting lots of sleep these days. It was great spending time with you over the holidays. If you practise your skating more you won't fall on your backside so often.

Hope your mom and the family are well. It's too bad Hughie doesn't live in town. He's a husky kid and would make a good hockey player. Is he going to attend school in Quebec next fall or will your mom home-school him?

I miss you a lot, Marianne. I don't see how I'll be able to go home before the Easter break, so we won't see each other very much till the summer. But I think about you all the time and hope that you will keep well and try not to dwell on the past.

Love, Francis

January 24th, 1957
Dear Francis,

I'm sorry I didn't answer you sooner but going to school and then doing the chores afterwards tires me out, so I really get lazy. I really enjoyed being with you over the holidays. You're so good to me, Francis. I promise I'll try to be a better skater. There's a rink at the camp and some of the girls go over now and then, so I'll try to join them.

Our family doctor says that I had a panic attack last week. I was sitting on the train after school on the way home and suddenly I started to sweat and my heart was beating like mad. I really got scared. One of the girls went to get the conductor and he gave me some water. But after a while I was all right as if nothing happened. But it's a terrible feeling, Francis. You feel like getting up and running away as fast as you can, but I was on the train and there was no place to run. I would have looked funny running up and down the aisles of the train. I told my mom about it and I took the next day off, and Mom brought me down to Loretteville to see Dr. Genest. He prescribed some pills for me. They're anti-depressants. I never thought I'd be taking pills at 17 years old. The doctor said that I might need to talk to somebody if the panic attacks continue. I guess he means a psychiatrist. I hope I'm spelling that right.

Uncle Ed is still coming over a few times a week to do some of the jobs that have to be done. The barn roof was leaking onto the hay so he climbed up and patched things up temporarily. We're glad he's around to help us. I couldn't see myself climbing up there.

I miss you a lot, Francis. When I'm with you, I'm so relaxed, it's not funny.

Mom sends her best regards and Gerald was asking if you were coming back. I told him you'd better.

Love and kisses, Marianne.

On the last day of January disaster struck Mrs. Taschereau when she fell down the outside steps of her duplex and fractured her pelvis. I was not there at the time and I partly blamed myself for the accident because I had allowed some ice to accumulate on the cement stairs. When I got back from our newspaper office, I noticed that all the lights were off in our section of the house. I let myself in to the darkness with my key, and the young guy from the downstairs apartment came to the door almost immediately and informed me about what had happened. The ambulance had taken Mrs. Taschereau to the Royal Vic Hospital, so I went up there that evening. Mrs. Taschereau was still in pain and lying flat on her back, sedated. The nurses told me that it was the sort of injury that likely would not be operated upon, but that the patient required rest and time and then therapy.

Mrs. Taschereau recognized me right away, although she was half asleep.

"Francis! You didn't have to come all the way up here! Don't you have assignments?" She spoke barely above a whisper.

What she said choked me up. That was typical of her. She cared a lot about what I was doing.

"Don't worry about the house, Mrs. Taschereau," I said. "I'll look after everything."

"Just make sure you pick up the mail and the newspaper, and see that all the doors are locked all the time. There have been a few break-ins lately on our street. That's all you have to do."

She sort of dozed off soon. After sitting there a while, I sneaked out without waking her.

Mrs. Taschereau was in the hospital for about a week. No one called the house to inquire about her health. No cards or flowers were delivered to her bedside at the hospital. She was utterly alone in her world. She was the first person that I had ever met who did not seem to have any family support system whatsoever. It was only after she got home from the hospital that her parish church people sent a bouquet of flowers with a "get well" card. For the next several weeks she used a cane to get around and moved rather slowly. I helped her out by doing the housework when I got home from school and went out to get the groceries.

One evening, after I had helped her cook supper, she said: "Do you have your driver's licence, Francis?"

"No, Mrs. Taschereau. I've never driven."

"Well, my husband left me his car when he died, but I've had it in storage. He always wanted me to drive, but I never got around to getting my licence. I thought that if you got your driving permit, you could take me to Mass. I haven't been there for the last three Sundays."

Within the next two weeks and with the coaching of Jake Zella, our newspaper editor, I passed the driving test down at the licence bureau and was driving Mrs. Taschereau's De Soto. This meant that I was back to Sunday Mass, a practice that I had neglected since I had started my college life. I would help her in and out of the car and up the outside stairs of the church. After Mass, Mrs. Taschereau liked to be driven for a spell to the north of the city, into the Laurentians where she could see the mountains, some bordered by snowfields, some filled with skiers.

Her De Soto was a large car, much like the Chrysler. I cannot tell you how much I enjoyed being Mrs. Taschereau's "chauffeur." She revelled in our little trips, telling me that I was a good driver and reminiscing about the long car rides she had taken with her husband, when she had driven to Florida with him on two occasions.

Mrs. Taschereau told me that, as long as she was disabled and while I was helping her with the chores of the house, I would not have to pay her any rent.

"You're my driver, you're my cook, you're my dishwasher, you're my errand boy, you're my chambermaid. Why should you have to pay me?" she said, accenting the "me."

Of course, I "insisted" upon paying her, but not for too long. I was happy that it would not be necessary for me to look for part-time work. It turned out that she refused to collect room and board from me for the remainder of the school year.

I had a pretty busy schedule during that time. After classes in mid-afternoon, I would head over to the newspaper office and work with Dave McAuslin. Then I'd go back to the house to help Mrs. Taschereau make supper and tidy up the kitchen afterwards. I was usually pretty tired by this time, but I still had to do my reading for the courses I was taking, and I would find myself falling asleep while I was trying to type out my assignments using my unique and stumbling two-finger method.

And then there was Sonia Martel. She would call me quite often during the evening while I was trying to stay awake and do my work. I'd been trying to wean myself away from her, feeling that I should never have attached myself to begin with.

"Francis, why are you ignoring me at the office?"

"I'm not ignoring you, Sonia," I lied.

"You're forever talking and laughing with David. Are you in love with him?"

"Do I have to answer that?"

"Well, are you?"

"Sonia, I'm behind in my assignments, and I'm trying to help Mrs. Taschereau here. So I've got my hands full right now."

"So, will we ever do something together again?"

"Maybe we could go to a movie sometime," I tried to pacify her.

I wanted to sever whatever I'd had with Sonia. Besides, Marianne was on my mind and I could not cope with the hypocrisy of pretending that I felt something for Sonia.

At the Easter break that year, Mrs. Taschereau suggested that I could drive her car down to Quebec City if I so desired. By this time, she was more mobile and felt that she could take care of herself. I telephoned Joey Ferrigan and asked him if he wanted to drive down with me, which he was gung-ho about. He told me that the railway owed him a few days off, which would enable him to stay till the following Wednesday when I planned to drive back to Montreal. So I picked him up on Holy Thursday and took the St. Lawrence north shore highway to Quebec. I would drop him off

..ay station in Quebec, where he would take the train to ..ne River. His older brother would pick him up from there.

Driving down the highway with Joey was a great time for me. It was nice to get away from school for a while, so I felt as free as a bird in Mrs. Taschereau's De Soto, a sumptuous auto with a smooth suspension and patent leather seats. The snows at the side of the road were melting. We also had the opportunity to do our "good deed for the day" when we helped an elderly couple who had a flat tire and were waiting at the side of the road, their emergency lights beckoning. Joey was rather amazing. It took him about ten minutes to jack up their car and change the flat tire.

As we approached Quebec there was the vista of the St. Lawrence in the distance, with lots of blue sky and cumulus clouds with their bulbous outlines. We talked about sports and Irish folk music. Our conversation was pretty positive, so we didn't dwell on the hurtful past. We were two young guys going down the road. It was exhilarating.

After dropping Joey off at the railway station in Quebec, I drove the car through the old city and swept up to the door in front of my house blowing the horn and revving up the motor. I rang the bell, then ran back and sat in the car again. My kid sister Eileen came down the stairway first and peered into the car window wondering who the visitor was. I got out of the car and swaggered over to her to give her a big hug. I had not told my family about the car. They'd expected me to come home by bus or train. It didn't take long for the De Soto to attract the attention of the neighbourhood, and a few kids gathered around the car. My two younger brothers were soon down on the sidewalk looking the car over and wondering how the hell it was that I was driving this big souped-up automobile.

My infantile exhibitionism was soon erased when my mom told me that Marianne was in a Quebec City hospital, being treated for severe panic attacks and depression. I had not received a letter from her in the previous few weeks, but I had just figured it to be because she was too busy to answer me.

After spending a brief time with my parents, I drove out to the hospital and found Marianne sitting on a chair in a semi-private room.

She stood up as I entered the room, but was attached to an IV. When I put my arms around her, I found her to be rather thinner than I recalled, and there was a pale look to her skin. But she still had that beautiful smile that I'd fallen in love with.

"So how are you feeling?"

"I'm fine. I don't know what I'm doing here, but the doctor says I should have my heart checked. He says I have a murmur."

"So what are they doing to treat you?"

"Oh, they're giving me all sorts of pills, and I've had a few X-rays and blood tests. I feel pretty good actually. My appetite is improving since I got here last Monday. But I have to put up with this drip all the time."

Her hand was bandaged to hold a needle that was feeding her intravenously, the sac of nutrients hanging on a roller allowing her to walk down the hallway if she wished.

"So why didn't someone call me about this?"

"Well, we knew you were coming down for the long weekend, so we decided to just wait till you got here."

"So you were having those anxiety attacks?"

"Yes, my heart was racing a lot of the time. I was getting a little worried and Mom was too."

I talked with her about what I was doing at school, about Mrs. Taschereau and the car I had parked outside the hospital but which we couldn't see from the room window. I'd wanted to take her for a ride more than anything else, but it wasn't going to happen.

Eleanor Connors soon came into the room with Gerald, Marianne's ten-year-old brother. There were a couple of other people in the room to see the other patient, so I withdrew and said I'd be back later. I offered to drive Eleanor back to Pine River later in the day since I planned to visit Tommy Kelly to say hello and show him the car.

So that was how I spent the Easter holidays: ferrying my brothers around and giving Eileen a few rides, dropping in to the hospital to see Marianne at least once a day. Tommy was very impressed with the De Soto. His dad lifted up the hood and had an up-close look at the engine.

I was not too concerned about Marianne. She was being well treated at the hospital and would stay about two weeks. She had a series of therapeutic sessions planned with a psychologist, talking about her anxiety. Marianne eventually made a complete recovery from this malaise.

Driving back to Montreal with Joey was an eye-opener. He seemed quite morose and did not talk a whole lot. He did say that his mother and older brother Stephen were running things at the farm and that everyone was well. I shuddered to think about how Maggie Ferrigan was dealing with a young family that had to be nurtured without a father. Three of the children were below ten years of age and three slightly older, all six living at the farm. It may not have been the most satisfying few days for Joey. I saw him as a very sensitive soul despite his impressive size and outwardly cheerful manner. After hearing him talk about his family, somehow I got the impression that Joey felt some guilt about not being there for them.

Joey Ferrigan, nineteen years old, was killed eight days later when hit by a freight train close to his workstation. No one was certain how the incident had occurred. Some police reports suggested that Joey may have thrown himself in front of the train as it picked up speed while leaving the railway yard. Others, including Joey's foreman, explained it as an unfortunate accident where Joey had walked across the multiple tracks, unaware of the approaching train. However it happened, it was a devastating blow.

When I first heard about the accident from my cousin, Charlie, I could not believe what I was hearing. This had to be incorrect. I had just been with Joey the week before and he had seemed quite normal, although a little perplexed at how he could be helpful to his younger brothers and sisters while he was working in Montreal.

An autopsy was held and it was discovered that Joey had been drinking quite heavily on the evening before his death. His body was then transported down to Pine River by train, accompanied by my cousin, Charlie Carroll, at the request of Maggie Ferrigan.

I met with Charlie at the Irish pub of the York Hotel a few days after the funeral. Maggie Ferrigan had asked Charlie to clear out Joey's apartment, so he planned to rent a small trailer and he wanted me to help him carry whatever there was out of Joey's place.

"What a shock, Charlie!" I said.

"Yeah, and how did he seem to be when you went to Quebec with him?"

"He was fine, that I could tell. I don't understand it!"

"You know, I'm not that surprised. He was a very up-and-down guy, if you know what I mean. You probably just saw his good side. But I was out with him just after Christmas and he started crying like a baby out of nowhere. I couldn't understand it. And he could really drink for a guy who was only nineteen years old."

"Do you think he intentionally walked in front of that train?" I asked.

"Well, we know he'd been drinking, so he just could have been suicidal."

The death of Joey Ferrigan rocked me considerably. I began to understand how fragile life can be for someone who has been directly affected by tragedy. Joey had lost his father at a very impressionable age, a period in his life when he already had great fear for the welfare of his dad, a man who held great sway and predominance over him. The state had chosen to execute his father and in doing so they broke the spirit of the executed man's children, the survivors who must forever live with the memory of the man who had nourished them. The Supreme Court of Canada had refused to reconsider the death sentence and instead subjected a wife and ten children to a lamentable abyss in their lives. There was no guilt in the behaviour of Michael Ferrigan's wife or children, yet they had suffered an irreparable wound that would forever torment them. Who could say how this horrific experience would stunt the emotional growth of these children?

Charlie and I went to Joey's apartment in Pointe St. Charles a few nights later. He'd lived on Centre Street, not far from where he worked. The man who owned the three-storey house where Joey had stayed was the first floor occupant. He gave us the key to Joey's two-room apartment on the second floor. Joey's "digs" had a typical bachelor's layout with a kitchenette–dining room and a small bedroom and bathroom. The miniature fridge and stove belonged to the landlord so we did not have to move them. The only bulky items we had to load into the trailer were the bed, a dresser, chairs and table.

There were smaller items: lots of LPs, quite a few books, kitchen stuff, and the clothes in his dresser and closet. Charlie drove the trailer down to Pine River and delivered Joey's belongings to the Ferrigan household.

Among other personal items, I found what turned out to be three letters addressed to Joseph Ferrigan, written to him by his father, Michael Ferrigan, whose name was carefully printed on the top left-hand side of each envelope. The letters were bound together with an elastic band, the paper of the envelopes a little faded and stained but having been opened carefully, probably with a letter opener.

I "recognized" these letters immediately, remembering that Joey had spoken to me about them and had offered to show them to me. Joey had obviously carried them wherever he went and no doubt had considered them to be a precious remembrance of the last weeks of his father's life.

Throwing any ethical feelings I may have had to the winds, I stuffed the letters into my shirt pocket inside my sweater. In the midst of the moving of furniture and clothes and books, Charlie was in no mood to notice what I had done. I wondered if Maggie Ferrigan or Joey's older brother Stephen were aware of the existence of these letters. I discovered later that Maggie knew of the letters but thought they had been mislaid somewhere and lost. She was the one who had delivered two of them to Joey after her visits to her husband at the jail. I sent the letters back to her, explaining that Joey had allowed me to read them. She responded, thanking me for helping Charlie empty out Joey's apartment. She had little else to say.

Chapter 25

September 25th, 1952

Dear Joseph,

I hope you are well and that you are taking care of things with Stephen. Your mother needs your help more than ever now, until I can get back home. The fall will be ending soon and the snow will start, so we have to get ready. Remind your brother that he has to cut enough wood to keep the house warm, and you can help to cut a supply of kindling to get the flames going during the cold weather.

I am waiting for the trial to start in a few weeks and the people here have been very good to me.

Thank you for your letter, Joseph. Your mother gave it to me a few days ago. It is very hard to stay at this place but I am hoping to be home for Christmas. It is not easy to get up every morning and find that I have to stay here, instead of walking out the door at home and going into the fields and getting the fresh air. I miss everything that I had to do every day. I miss the daylight most of all. It's pretty dark here.

Joseph, don't forget to wash the pails and the separator before every milking. That's your job. They have to be kept clean at all times, including the two spouts at the bottom of the container. Everything has to be free of germs. We don't want anyone in the house to get sick. I know you don't like to milk the cows, but you could give Stephen and your mother a hand in the stable. Make sure to remind Stephen to put the cream in the dairy as soon as it's ready. And help your mother with the churn. It's tiring work for an older person. Don't forget to go through the garden and make sure that the potatoes are all picked out and save the small ones for the pigs.

I want you to go down and see that the fence is kept closed every time you see someone pass up by the track. I know that the oats are all cut, but I want that fence closed at all times.

Your mother tells me that you are doing very well with your reading and writing. Maybe we can arrange for you to go to town for school next year like your sisters. I know you would be a very good student, Joseph.

Tell Patrick, Johanna, and Ellen that I will be away for a while. Tell Patrick not to cry, that I will see him soon. I know that your mother is very upset about what happened, but it's over with now and I have to deal with it. I am sorry for what was done and for putting your mother and everyone through all of this.

Mr. Nolan has told me not to write down anything about the case before the trial, so I won't say anything more about it.

The guards here are very good to me. I go out every day to the yard and walk around. They are all family men with children of their own and we talk about things when we get together in the yard.

I am looking forward to the trial and telling my side of the story if I get the chance.

I miss all the family very much. It is hard to think that I will have to be here for a few more months until the trial is over, but Mr. Nolan is very hopeful.

Goodbye for now.

Your father, Michael.

This was the first chatty letter to Joey. It seemed to be written by a man who was in full control of his senses. He sounded contrite, optimistic, and worried about the feelings of his children now that he was not present at home. There appeared to be no hint of any delusion of persecution, the events in his life perhaps having sobered him up.

The second letter written to Joey was dated early December, a few weeks after the trial ended, after Michael Ferrigan had been sentenced to death. The letter had to have been hand-delivered to Joey by Maggie Ferrigan upon her return from a visit to her husband. There was no indication that it had been posted. The letter had been sealed in the usual envelope, and certainly proved to me that Michael Ferrigan harboured a deep and unbounded love and respect for his son Joey.

Dear Joseph,

It was nice seeing you last week. You grew at least a few inches since I saw you last, I am sure. I think you will be taller than your Uncle Jim when you finish growing.

The trial did not turn out to what I wished for, Joseph, so Mr. Nolan is working hard to try to get another hearing. I am very hopeful that the court will grant us another trial and we will have to go through everything again.

You will soon be fifteen years of age so I think I can talk to you about these things. Joseph, I did not murder Paddy Connors. I did not want to see him die. But it was a terrible mistake on my part. I could not seem to manage my anger and everything went out of control for me. I do not want you to go through life thinking that your father was a murderer. You must be brave no matter what happens, and live your life as a normal man would do. I always meant well for you and the family. I am proud of what I was doing and I am proud of all of you.

Your mother and I were very happy when you were born because you were our second son and such a strong healthy boy. I know that your brother Stephen has the farmer's blood running through him, so if things don't turn out right for me he will be able to handle the work. I hope that you will always stay close to your mother because she is very fond of you and depends on you so much. Your younger brothers and sisters look up to you and Stephen. You should always help them with their schoolwork and show them the things you learned with me.

I don't want you to think that I am losing courage, but it is possible that I will not be around for too much longer. It is hard to imagine myself being free of all of these things. If Mr. Nolan cannot get a new trial for me in the courts, then I don't know what can happen.

But keep your chin up and say a prayer for me.

Your father, Michael.

And finally, the third letter was delivered to Joey several days after his father's execution at Bordeaux Jail. This letter had obviously been sent by mail, with the date printed over the postage stamp.

January 6th, 1953

Dear Joseph,

I am in Montreal now as you very well know. Your mother has been visiting me for the last few days and she tells me that you are all in good health.

Mr. Nolan is working hard to get me a stay, and my hope is that I will still be on this earth for some time to come. It is hard to understand that I am in this situation, but I must show some courage. I will have to face my destiny if nothing can be done.

Joseph, I would like to say again that I regret what has happened to me over the last few months. If it is God's will that I must go, then I must face the future.

I want you to take good care of your mother. It's up to you and Stephen to help her in any way you can if I am not there. I don't know if you would like to stay in Pine River and make your living as a farmer. If not, I know that you are very smart and could do anything you put your mind to. You are already very good with motors and machinery, even better than me so I am very proud of you. If you should decide later to leave the farm, I hope you will always keep in touch with your family.

Joseph, I want you to take care of your younger brothers and sisters. They will wonder where I have gone, so you can tell them that I went to a better place. I love them all very much and will miss them terribly wherever I am going. As long as you are living at home, I hope you will help your brothers Patrick and Sean with their reading just as your mother helped you. I know that your mother will be working with Ellen and Johanna. It is very important to be able to read well in life so you can make a good future for yourself.

This may be my last letter to you, Joseph. It is very hard to say such a thing, but I must accept what has been given to me. I will miss walking in the fields and doing all the things that I've done since my father died and left the farm to me.

I will miss you and all your brothers and sisters. If I cannot get a stay I will have to say goodbye to your mother.

I hope that you can understand my writing as this is very hard to do.

So say another prayer for me, and if I cannot change what is planned for me, then I must face the music.

Your loving father, Michael.

I had to fight to hold back tears, especially when I finished reading the last of the three letters. I wonder why I didn't just allow myself to cry. It would have been worth it.

Life has been good to me thus far. Good fortune has smiled on me. I graduated from college in the summer of 1959 with a Bachelor of Arts, my major being Political Science. I don't suppose that I will ever put my interest in politics to any practical use, yet I enjoyed taking these courses and most of the teachers who taught them. My minor, of course, had to do with drawing and design. All of my elective courses involved using my creative juices to a certain extent.

1962 was a great year for me. I married one Marianne Connors in the small church in Pine River. We were married on August 10th on a beautiful Saturday morning just over four years ago now. We did not want to delay our marriage any longer. It was really the only way that we could please both her mother and my parents, together with seizing the moment.

I don't get to do what I would ideally like to do. I have to earn a living. My dream is to have an ocean-side cabin and go out and paint seascapes with sailboats in the distance, then journey inland and sketch the tree-filled countryside and finish off painting the scenes in my studio. But that's not likely to happen any time soon.

Unfortunately, although I have a consuming love for art and painting, I did not have the courage to forge ahead and become an independent artist. I was much too mercenary to take such a precarious step. I have been employed with an advertising firm for the last almost seven years here in Montreal. I was serving a sort of internship with the firm even before I finished my college courses. They appreciated the fact that I had worked on the college newspaper and that I appeared to be informed about the political and social trends of the country. There is a negative side to working for an ad agency in that you must have the confidence of your "accounts," some of which are merchandizing products that might not be appealing to you. For instance, I find myself lately having to sketch women's undergarments to provide patterns for retail stores that wish to advertise. But on the other hand I enjoy the creative side, such as writing dialogue for radio ads. One of my duties is to hire actors for media publicity, a task that I find very interesting.

After our marriage in 1962, Marianne and I settled in Montreal's west end, where we have a fairly spacious rented apartment. She is a Registered Nurse and works at the Montreal General Hospital. Marianne trained at the English hospital in Quebec City for three years before agreeing to move up to Montreal to be near me.

We are also the parents of a two-year-old boy whom we have named Liam and who is cared for, while Marianne and I are working, by a French-Canadian woman, Françoise Bégin. She lives close by and arrives early every morning to take over. She is wonderful with Liam and we have grown very fond of her. An added bonus is that she speaks to Liam in French at all times.

Both of my parents are in good health, my dad still teaching History and Literature in high school, and my mom doing a lot of painting. In their new house, my mom also now gives art and sewing craft lessons to anyone who is interested.

My two younger brothers have also done very well. Steven is now in his last year of college after playing hockey for two years with the Quebec City Junior A team and then playing hockey for the University of Minnesota on a scholarship. But civil engineering seems to be his strong suit and he says that he doesn't think that a career in hockey is a probability. He thinks he will stay in school next year and do post-graduate studies in his favourite field. My brother Eamon works as a salesman for a ball-bearing company, travelling around eastern Canada a lot, and he claims to love his work. He dropped out of college a few years ago. Kid sister Eileen has decided to become a teacher like her dad and is presently attending normal school.

My maternal grandfather, George Lawson, died two years ago after coming home from playing a hockey game with a bunch of resolute old-timers. He was 73 years old and had been told by his doctor to stop raising his heart rate at the local rink. Surprisingly, my grandmother Meg, incapacitated by a stroke, is still alive and living in a home for old folks in Montreal. My mom and dad drive up to see her about once a month. She has refused to move to Quebec City to be closer to my mom and prefers to stay with her Irish friends at the home.

Mrs. Louise Taschereau, my friend and former landlady, is still going strong and presently seems to have the company in her house of an elderly gentleman. How she worked this out, I have no idea. Who he is, I haven't a clue. When I call her up to say hello, she won't talk about him. But now, at last, she has someone to assuage her loneliness and a viewer for her vast collection of slides of the trips around the world she took with her former husband.

Epilogue

The year 1965 will live forever in the minds of Pine River residents as the year that the federal government decimated their community. It was the year when the expropriation of thousands of acres of land was destined to deprive the descendants of the Irish settlers of a heritage that was certain to have cumulative value, not to mention the intrinsic cultural legacy thrown "to the four winds." This was a thoughtless policy that gave no respect to the original pioneers who had uprooted their lives in Ireland and had taken the gigantic step to establish a foothold in Canada.

Some of the farmers in the Pine River area had warned of the strong possibility that the government would covet this precious territory to expand their military facility. In the 1820s there were few people who were willing to consider developing the primeval land north of the old city of Quebec. The families that undertook this momentous mission did so at great cost and with the ultimate sacrifice. Who would be willing to inhabit a forested terrain, spend years clearing out space for crops, and live in primitive conditions throughout the frigid winter months without the benefit of basic social aid? Who, after a treacherous voyage across stormy seas, would be willing to walk many miles, perhaps with their young children, to an area that awaited them, to live in crude log huts? The early settlers made these definitive commitments. After decades, the fruit of their toil began to reveal itself in the well-groomed fields and sturdily built houses of a community that was productive and self-sustaining.

How was the government able to impose its will upon a modest group of people who were without wealth but who exuded the independent spirit of all free men? And the government did this not once, but twice. This government was made up of men who professed to believe in the sanctity of liberty and choice in a democracy.

In the early sixties at Pine River, the future held great promise. The white clouds of summer overlooked a truly nurtured community with a set pattern of work and activity amidst the farm families. Still humble and modest in their style of life, the residents invariably saw the heritage of Pine River as something they would hold in perpetuity. The installation of electricity had enabled them to modernize their lives and work practices. Some of the roadways were being paved and people from the city began to look upon Pine River as an attractive and nearby area that they might seek to develop. The small towns that had once surrounded Quebec City were expanding into larger boroughs at an increasing rate. There seemed little doubt in the minds of Pine River's farmers that the inherent value of their properties would escalate exponentially as the boundaries of the old city expanded.

And why should this not have been so?

This territory, set amidst the lower Laurentian hills, with the tall dark coniferous trees surrounding the broad flat fields, had been home to its Irish inhabitants since the early 1800s. Each property had it own unique features and each family had a matchless story to tell about the ancestors who had made the farms what they were. These were not stories of materialistic people seeking mercenary acquisitions, but rather, accounts of how a community was developed by citizens striving to build a sustainable existence. There was little political power or influence among these farmers. They were the salt of the earth and had scratched out a living for generations in a land that, at one time, no one wanted. As a result of this, the farmers of Pine River were vulnerable. How would they be able to fight the encroaching wishes of the policy-makers in the government? If they thought that they could oppose the expropriation plans of the military establishment, who was there to back them up?

It is astonishing to think that in 1965, one hundred families in the area surrounding Valcartier Camp were informed that the federal government had expropriated their farms for the purpose of expanding their training grounds. This latest expropriation was the second one imposed upon the people of Pine River, the first one having been decreed in 1914. This latest expropriation took in over 38,000 acres of farmland and forest.

The news of this government policy was initially relayed to the farmers through a high-ranked military officer from the camp. The need for the new territory had been necessitated because of the upcoming introduction of new weaponry, the use of which required a "safety corridor."

The information about the latest expropriation, emanating from a military correspondence, had its desired effect. The farmers, for the most part, considered the government policy as a fait accompli, something they could do little about. The notion that government policy required its introduction by military officers was intimidating, to say the least.

Basically, the farmers were told that they would be compensated for the loss of their holdings, the value of which would be decided by the government.

How are farmers to react when told by "authorities" that they will soon have to leave their homesteads, heritages that they have held for generations? What would be the effect upon a farmer who has given his life to his property and hopes to pass it on to his children?

After such a take-over by the military, the Pine River settlement would be reduced to a fraction of its former self. Who would have thought it possible that the government could do this to its citizens? What sinister manipulation was at work, where a government could wipe out the toil and tears of generations of Irish settlers? It was not that the military could not have expanded in a different direction. The areas north of the camp were uninhabited, a vast territory available to the development of the military establishment. But most of all, it was the sheer dishonesty of this latest manoeuvre where the descendants of these farmers were deprived of the future accumulating value of the properties.

The Quebec City English newspaper took up the cause of the Pine River farmers with story lines and interviews and editorials.

This public knowledge of the situation led to debate in the House of Commons in Ottawa, where the issue was discussed for many hours over several days, with the members of the New Democratic Party and the Conservative Party excoriating the Liberal Government and the Department of National Defence.

The attack on government policy with regard to the expropriations in Pine River began in earnest on February 21st of 1966.

> I refer [began Ed Schreyer of the NDP] to the decision of the Department of National Defence to expropriate several thousands of acres of land, including an entire village, in order to enlarge the area of Valcartier Camp . . . . Could not the department have acquired that land in more unsettled areas where the land is not being used? . . . To expropriate first and then approach the owners as to the price to be paid seems to me to be an abuse of this power . . . . I think we have degenerated into a sorry state when we give preference to administrative convenience over the rights of individual small property owners . . . . It is my impression that no high ranking official of the department has bothered to go to the area to meet with the people who are affected and no attempt has been made to discuss the necessity of the undertaking or relocation plans . . . . One other aspect of this whole program of land acquisition which rather intrigued me relates to the fact that it was a military person who got in touch with the people to inform them of the need for this land . . . . What possible justification can there be for having military personnel involve themselves in what is essentially a transaction between the government and the property owners?

The next day, February 22nd, John Diefenbaker entered the fray:

> Surely those who opened up this country, the pioneers who have been there for generations and whose ancestors came even before the Potato Famine, are entitled to be treated in a way that has not been accorded them . . . . These are human beings, they are Canadians and I hope this government will have some recognition of the inhumanity that is inherent in a mass evacuation from an area . . . . They suffer the indignity of a community being shoved and pushed about with no regard paid.

It was not surprising that John Diefenbaker would support the farmers of Pine River. Although born in Ontario, this author of Canada's Bill of Rights was a criminal lawyer who had been educated for the most part in Saskatchewan, from whose fields had emerged the genesis of Canada's reputation as "one of the breadbaskets of the world." No one had more respect for the plight of the farmer than this former Prime Minister of Canada. In his mind it was the farmer who saw to the sustenance of the population, the undermined worker who provided the fuel that propelled a nation forward. It is the farmer who has toiled the fields and who must be given precedence over other considerations.

"The people understand they have to move, and they've no kicks," said the mayor of St. Gabriel West, the adjacent community.

Why the farmers of St. Gabriel West did not choose to fight the government policy is a mystery. The majority of the people in his municipality, said the mayor, "would like to get jobs with the government and relocate as near to their own homes as possible."

"But the government fellow said anyone who wants a job will get one and we don't have to worry," said the mayor.

I do not know if the "government fellow" eventually allowed the expropriated residents to realize their expectations, but it is beyond me as to why the farmers of St. Gabriel West did not put up a bigger fight to maintain their holdings. Did they not also have their own heritage to protect? Did they not also have a profound appreciation for the toil of their forebears?

Excerpt from the Quebec City newspaper editorial: "The land, Ottawa told them, was needed for much more important things than raising people."

"The homes are no mansions by any means, but at least the people can live in them comfortably. Likewise, income is not that good but they manage to earn enough to live happily and bring up children," said one resident.

"I won't be able to put my kids through college now. I'm going to have to go to work—if I can get a job," said another farmer, who has five children.

"After having made so many sacrifices during the Depression in order to have a home in my old age, the government steps in and tells us we just have to get out," was another complaint.

The compensation offered to the residents of Pine River for the expropriation of their properties was a mere pittance if one considered the potential and future value of this land.

"The price we were offered was ridiculous considering what we were being deprived of," said one local who had to give over 180 acres.

"We may not be college graduates, but at least we are educated enough to know when people are being cheated," said a councillor of the municipality.

The appeals by members of the opposition did not hold much sway with Defence Minister Hellyer and Associate Minister Cadieux. An earnest invocation to the Canadian Prime Minister Pearson himself could not dissuade the powers-that-be from implementing their policy, depriving the farmers of Pine River of their long-held homesteads.

> This whole matter of expropriation [explained Associate Defence Minister Cadieux in the House of Commons] has been considered at length . . . . There have been recommendations to expropriate an area of about 60 square miles . . . . We received protests from this community . . . which is not a village but a group of small properties . . . if these people are not relocated, they would be in a danger zone when there is long-range mortar, arms and cannon fire practice . . . . I understand that when expropriation was decided on, these properties were included in the expropriation, and that, consequently, they are expropriated.

> . . . It seems to me [said Ed Schreyer of the NDP] that a genuine attempt should have been made to negotiate price and reach a settlement before any resort to expropriation took place . . . .

> Mr. Cadieux: If the Department of Defence were to announce in advance that 60 square miles of land are to be expropriated and then tried to negotiate prices before filing its expropriation plan, prices would go up of course . . . . One must presume that the Department of Defence is not out to rob property owners by offering unacceptable prices.

Gordon Minto Churchill, another member of the opposition, a former Cabinet minister in the Diefenbaker government, was another vociferous voice against the expropriation. He was a man who had served in both world wars.

> Mr. Churchill (of the Opposition): Therefore a shotgun has been placed at the heads of these people. They are told, "You are now in a danger zone; it is too bad but in order to protect your safety, it would be advisable for

you to move." This is a scandalous thing to do. Twenty-five families whose ancestors have been living in this area for 150 years are suddenly to be moved by arbitrary action by the Department of Defence . . . . I think that this is a shocking piece of bungling . . . . It just happens that most of these people are Irish . . . . What has the Minister got against the Irish? They are the best fighters in the world, and he knows it.

Mr. Diefenbaker: Mr. Chairman, I think that the government should reconsider this matter. This is a totally unjustified action and has all the earmarks of administrative lawlessness and contempt for the rights of the individual. . . . Is there no heart in the Department of National Defence? . . . What is going on here? What are the rights of the people? . . . Families who have not got the best land in the world but have lived there for generations are to be uprooted . . . .

Mr. Churchill: . . . Has the Minister [of Defence] had time now to consider these questions and will he indicate to the House that these expropriation actions will cease forthwith so that the 25 families who are now in a state of dismay may be assured that they will be allowed to remain in possession of their homes and property . . . ?

Mr. Cadieux: I said, before the adjournment, I believe, that I was prepared to reconsider the whole matter with the parties concerned . . . .

Mr. Churchill: Mr. Chairman, one must examine carefully the words used by the Associate Minister [Cadieux]. Before our supper hour he said he was willing to negotiate a just settlement with the people con-

> cerned. What I want to know is whether the whole operation will cease and whether the expropriation will be cancelled so that these people may be left where they are . . . . We are talking about justice and equitable treatment for these people, leaving them where they are and establishing the mortar firing range somewhere else . . . . May I ask the Minister [Hellyer] whether any part of the camp . . . is used for artillery practice? If the answer is yes, then he already has in effect a mortar range there. If the answer is no, I would ask the Minister why he does not shift this mortar practice to places where artillery ranges are already in operation . . . .
>
> Mr. Hellyer: Mr. Chairman, there is no artillery range at camp Valcartier. Indeed, there was nowhere near sufficient land, until this expropriation took place, to permit either mortar or artillery fire of any kind . . . .

This was blatant "mis-information," whether intended or not. It was incredible to think that the Minister of National Defence was unaware of the lengthy history of artillery shells falling on the scar of Pinkney's Mountain, or that none of his advisors were on the job in Parliament to clue him in. I do not know what effect this untruth had upon the final outcome of this dispute.

> Mr. Diefenbaker: . . . I have already placed on the record the views of certain of the people involved in this move. The Prime Minister was communicated with. These people gave up trying to soften the adamant attitude of the Minister of National Defence . . . and made an appeal to the Prime Minister of Canada to look into this matter. A protest was organized . . . and a petition was sent to the Prime Minister. It was duly acknowledged. One of the letters was actually answered. . . . These people are just being told, "Get out of here. Away

with you. We are going to give you the proper value for your land." . . .

Mr. Cadieux: . . . As I said earlier, I am ready to renegotiate with these people and their representatives and to re-examine the whole question, and we shall see then. I explained at the outset how this whole situation came about. Unfortunately, these people live in what is considered a danger zone. That is why, at the time, we decided it might be better to expropriate them along with the others. We have never closed the door on a reconsideration of the whole matter. But they did not come back to see us. I saw these people only once. I am willing to meet with them at any time to review the whole matter.

Mr. Schreyer: . . . When large bodies such as governments deal with holders of small plots of property and impinge on their rights, it is necessary to take as firm a stand as possible against any infractions by what the Leader of the Opposition called autocracy. I sincerely hope that the Minister or the Associate Minister will look at the file once again to see whether the course of action they have taken was necessary in the first place.

In response to the criticism of the members of the Opposition, Minister of Defence Hellyer seemed to be willing to compromise.

Mr. Hellyer: . . . After close examination over a number of years it was concluded that the expansion of this camp was essential in the national interest—that increased training facilities should be provided there and that a large area should be set aside for the training of a substantial portion of the Canadian army which is

> stationed at this camp . . . . The Associate Minister [Mr. Cadieux] would be glad to look at this question . . . .

For all their good intentions, the members of the Opposition also seemed to be mis-informed. The army facility next to Pine River had been used for artillery training since as far back as the Second World War. The daily, constant, and irritating boom of the cannons during the spring, summer, and fall was a constant reminder to all the residents that the army was at work.

> Mr. Groos: Mr. Chairman, I merely wish to say that in considering the attitude taken by hon. members opposite when we were considering the Columbia River development proposals which required the dispossession of 500 families in the national interest, I find that attitude in strange contrast now when we are talking about the same sort of thing but where only 25 families must have their land expropriated in the national interest. We are now being told that this was a terrible thing to have done.

The following day, February 23rd, debate continued wherein Defence Minister Hellyer was asked a pointed question about the history of artillery practice at the camp.

> Mr. MacInnis (Cape Breton South): Can the Minister explain his reference to the fact that the range at Valcartier is congested with unexploded shells, and practically no firing can be done? Since there is no artillery or mortar range there can he explain why unexploded shells are congesting that range and how they got there?

> Mr. Hellyer: Well, I understand there is a variety of shells of various kinds going back the whole 50 years

since the camp was in operation, and that they are pretty well concentrated in one major hill which exists in the present camp.

On April 28, Mr. Diefenbaker rose in the House of Commons and directed a final question on the expropriation issue to Associate Minister of Defence Cadieux.

Mr. Diefenbaker: . . . I should like to ask the Associate Minister of National Defence, following his recent pilgrimage . . . to Valcartier camp, what his view is as to the reaction of the people, whether any decision has been made and what action the government will take.

Mr. Cadieux: Mr. Speaker . . . . On Tuesday, April 26th, I visited several of the residents . . . and inspected the entire new training area by car and by helicopter . . . . I have decided . . . that a somewhat lesser area will meet current operational training land requirements in an optimum if not a maximum manner . . . .

Mr. Diefenbaker: Mr. Speaker, this is certainly a step in the right direction. Perhaps I should ask the minister to what extent there has been a reduction in the acreage originally decided upon for expropriation . . . .

Mr. Cadieux: It will be reduced by about one quarter.

Mr. Starr: . . . Does this mean that only one quarter of the land originally intended for expropriation will not now be expropriated and is the department now going to expropriate three quarters of the original?

Mr. Cadieux: . . . The land to be expropriated will be one quarter less than that originally projected.

The final result, in the Pine River area, was that about 9,000 acres of land were expropriated, affecting fifteen families. There was no change in the expropriation tally for the farmers of St. Gabriel West, over three hundred people being affected. The total expropriation of land in that sector was over 28,000 acres.

Initially, my Uncle Mike Carroll's farm was part of the plans of the federal expropriation of 1965. Thankfully, most of his acreage was "returned" to him as part of the reduction decided by the Minister of Defence. He was compensated for part of his holdings taken in the expansion of the Military Camp. My uncle has cut back on his farming workload over the past few years. Since the plan took much of his forest acreage at what he considered an unjust amount of compensation, he virtually has ceased the selling of wood, an income that helped to provide him with security for many years.

Included in the fifteen families who lost their homesteads to the expropriation at Pine River were two families of the Ferrigan clan. It is said that most of them moved to Wisconsin in the U.S.A., where relatives have already been farming for three generations. This family name has now completely vanished from the Pine River area. Some residents have said that Maggie Ferrigan was happy to leave Pine River, but this has not been really verified.

Marianne's mother, Eleanor, has lost her farm close to the lakeside where the generous supply of tall pine trees grace the edges of the rolling fields not far from the Rivière aux Pins, a beloved stream of brown and blue water so often visited. She has rented a house close to my Uncle Mike's property, one of several lots that have been sold from the original property of Willie Connors, her father-in-law. He is in his declining years now, seldom moving out of his house. Eleanor can easily visit him and help to see to his needs. His property has risen in value, of course. Army personnel who wish to live away from the camp are seeking to build on his land near the road.

All of the farms north of my Uncle Mike's remaining property in Pine River have been affected. As a result, the Coughlins and the Hayes family (my Aunt Mona) and the Dunigans and the Clearys and the O'Mearas and the Farleys and the Fogartys, as well as eight other families, were all completely expropriated, and must decide what they are to do with their lives. Some are searching for alternative farm properties west of the Pine River area. Others, whose children have grown up and moved to urban centres, have given up farming altogether. A few of the expropriated residents have acquired employment at the Military Camp.

Alan Kelly, Tommy's father, has been lucky to escape the selection process. His farm was part of the adjustment in the government's plan in the same case as my uncle's.

There is little doubt that Pine River will soon be a close suburban extension of the Quebec City sprawl. But when Marianne and I visit, there is that same scent of spruce and balsam in the air as the evening settles on the sullen scar of Pinkney's Mountain.

At my Uncle Mike's, we sit on his balcony and survey the dark green line of trees bordering the Carroll homestead. There is always a lot to talk about, especially relating to all the changes over the last few decades. It is a cycle of conversation not devoid of a certain nostalgia, tinged with some emotion.

My Uncle Mike and Marianne's mother are living close to each other, just a ten-minute walk apart. We have heard that they see quite a lot of each other. Could there be something going on there? Time will tell.